The Way of the Bees

A P Clarke was born in Singapore under the sign of Aquarius. At seventeen she came to Europe and undertook to find herself. This quest began on an Irish campus, rowed itself along many rivers, and found Amazons who taught her about the stars, the nightclubs, the goddess and Her creatures. At twenty-eight, she abandoned her studies and moved to Cork, the true capital of the world, where she became a welfare dyke with capitalist intentions. Then, one very karmic day, a fish tank landed on her head, releasing the energy and time to write a book.

The Way of the Bees
An Ovarian Yarn

A P Clarke

Basement Press
DUBLIN

First published in Ireland in 1995 by
Basement Press
an imprint of Attic Press Ltd
29 Upper Mount Street
Dublin 2

A catalogue record for this title is available from the British Library

ISBN 1 85594 180 5

The moral right of the Author has been asserted.

Cover design: Michael O'Dwyer
Typesetting: Verbatim Typesetting & Design Ltd
Printing: The Guernsey Press Co. Ltd

This book is published with the financial assistance of the Arts Council/An Comhairle Ealaíon, Ireland.

For Swee'Pea
With all my love

Cast of Characters

The Mainlanders

Mother Nature	The Creator of All Things
St Gubnet	Of Balleyvourney
Maryann Leaf	Horticulturalist
Professor Louis Sterne	The Paris Institute of Genetics
Captain McCarthy	Captain of Mother Nature's private yacht

The Island of Ascourt

Queen Bea	The Queen
Princess Vee	Her middle sister
Princess Min	Her youngest sister
Queen Charlotte	Their mother (RIP)
Dr Heron Home PhD	Island Manager of Ascourt
Delia du Pont (MD)	Ascourt's State Pathologist
Montague du Pont	Delia's sister and local journalist
Yossarian	Queen Bea's Nanny
Cook	Cook
Sorrel	Guardian of Ascourt's Northern Territories
Dame Clemis	Head of the Old Dames Breakfast Club
Dame Agnetha	Counsellor
Dame Thwaites	Proprietor of Swann's Hotel, Ascourt
Dame Toplis	Dame Thwaites's bridge partner
Dame Murphy	Mechanic
Dame Meleka	Medical Herbalist

The Island of Porschia

Porky	The Queen of Porschia
Princess Tamarind	Porky's daughter
Hayde Lewis	Island Manager of Porschia

PART ONE

PART ONE

CHAPTER ONE

Mother Nature

In the beginning,
Mother Nature emerged from her chrysalis. She filled all of space with Her thoughts and feelings. She had created Herself and She knew it was good.

In the second age of creation,
Mother Nature marvelled at every turn and fold of Her infinite complexity. She realised the intensity of Her thoughts and feelings as events; and from each event sprang thoughts and feelings anew. She had created infinite creativity and She knew She was a genius.

During the third age of creation,
Mother Nature imagined others like Her, yet there was no other like Her.

She filled the universe with the soulful echoes of Her longing – but She was all that was. On the verge of deepest despair, the breath of creation rushed out of Her lungs in a terrible sigh; and when at last She opened Her eyes, the world had been born and its inhabitants too, in the likeness of Her very own image.

She watched as they stirred into life, just as She had Herself on Her own first wondrous day. She saw that desire was the key to creation, and She was inspired to think Her desire could produce such beauty and happiness.

Over the course of the fourth age of creation,
Mother Nature realised that a serious problem was developing. The world and its beautiful inhabitants were basking in the lights of Her own creativity. They did not seem to know that they were meant to be separate from Her. They felt every thought and feeling of Hers as their own. There were no boundaries between them. Painfully, She realised what She

must do. She called the people unto Herself and told them of Her intention.

'I feel deeply about you, as you do about me. But I must leave for fear that you will never come to know yourselves in my presence.' As She exhaled a swarm of bees emerged from Her nostrils. 'The bees are here to teach you. Trust in the order of Nature. You must each one learn to be about your Mother's business.'

When She finished speaking, a bee landed on Her hand and stung Her. The world cried out with the intensity of Her pain. All was thrown into chaos. Mother Nature held out Her throbbing hand and tried to make them understand.

'The greatest gift I have to give you is each of yourselves. Let The Way of the Bees remind us of the pain of our separation and of the perfection that once was between us. Follow their ways and you shall know Mine.'

Sadly and lovingly, She left them, knowing that they would not choose to become themselves until they felt the pain and chaos of a world without Her. Paradise was lost. It did not feel good. It was a choice that was no choice. She felt bound to give them what She had given Herself – the gift of creation; their Mother's business.

But still She was linked to their every thought and action, and at first, She did not go away completely. She hid nearby and listened with all her rapt attention. The world was consumed with its newfound pain and chaos. They talked of nothing else. Soon Her head pounded and Her ears rang. She knew She must release the untenable reins of responsibility.

Mother Nature closed Her eyes and ears and imagined a place called the overworld, high above the disillusionment and haste. It was a place for the mind to rest. It was heaven, and She wanted to be there.

Throughout the fifth age of creation,
Mother Nature sat in the spacious library of the overworld, contemplating the pain and suffering of Her people on earth. They looked up to Her, they saw Her in the stars, the sun and the moon. They said She was the one true goddess and creator of all things. They dreamed of dying and being reunited with Her in heaven.

Mother Nature shook Her head wisely and saw the

nature of their misunderstanding. She was no more 'all that is good' than they were 'all that is not good'. She alone knew just how difficult it had been to create anything at all – movement, thought, desire, love, Herself, the whole damned blessed world. The people could gaze at the stars all they liked, but to die seeking Her pristine perfection would mean nothing less than a moribund eternity in heaven. And it was such a boring place!

To redress the imbalance, Mother Nature created the underworld. In its centre, She carefully placed the Seven Rules of Creation and surrounded it with the cryptic maze of human suffering. Those few who would willingly go through hell to seek out the underworld would find valuable insights and nuggets of wisdom strewn all along its tortuous path. Those who died searching would gain the Rules and be miraculously reborn with Her blessing.

It was the fifth age of creation. Mother Nature had created Herself, the world and its creatures. They had no idea how much She was missing them, for She Herself was made of the same stuff – the same flesh and blood, lust and lovingness. She had created the overworld and the underworld, but if She stayed much longer, She would become rigid with their dreams of a perfect Mother.

No, She decided, She would return to earth and live Her own life. She had more *joie de vivre* and mischief than the whole lot of them put together. What was the point in people worshipping the one true goddess in the overworld? Life was for the living and, anyway, nobody would know She was gone.

To herald the sixth age of creation,
Mother Nature returned to earth and was appalled to discover that nobody remembered, or had even heard of, The Way of the Bees. It was an interesting position to find Herself in – for without even one person to believe in Her, She supposed that it might also be true that She was technically, at any rate, no longer a goddess. Nobody followed Her around the world, save the odd companionable bee.

Mother Nature travelled to Ireland because She had heard tell of a woman who lived among the fairy people. When She reached the isolated village of Balleyvourney in

County Cork, She received a hearty welcome and was pleased to hear that the story was not only true, but the woman was also immortal – a gift bestowed on her by the bees to whom she had shown an extraordinary devotion. Even the Church was enamoured, for St Gubnet of Balleyvourney had been christianised, after the fashion, and named the patron saint of bees. Mother Nature shook Her head. It was too good to be true, but She wasted no time finding the lake where the holy woman prayed.

By the shores of tranquil Gougonbarragh, Mother Nature was transfixed by the figure of the kneeling saint whose life so obviously exemplified The Way of the Bees. Before long, the woman stood up and boldly swept round to face Her. The features on the exquisitely chiselled face were enough to take Her breath away. She wore red curls, hooding dark green eyes, and had the laugh of a lark in spring. But whether it was in the toss of the locks or the play of an eye, Mother Nature was quite overcome with the strength of a sexuality as lustful as Her own.

'Where are the fairy people?' enquired Mother Nature politely, looking to left and right.

'They're not fairies!' laughed Gubnet, 'they're Bee People!'

And Mother Nature was entranced by their story. And with each word, Gubnet drew closer until they were hand-in-hand, strolling in the wake of a pair of swans: two timeless couples whispering, nudging, confiding and agreeing on the peaceful shores of the holy lake.

'I am only a human,' told St Gubnet, 'yet I learned everything I know of the Way of the Bees from those you call the fairies. But long ago, they were revered as the mighty descendants of a cross between a human and a bee. Now the Bee People are hunted and persecuted in these most christian lands. They hide, for fear of being seen. They are misunderstood – for they look like humans but they live as bees.'

Mother Nature vowed most solemnly that She would protect the Bee People, 'For they are My Chosen Ones.'

They left the lake and crossed silently into the forest to the cottage where Gubnet lived. The birds took a keen interest in their embrace, commenting on every aspect of their kiss until a hundred songs were composed and sung, wishing them and their children's children sound hearts and sturdy nests.

It was an age of productivity and predictability. Mother Nature and St Gubnet founded the Convent for the Keepers of Bees, they built the Great Apiary and owned every business in the tiny village of Balleyvourney. The local people became skilled in the distilling of mead, the art of candlemaking and the carving of waxseals. Tourism flourished and hostelries sprang up all over the burgeoning town.

Mother Nature cleverly bought up islands off the coast of Ireland where Her Chosen Ones could live and work according to the Way of the Bees. In return, the Bee People were a grateful hive of industrious activity, and by the end of the sixth age, She had undisclosed personal wealth, worldwide interests and a life and love of Her own.

It would be easy to underestimate the magnitude of such a feat in an era obsessed by the triple god. Naturally, She was tactful about blowing Her own trumpet. But She was, after all, the one true goddess, and She was very much back in business.

The seventh age of creation began in 1781,
coinciding, in Mother Nature's mind, with the 'eruption' of Uranus into the cosmos, demanding a premature end to the age of Pisces. From thereon in, it was change, change, change. In some respects, She gave in. Technology was a tremendous boon to margins. By the end of the nineteenth century, She and Gubnet formed a limited company to keep abreast of the changing times. They poached the best university graduates to run it and by the middle of the twentieth century, Mother Nature International had offices in Dublin, London, New York and Balleyvourney, Co. Cork. It was a giant in an age of corporate multinationals.

Mother Nature was adamant, however, that the Way of the Bees was a predictable, productive, holistic system that defied scientific advancement. And up to the 1960s, She was probably correct in that assertion. While Mother Nature International diversified, the remote island colonies of the Bee Peoples remained untouched, and, in consequence, became an economic liability in an age of technological specialisation.

In 1961, after Gubnet had earned a Degree in Business Studies from MIT, she persuaded Mother Nature to appoint some of the highly qualified graduates in her class as Island

Managers. Her argument was a convincing one: each Island Manager would be paid on an incentive scheme, their job to assess the best specialist industry for each island in concert with the Way of the Bees. Gubnet cited the recent market research on royal jelly to augment her case. Mother Nature expressed reservations. A sophisticated human presence might contaminate the Bee People. She was right, insofar as it did – but the real problems began when the newly appointed managers argued that a rationalised, streamlined industry could not possibly emerge from the island colonies without electricity. It was duly installed. Business boomed. The Island Managers took a percentage of the gross earnings and for the first time ever, the Bee People were paid a wage. They became consumers, buying televisions and washing machines.

The visible signs of unrest did not emerge fully until 1978, when Mother Nature paid a courtesy visit to Queen Charlotte of the island colony of Ascourt. The meeting was an eye-opener. There was no reasoning with the misguided and rebellious Charlotte. Even the Island Manager seemed completely under her spell. In an act of shortsighted defiance, Ascourt had abandoned the Way of the Bees.

It was the seventh age of creation, and Uranus was conspiring against Her. Change for the sake of change. Free love, feminism, ban the bomb, artificial insemination... It was all very well – and there were profits to be made! – but where would it all end? It was an imperative bee in Mother Nature's bonnet that one small corner of the world remained faithful to Her ideal. The Way of the Bees was perfect, predictable and productive. In 1984, the renegade Queen Charlotte died at the fortuitous age of forty-six, and by the end of the 1980s, all the island colonies were in profit, with the conspicuous exception of Ascourt.

St Gubnet met her new class under the majestic old linden tree in the opulent grounds of Balleyvourney's Convent for the Keepers of Bees. The course was experimental and entirely new. It was the first of its kind in the country. There were bound to be teething problems, but Gubnet felt prepared for all eventualities.

'Now, I've been informed that none of you have had any previous experience with apiary work, that is to say, the art of beekeeping,' she beamed. 'So we had best start with a few basics.' Facing her was the convent building, and two floors up Gubnet could just make out Mother Nature's handsome profile looking down upon her. *In wickedness and in wealth...* She was never prepared for the fiery shiver that her lover's gaze still sent through her.

'There are two types of bee,' she began, 'male and female. First, but not foremost, is the male bee, or drone. You will always know him as he has a distinguishable drone mark – a widow's peak, or as some like to say, a heart-shaped face – and indeed he is a fun-loving playboy. He has never been known to hurt anyone, but he has also never been known to do any useful work – apart, that is, from fertilising the Queen.'

There were noticeable deep guffaws from some of the students. Gubnet did not approve of co-education. Fortunately, this revolutionary new training course was only six weeks long. Thereafter the sixty-four inmates would leave the sacred grounds of Balleyvourney Convent to be scattered around the country, at the government's pleasure, for three years' valuable work experience.

'Drones are fed on demand,' continued Gubnet. 'Whatever they want they are given, without question, by the female bees, the stalwarts of the hive. And this brings me to the fair sex. Both Queens and Workers are female. Now a Queen's job is to lay eggs, both male and female. A female egg can become a Queen or a Worker, depending on the diet it receives in its first week after hatching. Lots of royal jelly makes a Queen, ordinary food makes a Worker. So perhaps we are what we eat, do you see?'

It was a close and humid September morning. Gubnet surveyed the shifting crowd before her, and beyond them, the reassuring ring of twelve-foot-high electrified steel and barbed wire fencing recently added to the perimeters of the convent grounds. She loosened the red silk cravat around her neck and breathed deeply to release the tension in her lower back.

'Without fertilisation by the drones,' pumped Gubnet into the unreceptive vacuum, 'the Queen can still lay eggs, but they will all be males – and that would be a disaster, for a hive full of drones is no hive at all. Proper fertilisation by the drones will allow the Queen to lay eggs of the female sex, and thereafter males, as the hive may require. Now, as soon as the young Queen is fertilised high up in the air, by five or six drones who sacrifice their lives and their genitals into her reproductive tract, she returns to the hive and is fed by her female Worker bees.'

Gubnet was not surprised to see that the class had shrunk noticeably since she last looked up from her lecture notes. It was to be expected. And it was just as well that the convent, in its transformation into a private-sector prison, had followed the eminently sensible guidelines of the Department of Justice. If any of them got beyond the fence, they most certainly would not make it past the bee hives.

'Now, where was I? Yes, some of you may well ask – can a Worker bee lay eggs? And the answer is that yes, she can. But she will never be fertilised, so her eggs can only be males. And that is why the Queen secretes a special substance which keeps her Workers' ovaries undeveloped. The Worker bee may have an individual function at a given time, but she never has any individuality, save her loyalty and service to the Queen whose job it is to regulate her community in a productive and predictable way. There can only be one Queen per colony, for she is the nerve centre of the hive.

'A healthy Queen, fertilised only once, when young, has to do no more than swell full of eggs and lay them over the course of her lifetime. All the resources of the hive are put at her disposal. Her job is simply to lay the eggs and secrete substances from her body which regulate the hive. She is constantly attended and groomed by the Workers who pick up her substances on their bodies and pass it to one another in the course of their daily tasks. It is a most ordered and elegant means of communication. Indeed it is the Way of the Bees.'

Her own first-day nerves and earlier feelings of nausea had eased somewhat. The dozen or so young faces left in the group were demonstrating a partial sentience. Yawning with them, Gubnet proceeded to wrap up 'An Introduction to Beekeeping'.

'There will be no more lectures today. You can amuse yourselves till after lunch and you may inform your missing colleagues that there will be a tour of the old convent and the Great Apiary beginning here at two o'clock sharp. Now before we go – any questions?'

'What happened to the lovely drones, Miss?' came a raised female voice.

'Who?' replied Gubnet absently.

'The drones, Miss, after they've had the Queen – you know!' giggled the student.

Gubnet was gobsmacked. 'Drones?' she quavered. 'Drones? Gone, gone, they eat too much. Out – kicked out. Gone, gone for good, good for nothing!'

*

The Convent for the Keepers of Bees
Balleyvourney, County Cork,
Republic of Ireland

Dr. Heron Home, PhD
Island Manager of Ascourt
c/o The Ascourt Institute of Technology
Ascourt Island

September 9, 1996

Dear Doctor Home,

It has been quite some time since we received any communication from the Island Colony of Ascourt. As you may remember, your terms of employment as a Manager of one of my Island Colonies includes an annual report, i.e., once a year.

Like you, Heron, Gubnet lived as a human being among the Bee People. Unlike Robinson Crusoe, she did not succumb to the idle folly of going native. We are really quite anxious about you. Are you being held hostage?

In your last report dated 1986 you mentioned that Ascourt was specialising in genetic engineering and we would be pleased to hear of any progress you are making in that area. Of course we understand that Queen Charlotte's death, twelve years ago, was a terrible shock to you, but surely you can appreciate that we must be furnished with the relevant financial details in order to ascertain our own tax position with reference to the domestic inland revenue.

Now, Heron, as you know, since Uranus was discovered in 1781, technology has been revolutionised and my name has not escaped the watchful eye of the computers in the Tax Office. I realise that Ascourt is the furthest of my Island Colonies from the mainland, and that you may not have heard the unfavourable news that since last year, islands off the coast of Ireland are no longer subject to the tax-free status that I negotiated way back in 1781.

My tax bill for 1996 is longer than the telephone number you would dial to reach me from Ascourt, and I would like to hear from you soon. I am not a vindictive woman but half a million pounds has been mooted to me by my accountants Gilbey and Lynch as a not unreasonable estimate as to the profits of any reputable establishment involved in the trade of genetic engineering *over a period of ten years*, Heron.

Do give my blessings to the new Queen of Ascourt – Queen Bea. Am I right in thinking she has recently come of age?

We are a reputable family business, and you have always been a friend to us both. We are keeping abreast of modern times and you wouldn't recognise the old convent. Gubnet is at this very moment lecturing our first batch of juvenile offenders. I can see her from my window as I write. We plan on an intake of eight six-week sessions of approximately sixty 'students' per year. The EU pays us a grant of £1,000 per client (see the European Co-Educational Juvenile Re-orientation Programme), which works out at half a million pounds *per annum*, Heron. It is indeed a very lucrative business, and much needed since vocations are down, and young girls have better things to do with their family's money.

Which reminds me, I would have liked to have attended Queen Bea's eighteenth birthday celebrations which I read about in the social page of the *Irish Herald* of 12.02.96. Perhaps our invitation got lost in the post; at any rate it never arrived.

You will be as proud as I am to hear that Gubnet was recently awarded her Masters degree in Genetic Engineering in Paris for inventing a revolutionary dual purpose 'super' drone, i.e. the Superdrone. She is very busy, dividing her time between me and the demands of research abroad. She has become quite the expert on French cuisine and I must say that the added weight suits her. My health is good but I am having my varicose veins done so I will not be accompanying Gubnet on our tour of the islands in a fortnight's time.

My last visit, as you may remember, was in 1978 – the year Queen Charlotte produced her first and last three eggs at the miraculous age of forty. I had been labouring under your assurances that Charlotte was completely sterile, and I do hope that she has not passed on this condition to her daughter, Bea. Needless to say, I informed the press of your gender when asked to confirm a report that the said Queen Bea was the love-child of a *totally inappropriate liaison* between the former and much respected Queen Charlotte of Ascourt and *you*, of all people, Heron.

Ascourt is always close to my thoughts, and never more so than now. I cannot find it in my heart to forgive Queen Charlotte for abandoning the Way of the Bees, but a new era is underway and I believe that the introduction of the Superdrone to Ascourt would be both timely and productive. It is in keeping with Charlotte's wish that the reproductive methods of the Bee People be revolu-tionised, and it is in keeping with mine that Ascourt become a flagship – indeed, a model island – for genetic advancement germane with the Way of the Bees. The Superdrones are absolutely free of charge – consider them a gift from Me. It is time to bury the hatchet, Heron.

Gubnet is looking forward to meeting you and exchanging some hi-tech shop talk on the state of the art with you very soon.

Yours in productivity and predictability,

Mother Nature

*

It was a fortnight later on the morning of September 23rd, 1996 when two voices rose and fell from the nest of a well-worn four-postered bed. The convent bells chimed six. The morning star was visible on the western horizon. Overlooking the college quadrangle was a window framed in leaves of ivy alight with the wind and the shadows of a dawn candle. The rest of the building was in darkness, its inhabitants still hostage to sleep.

'I simply can't get used to us being a prison,' came the first. 'It's intolerable. I want us to move out. Could we not live in my old cottage by Gougonbarragh Lake?'

'But you thought it was the height of luxury when we bought this old convent in the sixteenth century,' reminded the second.

'That was different. There were no men, for a start... you

know I'd rather be a gannet with a broken wing than a prisoner in my own home,' came the plaintive response.

'I know, I know. But it's the industry of the future, my love. There are only two growth areas in Ireland – '

'Unemployment and crime,' intoned the other as if by rote.

'Yes, and now the private sector has stepped in. It's cheaper for Europe to pay us a grant for every prisoner we house than to build more prisons. The private sector is simply more efficient and economic. I mean we're even providing training schemes and jobs for the country – '

'Why on earth could we not have been a women's prison? Why all these revolting men? I feel as if I hardly know you these days.'

The second voice remained calm and reasonable despite the early tirade. 'You haven't seemed much yourself lately either…'

'I want us to move out of this rat-trap and set up home like a normal family,' stung Gubnet.

'Don't I want you to stay at home and be with me like a normal family,' remonstrated Mother Nature. 'But you'd rather be in Paris eating croissants. That's hardly my fault!'

Gubnet leapt up and started rummaging in her wardrobe. She found the suitcase she so recently unpacked and threw it open on the bed.

'I'll gladly quit my research in Paris if you agree to retire from Mother Nature International,' challenged Gubnet angrily.

'Retire?' boomed Mother Nature. 'Retire? The seventh age of creation is barely in swing and you want me to retire?'

'For the last two weeks,' lectured Gubnet icily, 'I have been in Paris getting the Superdrones ready for transport to Ascourt. This morning I'm up at the crack of dawn on a business trip paying courtesy calls to your bloody islands, on your bloody yacht with a load of bloody Superdrones that I couldn't care less about. I am tired of doing business for you. I am sick to death of playing second fiddle to Mother Nature bloody International.'

Mother Nature recoiled at the sudden twist. She felt a loneliness from a long ago and faraway place which was deep inside herself. There was a strangeness in her voice which spoke, 'I have never before felt so far away from you. What is wrong? What has become of the Gubnet I once loved?'

'I want us to have a daughter,' pleaded Gubnet emotionally.

'But that's impossible!' exclaimed Mother Nature quite rationally.

'Nothing is impossible if you desire it enough,' retorted Gubnet as she smartly zipped up the bulging suitcase. 'The only wonder is that we have a relationship at all.'

'I do not desire children,' stated Mother Nature defensively, 'I do not wish to retire and I do not want to continue this hysterical line of conversation.'

'Well if that's your attitude,' said Gubnet heading for the door, 'then put this in your pipe and smoke it. Either you agree to have a child with me or I'm leaving you – '

'Don't you want breakfast before you go?' interrupted Mother Nature, grasping for straws.

'No!' screamed Gubnet, her green eyes sparking with fury, 'I just want an answer!'

The door slammed shut and a great tear rolled down Mother Nature's face. A vast expanse of lonely bed enclosed Her. *What a fool I've been*, She snuffled miserably, *what a happy deluded old fool I've been*. And then for one small moment She allowed herself to imagine the unimaginable joy of Gubnet carrying their very own child. But Mother Nature had not got to where She'd got by dwelling on the impossible. And then suddenly it became crystal clear. Of course, that's why Gubnet had spent so long 'studying' in Paris – and no doubt she'd be hurrying back to join the father of the child. The change, the difference in her since she'd come home, of course! *It's so sad*, howled Mother Nature. *It's so sad and I'm so lonely*, She choked convulsively. *I'll never trust anyone again for the rest of my life*, She wailed.

And the world was cast into darkness. It was the seventh age of creation; and everything was impossible.

CHAPTER TWO

St Gubnet's Voyage

September 23 – November 11, 1996

The great white yacht was the pride of Mother Nature's shipping fleet. It was anchored just off Whiddy Island as its size proscribed a berth in any of the smaller, more idyllic harbours off the rugged coast of West Cork. Gubnet sat into the motor launch which bravely chopped its way past Whiddy, and within ten minutes she was clambering aboard to begin the long-planned tour of the islands, *sans* Mother Nature, very possibly *sans* relationship and if so, almost certainly *sans* the future she wanted with the woman she loved.

Gubnet ran her hand along the freshly polished railing of the gleaming white boat. The full implication of this morning's argument was clear: their relationship was not a priority in Mother Nature's ordered existence. But if that were true, mulled Gubnet, then things were doubly uncertain, for until this morning she would have had no reason to suspect otherwise. If she was not a priority, then who or what was? Gubnet noted that the door to the ship's boardroom was sticky with brine. Had there been a myriad such telltale signs of neglect? She looked out to sea and at once she felt guilty for wishing Neptune's vast forgetfulness between herself and the mainland.

The Captain joined her immediately in the tiny but elegantly furnished boardroom.

'Saint Gubnet,' said the Captain, smoothly pulling out a highback Windsor chair, 'could I recommend a brandy to settle the stomach, perhaps?'

'Madam will do,' replied Gubnet, taking an immediate dislike to his unsolicited familiarity. She could hardly remember what it was like to be in good form and she was not about to take a slack attitude from subordinates. She pointed at the chair, still in his hands. 'Sit,' she commanded.

The Captain sat staring out the porthole in manly disbelief as Gubnet paced around the elliptical mahogany table instructing him on the details of the six-week voyage. He had quite genuinely anticipated that the trip would be a gentle cruise, a semi-official holiday: a reward for a long and dedicated service to the firm. For the first time in his life he felt queasy. He was only half listening when a droning began in his head. He was sure he was going to be ill. Gubnet worked her way steadily through the itinerary, island by island: the list of cargoes to be collected and supplies to be delivered, the order of filling in the dockets, the ship's log which she would check every night and the protocol the ship's crew were to follow depending on island custom. She had assumed her lecturing voice.

'Madam,' interrupted the Captain suddenly pointing to the porthole, 'I should tell you that we have just been surrounded by an army of hostile rowing boats. It may be wise to…'

'The Superdrones,' remarked Gubnet sourly. 'They are coming on board and will be housed in the lower decks for the duration of the passage.'

The Captain stood up weakly and put his swarthy hands against his ears. The droning was now unmistakable.

'They're all for Ascourt,' she said wryly.

'But that's the last stop,' groaned the Captain. 'You mean we have to put up with that cacophony for the next six weeks?'

'It's like this,' began Gubnet in a conspiratorial whisper. 'These Superdrones are laboratory-bred creatures, d'you see? They've never laid eyes on a woman before, so we'll have to operate a policy of strict segregation – with you being the only qualified male on board, so to speak, I think it best that you take sole charge of their welfare during our voyage. If you think you're up to it, of course.'

'But I don't know anything about drones,' fumbled the Captain nervously. 'We seem to be in something of a dilemma.'

'The Superdrones are programmed to imprint on the first woman they come into contact with, and since I'm the only woman on board, I see no dilemma whatever.' The most senior member of the crew moaned softly as Gubnet swept past him. 'I'm told a double brandy works wonders for a nervous disposition, Captain.'

While St Gubnet and Captain McCarthy sought refuge in their respective cabins, it was left to an inexperienced crew to escort the Superdrones safely on board. Due to the high spirits of the cargo, it was well past noon before the great white yacht began its journey out of Bantry Bay.

As the ship sailed, Gubnet sat recovering on a deck chair, taking in the marvellous view of the lush green hills sloping down towards the sea. In the distance she spied a small motor launch advancing on white foam at a terrifying speed. She took off her sunglasses and peered through her binoculars. Within minutes, it was alongside the yacht.

'This is the Irish Navy,' barked the loudhailer. 'I repeat, this is the Irish Navy. Slow down to two knots. We are boarding your vessel.'

A rope ladder was immediately thrown over the side; the commando clambered on board and handed a sealed document to the Captain. It was an order from the Admiral of the Irish Navy that all private vessels sailing in Irish waters would henceforth and herewith be escorted by Navy personnel. It was a reasonable precaution, the letter went on, a security measure against unforeseen threats from foreign powers.

The Commando lowered the automatic rifle, took a step towards Gubnet and saluted before curtly dismissing the launch.

'Lieutenant Min. At your service, Madam.'

Gubnet looked straight into the Lieutenant's steely eyes. She found herself trembling.

Gubnet watched the young officer's every move from the closed circuit TV monitor in her cabin. She ordered a small tray of tea and toast and sent an apology to the Captain's dinner table for her absence due to fatigue. After the light but refreshing repast, she put on her reading glasses and examined the letter from the Navy Admiral. There was no doubt in her mind that Mother Nature was responsible – Navy Admirals simply did not sign themselves *Yours in Productivity and Predictability*. The letter had been forged. Gubnet was now certain of one thing. Whoever Lieutenant Min was, he was in the employ of her former lover. These words were new to her. They were distinctly unpalatable. *My former lover*. It bequeathed the astringent taste of deceit.

The presence of the young man strangely unnerved her. Gubnet watched him closely through the TV monitor. The lieutenant had dressed for dinner. Gubnet gasped. His slim figure was sheathed in a flowing black Aikido robe, a trailing white sash circling the forehead, almost crowning a head of finely shaved black stubble. As he moved, she could feel his vibrations inside her. She was overwhelmed by waves of panic and confusion. The electronic spy bore witness that Lieutenant Min was in the grips of a similar discomfort.

Gubnet watched the screen hesitantly. First, he plugged his ears with cotton wool. She could hear it too – there was an unnatural vibration in the boat. It was a swelling sound which made its way to the centre of the brain and from here, set up its own pulsating resonance. It felt exactly as if one were being insidiously overtaken by an alien force. Gubnet followed with her eyes, and when the Lieutenant descended the lower decks, the subsonic din became unbearable.

Lieutenant Min centred himself and breathed deeply to counteract the nausea. Ten years training at the Kyoto Military Academy had prepared him well. He unsheathed his sword and flung open the only cabin door on the otherwise deserted corridor. He could not believe his eyes.

'Drones!' he muttered incredulously above the noise.

For a faint second he felt himself losing control of his motor nerves. He knotted his eyebrows in concentration and began a slow dance with his sword cutting the figure eight high above his head. He moved with the agility of a cat, and every drone watched him nervously.

Lieutenant Min understood men. Teach them who's boss. He had left home when he was six years old and lived in an exclusive world of blood, sweat and Aikido. He did not know that drones were passive by nature. More seriously, he did not know that the drones were vying to disrobe their queen, whose scent had overpowered them completely. As far as they were concerned, the queen had danced for their eyes only. They were in the presence of a regally dressed and intoxicating beauty whose every action affirmed their passionate existence.

'Take off your trousers and stand up in a straight line!' he barked.

The drones tittered and blushed.

Lieutenant Min coolly inspected them, one by one. He seemed surprised at the microscopic nature of their nether regions. Trained in the correct use of weapons, he put his long sword back into its sheath and produced, instead, a schoolboy's penknife.

'Any more of that racket and I'll cut off your balls, understood?'

Lieutenant Min slammed the door behind him and made his way towards the bridge. He stopped for a moment to listen but the droning had well and truly ceased.

The drones, one and all, slept peacefully. Their queen was imprinted in their noses, minds and hearts. And they would follow her wherever she went.

Lieutenant Min acknowledged to himself a slight disappointment; he had been denied a fight. He shrugged his broad shoulders. These drones were dishonourable, after all.

Gubnet switched off the TV screen. It was just as well, she supposed, that he had taken an interest in the Superdrones. She tried to put him out of her mind, but he just wouldn't go. Eventually, she reached for her needlework and crocheted like a demon, knotting waves and spirals where no man could follow.

Through the porthole in her cabin, all gave way to darkness. But Gubnet slept fitfully; she was prescient of danger. She went through every detail of her argument with Mother Nature. *It's all my fault*, thought Gubnet ruefully. *I bred the Superdrone.* And Mother Nature had been so enthusiastic, for nowhere on earth existed a dual purpose drone that would work as well as reproduce. What a boon to the island economies – and what a mark of progress. Mother Nature suggested a pilot project – a suitable island to test the efficacy of the revolutionary Superdrones. Gubnet favoured the island of Porschia, a wealthy economy which was well run and always hungry for new ideas and methods. But Mother Nature wanted the Superdrones on Ascourt. She was adamant – Ascourt must revive its economy and return to the Way of the Bees. Young Queen Bea was eighteen. She was ready to reproduce and Ascourt desperately needed to be populated with young, healthy workers. Gubnet had been left with no choice but to agree. To do otherwise would have raised Mother Nature's suspicions. It was a hideous mess.

The dawn enlightened her spirits with a simplicity of outlook. The young man was obviously on board with his firearms to carry out Mother Nature's orders – to ensure that the Superdrones arrived at their destination. The bones of their decaying union were finally showing themselves for what they really were. Mother Nature no longer trusted her. Well, the mistrust was mutual. The Superdrones were a real liability now that she needed Ascourt more than Ascourt needed her. She would not go back to Mother Nature; things had come far too far…

Gubnet washed, dressed and viewed herself uncertainly in the mirror. She vowed to rise each morning with the sun. She strolled up to the main deck. You are not a quitter, she told herself.

Each morning Lieutenant Min woke at dawn, rounded up the Superdrones and took them out on the main deck for a five-mile run before breakfast. The Captain adopted a policy of non-interference and diplomatically stayed out of the way, thanking his God for minor miracles. The dinner table remained an all-male concern with the lieutenant proving to be an amiable sort of chap.

On the morning of Friday, November 8th, the Captain entered the harbour of their penultimate destination. The Porschians ran a model island. The Island Manager, one Hayde Lewis, spent more time abroad than at home, negotiating international contracts for the sale of royal jelly, the lucrative local product. The island was run in the traditional Way of the Bees, and the Queen of Porschia greeted the arrival of the ship by announcing a long weekend of feasting and fun.

Gubnet did not feel up to it, but her official duties could not be shirked. The Queen of Porschia was avid for news of the Superdrones and conveyed her disappointment that Porschia had not been chosen for the pilot project. She expressed the opinion to Gubnet that in Ascourt 'the poor lads' would very probably be 'hurled off the cliffs by fairies'.

The weekend seemed never-ending to Gubnet. She found

their food too rich, their rituals too long and their speeches ideal for a restorative catnap. She wasn't allowed a moment to herself. Lieutenant Min avoided the festivities and maintained a routine vigil along the corridor of the Superdrones. The Captain was taken in by a coquettish invitation to spend the weekend in the Queen of Porschia's private ranch, resulting in a scattering of the rank-and-file crew and a concomitant shortfall in security.

On Sunday afternoon, an unauthorised visitor emerged from the engine room of the yacht. The Queen of Porschia was not aware that she was being followed by Lieutenant Min who, shortly afterwards, apprehended her breaking and entering the Superdrone quarters. The incident was tactfully handled, and the bribe diplomatically refused. Later that evening, Porschian worker females loaded the boat with crates of Royal Jelly and the great white yacht left their prosperous shores for a route due north.

From her private TV monitor, Gubnet watched as Lieutenant Min released the cabin-bound Superdrones on to the deck for a reviving circuit of fresh air and healthy callisthenics. With him safely out of the way, she entered his cabin and instigated a thorough search of his belongings. There were no papers of identification, not even a driver's licence. She subconsciously sensed, but did not note, that the usual manly toiletries were missing. Gubnet turned a small rucksack upside down. Out tumbled three items. An old sepia photograph of three small children on a beach. There was a pack of dehydrated vegan sushi and a box of battered tampons. Gubnet picked up the photo and read the faded inscription on the back. *Bea, Vee and Min, 1984.*

Gubnet lay in wait. She picked up the automatic rifle which the Lieutenant had conveniently left in the cabin and sat pointing it towards the door. At three minutes to eight, the door opened. Before Gubnet had time to announce her presence, Lieutenant Min had stripped off and was heading for the shower.

'Ahem!' coughed Gubnet loudly.

The Lieutenant turned round.

'Holy Mother, you're a woman!'

'The Japanese Navy is an equal-opportunities employer, Madam,' grinned the naked Lieutenant.

'Who are you working for?' rapped Gubnet impatiently on the automatic weapon.

'The gun isn't loaded, Madam,' said Lieutenant Min politely, disappearing into the shower.

Gubnet threw the gun to one side. She was beside herself with rage. She felt like an indignant lioness but there was nothing she could do until the young Lieutenant reappeared, showered and dressed with a radiant smile.

'You're a spy!' accused Gubnet hotly. 'You've been sent to guard the Superdrones and report my movements to Mother Nature!'

'I'm not working for Her,' replied the bemused Lieutenant. 'I'm on indefinite leave from the Japanese Navy – it was only thanks to Mother Nature I heard that my sister is ill. I'm on my way home to Ascourt to look after her.'

Lieutenant Min rolled up the sleeve of her shirt and pointed to her forearm. On it was an ornate tattoo of three bees around the letters, B, V and M.

'Look, see – I'm the Princess Min of Ascourt, Queen Bea's youngest sister.'

Gubnet stared in disbelief. 'Then why all the pretence? If you are who you say you are, then why the uniform, the gun, the carry-on – for the Goddess' Sake why not just come aboard like any decent VIP?'

Princess Min considered this carefully. 'I was led to believe that my life would be in danger if my royal identity was revealed. I was told to stay in uniform for my own protection.'

'By Mother Nature,' concluded Gubnet tersely.

'Yes,' replied Princess Min.

Gubnet sank back on the bed. 'My dear, She was protecting your identity from me. Evidently I was not to know...'

'I don't understand,' said Princess Min. 'You are her girl-friend, aren't you?'

'No. How could you possibly understand,' she stated finally. 'You're not going home to protect your sister, Princess Min. You're being sent to Ascourt by Mother Nature to depose your sister.'

'I don't believe you,' said the Princess sceptically.

31

'You'd better believe it,' said Gubnet urgently, motioning the young woman to sit on the bed beside her. 'Princess Min, listen to me. Mother Nature is the cleverest woman on all earth. I have been completely misled myself. You were disguised in such a way so as to lead me to believe you were a man. I thought nothing of it when you showed an interest in the Superdrones. In fact the Captain and I were quite relieved. Yet Mother Nature must have known that you would have found them. You are a Princess – and the first woman the drones came into contact with. Mother Nature must have planned this right down to the last detail. They have bonded to you – they consider you their Queen. Don't you see?'

Princess Min put her strong, sinuous hand into Gubnet's, like a small child.

'Mother Nature was not invited to Queen Bea's coronation – I suspect She will never forgive that and She cannot accept Queen Bea as the ruler of Ascourt. Now do you see? Mother Nature has chosen you instead. You are being sent back to Ascourt with a bevy of Superdrones who are ready to mate with you. Your people will know it is a sign from Mother Nature. She has ruthlessly and deliberately selected you, a Princess of Ascourt, to tell your very own people, "Return to the old ways, return to the Way of the Bees." Princess Min,' implored Gubnet, 'we both know your people will never accept the Old Ways again – what are we to do?'

Princess Min stood her full five foot two inches and concentrated on Gubnet's tired body.

'First,' she said, 'we must take care of you.' And Princess Min boldly picked Gubnet up off the bed and carried her into the ship's galley. She made Gubnet a glass of warm raspberry leaf tea while she busied herself making a very special macrobiotic broth.

'It'll help,' observed the Princess mysteriously. 'I'd guess you were six months though it hardly shows.'

'It doesn't?' asked Gubnet edgily.

'You're tall and big-boned,' replied Princess Min matter-of-factly.

CHAPTER THREE

A Queen in Love

Tuesday, November 12, 1996

Queen Bea sat thoughtfully in her bed with a mug of thick, black coffee and a French cigarette. Through the long bay window, which was twice as tall as herself, she contemplated the marvellous sight of the sprawling city and the rolling hills beyond. She wondered if she were in love.

On a Sunday morning the queen lingered, making the future. She might add an extra day to the week for instance. It was a special day to make right the time ahead. She could make nights longer, so that people could stay out, party, and sleep in late. She was completely tuned in to their happiness. She had been trained that way since she was young.

But it wasn't Sunday, it was Tuesday...*The Women's Group*. And that she had to face them was exactly the thought which caused her to do something she had never done before. She ordered another cup of coffee and lit a second cigarette.

Ascourt was a long cigar-shaped island, the mighty hills of the East descending gently towards the setting point of the sun. The River Naiad assumed its source from the spas and geysers of the Eastern chalk hills. It cut a steady, latitudinal path across the island, delivering a spectacular waterfall of pure spring water before a sudden dip into the golden beaches of the West. The river cut the island into two equal lengths, the southern half being the townsland from which Queen Bea was presently enjoying the view.

The previous Tuesday had been difficult. The women were angry and frightened about the future. They had sung songs and howled.

The queen had been ill for the rest of the week. Naturally, for she was saddened and confused by their unhappiness.

'I am the will of the people,' she had reminded them. 'I am

the instrument through which you realise what surrounds you.'

Each and everyone of them had fallen silent.

'I can only manifest what you have already decided. I am not the decider,' she finished simply.

What the workers actually decided was to vote on whether or not the queen should be asked to leave the group permanently. As they took the vote by secret ballot, the queen went deep into herself. They had forgotten that no matter what they chose, she looked on it with love, and facilitated them always. She had agonised that she would always *feel* different. Her every cell was the assembly of a long and regal lineage. She was not indifferent to the fact that not one of the women in the group had ever acknowledged what a gargantuan effort she had had to make. It went against the grain for a queen to grapple with notions of equality. Yet like her mother Queen Charlotte before her, she had eschewed personal power, risked the wrath of Mother Nature and actively endorsed the frontier values of Ascourt. No other colony held their females, the workers, in such high esteem. No other colony had committed itself to a change so profound that every asset had been invested in the scientific research to provide the necessary physiological breakthroughs. What other colony could boast, as Ascourt so proudly could, that it had succeeded in doing away with drones? *What other queen*, thought Bea to herself, *would give up an entire Tuesday to discuss feminist socialist politics?*

She got out of bed and struggled to get into her jeans. *Perhaps it's time I laid an egg*, she thought, fighting a feeling of impending failure.

Closing the heavy double doors behind her, Queen Bea inhaled the tranquillising scent imparted by the last few precious blooms of honeysuckle which entirely clothed the walls of the diminutive palace. From this vantage, she could appraise the blue glaze of sea which lay beyond the fertile hills of the uninhabited Northern Territory. The imminent winter gales showed no sign of an early appearance. It was a calm, if slightly dull, November day.

She counted the steps from the front doors of the palace to the Town Square beneath her. At one hundred and six, she stopped and closed her eyes momentarily. At one hundred and seven, she opened them and looked down. It was never, never until one hundred and eight that the River Naiad sprang out and sparkled from the deep, nested cleavage dividing the townsland and the Northern Territory. It was a spectacular descent. By two hundred and sixteen, Queen Bea had recovered her good humour and arrived on *terra firma*.

The plump, bespectacled figure strode across to inspect the sundial in the middle of Town Square. Being overcast, no apparent time could be calculated, gauged, hinted or guessed at. *I cannot possibly be late*, concluded Queen Bea optimistically.

Dame Agnetha's unquestionable skills in the field of consciousness-raising were based on her decision to reverse the normal principles of group dynamics as she understood them from a limited selection of specialist books in the local lending library. The justification for this was that Bee People were oversocialised to the point where, as a local adage had it, 'The most uncomfortable position for a Bee Person to be in, is herself.'

In the community's struggle towards a New Order, it was Dame Agnetha's personal mission that the Bee People of Ascourt learn to become individuals. The problem was that the Way of the Bees was predictable and harmonious. The citizens knew that their feelings and thoughts were automatically linked to the queen whose actions, though unaccountable, represented the sum total of her community's desire. Everyone agreed that some form of decolonisation was necessary, but it was a matter of national obsession as to what the logical first step should be.

The popular opinion was that the Queen should be deprogrammed, after which everyone else could get on with the job. The more sensitive opinion was that the workers should partake in programmes for individual consciousness raising, which in itself would take care of the Queen.

While Dame Agnetha would belong to the second school of thought, she refused to be a party to chicken-and-egg politics. Whatever her critics might think, Dame Agnetha could see for herself that the group were becoming openly critical of the Queen. Progress was being made. It was a first step, however small, towards collapsing the collective Bee Person myth that harmony must at all times prevail. Queen Bea's non-arrival at the first session had presented a fortuitous opportunity for the group to express some significant individual feelings as a result of their disconnectedness from her.

After lunch, Dame Agnetha had carefully selected a moody green kaftan which matched her full head of soft henna curls. The wooden beads around her neck clicked softly as she assumed the lotus position. She initiated the afternoon's session with promptness and sensitivity.

'Now, you all did really well this morning. You focused on Queen Bea as a source of power and you all had to feel what it was like to be out of touch with her, which gave rise to feelings of hate and destruction towards her. But what is hate other than a desire to return to love?'

The group accepted Dame Agnetha's words without so much as a murmur of dissent. They knew she was telling them not to be afraid. But Agnetha challenged them again.

'Now can anyone tell me why we all felt so powerless when we could not be at one with Queen Bea's harmonious love?'

Queen Bea considered this a difficult question. She did not feel powerless, but neither did she feel harmonious, and since both these feelings had more to do with everyone else, she wondered if the very attractive newcomer might be nicer to her than the others.

And it was, in fact, the tall, dark stranger who spoke. 'I suppose one would feel lost without it, once having experienced it, which I have yet to do,' she said, lowering her eyes at Bea whose heart thumped wildly. 'But then again, Queen Bea might like to check out my centre which I think is equally as beautiful.'

Dame Agnetha clapped her bangled hands with delight. But she wasn't the only person impressed by the new arrival. Queen Bea was in love and she hung on every word.

'If I resented you it would surely be because I didn't know the equal potential of my own essential self,' continued the stranger, never once wavering from Queen Bea's attentive gaze.

Dame Agnetha smiled in wise agreement. 'And I can tell at once that you're not from these parts. You see, we in Ascourt are so used to focusing all our activities around our Queen that it is hard to change our ways. We must begin to look at each other with the same respect that we are used to giving our Queen. So this is what we are going to practise this afternoon.'

A vibrant buzz of appreciation went round the room.

'Women, pair up with a partner and sit on the floor with a lighted candle between you. Try not to blink as you stare into each other's eyes. You may begin to see the huge and unsuspected potentials in your partner. Do not be frightened. Try not to make judgements. And no talking from now on, please.'

The women quickly paired up, leaving Queen Bea and the stranger to the last empty mat. Queen Bea smiled awkwardly, removed her spectacles and laid them on the floor beside her. Without her glasses she couldn't see a thing. Bea concentrated on the candle, remembering not to blink. She could feel her eyes sting. It was very romantic to be in a dark room with flickering candles and the one you loved, but she couldn't actually make out a single feature on the stranger's face. After a few minutes, Queen Bea found that her eyes were regularly blurring in and out of focus. Her breathing got slower. With each wave, she saw something different sitting in front of her. At first, it was just a lion, but then it was a crow, and a snake and… time seemed to have taken on a different dimension.

Queen Bea found herself up on a cloud travelling away from Ascourt over an angry black sea. The cloud rolled faster and faster until she was on top of a large white yacht. The stranger held her safe on the cloud, stroking her cheeks and brushing her lips until all they knew was one another. But the excitement gave way to danger when a horrible buzzing started in her ears. A vicious black bee was darting at her true love.

'Don't go!' screamed Bea, but the stranger had jumped off the cloud in fright and all Bea could see was her body plummeting towards the boat. 'No, no, no!' screamed Bea, but it was too late. The bee transformed itself, growing bigger and bigger until right in front of her very eyes was Mother Nature dressed in a long black cape; her face twisted into a vicious snarl.

'What have you done to my friend?' cried Bea miserably.

'Love,' spat Mother Nature, 'is a fool's game, and yours is an ill-fated fortune, Queen Bea. You have forsaken my ways, and as long as you dare to call yourself Queen, I will seek you out and destroy you. You stand horribly cursed!'

And with that Mother Nature jumped on Queen Bea and stung her until she passed out with pain.

*

When Bea came round, she found herself safe in her own bed in the tiny North Wing with a fearful storm raging outside and Nanny Yossarian making a great fuss of her. Bea felt hot tears welling up in her throat. 'It all happened today, Yossarian. I found love and then Mother Nature took her away and She told me I couldn't be Queen any more and She said love was a fool's game and then She cursed me forever – '

'Hush now, you've had a bad fright. Have a drink of this, now there you go,' clucked the deep, matronly voice.

'Yossarian, She stung me all over, here look.' But there wasn't a mark to be seen on her young, smooth skin. 'I'm not making it up, I promise, you have to believe me…'

'Hush, child, settle down. Of course I believe you. How about our favourite bedtime story about your mother, Queen Charlotte?'

'Oh yes,' said Bea glad of the diversion.

Yossarian took Bea's tiny hand in her own. She began in a low melodious voice. '*Once upon a Time*… there lived in Ascourt a brave and beautiful Queen called Charlotte.

'From an early age, she was rational and scientific, an unusual way for a queen to be, because as we all know, a queen's brains are smaller than a worker's. Queen Charlotte spent most of her time peering through microscopes, studiously ignoring the young drones-about-town, any one of whom would have gladly laid down his life just to be seen out with her.

'In despair, her mother took her to one side and gave her a lecture on the Way of the Bees.

'"Charlotte, Ascourt must recognise its Queen. This juvenile behaviour cannot go on much longer – you are twenty-five years old and it is time you reproduced."

'"Well, I just won't," said Charlotte defiantly, 'And you can't make me!"

'"Charlotte, you will listen to reason. If you insist on ignoring the drones, your body will soon start to make it's store of eggs. If these precious eggs are not fertilised by a drone, then you will only be capable of laying male eggs. In time to come you will be held personally responsible for populating Ascourt with nothing but layabout drones demanding food and attention – what precious few worker females are left will die of exhaustion trying to keep their boundless appetites satisfied." Charlotte's mother looked at her sternly. "Now you

38

wouldn't want that, would you?"

'"It's so unfair, mother. How come aphids don't have to mate with drones? How come if an aphid just goes about her business and lays a few eggs they'll all be female? How come if I just go about my business and lay a few eggs they'll all be males, how come?" wailed Charlotte miserably.

'"I'm sure I don't know, Charlotte, I'm sure Mother Nature has her own good reasons for the way She chose to create us and I'm sure you'd be much happier if you didn't question the Way of the Bees so much."

'Charlotte wept tears of uncontrollable anger and frustration. Her mother tried Common Sense.

'"Well, aphids have their problems too, you know. Just think, they're all the same; they look alike, they talk alike, they think alike, they dress alike – they're all identical clones of their mother."

'"Lucky them!"

'"My poor dear," she crooned, squeezing Charlotte into the folds of her ample bosom. "You only have to go to bed with him once ,darling, and you'll never have to see him again."

'"Is that a promise, mother?"

'"He'll be dead as a drone, poor boy, and you'll have enough eggs in your womb to be laying worker females for as long as you live."

'"O mum, it'll be so humiliating!" sobbed Charlotte whose concession, slight as it was, did not go unnoticed.

'"I'll make the arrangements immediately," said her mother wasting no time.

'By nightfall, a hiatus of droning had filled everyone's ears. Only one of them would succeed in mating with the Queen, and for his devotion to duty the prize was great indeed. He would join the list of Great Drones, a statue would be erected to him in the grounds of the palace, and he would die in certain knowledge that he was undisputed father of every egg laid in the queen's lifetime. The drones could not contain themselves. The town's taverns were filled to capacity and the drains were running with mead. The young men talked incessantly of the Great Drones before them, of honour and glory, and of death and destiny. They advised each other in a spirit of masculine generosity as to how best they might prepare themselves for this chance of a lifetime.

'"Remember Valentino? Now he got it right – you see what

a queen wants in a man is that he's dressed smart, smells good and has nice manners in bed. Dunno about you but I'm spending the next few days in the beauty parlour."

'"Na, na, after tonight I'll be in the gym – no boozin' and no birds. Coach sez that you gotta do it at an altitude of three thousand feet mate, now that means training, my old man. No point in bein' all tarted up if you can't take the pace, what?"

'By sunrise, Ascourt was littered with snoring drunken drones. The female workers rose early and began to clear up the debris.

'High up in the palace, Charlotte rose to the majestic sight of Ascourt's flag being raised outside her bedroom window. As the wind released the waxcloth, she watched Mother Nature's face unfold over the words 'Productivity and Predictability'. The words somehow inspired her. Before the awful droning began again, she put on her thinking cap and resolved to find an answer.

'Ascourt was a hive of activity. The drones were being fed on demand and all the reserves of honey had been fermented into mead for their benefit. After the mating had taken place, the drones would not be fed any more, nor given hospitality or shelter. Not one would survive the winter. There were lean times ahead. For while their brothers were talking of dedication to duty, many sisters would die too – for they would refuse food in favour of Queen Charlotte's young. These were exciting times, but the collective instinct of the female workers kept them objectified and distanced in a milieu of angst-ridden signals. They organised themselves into workgangs. There was much to be done.

'To reach the queen, the drones would have to climb to the top of the three thousand-foot tower being built by the female construction workers that Queen Charlotte's mother had hired. The tower was a tube of hexagonal wax cells laid one on top of the other and would, when complete, be three times taller than the palace itself and festooned with flowers from all over the island. Florists and dressmakers were in equally high demand. And no chef was working less than twenty-four hours a day.

'Queen Charlotte plugged her ears with wax, locked herself into her bedroom and refused to read the sycophantic telegrams arriving without respite from lovesick drones. But by night, she frequented a gay bar cleverly made up as a drone. There she would rendezvous with the Island Manager, Dr Heron Home, PhD. It was the quietest spot in town. There wasn't a drone in sight. They sat and talked in total privacy, working out the details of their plan. They were in love, but time was running out for them.

'Then just two nights before The Mating, in walked two gloomy drones. "Psst! I think they're gay," whispered Heron, perking up. Their plan depended on it. Before long, Peter and his sylph-like lover, Daniel were seated and in deep conversation with the two girls who had removed their disguises and revealed who they were. As their stories unfolded, both couples realised an instinctive empathy for each other's impossible plight. Peter and Daniel were lovers and they knew that these few days together would be their last. And when Charlotte and Heron revealed their plan, the two boys immediately agreed, saying that it was "the only reasonable course of action" and they were both "doomed anyway". Peter and Daniel were given instructions for admission into the royal grounds the very next day.

'As planned, Charlotte rose early and joined her mother at the gates of the palace where specialist staff were being recruited to finish the tower and complete last-minute domestic duties.

'"I'm glad to see you taking an interest, Charlotte," said her mother. "Now, what do you think of this one – she's fine and strong, isn't she?" He had followed her instructions to the letter. His hard hat, pulled close down over his forehead, completely hid the drone-mark. Charlotte winked at him, saying, "Have you done this kind of work before"' Peter nodded confidently. "But are you afraid of heights?" enquired her mother. He shook his head shyly, remembering not to speak. "Mother come on, do make up your mind, we're late for breakfast as it is," implored Charlotte. "Yes, yes, very well, you'll do."

'Peter positively skipped through the palace gates, looking round just once to give Daniel the thumbs-up. Charlotte followed her mother to breakfast and breathed a sigh of relief – she had been particularly worried about Peter, but thankfully her mother's appetite was keener than her eyesight.

'Along the queue for Domestic Duties, Daniel struggled to open his handbag and produce a sample of needlework for inspection. But the Head Chamberworker put a restraining hand on his arm and said impatiently, "No seamstresses today.

41

Chefs and florists only." Daniel didn't dare say a word in case he gave himself away, but the woebegone look on his face must have touched the Head Chamberworker's heart. "Come back next month we might find something for you to do, alright love?" Daniel lowered his head and started miserably down the two hundred and sixteen steps of the palace.

'By the time Charlotte discovered that Daniel was missing it was already past suppertime that evening. She and Dr Heron Home once more donned their drone disguises and went about the town in search of him. He did not turn up at the gay bar. Nobody they asked had seen anyone matching his description. By midnight, they admitted defeat. The town was half empty anyway and the droning could hardly be heard. Any of them that fancied their chances were in bed getting a good night's sleep before the rigours of the day ahead. Daniel must have panicked and was probably hiding out somewhere. "He's very thin, Charlotte, and when they stop feeding the drones after The Mating, he'll be among the first to die of starvation – he won't last more than a week, I'm sure," said Heron sadly.

'Finally the day of The Mating arrived. Neither Queen Charlotte nor Heron Home had seen Peter, as he had cleverly built himself into one of the wax cells in the Great Tower. Queen Charlotte's mother shed a tear and gave her daughter a crushing squeeze. "Remember every moment, Charlotte, for this will be the most exciting day of your life. Good luck and may the best man win!"

'Charlotte suppressed a swear word, defiantly took Heron's hand in her own and waved the excited crowd goodbye. As she climbed to the top of the tower, Heron pointed towards the Eastern Chalk Cliffs where the young drones were getting themselves ready for the start of the race. There was a faraway low droning noise and by mid-afternoon it would reach a fever pitch. They hadn't a minute to waste. It would take even the fittest of the drones only three hours to complete the circuit of the island before they began to scale the dizzy heights of the tower in their attempt to be the first to reach Queen Charlotte and fertilise her.

'Heron tapped lightly on the floor of the chamber. Two taps rapped back at her smartly. "Well, he's still alive, thank the stars," breathed Heron heavily. She took out a chisel from her tool kit and began to carve out an escape hole for Peter. Charlotte unpacked a hamper of food. He would be starving by now and he had a long night ahead, if all went according to plan.

'Peter emerged and shook off the waxy flakes of dust. For an instant the little chamber on the top of the tower looked like it had been hit by a blizzard. They all laughed, relieving the tension of the last few days. Peter gobbled a sandwich greedily while Heron boiled a kettle to sterilise the terrifying tools which were emerging from her toolbag. Scalpels, hypodermics, forceps, needles and surgical thread.

'"Now," she said with an air of authority, "I don't want either of you to be in the least bit afraid. You'll each have an anaesthetic and you won't feel a thing. I'll operate on Peter first, removing his genitals. When I've stitched him up, I will insert his genital system into Charlotte's reproductive tract. When the first of the drones starts to arrive, they will assume that Peter is dead, the glorious victor, and that Charlotte is in a state of bliss. I will put Peter's body into the State Coffin and when the party gets under way, I will accompany him to the boat where he will make his escape from Ascourt by dead of night. Is that understood?"

'The frightened pair nodded. Heron loaded the syringe and motioned Peter to roll up his sleeve. She inserted the needle and slowly began to inject the anaesthetic into Peter's arm. "Now count to ten," she said.

'"Where's Daniel?" said Peter suddenly. He struggled against the anaesthetic, but to no avail. He mumbled "Daniel" three times and these three words were the last he ever spoke.'

When Queen Bea looked up, her elegant nanny was pouring tears in great snuffling breaths. Bea handed her a hanky and squeezed her arm. 'It's a very sad story, isn't it?' she said by way of sympathy. 'Peter never got on that boat did he?'

'No, my little pet, he didn't. And there wouldn't have been any point. I'm sure Peter would rather have died than to go on living without Daniel. And Heron and Charlotte knew that too. So when his operation was done, Heron just gave him a little more of the anaesthetic, and you know, well, she didn't do the rest of the operation, so Charlotte was never fertilised and Peter never woke up.' The tears poured down Yossarian's face in a steady stream. 'He's a great Hero now and his statue is so brave and beautiful…'

Queen Bea knew that the story of Peter, the Last Great

Drone of Ascourt, always made her cry. But the story was never over until Bea asked, 'And what became of Daniel?', to which Yossarian always replied, 'The winter of 1963 was the worst winter in living memory. By the following spring, the workers had found over two hundred bodies, one of which was Daniel's. He was buried with all the others in the old drone cells in the Northern Territories. May he rest in peace.'

But tonight the petite nanny, who always underestimated her strength, gave Bea a rib-cracking hug and a lecture instead. 'Your mother Charlotte said to me that no daughter of hers would ever have to endure what she had to go through. The old ways of Mother Nature are lonely and cold. There can be no personal love in the ordered and predictable Way of the Bees. And that's why Charlotte dreamed of a New Order. She said she didn't give a fig for what Mother Nature thought. She said we'd get on better without drones and just muddle along our own way – and she said that love would win in the end.'

'Do you really believe that, Yossarian?' asked Bea intently.

'I try to my love, I try to. And don't you be afraid of Mother Nature. She's afraid too, She's afraid that we're changing the old ways, the tried and tested methods, and like children we'll only end up hurting ourselves. She's just like all mothers really – comes a time you just have to let go. You're just always convinced that you've lived longer, you've seen more and in the end it can tie you in knots because all you're really afraid of is the power of change. And when the fear becomes more than the love, then you end up hurting your own children and I think that's what's wrong with Mother Nature right now. Charlotte wasn't afraid, and you mustn't be either.'

'I found out today that love is painful. Did you know that Yossarian?' said Bea sleepily.

Nanny Yossarian nodded her perfectly held hairpiece. At fifty-one years old she had not forgotten what it felt like to be eighteen and in love. In fact, it haunted her every dream…

'What's her name?' divined the nanny astutely.

'I didn't get a chance to ask her. How come you're so wise and you know everything, Yossarian?'

'Because I'm a nanny and it's my job.' She kissed Bea goodnight and pointed an elegantly manicured finger at her young charge. 'No reading now, you've had a long day. And whoever she is, she can wait till morning!'

CHAPTER FOUR

A Tall Dark Stranger

Thursday, November 14, 1996

The storm which had broken out on the afternoon of what became known as Queen Bea's Premonition did not abate for two days. In Ascourt, the natural forces were taken seriously and interpreted as 'essences', which were akin to messages from the goddess. No one was in any doubt that the elements had been vigorously exercised by Mother Nature to inform the citizens of Ascourt that She Was Not Pleased.

The Old Dames Breakfast Club took a pragmatic view. If Mother Nature was angry with Ascourt, then the first logical step was to find out exactly what She was angry about. If an exact message could be deciphered, then where better than the uninhabited Northern Territories to begin? If there were clues to be hunted, then only here would they be found in pristine condition, and only here would the earth impart her secrets to those whose knowing knew. Such a highly trained Bee Person did exist. And when the last drop of rain had fallen and the last breath of wind expired, the Old Dames Breakfast Club set out towards the small wooden homestead of the sole inhabitant and Guide of the Northern Territories.

As was the custom, meetings began with a hearty breakfast gathered from the wild. The reclusive Guide informed the Breakfast Club that she had already noticed a change in the hills. There were unaccountable disturbances to the local fauna and flora. Her own bees were swarming. The Dames discussed tactics and as the sun rose up towards the meridian they broke up into pairs and scattered among the hills.

The search proved fruitful. Every bird and plant revealed that there was a stranger living in their midst. Eventually their separate journeys led them one by one to the edge of the Spruce Forest. Tucked behind the first row of trees was the entrance to the old drone cells. There were footprints leading into them. There were also several sets of footprints leading away from the ruined cells around the edge of the trees. One trail led them to a neat, oval heap of old leaves and twigs. By the Guide's reckoning it was less than a few hours old; it could only have been made this morning when the storm winds had died down. The Dames tentatively uncovered the mound to find a glider, neatly buried with one broken wing. They were now of one mind. Mother Nature had clearly sent a messenger. And the essence was with whoever was sheltering in the old drone cells.

Dame Agnetha could hardly believe her own absent-mindedness. There was no ferry service to Ascourt and casual tourists were as rare as the corncrake. As she came to her senses she remembered that the strange woman who spoke at the Women's Group had also inexplicably disappeared after Queen Bea's collapse two days ago. There was such a commotion that no one had noticed, nor thought to ask any questions. Queen Bea had been very badly frightened. It was quite possible, thought Agnetha, that the stranger had intended to harm her from the outset.

Dame Agnetha immediately called the group to order and informed them of her thoughts. Like stalking cats, they entered the spooky dark cells, quietly but effectively combing every possible nook among the lifeless skeletons of the old drones. There was nobody there. Back in daylight, their hearts pounded wildly. They rebuilt the stack of leaves and twigs over the glider, covered their tracks and expertly left the area as if they had never been there.

By evening, the immediate essence was clear. Queen Bea was in danger. There was a hired assassin stranded on the island, a tall dark stranger on Mother Nature's payroll.

While the Old Dames investigated the 'essence' of the storm, a line of wellwishers made their way up the two hundred and sixteen steps of the palace. By noon, the heavy oak doors of the front gates were opened and a crowd had gathered hoping for a glimpse of Queen Bea. The cheering stopped as soon as they realised that the Queen herself was not present. The mob pushed its collective way towards Queen Bea's Nanny with cards and presents, some with elixirs and homemade remedies.

A heavy-set woman in tweeds elbowed her way to the front and the crowd obligingly made way for the convivial figure of their local journalist. Montague du Pont was the editor of the *Ascourt Echo*, a bimonthly newsheet which survived on local scandal and the odd scientific scoop from the Ascourt Institute of Technology.

'Is there a statement from the palace?' she shouted, waving her notepad in the air.

'Press can get a statement in the main reception,' nodded Nanny Yossarian. 'Through the front doors and turn left, Montague – you know where it is – and would you mind reading it to the citizens as soon as I've finished up here? Queen Bea is not well enough to see anyone today.'

Montague du Pont casually sauntered through the palace gates and made her familiar way to the entrance hall. As she went through the swing doors, she realised that someone was beside her: a tall dark stranger with a copy of the *Irish Herald* tucked casually under her arm. Montague's heart nearly missed a beat when she saw the tip of a sharpened pencil peek out from the breast pocket of a telling beige raincoat. The salubrious suntan and weather-beaten good looks left Montague du Pont in no doubt as to the identity of her companion.

She recovered her composure and explained to the foreign correspondent of the prestigious mainland daily that palace statements were notoriously slow in arriving. She then politely asked if she could have a look through the *Irish Herald*, and the stranger willingly obliged.

Not a word was passed between them. The stranger took out her notepad and began scribbling. In companionable silence Montague scanned the newspages avidly. She had not seen a copy of the *Irish Herald* in over a month. In the scientific columns, a headline caught her attention. *'SUPERDRONES FOR ASCOURT'*. She checked the date of the newspaper. It was only three days old. *'Mother Nature, Head of Mother Nature International, has successfully bred a Superdrone intended for experimental use on the island colony of Ascourt. This research station has been specially selected to test the efficacy of the Superdrones on an ageing population which has resulted largely from the sterility of native Queens.'*

The article answered all of Montague's questions at once. It wasn't everyday that a big-shot reporter arrived on the otherwise unnewsworthy shores of Ascourt. This Superdrone thing was a bombshell! As editor of their own humble newsheet, she would, of course, do everything in her power to facilitate the foreign press. She would cooperate in every way…

*

It was past lunchtime when the palace porter shuffled in with the statement.

'Did you make this up yourself?' demanded Montague of the weary porter.

'Nobody else was available, Madam, they all seem to have disappeared.'

'Humpph,' snorted Montague. 'QUEEN SENDS LUV, WILL BE OK SOON. I'd better learn that off by heart so's I can recite it to the crowd outside and not mess up my lines,' she said rather pointedly.

The porter was about to shrink back into the labyrinthine corridors when the stranger spoke up.

'I wonder would it be possible to gain a private audience with the Queen?' intoned the rich, mellifluous voice.

The porter shook her head quite firmly. The stranger handed over a sealed envelope. 'I would be grateful if you would use your influence to see that Queen Bea receives this personally. Thank you.'

Montague and the stranger left the palace together. With mercurial quickness, she decided that the best course of action would be to invite the stranger to dinner. An honest reporter would never refuse a free meal and Montague's curiosity was fully aroused. In fact she was bursting. She made a mental note to book a table for two at Swann's. The stranger seemed reserved but the local hospitality would help to loosen her up.

On the steps of the palace, the crowd gathered round and Montague delivered her speech. She neatly folded her reading glasses and tucked them into her breast pocket. When she looked up, the foreign reporter had vanished.

The Island Manager of Ascourt sat behind her untidy desk at the Ascourt Institute of Technology from which she enjoyed a comfortable vantage of the palace, strategically aided by a rather large telescope which, for this evening's purposes, was unerringly trained into the bedchamber of Queen Bea. This direct means of enquiry had been abandoned due to the fact that the Queen's curtains had been drawn all day.

Dr Heron Home disbelievingly reread the facsimile which had arrived that Thursday afternoon. It seemed that St Gubnet was to visit. *The introduction of the Superdrone to Ascourt would be both timely and productive...* wrote Mother Nature in a letter which was hectoring and confused except, it would seem, on financial matters about which the old curmudgeon had acquired new standards of cupidity. *'I am not a vindictive woman but a half a million pounds has been mooted to me by my accountants Gilbey and Lynch as a not unreasonable estimate as to the profits of any reputable establishment involved in the trade of genetic engineering* over a period of ten years, *Heron.'*

As Heron Home had received neither communication nor remuneration from Mother Nature International in the said decade, she contemplated the mystery, slander and complete lack of ethics inherent in Mother Nature's unsolicited and mis-anthropic dispatch.

Furthermore, the letter was dated September 9, 1996, yet it had arrived only this afternoon, some two months later, on November 14. It seemed certain that the timing had been carefully arranged so that Ascourt would have no chance to prepare itself against an imminent invasion of Superdrones. Heron sucked her lips. With an IQ of one hundred and twenty-nine, she correctly supposed that there were no rational answers to hand.

Heron addressed the smudged photograph of Queen Charlotte which sat on her desk in a heavy silver frame. *My darling, I think we've run out of time. Mother Nature is forcing my hand. To think, Charlie, I'm sixty next month. I want to come home! Half a century and a promise. My love, what will we do? Timing, timing, timing!*

Queen Charlotte smiled back as wryly as ever. Heron twitched. She was an optimist by nature. She drummed a slow beat on her desk, appealing to the cosmic sympathy for enlightenment. It came in a flash. If timing was Mother Nature's weapon, then it was to timing she must turn in her hour of need.

She reached into her desk drawer and unglued a sticky sweet from the corner of her birth chart. She checked the ephemeris and did a quick calculation. Transiting Venus was within moments of entering her Seventh House in Sagittarius.

She crossed the room to the dusty bookshelf and dragged out a copy of Penzance's *Compleat Planets in Transit*. Flicking through the well-worn tome, she found the heading 'Transiting Venus in the 7th House of Sagittarius'.

Heron Home, PhD, sat at her desk and reread the cryptic interpretation. 'You will meet a tall, dark stranger.'

*

In full evening dress, Montague du Pont ordered from the set menu and was sipping the house wine when the six Old Dames entered the dining room and solemnly took their places in the ritualistic splendour of the traditionally run Swann's Hotel. It was not the first time she had witnessed a gathering of the Dames, but it was a very special privilege, causing Montague to look ruefully at the lonesome top hat which sat in place of her anticipated evening companion. It was a great honour and responsibility to be an Old Dame and Montague had always found it impossible to explain them to the foreign Press. Still, she would have relished that prospect tonight, but her every effort had failed to locate the visiting correspondent for whom she had booked an extra place at her table.

The Old Dames were originally recruited by Queen Charlotte as women of action and consequence. The minimum entry requirement was conditional on the experience of at least ten relationships of no less than eighteen months' duration each. It had been a key part of Queen Charlotte's Dream that all matters of importance were Personal, and the Personal was Political. Since the Old Dames were the living essence of this principle, their function was to interpret the essences and make their decisions accordingly. For brevity's sake, Montague likened the Old Dames Breakfast Club to a parliament, particularly for the foreign Press, who had trouble understanding their role.

Dame Clemis stood up, in the time-honoured custom, and tucked the starched white napkin under her gaunt collar. The hotel staff discreetly poured a chilled white wine and unobtrusively served the starter. Six forks dipped into the antipasta. After each course, Dame Agnetha stood and said, 'In memory of Charlotte, my dears,' and when the last piece of cutlery had been discharged, the Dames would look forward to Swann's finest chocolate cake, served in the private lounge with a coffee and port by the fire. It was part of the ritual. It never differed. It was twenty-odd years since Charlotte passed on, and not one of them had lost her appetite at an average age of seventy-six.

Montague likened Clemis to the Prime Minister, the first of the Dames chosen by Queen Charlotte on her deathbed. Clemis was the most powerful citizen of Ascourt, and even Dr Heron Home, PhD, deferred to her wisdom and experience. As Island Manager, Heron was in charge of the Ascourt Institute of Technology and as such dealt officially with the non-personal matter of Science, a realm in which Charlotte had reserved a special place, a place where progress might be made in order to enhance the personal relationships of one to another in her dream of a New Order for Ascourt. Although Dr Home was, strictly speaking, both a human being and an employee of Mother Nature International, she had been awarded the honarary title of 'Islander' by the Old Dames Breakfast Club, an appelation which Montague considered both reckless and impetuous for a blow-in who had taken up residency only since 1961.

Montague licked the last of the gravy off her forefinger and reminded herself that to disagree with the Old Dames was a mark of her own superior intelligence, which the Old Dames, and Dame Agnetha in particular, could not deny, given their mandate to foster an individual viewpoint for the average communal citizen of Ascourt. Each Dame, therefore, exemplified a characteristic personality, unmistakeable to the general populace. Dame Thwaites was the proud and aristocratic owner of Swann's Hotel. Dame Meleka was a midwife and medical herbalist. Dame Murphy's 'do-it' philosophy was the result of a mechanical bent of mind, and Dame Toplis spent life in pursuit of Dame Thwaites.

Montague du Pont would have given her right cufflink to see the expression on the face of the foreign correspondent when she wryly confided that to the discerning mind, one Old Dame was very much like another. But not so Queen Bea, who was undoubtedly the most difficult phenomenon of them all, ruminated Montague who was patiently awaiting her dessert. Queen Bea was the manifestation of everyone's desires and as such had no special area of responsibility. At least in theory. The fact of the matter was that nobody really knew what Charlotte's intent had been in the matter of her three daughters. It was said that the contents of Charlotte's Will contained specific instructions, but the whereabouts of both the Will and the remaining daughters was yet another local mystery...

Montague's pudding arrived on a silver salver with her bill and a note from the Old Dames requesting her copy of the *Irish Herald*, which was duly conveyed to Dame Clemis, who ceremoniously handed it to Dame Agnetha, who read it out loud to the others.

'*Mother Nature, head of Mother Nature International, has successfully bred a Superdrone intended for experimental use on the island colony of Ascourt. This research station has been specially*

selected to test the efficacy of the Superdrones on an ageing popula-
tion which has resulted largely from the sterility of native Queens.'

On the way to the lounge, several Dames took a timely detour by way of the powder room. Montague avoided the jam by using the guest's facilities which were situated on the first floor.

It was almost midnight. Montague sensed a purposeful activity coming from the usually unoccupied bedrooms of the November off-season. Poking her nose into an opened door, she caught the scent of honeysuckle and observed from the opened window that the room was being aired. She loosened the leather belt on her trousers by three notches. There was more to go, for she had been unexpectedly invited to attend the lounge. This precedence could mean only one thing, and Montague quietly congratulated herself on her forthcoming invitation to become the seventh member of the Old Dames Breakfast Club. It was merely a recognition of services rendered down the years, but the formality was long overdue. Montague let out a little whoop of delight. She rehearsed an impromptu speech of thanks and checked her tails for tenacious pudding crumbs. As she turned to leave the room, she bumped into a linen trolley.

'What on earth are you doing here?' expostulated Montague, recognising the person in charge of the vehicle.

The tall, dark stranger smiled uncomfortably. 'I'm helping out – the Queen of Porschia's arriving tomorrow and she's booked up the entire hotel for her entourage.'

Montague raised an eyebrow. It was the first she'd heard of the Queen of Porschia's visit. 'I see,' she said. 'You are cleaning bedrooms in exchange for your board. You know you could have stayed with me, foreign Press always stay at the cottage with my sister Delia and I. You could always come home with me tonight, you know it wouldn't be any bother, and I could give you reliable background on the island and we could discuss your article on the Superdrones…'

The tall, dark stranger was puzzled. 'Superdrones? Never heard of them! I'm a horticulturalist myself.'

'*You* are the gardening correspondent?' enquired Montague somewhat mystified.

'I intend to ask the Queen of Porschia about her under-water camellias, if that's what you mean,' replied the tall, dark stranger, hurriedly checking her wristwatch. 'Look, why don't you come too? Dame Thwaites is throwing a dinner party in her honour here tomorrow night.'

'Of course,' said Montague, forgiving Dame Thwaites for the oversight. 'Well, we've never done a gardening column in the *Ascourt Echo*, but I'll certainly publish your interview and we'd pay you something of course…'

'I'll see what I can do,' conceded the stranger, in a final attempt to squeeze her trolley past the obstruction of Montague du Pont.

Following the article in the *Irish Herald.*, there was a lively discussion in the lounge. If Mother Nature was sending Superdrones to Ascourt, then the New Order was in jeopardy. It was war and nothing less. Mother Nature was demanding a return to the Way of the Bees.

'Perhaps She really is concerned about our steadily falling population rate,' tempered Dame Agnetha.

'Insensible nonsense!' rasped Dame Clemis. 'Have you forgotten what Mother Nature did to the young Princesses?'

It was no secret that Mother Nature had not seen eye to eye with Queen Charlotte. Everyone on Ascourt knew that Charlotte had agonised over splitting up the three young Princesses. Mother Nature had been ruthless. In the Way of the Bees, there was only room for one Queen per colony. Charlotte had chosen Bea among her three daughters to remain.

Montague knew, like the other Old Dames, that Ascourt was on the brink of disaster. She was deep in thought when Dame Agnetha handed her a glass of port. Ascourt was devoted to Queen Charlotte's Dream. There were no dissenters in the plan for a New Order. How could there be? Their loyalty was unquestionable. But were the Old Dames prepared to grasp the awful nettle that, like Charlotte's Will, the plans for the New Order had never actually been seen?

'It seems to me that our only solution is to find the Princesses Min and Vee and reunite the three royal daughters of Queen Charlotte,' concluded Montague to the presently gathered.

'It would also seem that we will be overrun by Superdrones before we can locate the Princesses Min and Vee,' cautioned Dame Clemis. 'I fear we have run out of time.'

'Yossarian is the Keeper of Charlotte's Will,' said Dame Thwaites flushing from the effects of a second tumbler of port. 'We could demand that she reveal to us its secret location.'

53

'I don't see what good that would do,' retorted Dame Clemis. 'After all, Queen Charlotte made it clear to me, *on her deathbed*, that the instructions in her Will would not benefit the New Order until her three girls were reunited.'

Montague held her tongue. It would not do to remark that the instructions in the Will might even tell them what the New Order was all about...

'And when do you suppose that will be?' ventured Dame Thwaites.

'When we are ready,' proposed Dame Agnetha philosophically.

The uncomfortable pause lent Montague a chance to rally against Dame Thwaites, of whom she acerbically enquired, 'I take it that your hotel will be inviting the local Press to dine with the Queen of Porschia here tomorrow night?'

Dame Thwaites did not take the bait. 'Change of plans, my dear. She will be attending Queen Bea's céilí at the palace tomorrow night. Invitation only, I believe.'

Montague knew that her place in the pecking order did not permit her the luxury of a further exchange, but it gnawed away at her, all the same, that the Old Dames had not seen it necessary to inform the local Press of the Queen of Porschia's visit. No, but they'd told the horticultural correspondent of the *Irish Herald*, an uninformed hack without the slightest interest in current affairs.

She listened with a growing cynicism as Dame Agnetha reported on the progress of the Women's Group, word for solemn word, and Dame Toplis called for a rubber of bridge. Montague did not contribute any further that night. She determined to call the Dublin offices of the *Herald* and check the bona fides of their 'horticultural' correspondent. Her journalist's instinct told her that Ascourt was hotter news than hell itself. She would conduct her own investigations as to the whereabouts of Charlotte's Will – oh yes, her day would come and no thanks whatever to the Old Dames Breakfast Club.

It was past two-thirty in the morning. Dame Clemis 'had work to do', and Montague made her excuses. They had not asked her to the lounge to propose that she join their ranks, and she'd be damned if she was going to make up a convenient fourth at their bridge table. On the way out, she retrieved her top hat, helped herself to a cigar and walked briskly home under a waning moon.

CHAPTER FIVE

Who Smashed Queen Charlotte's Statue?

The Morning of Friday, November 15, 1996

Early next morning, Montague du Pont was called to the palace to investigate a break-in. Queen Bea claimed she had hardly slept a wink that night but she was certain she had heard nothing unusual.

'When did it first come to your attention that something was wrong?' asked Montague, notepad poised.

Yossarian answered without hesitating. 'I went to bed at three in the morning, was up by five and left my room by the back staircase, as usual. On my way downstairs, I noticed that the door to the west wing was open. I'd locked it behind me when I went to bed last night, so I went in and then – O Goddess – the statue of Charlotte…'

'Our bedrooms are side by side,' explained Queen Bea. 'Nanny uses the backstairs in the morning, so's not to disturb my beauty sleep.'

'I'm a bit heavyfooted,' apologised Yossarian, tucking her feet into the folds of her pristine white bathrobe. On the point of tears, she calmed herself and continued, 'The statue of Charlotte was smashed to smithereens – it's completely destroyed…'

Montague estimated the time of the break-in at around three or four in the morning. It could not have been earlier. She had noticed the palace lights still burning in the west wing sometime between 2:30 and 3:00 a.m. on her way home from Swann's Hotel the night before. Apparently Yossarian had been unable to sleep, and in view of the Queen of Porschia's visit, had occupied herself with some late night cleaning and polishing.

'Was there anything missing, Yossarian?'

Queen Bea shook her head. Yossarian was sobbing uncontrollably. Both women were badly shaken.

'Is it possible that somebody unknown to you was in the palace last night?' queried Montague.

Yossarian looked reproachfully at her young charge.

'The Queen of Porschia will be here in thirty minutes and we can't even decide which bedroom she should have,' said Queen Bea, as red as the check on her flannel pyjamas.

'My deepest sympathies,' replied Montague tactfully. 'This incident will surely leave you in no humour for the céilí tonight.'

'Do join us,' said Queen Bea unexpectedly.

'Well, thank you – I'll collect my personal invitation from the porter,' smiled Montague, who had no time to gloat.

Queen Bea looked puzzled.

'Do you think I might bring my sister, Delia, along?' supplicated the editor of the *Ascourt Echo*.

'I'd be delighted,' granted Queen Bea magnanimously.

'It is by invitation only, isn't it?'

'Oh yes of course,' confirmed Queen Bea uncertainly. 'I've invited the whole island.'

Montague du Pont had a hunch, and she needed to reach Heron Home before the news of the break-in got out. If she were right, then Yossarian was not the only person in Ascourt who knew the whereabouts of the Will. There are morbid matters about which lovers will conspire, and while Yossarian was the Keeper of Charlotte's Will, Dr Heron Home PhD had been her lifelong lover. When Charlotte died, it was Heron Home who had commissioned the very statue which now lay in a thousand pieces in the west wing of the palace.

Montague du Pont thought up a clever ruse. In order to solve the crime, she would get Heron Home to confirm her suspicions that whoever broke into the palace the night before had had reason to believe that the statue was in fact the repository of the Will.

Montague intercepted the Island Manager ascending the steps of the palace. Heron Home was on her way to join the group of dignitaries about to gather on the palace lawns to welcome the Queen of Porschia. Montague's heart beat wildly.

'Dr Home, I presume?'

'Oh very funny, Monty. You seem to be going the wrong way – aren't you going to this bloody thing?'

Montague faked a casual grin. 'No actually, I'm off to settle a bet I made last night.'

'Oh?' enquired Heron Home. 'Didn't think bridge was your thing, dear.'

'How on earth–' spluttered Montague disingenuously.

'I don't have to tell you how it is,' said Heron, rubbing the dark rings under her eyes. 'Dame Thwaites rang me about four in the morning, couldn't sleep poor old thing. Needless to say, didn't get much sleep myself. Island's in a fearful mess, she said, much worse than three-handed bridge, and you'd been awfully helpful or words to that effect.'

'Well what a coincidence,' said Montague carefully. 'Dame Thwaites didn't tell you about our little bet then.'

Heron Home shook her head and widened her tired eyes.

Montague adopted a conspiratorial tone. 'Well, we were discussing what was to gain by looking at Queen Charlotte's Will. I said there wouldn't be much point in destroying Charlotte's statue just to get a look at it, and Dame Clemis said that reading the Will would make no difference until the three princesses were reunited. And when I said that you said that Charlotte had said so on her deathbed, Dame Thwaites said that nobody could possibly remember such a thing, it was all so long ago. I made a bet with her that you'd remember.'

Heron screwed up her face and laughed. 'Well, you crafty thing, Monty. You had me worried. Still, you're quite right. Charlotte did say that. You've won your bet, my dear and if Dame Thwaites gives you any argument, she can answer to me.'

Montague descended the two hundred and sixteen steps of the palace, turned left at Town Square, walked past Dame Thwaites's Hotel and headed straight down the hill towards the Ascourt Institute of Technology, where her sister Delia was employed as the senior pathologist. It was all falling into place. Heron had indirectly confirmed that Queen Charlotte's Will was hidden in the statue commemorated at her death. That's why Yossarian had been so upset. Whoever smashed the statue had stolen the Will from under her nose. There was only one suspect – a tall, dark stranger masquerading as a foreign correspondent. It had not fooled Montague du Pont. Nor would it fool Delia, who was skilled in unravelling even the most molecular of clues. More to the point, Delia had a telephone in her office.

The palace lawns were immaculately kept by the Head Gardener who was busy chalking a perfect round circle in anticipation of the arrival of the Queen of Porschia's helicopter. Peripheral to the horticultural focus, small enclaves of Ascourt's Welcoming Committee were enjoying light refreshment and gossip. It was an invigorating morning with uplifting winds. The southerly view of the ocean was a spectacle to be enjoyed on such a day as this, and particularly from the lawns of the palace which still sported an antique cannon for much the same purpose.

Dr Heron Home resolved not to partake of champagne, but vaguely suspected that she might do so anyway. She inhaled a deep breath of salty air, adjusted her crumpled yellow cravat and made her way to Dame Thwaites who had caught her eye with a friendly wink.

'You're all the business this morning,' cajoled Dame Thwaites.

'Well, yes,' muttered Heron uncomfortably. 'I'll have to tap the Queen of Porschia for another loan – our tax bill, half a million apparently.'

'They've got so much money in Porschia they don't know what to do with it,' bolstered Dame Elma Thwaites. 'A mere drop in the Porschian ocean, what?'

'Charlotte did say the Will wouldn't make sense to anyone but the girls, Elma. I was there when she died, you know.'

'Of course you were, dear.'

Dame Thwaites rummaged in her large handbag and proceeded to swallow two capsules which were a perilous shade of pink. She offered two to Heron. 'Here, these will help you Herry, you are not making sense. Now get those down you and let me tell you what I've just heard.'

It wasn't that anything was wrong *exactly*, but ever since she was a child, Dr Heron Home sometimes, and sometimes for days at a time, had experienced the rare phenomenon of exclusive right brain function. It was during these times as a child, barely able to tie her shoelaces, that she uncovered the profound harmony of a cosmic symbology. Had she been aware that today was such a day, or had she just been more alert to herself on awakening, she might have proceeded to erect an astrological chart for the day ahead. She might have been better prepared. Heron removed a glass of champagne from a travelling silver tray and swallowed the tablets in one gulp. She hoped they were amphetamines. Or at the very least, memory enhancers.

'Queen Charlotte's statue – you remember the one Heron, the one you had specially designed for the west wing – well, it's been criminally vandalised!'

'Oh no,' moaned Heron, finally grasping her earlier failure to realise what Montague had been fishing for.

'Yes!' cried Dame Elma Thwaites. 'And we know who did it too!'

Heron sighed. 'It wasn't me, Elma, really.'

Dame Thwaites looked puzzled. 'Whatever made you think it was?'

'It seems that Montague must have guessed that I was privy to the whereabouts of the Will. Of course now she thinks I did it, it'll be all over the *Ascourt Echo* by tomorrow morning.'

'What rubbish, Heron,' said Dame Thwaites impatiently.

'Elma, the point is whoever smashed the statue also took the Will.'

'My dear, listen up – can't you hear the helicopter? Listen, look!'

Dame Mary Murphy was grazing vol-au-vents off the long table under the South Wall. Dame Mary Murphy appeared to be listening to Dame Toplis.

'Dame Thwaites told me so herself. The tall, dark stranger was not in her hotel room this morning and her bed had not even been slept in. It can only mean one thing. As soon as Porky's visit is over I'm off to the North Island to check up on that gliding aeroplane.'

'We should have removed the carburettor while we still had the chance,' said Dame Murphy with her mouth full. 'Damn cheek if you ask me, landing without permission.'

'I'm not sure I agree with you. I like her. She seems honest, open and sincere – not at all the type who would be working for Mother Nature. I would go so far as to say that if more of Ascourt's citizens were as consciously raised as she, this island would not be in the state it's in,' said Dame Agnetha passionately.

'Bit of a turnabout, Aggie!' said Dame Toplis provocatively. 'One might think you were sporting a crush on a handsome aviator, what!'

'No, no, no. I am simply presenting another point of view. All our opinions on the matter are based on circumstantial evidence,' stressed Dame Agnetha carefully.

The chopping purr of the helicopter provided an audible impact to the approach of Dame Thwaites's flapping electric-blue gown. 'Listen up, girls. The Will's been stolen!' she shouted over the noise.

'What?'

'Yes, it was in the statue all along!'

Dame Agnetha wasn't certain. Dame Clemis said she needed more information. Dame Thwaites fancied that the tall, dark stranger was not their only suspect and they should keep an eye on Heron Home, just in case. The remaining three Dames were unequivocal in their view that nothing should be done until morning cocktails were over.

When the helicopter had been safely landed on the white chalk circle, a cheer went up as the Queen of Porschia emerged. Two very bedraggled-looking creatures followed behind her. The Queen of Porschia swept up the VIP carpet dressed in an outsize red rubber diving suit, and crushed Queen Bea against her firm, wet bosom. Although the royal greetings were drowned out by the whirling blades of the helicopter, the Welcoming Committee were awed by the solemnity of the occasion.

'New girlfriend, Beatrice?' enquired the Queen of Porschia of Bea's tall, dark companion.

'I wouldn't say that,' blushed Queen Bea, who had never, ever had a girlfriend. But she did not forget her manners. 'Porky, meet Maryann Leaf. Maryann, meet Her Royal Highness the Queen of Porschia.'

'Oh call me Porky, everyone else does – if not to my face then at least behind my back.'

'Maryann is an admirer of your underwater Camellia, Porky – she's been asked to do an interview for the Press,' hinted Bea.

'Oh my,' said the Queen of Porschia who simply loved publicity. 'Could it possibly be the *Irish Herald* Gardening Supplement?'

'No actually, it's for the *Ascourt Echo*,' explained Maryann quickly.

'Never heard of it,' said the Queen of Porschia who turned her back and unceremoniously shouted, 'Tell them to turn off that damn machine, I want to make a speech.' She huddled the two dripping-wet women beside her.

'Hush please, everybody. I have a bit of a story to tell. On our way over we spotted a lifeboat in distress. Naturally we went to the rescue. It turns out that these two wonderful people were just on their way to Ascourt but they were very lost. Please extend a warm welcome to Saint Gubnet of Balleyvourney and–' An aide whispered into her ear. 'Yes, and the Princess Min of Ascourt – that must be a sister of yours, Beatrice. Now hot mead all round and let's get changed into something a little less – wet! Let the celebrations begin!'

Queen Bea flung herself into the arms of her sister and wept for the fact that she had not recognised her and then wept for the twelve cruel years in which they had been separated. Gubnet looked for Dr Heron Home, but did not find her among the personnel of the Ascourt Institute of Technology, because the Island Manager was hiding under the ornamental cannon struggling to remember something very important. Which she did.

When Dr Home returned to the main lawn, she wondered whether she might be experiencing a visual impairment as a result of her earlier cocktail. There appeared to be an obstructive kaleidoscope of Old Dames arresting the stranger whose identity she had finally remembered in a painstaking search of her memory banks. Dr Home broke through the circle and announced herself.

'You're the tall, dark stranger who appeared in my horoscope reading last night!'

'I can't tell you how relieved I am to meet you at last, Dr Home,' said Maryann, reading the official nametag pinned to the collar of Heron's unironed blouse. The Old Dames each took a defensive step backwards.

'But I was expecting you ages ago – when you didn't show up I assumed you weren't coming. Did the storm delay you?' asked Heron.

'Not quite. You see I was flying a little low, looking for a spot to land, when I clipped the starboard wing on a tall tree. And that was exactly three days ago!'

'Well I never, I do hope you weren't too badly hurt,' said Heron kindly.

'No, and everyone has been so kind. Of course I meant to drop by the Ascourt Institute and introduce myself but so much has happened in just a few short days. I was waiting for the dust to settle!'

Montague du Pont was out of breath. She had practically run all the way. The *Irish Herald* confirmed, over the telephone, that they had no correspondent in Ascourt and were not planning on sending one. Montague reached to the bottom of her reserves, flung herself through the circle and gasped painfully, 'She's not a correspondent, she's an imposter!'

'I told you last night I'm a horticulturalist!' chided Maryann with an outstretched arm towards her accuser.

'That is correct,' said Heron loudly and slowly for all to hear. 'Maryann Leaf's application won the approval of the Ascourt Institute of Technology and she will be starting her work here straight away. We are researching an alternative, sustainable agriculture and we've just hired the best advice we can get.'

Montague's cause was not helped by the fact that the imposter had singlehandedly picked her up and dusted her off in front of the Old Dames before whom she was not prepared to lose further face.

'And just how many applications did you get for the job, Heron?'

'Just the one,' admitted Heron equably.

Dame Toplis coughed. 'You mean this person is employed by us?'

'Her credentials are impeccable,' returned Dr Home officiously. 'Maryann Leaf is a founder member of WITCH.'

Maryann nodded and swept an arm around Dame Toplis's

shoulder, manoeuvring her into the conversation. 'That's the Women's Initiative in Trade and Collective Horticulture.' At her full five feet and ten inches, Maryann was a woman in her nascent prime. Her dark glossy hair fell in long waves around her shoulders. Her anemone-green eyes sparkled with life. She was irresistable to the touch and could have passed for any age between thirty-four and fifty-two.

Dame Toplis acquiesced, feeling a liquid warmth running down her shoulder blades. 'You are a busy bee, as we say in these parts.'

Maryann Leaf smiled self-effacingly. But she meant every word. 'I really believe that the garden plot will revolutionise women's lives.'

'You're so right,' said Dame Agnetha already won to the cause. 'It is empowering to see a plant grow.'

'I believe,' said Dame Agnetha later that day, in a quiet aside to Dame Clemis, 'that that young woman will play a critical part in our development towards a pride in ourselves and the achievement of self-sufficiency on this island.'

'But what do you really know of her?' asked Dame Clemis tersely.

'Psychologically she strikes me as a wholesome and rounded personality.' Dame Agnetha paused to find the right words. 'And professionally she is mature, experienced and committed to women.'

Dame Clemis did not normally entertain emotion during her working day, but Agnetha was sure something was wrong. Clemis had missed the morning's ceremonies and seemed visibly agitated.

'Only two days ago you told us she was a hired assassin,' said Dame Clemis pointedly.

'I know,' wavered Dame Agnetha. 'But I think I should have trusted my first impressions which were – '

Dame Clemis caught her hand and almost spat the words out. 'She is forty-two years old. She has two daughters, by fathers unknown, of sixteen and fourteen years of age, who are currently living, unsupervised and unparented, in a West of Ireland commune. She is also due to make a court appearance facing charges of the illegal cultivation of *Cannabis sativa*.'

Dame Agnetha was horrified. 'The Goddess, Clemis – what on earth possessed you?'

Dame Clemis looked coldly at her. 'I'd make it my business to know the facts about anyone who is fucking the Queen, wouldn't you?'

The girl from the Cat Club followed Her on to the balcony. She reminded Her of Gubnet. Gubnet in biker's leathers. She nibbled Mother Nature's ears. 'I can tell you like it rough, darlin'.' Mother Nature could not believe it when She heard Herself invite the woman in black leathers to come home with Her. More to the point, She left Her BMW parked in the lot and travelled at high speed through the late night streets of New York on the back of Pearl's Harley Davidson. The apartment was hot. Pearl was hot. Mother Nature had never engaged in casual sex but She wanted this woman like a panther wanted its mate. They were matched in strength and physique. They fought for dominance, but neither would give in. The smell of blood and cunt was intoxicating. They hurt and scratched and ate and drank one another. It was long and deep and satisfying. When Pearl finally fell asleep beside Her, Mother Nature wanted to cry: great heaving sobs. But She couldn't release them, for Gubnet was strangled inside Her.

Mother Nature woke from the dream as Her alarm bleeped an electronic greeting. It was seven a.m. on Friday, November 15th in the Big Apple. She opened one eye and turned it ruefully towards the other side of the double divan. It had not been slept in. She was hungry and jetlagged. Her stomach reminded Her it was lunchtime back home.

By seven-thirty She had washed, showered and dressed. Breakfast was the usual chilled nectar and two slices of toast, well turned and dripping with honey. She padded across the penthouse apartment on the top floor of Mother Nature International and found the *Financial Times,* as usual, slipped under Her door. Turning to the Dow Jones She was not surprised to see that the share prices of MNI were down after the news broke out about the yacht sinking off the coast of Ireland. Lloyds, who had underwritten the yacht and its cargo, were investigating the claim. So far, they did not suspect foul play – there were gale-force winds in operation which would wreak havoc with a yacht that size.

In any case, it wasn't the outcome of an insurance investigation that was worrying Her, even though She stood to lose a great deal of money if Lloyds ever came to believe, as She did

Herself, that the yacht had been bombed. If She got Her hands on the culprit, She would...

She would have to move more quickly than anticipated. It was a matter of containment. As a shrewd businesswoman she knew that the faintest whiff of a maritime misconduct would alert the international community and attract unwanted publicity to the islands – a fate which would hurt MNI far more than any financial consideration at this sensitive stage of Ascourt's development.

The telephone rang. After three rings, it stopped. A few seconds later, the phone rang again. After five rings, Mother Nature picked it up, sat back on Her leather recliner and cradled the phone to Her shoulder as She began the cryptic crossword puzzle on page three.

'Codeword,' She asked peremptorily.

'Agent Drone,' came the reply.

'Proceed.'

'Superdrones have not arrived, check? Stress will not arrive.'

'What does the rest of the cargo look like?'

'It's in good order – Princess Min and Gubnet are here, thank the Goddess.'

'Stick to code. Anything else?'

'Documents from statue presumed officially missing – are you with me?'

'Excellent, excellent. Good work. Have you covered your tracks?'

'I have a guilty party. It'll never be traced.'

'Five letter word, second letter O, "Cut it fine with question about hive", any ideas?'

'"Fraid not. And you?'

'Proceed to plan B.'

There was a startled silence over the line connecting New York to Ascourt.

'Did you hear me?' reiterated Mother Nature. 'Proceed to Plan B.'

'But it's too late for Plan B!'

'It's what you were born to do. And the answer to the clue is "honey"; finely cut is hone, with a Y on the end for a question,' concluded Mother Nature. 'When there's honey in the hive, then it's good to be alive, eh?'

'But if I succeed, I won't be hearing from you again,' said the voice, heavy with consequence.

'And if I don't hear from you again, I'll know you have succeeded. Good luck, Agent D, you will be rewarded for preserving the Way of the Bees.'

'Right. My last goodbye then.'

'And have a nice day, y'all,' concluded Mother Nature in the pleasant tones of her adopted city.

CHAPTER SIX

The Celebration Buffet Lunch

The Afternoon of Friday, November 15, 1996

The celebration buffet lunch in the Long Room of the east wing was hosted by Queen Bea and attended, in order of age, by St Gubnet of Balleyvourney (age unknown), Dame Clemis, head of the Old Dames Breakfast Club (eighty-two), Dr Heron Home, PhD (fifty-nine), the Queen of Porschia (forty-one), and Princess Min (eighteen). Combining the best of oral tradition with the best of a bargain, a diverse range of subjects were chewed and haggled over. All told, it was a marriage of business and pleasure, and the chat was as good as the food.

The Queen of Porschia revealed that under Maritime Law, cargo floating away from the wreckage of a vessel was classified as flotsam which became the property of whomsoever took possession of it.

St Gubnet disagreed in the strongest possible terms. The Superdrones may have been floating, but since Mother Nature owned the island of Porschia, wherein the Superdrones were now domiciled, it followed that Mother Nature still owned the Superdrones.

The Queen of Porschia was vehement. She did not use the word *oppressor* to Gubnet's face. She said, 'You are challenging my sovereignty in terms that amount to abuse, Madam. I pay my taxes punctually. In a private capacity I am a majority shareholder of Mother Nature International. I will rule my island and my property as I please.'

'Be that as it may,' countered St Gubnet, 'it was I who bred the Superdrone and it is I, in a sole capacity, who owns the genetic copyright to the Superdrone – a copyright which would be upheld in any court you so choose to contest the law with me in.' Gubnet avoided the word *piracy* but made her point nonetheless.

Heron Home inwardly sighed at Gubnet's bludgeoning mainland methods. It was clear to all present, bar St Gubnet, that the Queen of Porschia had arrived with substantial assets in exchange for the Superdrones. But just as Ascourt would deny its displeasure of drones, the Queen of Porschia would deny that she stole them in full knowledge of this fact. In the language of oppression, discretion is employed as the better part of valour and had St Gubnet left well alone, Porky would have agreed to a half million 'loan', with pudding in her mouth and not a word about drones.

The stalemate was quickly breached by Dame Clemis, who also saw the folly of allowing St Gubnet peremptorily to assume the spokespersonship of Ascourt.

'Notwithstanding the proper assertions of St Gubnet, we of Ascourt would personally be delighted to have the Queen of Porschia assume the temporary custodianship of the Superdrones, given our,' and here Dame Clemis stressed, *'ongoing mutual respect* and financial cooperation, which we should like to broaden into a more political perspective.'

Dr Heron Home PhD gritted her teeth in suspense. Clemis was not the Head of the Old Dames Breakfast Club for nothing. The Queen of Porschia accepted the gracious apology, and expertly made eye contact with all present except St Gubnet.

'I think we would all agree that the Superdrones are somewhat peripheral to the main issue, which is far closer to the bosoms of Ascourtians and Porschians alike. I have long hoped that a marriage would cement the age-old relationship between our two islands and give us the 'political platform' from which we could mutually forge a joint and prosperous future.' The Queen of Porschia paused for effect and then resumed in full volume. 'However, merging our two cultures may be difficult in view of the Sapphic rigours exercised since the time of Her Majesty Queen Charlotte, may she rest in peace.'

But the Queen of Porschia was very interested in the notion of a marriage. She had one political reason – The Way of the Bees was over, but to say so publicly was treason. On the other hand, it was widely rumoured that Ascourt was developing genetic technology which could lead them into the future. She might have made an enemy of St Gubnet, but she was not ruler of the richest island colony for nothing. Ascourt was penniless, and Porschia was in a position to invest at a propitious price.

Queen Bea handed back the advantage to Ascourt when she inadvertently exposed the Queen of Porschia's second and more personal reason.

'Porky,' she said thoughtfully, 'your Tamarind's a dyke, isn't she?'

'Tamarind?' quavered the Queen of Porschia, defenceless in memory of her eldest and disinherited daughter. 'I haven't heard from her since she was – that is, since she left Porschia. I believe she's in –'

'London. And she's not very happy,' said Queen Bea insistently. 'You know how difficult it is to get a decent job over there these days. I got a letter from her just the other day. She's split up with her lover and she can't afford to get counselling and she's just about to get thrown out of her flat. I wrote straight back and sent her the fare to Ascourt.'

Princess Min snorted loudly.

Queen Bea kicked her under the table.

The blood drained visibly out of the Queen of Porschia's face.

'She's been a bit of a headache to you, I know, Porky, but I'd be delighted to call her my sister-in-law and she'd be a kindred spirit in Ascourt,' said Queen Bea, adding, 'We're all about the same age, too.'

'Would she really fit in do you think?' asked Porky nervously.

'Without a doubt,' said Queen Bea smiling romantically at her sister. 'And I'm sure Princess Min and Princess Tamarind would be very happy together.'

Princess Min stopped grinning.

The shock waves of this announcement did not affect Heron Home, who manoeuvred gracefully among the myriad blades of inter-island diplomacy. 'And so to formalise our joint commitment, it remains to agree on the terms of Princess Tamarind's dowry.'

'Right,' said the Queen of Porschia, mentally re-inheriting her eldest daughter. 'How much then?'

'Half a million pounds,' said Heron Home without inflection. 'Sterling, that is.'

'And a fifty per cent share in any genetic breakthroughs,' bargained the Queen of Porschia.

'Your future, Majesty, is our future,' concluded Dame Clemis on an even score.

The business done, Queen Bea and Dr Heron Home discreetly left the celebration buffet lunch to check up on Nanny Yossarian, who was in a state of collapse following the theft of the Will from Charlotte's statue. Queen Bea was genuinely worried. She had never seen Yossarian without her make-up on, and this morning, she had refused to come downstairs.

'I've put her in my bedroom in the north wing,' confided Queen Bea.

Yossarian perked up when her two favourite people entered the room and sat either side of the bed, each holding one of her hands.

'Doesn't this remind you of something, Heron?' reminisced Yossarian under a wrinkled layer of night cream.

'We both held Charlie's hands in this very room when she was dying,' said Heron sadly.

'You're not going to die on us, Nanny, are you?'

Nanny Yossarian shook her head weakly. 'No, my love, I'm just feeling a bit off colour – like you did, the day you fainted at the Women's Group.'

Queen Bea understood and ordered a large pot of weak tea to be brought up to them. When it arrived, she poured them each a mug, sweetened with fresh honey. She climbed in beside Yossarian who moved up to make room for her.

'Auntie Heron, I think it should make Yossarian feel much better if you told us a story. How about the story of Queen Charlotte's Eggs?'

'All right,' agreed Heron amiably. Queen Bea lit up two French cigarettes, handing one to Yossarian while putting the crystal ashtray on her lap between them.

'Once Upon a Time,' began Heron in a fog of aromatic fumes, 'eighteen years ago, to be precise, it came to the notice of Queen Charlotte that there wasn't a child to be found on the whole of the island of Ascourt. Since she had never been much of a one for laying eggs, she visited Dame Meleka in the high hopes that the herbalist might have a suggestion. Of course she didn't, because as we all know, Charlotte was never

70

actually fertilised by a drone. What's more, the herbalist told her that she was going through the menopause, a sign that her body had run out of eggs. Queen Charlotte was shocked. No eggs, royal or otherwise, had ever been laid or brought up by her, and now it seemed as if even a miracle might be too late. It worried her for days and nights and she started to go grey.

'One night, lying in bed with her, I couldn't sleep. There was a full moon shining into our bedroom window. I looked at the moon and I looked at my Charlotte and suddenly a scientific idea came to me. I realised by the deep round glow of the moon that a woman never runs out of eggs, she only runs out of the hormones which release them from her ovary.

'Excitedly I realised that I could very likely recover a few eggs still embedded in her ovaries; but it would involve surgery and Oh! how Charlotte hated the idea of that. Do you remember, Yossarian?'

Yossarian smiled for the first time that day. 'Indeed, what a performance she gave!'

Heron continued. 'Well we eventually persuaded her that all she would feel was a tiny dart and it'd be over. I injected her and all Charlotte managed to say was, "I want you both to know that – " and then I went to work.'

Queen Bea interrupted Heron, unable to contain her curiosity. 'What do you think she was going to say, Auntie Heron?'

'Oh probably, "I want you both to know that this procedure is in direct contravention to everything I believe in" or something very similar, knowing Charlie.'

'I think she said, "I want you both to know that I love you very much",' said Queen Bea whose eyes were misting over with emotion.

'Your mother,' continued Heron sternly, 'had thirteen unfertilised eggs on the surface of her left ovary. I examined them under my microscope and found three that were perfect in every way. I conducted an *in vitro* fertilisation, using some leftover drone sperms in my laboratory, the results of which were you and your two sisters.'

Queen Bea gasped, 'You mean I'm a test-tube baby!'

'You were a beautiful baby,' reassured Yossarian. 'You never cried, you slept twelve hours a day and you always ate your food.'

'Yossarian fed you all royal jelly to turn you into strong princesses. When you were twelve days old, your mother and I named you Beatrice, Virginia and Minerva, and you had your Royal Tattoos put on your arms. And that's the end of the story.'

'Tell the *whole* story, Heron,' said Yossarian meaningfully. 'Go on, Bea, and pour us all another cup of tea.'

Heron steeled herself. 'You mean –?' she asked, unable to finish.

'Yes, the story of Queen Charlotte's death. Queen Bea is old enough to know.'

Heron looked askance at her oldest friend, whose arching brows raised the matter of an ancient pact between them. Heron acquiesced. She questioned no further.

'Well, six years after you three were born, Mother Nature sent an edict to Ascourt ordering that only one of the little princesses could remain on Ascourt, for that is the Way of the Bees. Charlotte was heartbroken, in fact, I dare say that splitting you up was what broke her heart and killed her that same year. Night after night she saw Banba, the spirit of Death, tapping her fob-watch by the window. It was a very hard thing for me to accept. I asked Charlotte to write down her dreams of Ascourt so that they would be preserved for all posterity. And night after night I scribbled down her words, so beautiful that even Banba paused to listen by the window sill, forgetting the time. Charlotte was so weak, I had to help her to do even the simplest thing. Not even for one minute did I have time to contemplate what life would mean without her. Queen Charlotte thought about you three girls all the time. She even designed three separate gardens for each of you to remember her by.'

'Well, Bea?' frowned Yossarian. 'Do you remember any of this?'

'No, I really don't!' said Queen Bea in amazement.

'Well, your garden was planted when she died, and the others were to be done only when Min and Vee returned.'

'That'll be something for Min to look forward to,' said Queen Bea, absolutely positive it would cheer Min up.

'But finally,' resumed Heron, 'time ran out. Charlie called Yossarian and me to her deathbed. We each held a hand and she said, "Heron and Yossarian, my two oldest friends, Ascourt will not be strong until my three girls are back together again.

Nothing will make sense to anyone except them. My eldest, B, is blessed with wisdom, she is older than her years. She will rule with vision as Queen. Listen and obey all she says. My middle daughter, V, now she is the Shaman. Under her rule, Ascourt will never come to harm. Question not her actions, for all she does is for the protection of this island. My youngest, M, will be the Mother of the future generation of Ascourt. She will conceive and abundantly bear forth my dream. Under her rule, Ascourt will overflow with bounty and joy." Then we all heard the impatient rapping on the window sill. "O time, time, time – I must go now!" So I said, "I'm going to miss you so much" and Charlie said, "I've left you too much to do Heron, you won't have time to miss me", and I laughed. Then she just got out of bed and walked – no, she actually skipped – over to the window and just disappeared with Banba to Tír na n-Óg.'

Queen Bea paused to wipe a tear off Heron's nose. Anticipating her thoughts, Heron said, 'You see, Bea, the Will was really everything Queen Charlotte said about the New Order during her last dying days. I wrote it all down and Yossarian put it into the statue to give to you three girls when you were reunited.'

'And someone stole it this morning,' said Bea sadly.

'You can be sure Mother Nature had a hand in it,' said Yossarian bitterly.

'Mother Nature would have no good reason to steal the Will,' said Heron rather sharply to Yossarian. 'Someone *has* stolen the original – but we published and distributed several copies of Charlotte's Will posthumously. I mean to say, in theory at least, if Mother Nature wanted to read it all she'd have to do is order a copy from our local library. Isn't that so Yossarian?'

Yossarian nodded with the uncertain air of one whose hairpiece might at any moment expose the truth.

Queen Bea squealed with delight. 'What's it called?'

'It's called *The BVM – A New Order by Queen Charlotte,*' said Heron simply.

'Well, Min and I are here – and when Vee comes home, we three sisters can sit down and have a good read of that book,' said Bea firmly.

Heron and Yossarian looked unconvinced of the words of the wise one.

'There's just no point in you being upset, Yossarian, everything's just the same as it ever was. Whoever took the original book won't be able to understand it anyway, and I'm going to do an evening course with Maryann in pottery this winter and we're going to rebuild Mum's statue. Everything is going to be A-OK. Now paint your face and get dressed, Yossarian, we're off to the Northern Territories this afternoon to see if we can patch up Maryann's plane. And Heron, we'll need some glue from your laboratory at the Institute.'

Heron sighed peaceably. Yossarian looked exactly as she felt herself – old and tired and longing for a pasture anywhere out of earshot of the brave New Order.

St Gubnet squirmed uncomfortably in her seat while Dame Clemis ambled through the interminable closing speech of the celebration buffet lunch. Guests were to be taken on an afternoon's tour of the island the description of which, ruling out any motorised means of conveyance, conjured in Gubnet's mind a gorse-ridden hike unacceptable to even the most enduring of mules. Dame Clemis went on at some length about the sunny day, the loveliness of the island and guests observing the most solemn Rule of Three. Gubnet's stomach churned horribly at the thought.

As soon as Dame Clemis stopped talking, Gubnet stood up slowly and painfully to find the exit jammed by an eager queue of Important People all hoping for a ride on the Queen of Porschia's helicopter. She held herself upright and willed herself not to faint. The ancient head of the Old Dames Breakfast Club patiently joined her at the back of the queue.

'The Old Dames are convinced that the Rule of Three is a ploy to stop them playing bridge,' joked Dame Clemis, making light of the burdens of responsibility.

'Is there any other way out of here?' pleaded Gubnet in desperation.

Dame Clemis nodded. She took a firm grip of Gubnet's wrist and walked her to the other end of the Long Room where a curtain concealed a hidden door leading down a passage which opened out into the main hall. Dame Clemis pointed a bony hand to a restroom across the way, and Gubnet made it just before her stomach heaved its contents into the pristine white lavatory bowl. Was it just her imagination or was it common knowledge that she and Mother Nature had split up? Porky, for one, would never have dared snub her on any previous occasion! Gubnet stood helplessly by the marble sink. The ancient water pipes creaked and groaned, producing a murky whoosh of filthy brown tapwater. By all accounts, she hadn't been in the least bit prepared for anything like the mess that Ascourt was in. One of the Dames had informed her that apart from Queen Bea and her sister Min, and here Gubnet flushed a little, there wasn't a single bee person on the island under the age of fifty! The water cleared, and Gubnet splashed her face and hands. She would just have to make the best of it. She didn't want to need Ascourt. She didn't want to need anything or anyone. And what of the child? *Who are you but an empty shell without Mother Nature?* she implored of her jaded image in the mirror. When the door finally opened, admitting the presence of Dames Clemis and Agnetha, Gubnet was frozen to the spot.

The two Old Dames brought St Gubnet to the private garden of Queen Bea, which was not really very private because the palace grounds were open to the public at all times. Gubnet began to recover her composure. The enclosed garden was cut off by an imposing hedge of spinous myrtle whose dour shade was radiantly uplifted by the late blooming flowers of a vigorous companion clematis. The two Old Dames were agreeably silent. Gubnet felt her body open up to the cool fragrant hues of the season's last offerings, but even their gentleness added to the swell and pressure against the dam of her heart. She would not give in to the overwhelming and indiscriminate desire to release the floodbanks in front of two perfect strangers. She braced herself and taped on a smile. She asked Dame Agnetha about the mysterious Rule of Three.

The Rule of Three, explained Agnetha, was that guests and islanders alike spend the day in groups of three, or multiples thereof.

'The world has been torn asunder by the exclusive Rule of Two – '

'As in Black and White, Male and Female, Positive and Negative – ' entered Gubnet tentatively.

'Good and Evil!' creaked the tall, stooped frame of Dame Clemis.

'The Rule of Two allows no other. Extreme perceptions

75

become norms, and the Earth has struggled for over two millennia to invite the fusion of extremes in a futile effort to achieve wholeness. It is an ill-thought-out theory which demands that shades of grey must liken themselves to an absolute black or a radiant white in order then to come together and reproduce itself as grey.'

Dame Clemis went on to expand Dame Agnetha's theory. Gubnet listened, but she became transfixed by the sound of water trickling into a cool, dark grotto.

'When two people talk, they behave mutually, they conspire, they will make an effort to balance. When three people get together, it becomes difficult to play such a game. Two will agree but three must cooperate in a far more conscious way.'

Gubnet's eye was drawn to the neglected grotto, which was in obvious need of repair. The well was choked up with a thick, green algae, and the wooden statue was deeply lacerated with the initials of hasty admirers.

'If one has a secret, the other two will sense it as surely as I know that something is troubling you, St Gubnet of Balleyvourney,' said Dame Agnetha.

At the mention of her name, Gubnet started out of her reverie.

'You may share your troubles with us, St Gubnet. But under the Rule of Three, Agnetha and I are obliged to suffer with you should you choose to keep things to yourself. It is better to come out. A secret is not long hidden among three.'

Gubnet appraised the women with sincerity. Dame Agnetha was as genuine as the spray of orange blossom in her hair and by now, even Dame Clemis's neat white bun was coming adrift, softening the angular face of a formidable command. The swing under the cherry tree rocked the two kind faces expectantly to and fro. She felt certain their hearts were in the right place, but could they possibly understand how complicated it all was? She had planned to explain things to the Island Manager, but she hadn't found an opportune moment to engage Heron's attention all day. Gubnet put her hand on her tummy and swallowed. This was going to be hard.

'Dames Clemis and Agnetha, we are among four. Myself and my baby have come to Ascourt to seek asylum from Mother Nature.'

Gubnet leaned back on her reclining chair and shut her eyes. It was an awful moment of truth. But when she opened them, the two faces were beaming with pride.

'St Gubnet,' spoke Dame Clemis officially, *'Céad míle fáilte!* A thousand welcomes to you and your daughter. Ascourt is honoured by both your presences.'

Gubnet smiled in a peaceful exhaustion, enjoying the warm glow of sunlight trapped in Queen Bea's garden. For the first time in over a year she felt carefree and *cherished.* At first she listened to what the Dames were saying, realising that by their words she had underestimated them both. It no longer mattered. By the Rule of Three, the Dames would sit with her until she woke. She was safe in the bosom of wise women.

'You see, Clemis, it is as I have always said. The numbers three, six and nine are magically intertwined. Mother Nature is a six. She is afraid of deviation. The Way of the Bees is a perfect hexagonal six. It is economic, it is guaranteed – but it can never transform. Now Mother Nature is like a great rhinoceros, she will instinctively dig in her heels and pitch her might against the winds of change.'

Clemis agreed. 'Yet we are by nature the number three. We are afraid of failure, so must we strive together for success.'

'But a six must follow the Rule of Three, or no change can ever take place.'

'And a three must learn the way of Nine – '

'Which is to handle conflict among ourselves and so attain tranquility and fulfilment.'

'The testing times have begun, Agnetha dear. Have you heard the Queen of Porschia's latest demand? Her daughter must be elected to the Old Dames Breakfast Club or the marriage will not be sanctioned!'

'What an undisguised slieveen the Queen of Porschia is,' remarked Agnetha impolitely, 'to ensure that if the marriage fails, the young Tamarind will of course remain in Ascourt with very special status.'

'The Queen of Porschia is simply insuring her investment in Ascourt's future.'

'I presume the young Tamarind plays bridge?'

'You presume too much, Agnetha dear.'

Aware that she was dozing in an uncomfortable position, Gubnet rolled over on to her side. She dreamed she was a great big basking shark. From her sideways position in the water, she saw the Queen of Porschia planting explosives through the porthole of the engine room. She nudged the yacht with all her might. She tried to alert them but no one would listen. She rose to the surface and opened her vast mouth at them but she could not seem to shout. Everyone was afraid of her gargantuan size.

She heard the report of a rifle and immediately went into labour. The cramps were unbearably painful so she turned on to her back and floated belly up. The white yacht sailed away from her. She thought she would die. Then came a spasm more powerful than she, and she knew that her baby had come. She rolled over to welcome her firstborn, a beautiful miniature of herself. She found herself cradling her baby, still covered in blood, the infant basking shark suckling on her human breast. Mother Nature sat beside her on her bed and She said, 'You have given birth to a monster – get rid of it!'

Gubnet woke with beads of perspiration running down her face and back. Piecing together the fragments of her dream, she called to the attendant Dames, 'Please Goddess that I am not miscarrying! I cannot look!'

But there was no sign of blood, it was a false alarm. They laid Gubnet among the marsh marigolds by the stream and quietened her. Agnetha took her head and Clemis the feet. They prayed and poured the energy of the cosmos into her shaking body. When at last she was still, Clemis spoke.

'St Gubnet, you must strengthen your bond with the child – you must name her without delay!'

Gubnet's comprehension was atavistic and immediate, for there are strange faculties stirred in a woman with child. Gubnet found the strength to point towards the statue in the grotto. 'Who is she?' she mumbled.

Dame Agnetha wasted no time. She nested one of each of their hands on Gubnet's abdomen and lifted her head to the sky. 'By the Spirit of Charlotte I name this child Athena, daughter of Gubnet and citizen of the New Order of Ascourt.'

Athena, Athena, Athena, swooned Gubnet. It was a heady name on her lips and when she woke much later that evening, she repeated it again. *Athena,* she said to her child and felt a stirring in her womb.

'No,' said the beautiful young brown eyes worriedly. 'It's me, Min – you're in my bedroom now, I'm taking care of you. Are you alright, my love?'

CHAPTER SEVEN

Queen Bea's Céilí
The Evening of Friday, November 15, 1996

Yossarian returned to her own room in the west wing late that afternoon. She was completely drained by the energy and enthusiasm of the people around her. The hunt for glue at the Ascourt Institute had turned into a guided tour of the laboratories, and by the time they had reached the Northern Territories, she had been too tired to help the repair crew in any way and had crept into the cockpit of the glider and fallen asleep. On the way back in the helicopter, Heron had said rather mincingly, 'I want a little chat with you this evening sometime'. Well, blow Heron! Heron didn't have to supervise the kitchen staff for this evening's event. Heron didn't have to organise the impossible sleeping arrangements tonight in the palace. Heron didn't have to make sure Queen Bea's pumps were polished or find a gown to flatter Min's muscular proportions – the Goddess! and such a feminine little thing she had been as a child.

Yossarian felt her chest tighten with apprehension. She wanted so much to look beautiful tonight. She had always prided herself on her carriage. It meant something to her. Unlike Heron, who didn't give a fig for appearances and who had bothered even less after Charlotte had passed on. *Well, it shows*, thought Yossarian resentfully. Heron would dress in the same old tweeds at tonight's céilí and probably not even wash. Her old friend Heron just couldn't make the effort to open her eyes to the obvious.

Yossarian poured herself a herbal mix of valerian and added two quick fingers of brandy. She sat at her writing desk where she had a view of the entire length of the island. Bliss crept through her veins. The rasp of her breath eased. Heron just didn't know what it was like to be a

79

nanny. *She doesn't have a maternal bone in her body*, thought Yossarian crossly. It was as plain as the nose on your face that Princess Min had a terrible crush on St Gubnet – and the cheek of that Maryann Leaf sashaying into the palace, swinging her beads at midnight. Was it any wonder she'd been unable to sleep – the moans and groans out of Queen Bea's bedroom were enough to have wakened the dead!

Yossarian drew a rough plan of the palace and set about the task of personally supervising the sleeping arrangements for tonight's guests. There would be no bed for the Leaf woman – her name was not entered on the official guest list. With that small matter out of the way, Yossarian turned her attention to the list and the sketch on her desk. She would donate her own single bed in the west wing to the Queen of Porschia. Queen Bea would have to move out of her beloved north wing. There were two single beds in the east wing, and as Gubnet was already occupying one of them, Queen Bea could just as well join her there. These manoeuvres afforded Yossarian the necessary excuse of having personally to share Queen Bea's double bed with Princess Min. It gave her a certain satisfaction that as Nanny, she was the highest-ranking employee of the palace. There'd be no hanky-panky in the palace tonight. She would see to it. Her word was law.

Yossarian unfolded the note she had found earlier that day under Queen Bea's pillow and read it once again.

Thursday, Nov. 14th,
Swann's Hotel.

Dear Queen Bea,

I hope you're feeling better – do you remember me? We met briefly at the Women's Group on Tuesday. I'm staying at Swann's Hotel where I've been made welcome by a kind but eccentric group of older women! If only I played bridge…! Bea – do you mind if I call you by your name? I know this is forward, but I would really like to see you. Do you feel the same way? Phone me tonight and tell me you do…

Yours truly, Maryann Leaf.

P.S. I have urgent news from your sister, *Vee – tell no one.*

80

Yossarian coolly folded the note and put it back in her pocket. Queen Bea would not be sleeping with Ms Maryann Leaf tonight, and by the time it was returned to the pillow, Queen Bea would be none the wiser.

By five that evening, Yossarian had bathed, shaved, perfumed, dressed and packed a small overnight bag for a change of bedroom. She poured herself a second cocktail and slipped on her stilettos. She sprayed the hairpiece into a soft wave which completely hid her forehead. Standing back, she appraised herself in the body-length mirror. Always the lady, she sighed.

Yossarian taped the Queen of Porschia's name to her own door and smoothly glided, drink and baggage, towards the north wing whereupon she deposited her belongings on to Queen Bea's double bed and taped 'Princess Min/Yossarian' on to the bedroom door.

On her way to the east wing, Yossarian felt the exhilarating effect of the valerian-brandy cocktail. Without knocking, she flung wide the doors to the bedroom apartments of the east wing.

'Princess Min,' she warbled gaily, 'your bags have been sent for. You will be housed in the north wing tonight. My apologies for any inconvenience caused by the overnight stay of the Queen of Porschia – we will all be back to normal by tomorrow.' Yossarian rather theatrically pasted the names 'Queen Bea/St Gubnet' to the double doors, brazenly enquired after St Gubnet's well-being and, without waiting for a reply, left much as she had arrived, returning the pair abruptly to their intimacy.

'If I were you,' said Gubnet crossly, 'I'd make some changes around here. Staff take orders, they don't give them.'

Princess Min knew that Gubnet was right. She would see to it as soon as the Queen of Porschia left the very next day.

Yossarian flowed down the stairs and apprehended the entire kitchen staff sitting at the table playing cards. She waited, with arms folded, for the Cook's usual explanation that everything was already done when Yossarian could see quite clearly that it was not. Their defiance of her authority was not without its source. Yes indeed, the culprit was Heron Home – interfering again!

'My dear Yossarian, I bribed Cook to feed me in exchange for a tarot reading, and as you can see everything in the kitchen is SNAFU dear; quite, quite in order,' said Heron momentarily laying down the deck of cards.

Yossarian flushed and wobbled ever so slightly in her high heels. Cook correctly surmised, for she possessed a very fine nose, that Yossarian's instability might be benevolently indulged by an appeal to approve the wine list for this evening's table.

'An excellent idea,' breathed Yossarian heavily. 'I shall go to the wine cellar and sample the grape.'

'What is SNAFU?' whispered the Vegetable Chef, who was consumed with curiosity.

'Don't you know?' said Heron.

A voice descending the spiral stone steps which led to the wine cellar echoed, 'Situation Normal, All Fucked Up.'

'Aha,' registered the Vegetable Chef, committing it to memory.

Cook cut the deck into three, Heron laid out the cards and all eyes were glued to the kitchen table. The first card was the shaman of cups, crossed by the priestess of swords. Heron then laid the root and crown cards.

'SNAFU,' remarked the Vegetable Chef keenly.

'The nine of swords and the seven of coins, reversed,' muttered the Pastry Chef ominously.

Left and right, Heron laid the past and future cards. 'The ten of rods, well that's not too bad,' said Heron. 'And in the future, oh dear, the death card reversed. I do hope, Cook, that this is not a personal reading,' hinted Heron helpfully.

'No, no,' lied Cook. 'I meant it for everyone – for Ascourt especially.'

'Just as well,' said Heron. 'This is the worst reading I have ever seen.'

The kitchen staff trembled in morbid anticipation.

'Come on then, Dr Home, no point in softening the blow – what does it all mean?' prompted Cook, determined to hear the worst.

'Well, I don't know,' admitted Heron. 'You see I usually refer to my textbooks which are not presently upon my person.'

The Pastry Chef, who was moderately acquainted with arcane matters, spoke up. 'The shaman of cups crossed by the priestess of swords, well that's obvious: someone in disguise is crossed by a bitter woman.'

Heron considered the interpretation and added, 'Or a kindly person has been crossed by a bitter woman.'

'At the root of the matter is a nightmare, the nine of swords, which is leading to the seven of coins reversed – yes, a nightmare pregnancy,' confirmed the Pastry Chef.

'Or,' pointed out Heron, 'a nightmare which may prevent a pregnancy.'

The irony was not lost on the Cook, who said in an irreverent American accent, 'May Myrtle the turtle be fertile.'

'And may the Goddess forgive you, Cook,' said the Pastry Chef in defence of Queen Bea.

'The ten of rods is a message, which is already received, because it's in the past, but it will lead to a, um, an immoveable sort of situation, a stalemate, a –'

Yossarian appeared once again at the door of the kitchen. She looked quite levelly at Heron and said, 'Which quite clearly leads to a death. Now prepare your glasses for a taste of the best wine ever produced in Ascourt!'

The cards were mercifully abandoned and all cups cheerfully drained. The Cook arose to work, and the rest of the staff followed suit. Heron looked at Yossarian worriedly. 'Let's have that little chat, shall we, dear?'

'You have no idea, Heron, do you?' snapped Yossarian suddenly. 'As it happens, I've far too much to do.'

Heron was mystified by the sudden mood-swings that Yossarian had evidenced all day.

'Why don't you get out of everyone's hair and get into a nice hot tub – I'm sure it would improve the way you feel about yourself,' said Yossarian unkindly.

'All right – can I have it in your room then?'

'Of course, Heron dear, but do clean up after yourself – the Queen of Porschia is sleeping there tonight.'

Yossarian left the kitchen and went out into the garden. It was six in the evening and the sun was just below the horizon. Yossarian was almost numb from the insistent welling pain in her chest. She raised her glass and toasted the Statue of the Great Drone. *They say you never felt a thing, Peter. But I know how brave you must have been. Dear Peter, give me strength to face this night!*

83

The inhabitants of Ambling Cottage, actually No. 37 Seaview Suburbs, were one of forty households preparing to make the long walk uphill to attend the céilí at the palace. As the crow flies it was exactly two miles from the western tip of the island to the palace in the east. On foot it took almost an hour, mostly up a treacherously steep and winding terrain.

Unlike ninety-five per cent of the residents of Seaview Suburbs, Montague was employed neither by the nearby Ascourt Institute nor the palace, at the other end of the island. Almost everyone who lived beside south harbour was a Worker, but Montague worked for herself, producing a newspaper, adding to the records at the local library and doing a spot of research in whatever interested her. Her exact function was difficult to pin down, but she had once described herself to her sister, Delia as 'a great nerve centre with a finger on the pulse of world affairs'. Like many restless spirits uncertain of their footing, Montague had an inner conviction that, one day, she would be famous for something. And every day, she was open and ready for what that something might be.

Montague du Pont left No. 37, Seaview Suburbs dressed in a serviceable tuxedo. She slipped two new batteries into her trousers pocket and lightly tapped her waistcoat to ensure that the portable cassette recorder was secure upon her person.

The walk up the hill would be sociable and good-humoured. Citizens would greet one another and exchange chitchat as they passed or fell behind another group. Apart from royalty, Ascourt was a classless society of Workers. But Montague felt a certain distinction. She closed the little gate on Ambling Cottage completing a picture which she stood back and admired. Being self-employed gave her more time than most to spend on her garden. She adjusted her monocle and critically appraised a shady bare patch on the whitewashed stone cottage. She made a mental note to ask the Queen of Porschia for a cutting of her underwater camellia. She left Seaview Suburbs, passed south harbour and began her ascent up the first steep hill.

Montague du Pont made it her business to be fair-minded and even-tempered. Dame Thwaites had tried, unsuccessfully of course, to sabotage her attendance at tonight's event, but Montague was a champion of the people. She spent the afternoon generously advising her neighbours on the correct form of dress and address for this evening's céilí. Every morning after Delia left to go to work, Montague tuned into the BBC World Service. She had gained a perspective on the world which the plain Worker of Ascourt lacked. She looked at the happy groups of citizens ahead of her into the distance and wondered how many of them could share her view that Ascourt was just a tiny piece of floating rock in a vast infinity of water. No; for they were simple peasant folk. The ground at their feet was the solid, firm lifegiving centre of their understandably limited universe.

As she ascended the hill, the sprawling length of the Northern Territories came into view. Ascourt was a very beautiful piece of rock, she had to admit. Montague took in a deep and unadulterated lungful of air. There was a greatness in the primitive beauty of the island, but there was also a greatness in the soul of Montague du Pont whose journalistic sixth sense told her that she was in the right place at the right time – and she had worked long and hard to be poised for the reward which she would shortly claim as her own.

As the night closed in upon them, she could see the twinkle of lights just ahead of her in the Ascourt Institute. She could hardly wait to tell Delia that she was hot on the trails of a crime. During the celidh tonight, Montague proposed to conduct a search of the aeroplane to recover the Will which Maryann had stolen the night before. There would be close to one hundred and fifty people at the palace tonight. For once, her absence would not be noticed. After she had recovered the Will and obtained a recorded confession from the criminal, she would sell her story to the mainland dailies. For an instant, Montague felt what it was like to be a household name. But the islander in her was incapable of abstraction. No, the real prize was the prescient picture of six humiliated Old Dames. Six arrogant Old Dames who had set up an exclusive club in a classless society. They had been taken in by a petty thief. And now she would expose them for the fools that they were. The rest was simply icing on the cake.

'Montague, how ought one address Saint Gubnet of Balleyvourney?' asked Delia, who had just joined her from the track which led down to the Institute. As they walked back on to the path they were joined by Sorrel, the unassuming Guide of the Northern Territories. Montague seemed to be in a sort of dream. She neither greeted Sorrel nor acknowledged her sister's question. Delia tapped Montague on the shoulder and repeated herself.

'Should she be addressed as Saint Gubnet or Madam?'

'On being introduced, one uses the full title, "Saint Gubnet", thereafter, "Madam".'

The three women ambled gently in the twilight, rising to the hill which left behind the imposing redbrick presence of the Ascourt Institute of Technology. Round the next sharp corner, they could see the lights of the palace towering above them, whereupon they caught up with the herbalist, Dame Meleka. The four were well acquainted and greeted each other in accordance with the festive mood.

'I do hope you haven't forgotten your *personal* invitation, Dame Meleka,' said Montague, noting, with some satisfaction, that Sorrel and Dame Meleka were identically dressed for the occasion, a fact which would embarrass them both, and all the more so since their drab choice of frock had been bought from the bargain bin of the local market.

Delia's forehead twitched in anticipation of a row.

'I've collected and dried the psilocybins you ordered for your apothecary,' said Sorrel, who never usually spoke out of turn, nor to Dame Meleka for that matter.

Delia relaxed and inwardly thanked Sorrel for her fortu-itous and sensitive interruption.

'How much do you want for them this time, then?' rapped Dame Meleka sharply.

Delia sighed. The price of dried mushrooms was a most contentious issue in view of the fact that Meleka and Sorrel had terminated their fifteen-year relationship over this same issue the previous November. Delia suggested that they talk about Something Else.

'I can't think of anything else to talk about,' said Dame Meleka, whose bile was up.

'Neither can I,' agreed Montague indignantly.

Sorrel remained characteristically silent and played a private game with a rat who was following them in the dark.

'Well, we *were* talking about St Gubnet,' suggested Delia, choosing a neutral topic of conversation.

'She's preggers, isn't she?' smirked Dame Meleka in a condescending tone of voice.

'I shouldn't think so,' replied Montague vaguely.

But in the course of her shopping that afternoon, Dame Meleka the herbalist had exchanged gossip with the head gardener in the market used by the residents of Seaview Suburbs, on the edge of the south harbour. Dame Meleka was insistent, the garden staff had been given the afternoon off and *they'd* heard it from the domestic staff at the palace.

'They say she hardly touched her food and then she threw up in the loos,' pointed out Meleka, who was knowledgeable in the affairs of women.

As the only person in Seaview Suburbs to have been officially introduced to Saint Gubnet, Montague tried to impress upon her companions the folly of idle speculation.

'I don't suppose the head gardener also informed you that Saint Gubnet narrowly survived an explosion aboard Mother Nature's yacht?'

'No,' said Sorrel who had also been to the market that afternoon.

'It could just as well have been a delayed reaction to the shock,' said Montague.

'Yes,' agreed Delia, who was a medically qualified pathologist at the Institute. 'Seasickness'.

'You know she and Mother Nature have just split up,' continued Dame Meleka unabashed.

'That is hearsay,' reminded Montague.

'I can't imagine being pregnant and dumped,' remarked Dame Meleka to Sorrel, her ex-lover of fifteen years.

Montague fidgeted nervously with her monocle. *It had never occurred to her to have a good look...*

'Believe me, if she's pregnant I'll know just by looking at her,' said Dame Meleka hitting her mark.

'And, pray, when was the last time you saw a pregnant woman in these parts?' volleyed Delia in defence of Montague's untrained eye.

'More recently than you've seen a dead one, I'm sure,' shot back Meleka unerringly.

The conversational deadlock was in part circumvented by the fact that the party had reached Town Square and were facing the aerobic prospect of the two hundred and sixteen steps. They climbed in silence. The palace clock struck eight when they reached the ascent. Above them, the black sky was encrusted with stars and a full moon emerged, still wet, like a newborn on the eastern horizon. It was an intensely personal moment for each of the four; a moment commanded by the majesty of nature. Slowly, the party turned towards the gates of the palace.

'I'm telling you, that's why she's come here – she's got nowhere else to go,' whispered the Old Dame loudly.

At twelve midnight, the céilí began. Accompanied by two fiddles, a mojun, bodhran and spoons, Dame Murphy called all present to form two circles, one moving counter-clockwise to the other. When the music stopped, those facing one another from the inner and outer circles paired up and danced to the next three fast reels.

The Cook was certain she recognised the woman in front of her in the white sable coat, but the name eluded her. No matter, for she was merry and the handsome visitor of ageless beauty agreed to join her for a glass of mead at the kitchen table. They made small talk and the Cook flirted as her work was done for the evening. Her companion idled with a brass fob watch, swinging it to and fro. The Cook became hypnotised. The woman asked her a question.

'Where is Yossarian?'

The Cook replied in a monotone, 'She is on the balcony of the north wing, overlooking the ballroom.'

'Thank you Cook. I will be back one day soon and we will tarry longer. When I snap my fingers you will count to ten and have no memory of ever meeting me.'

From the balcony of the north wing, Yossarian had a bird's eye view. After the first flush of dancing, the two circles reformed and spinned against each other like a roulette wheel. Yossarian felt woozy. Dame Murphy's mouth moved incessantly, urging the dancers to spin and to whirl as she conjured the soul of the dervish.

From the corner of her eye, Princess Min caught a slight movement on the balcony. She was a fourth Dan Aikido and her reaction times were a testimony to ten hard years from the tender age of six in a demanding and regimented Japanese dojo. She bounded up the staircase and caught Yossarian before she fell to the floor outside the door of Queen Bea's bedroom. For two years running, she had been the hundred-metre sprint champion in the Japanese Navy. Yossarian was as light as a feather. Princess Min lifted her on to Queen Bea's bed and took her pulse. It was pumping.

Yossarian mumbled incoherently. Princess Min put her ear to Yossarian's mouth.

'She's coming to get me,' whispered Yossarian weakly.

Princess Min examined her pupils. They were widely dilated.

'Please don't leave me here on my own, I'm so frightened', whimpered Yossarian. *And experiencing paranoid delusions as the result of chemicals*, reasoned the Princess, who strongly disapproved of drink and drugs. But there was no point in being stern with someone this far gone. It was probably best to let her sleep it off.

'I'm here,' said Min. 'Nobody's going to get you as long as I'm here, all right?'

Princess Min thought about Gubnet's remark earlier that afternoon. Queen Bea had no control over her staff. The staff had no self-respect, no honour and no discipline. Yossarian would be replaced after morning exercise tomorrow.

At two-thirty a.m. Dame Murphy called everyone together for the *Bróg*. The walls were suddenly emptied of bystanders taking refreshment. Two circles formed in great excitement, for the *Bróg* was the highlight of the autumn dance. And the tale of each *bróg* or shoe would be proudly or boldly or shyly or slyly told by the fireside of its owner during the long winter months to come. Nobody wanted to be left out of the *Bróg*.

They listened to Dame Murphy's instructions intently. Following this, each member of the inner circle removed a shoe and placed it on a heap in the centre of the room. The outer circle were instructed to turn their eyes to the wall as those from the inner circle left the ballroom to hide. At the count of ten, only those from the outer circle remained in the ballroom. Dame Murphy gave her last words. 'The first couple to return with the right fitting shoe will lead the dance of their choice!'

At this, the shoes were pounced on. The heap was cleared and the hunt was on. With screams and hoots the ballroom was emptied, save for the band, who played on.

Montague du Pont was not hiding in the garden. She hobbled in full view, anxiously watching for anyone bearing a white Adidas with leather uppers, size three. She was only too aware that travelling on one foot was infinitely slower than on two. It was after three in the morning and she had a Will to find on board an aeroplane nested in the rugged Northern Territories.

'Damn, damn, damn!' she almost cried. She thought of her twin sister, Delia, but gave up on the idea, as Delia had also been among the sacrificial inner circle and was therefore bereft of the vital left shoe. The hunt for the shoe usually went on until daybreak, with much mischief and cavorting as an excuse for high spirits and unvented lust. In fact a wholly indecent interval would have to pass before anyone would have the temerity to report back to Dame Murphy and claim the dance.

'Have you seen Maryann?' asked Queen Bea.

'No,' said Montague, catching her hand. And in it was Montague's shoe.

'That's mine,' said Montague possessively.

'No, I'm sure it's Maryann's,' said the Queen, unwilling to let go.

'It couldn't possibly fit her!' spluttered Montague. 'Maryann was wearing Doc Martens, about a size eight, I'd swear to it.'

'Well you just can't have it Montague, it's not convenient.'

'It certainly isn't, Your Highness. I really must be on my way and you really must give me that shoe.'

Montague tugged, but the Queen would not let go.

'Let go!' ordered the Queen. Montague reluctantly obeyed.

Queen Bea looked at the plaintive subject before her and shook her head. 'You can go up to my bedroom and help yourself to any pair of shoes you like and if it makes you feel better you can keep them.' She stuck her hand out. 'Don't be resentful, Montague. Now shake hands and make friends.'

Princess Min stalked the white sable coat in possession of her sandal through the palace. The heavenly apparition floated through walls and glided down long corridors but Min never lost it for long. Eventually, it stopped at the backstairs of the west wing and winked at Min who grinned ruefully back at her. What a worthy opponent this adversary was. Without warning, the glamorous coat suddenly whisked itself down the secret passage to Queen Bea's bedroom and Min found herself in hot pursuit.

Min was certain that the woman in the white sable coat had allowed herself to be caught in Queen Bea's bedroom. When the sandal had been graciously handed back, Princess Min found herself in a quandary. Was she supposed to seduce her?

Min looked around nervously, but it was dark and she couldn't see whether or not Yossarian was still in Queen Bea's double bed.

'I don't think we've been introduced,' murmured the Princess shyly.

'No, you and I have never met – I'm an old friend of your mother's,' came the casual reply.

Princess Min blushed violently in the dark.

'I'm so sorry,' she blurted.

'Sorry for what?' teased the white-coated one.

'I wasn't sure what you wanted,' said Min edgily.

'I won't be wanting you until you're a bit more grown up,' she laughed.

'I am eighteen!' protested Min.

'And very courageous, I can tell. By the way, my name is Banba. I am the Spirit of Death.'

Banba opened the windows, allowing the moon to softly illuminate the room. She removed her brass fob watch and dangled it before Princess Min. By way of explanation she shrugged unhurriedly and said, 'I'm running a bit late…'

Maryann and Queen Bea held hands and sighed upon the easy chairs in Queen Bea's moonlit garden.

'I feel like an overgrown Cinderella,' said Maryann, dangling a petite white runner from her left big toe. 'The slipper doesn't fit, milady!'

'Well then, we'll bind your feet, and you won't be able to run away from me,' joked Queen Bea seriously.

'Bea, I know I should have told you this before but I didn't want to upset you – why can't we say goodbye properly?'

'Because it's only a tiny palace and all the rooms are full. Why must you go so soon?'

'Why don't you come with me? You've never been out of Ascourt, have you? There's a whole wide world out there – come with me!'

'And just fly off into the sunset?'

'Sunrise,' said Maryann. 'Six in the morning!'

'But I'm the Queen – I can't leave!'

'And I'm better paid than you are, Bea – I 'd support you.'

Nearby a hedge of myrtle sneezed.

'It's just the wind.'

'What if your children don't like me?' asked Queen Bea nervously.

'Then I'd pack them off to a boarding school.'

'That's a terrible thing to do to children,' ached Queen Bea.

'I didn't mean it, they live with their fathers really,' said Maryann desperately. 'Why does true love hurt so much?'

'I'll only be half a person without you,' sorrowed Queen Bea.

'I'll be back as soon as the Institute gives me an official contract to begin work on the island. It can't be helped, Bea, I've got to go home.'

'Well don't forget to give my love to – '

Maryann closed Bea's mouth with her finger, 'Just kiss me love, no more words…'

Under the myrtle hedge, Dame Clemis rubbed a frozen bare foot. She was catching a cold.

Montague did not knock before entering Queen Bea's bedroom. She flipped the light switch, saw the wardrobe straight ahead of her and ran towards it. She bent over and rummaged through the shoes. As luck would have it, she spotted a pair of size three mountain boots which would be perfect for the long hike ahead. She frantically unlaced her right shoe but lost her balance. Her head hit something very hard and metallic. The night burst into stars and before the lights went out completely, the door to the wardrobe was clicked shut and locked.

The Queen of Porschia cheated. Cook had been rostered for

staff duty during the *Bróg* and was certain that someone in a white coat was coming to get her. The Queen of Porschia took advantage of Cook's poor mental state and bribed her with an offer of a job in Porschia with better and brighter prospects.

Cook removed her left shoe in the kitchen and handed it to Porky. Porky handed Cook an unclaimed size eight Doc Marten boot and told her to get rid of it. Cook tossed the boot into the flour bin, removed her apron and ran into the ballroom with Porky where they were announced as the winners of the the *Bróg* at precisely five-thirty a.m.

Porky requested the band to play 'My Way'. Under the compliant baton of Dame Murphy, the portly pair swept skilfully around the ballroom to a gathering crowd of admiring party-goers. The band played it twice and everyone joined in. At 5:20 a.m., Dame Murphy laid down her baton and announced that the céilí was officially over.

Delia returned to Ambling Cottage alone. It was after six in the morning when she turned off the bedside light, but she couldn't sleep. She was worried about Montague. She set her alarm for seven-thirty. If Montague had not returned by then she would set off alone for the Northern Territories in search of her twin sister. Montague had told her everything. There were no secrets between them. Delia berated herself for not being more insistent about accompanying Montague on her mission.

She slept for what seemed like a moment before the phone rang waking her. But when she looked at the clock, an hour had passed. It was seven in the morning.

'Delia?'

Delia nodded sleepily into the receiver.

'Delia, it's Dr Home speaking.'

'Something has happened to Montague, I know it!'

'You've got to get up to the palace as fast as you can.'

'Where is Montague?' wailed Delia hysterically.

'Delia, listen to me' shouted Heron down the receiver. 'There's been a murder up here – '

'It's Montague, isn't it?' said Delia suddenly steadying herself.

'We'll start again, Delia. I will speak slowly and clearly so that you will understand me, all right?'

Delia closed her eyes hard.

'I don't know where Montague is. Now could I please talk to the State Pathologist?'

'You know very well who you are speaking to Heron,' said the State Pathologist with her eyes still shut.

'Delia, please, we need you up here – '

'Who – '

'Yossarian.'

The phone went dead.

PART TWO

CHAPTER EIGHT

A Murder

Saturday, November 16, 1996

Mother Nature boarded Her private jet at 00:56 hours, New York time, within a half hour of Agent D's last and final phone call from Ascourt. The five-hour transatlantic flight had given Her time to think. Now that Ascourt was caught in the merry web of its own demise, they could just sit there and rot. Meanwhile, She needed to press on with Her plans. Her first stop was the island which would be replacing Ascourt as the pilot project for the Superdrones – Porschia. At noon, She would go on to give a lecture entitled 'Recent Advances in Genetic Apiculture' to a group of influential and well-funded researchers in Oxford, England. The pilot of the jet interrupted Her thoughts with an announcement that the island of Porschia was in sight, and that it was 11:05 a.m., local time. Mother Nature ordered a glass of ginseng tonic and stared, deep in thought, from the starboard window.

She was sensitive to the marriage between science and economics. The Superdrones were a shot in the arm for an ailing international bee industry. One didn't go in shouting about sole rights and big bucks. No, Mother Nature knew the game and played it for every cent it was worth. The first step was to court the boffins and get the rubber stamp of approval. She was going to sell them the blurb which described the revolutionary Superdrone and its capability as both a worker and a drone. If Oxford agreed to perform academic trials, the whole world would soon be looking for a slice of the action. The copyright was technically the property of Mother Nature International. Nothing could go wrong except, of course, a leak of bad publicity from Ascourt...

Which was why She was going to fly straight from Oxford

to Dublin to meet a senior figure of the Irish cabinet for an early-evening appointment. Ascourt would be sewn up tighter than a tick's ass. Only then would She take a rest, a much-needed rest, back in the luxuriant folds of her London penthouse.

The Porschian Island Manager stepped on to the VIP carpet within minutes of the jet landing. Mother Nature had a good look at Hayde Lewis, briefcase in hand, striding confidently towards Her. She had a certain admiration for this woman who had graduated top of the class of '61. Hayde had a reputation as a dealer and a girl about town. Under her skilful management, Porschia outstripped all other island colonies in earnings, efficiency and investment policy. Profits were regularly ploughed back into new technology which, in return, made more money for Mother Nature International.

Mother Nature knew three important facts about Hayde Lewis. One: the lodgements into her private Swiss bank account exceeded her salary. Two: she had cheated in her final exams in MIT. Three: Hayde knew Mother Nature knew, and that made her a valued employee.

When the Island Manager came aboard, Mother Nature replaced the smile with a frown of displeasure.

'Where is Her Majesty, the Queen of Porschia?'

'To the best of my knowledge, Your Eminence, she is in Ascourt.'

Mother Nature turned purple. 'Ascourt? What is she doing in that hellhole?'

'I believe, Eminence, that she responded to an SOS from your private yacht and headed a rescue team to save the lives of drowning passengers and crew, most of whom were headed for Ascourt.'

Mother Nature did not invite Hayde to take a seat. She looked out on to the runway and twiddled Her thumbs slowly. Agent D had neglected to mention the Queen of Porschia...

'And the rest of whom are here,' stated Mother Nature turning back to the pellucid blue eyes.

'I was away on business at the time, Your Eminence. I wouldn't presume to know the facts.'

'Very well, Hayde. We'll get down to straight talk. My theory is that the yacht was deliberately sunk by a timed explosive which was planted by someone while the yacht was anchored here in Porschia. Now who do you suppose did it, Hayde?'

Hayde silently ran her fingers through her short blond hair.

'The Queen of Porschia did it, Hayde, in order to get her hands on the Superdrones who are somewhere on this very island. Perhaps the Captain is here too. Did you know that the yacht is insured with Lloyds for ten million pounds? What d'you suppose they'll think when they find a large hole blown out of the bottom of it, Hayde?'

Hayde studiously concentrated on her fingernails which were clean and short.

'Didn't you know that the Superdrones were useless to you?' goaded Mother Nature furiously.

It was clear from the astonished look on Hayde's face that she did not.

'We're not fools in MNI,' lectured Mother Nature scathingly. 'The computer industry could learn a thing or two from us. The Superdrones can't be ripped off – they're designed with an inbuilt genetic copyright. They imprint on only one royal female, and the ones you pinched, Hayde, well, they already have – on Princess Min of Ascourt. So what do you propose to do with them now?'

Hayde Lewis, a percentage tennis player, elected to remain silent.

'All right – let's try an easy one. Who's Porky's eldest daughter?'

Hayde Lewis repeated the deadpan official line. 'Princess Tamarind, Your Eminence, eighteen years of age, currently researching Alternative Culture in London.'

The pilot of the aircraft poked her head around the cabin door. 'Ten minutes to take-off, Your Eminence.'

Mother Nature returned a scorpionic gaze to the pampered figure of Her overpaid employee.

'Start a full reproductive programme with this Princess Tamarind and the Superdrones. I want results, Lewis – a full report every three days, media coverage and healthy statistics. I want a model island Hayde, and if Lloyds don't pay up for the yacht I'm going to hold you personally accountable.'

Hayde Lewis pondered the finger pointing at her. The odds on getting a bunch of Superdrones interested in a second party did not sound promising. But it was the odds on getting the exiled Tamarind interested in the Superdrones that really worried her...

'Just make it *look* as if it's working, for Christ's sake,' said Mother Nature impatiently. 'I want the investors impressed, Hayde – just like the examiners were at MIT, remember?'

Being a Gemini, Hayde did remember – only the past never interested her as much as the future, and it was in this latter domain that she foresaw the effects of the Queen of Porshia's most likely reaction to the news of Tamarind's return.

'What is my position *re* the present Queen?' asked Hayde, calculating rapidly.

'Who are you working for – her or me?

'So you mean Porky will be –'

'Retired, Lewis. Like you will be if this doesn't work out.'

'Long live Queen Tamarind!' said Hayde Lewis.

'Out of my sight,' said Mother Nature, waving a hand in dismissal.

The burly figure of Hayde Lewis emerged and stood hunched on the red carpet as the light aircraft taxied down the runway. Out of the corner of her eye, she spotted a red helicopter on the northern horizon. The Queen of Porschia had timed a perfect return. Hayde looked up and prayed for a collision.

Mother Nature embarked from the jet in Dublin Airport at four o'clock and was whisked to Kildare Street in a black Mercedes. The Minister for Agriculture greeted her warmly.

'Killian, I need a favour – ' began Mother Nature.

The Minister graciously gestured Her to continue. It was difficult not to. Mother Nature International was an Irish-registered company with an export base large enough to keep the national economy afloat.

'One of my Island Colonies, Ascourt – I doubt you've ever heard of it, dear – has reported a death from the BADS virus. We are doing all we can to contain the outbreak, but until it is safely under control, I am forced to comply with your own departmental guidelines and put the island into quarantine for an indefinite period.'

Mother Nature squeezed a tear which She patted dry with a black lace West of Ireland handkerchief.

'Your Eminence,' squirmed the Minister, 'Bee and Drone Sickness – how embarrassing for all of us. I'll have to notify the World Health Organisation, there hasn't been an outbreak since the 1950s.'

'Quite,' agreed Mother Nature. 'And as you may know, Killian, I have only just launched the Superdrone in Oxford this very afternoon – a project that is one hundred per cent Irish and will most certainly displace the balance of trade in favour of exports for your foreseeable political future. A mere whisper of BADS and the entire gross national product will be in jeopardy...'

Killian Walsh, Minister for Agriculture, wasted no time interpreting the economic jargon. 'What can I do for you, Mother Nature?'

Mother Nature sipped Her cup of tea thoughtfully.

'I thought you might suggest that we get on to the Minister for Defence and have the island of Ascourt ringed by a few gunboats...'

'We'll take the usual precautions. No one in or out of the island. We could call it a top-secret naval exercise – it'll give the lads a bit of practice before their tour of duty in the Gulf next month,' reasoned the Minister.

'Naturally I didn't think it necessary to suggest that you also have a word with the Minister for Posts and Telegraphs...', prompted Mother Nature diplomatically.

'You took the words right out of my mouth,' blustered the Minister. 'Sure it's in the national interest that the island be cut off from all communication. Do you think that will be all?'

'Well, as I said, Killian, I need a small favour...'

The Minister nodded hopefully.

'I may need someone presently on Ascourt to be quietly and discreetly removed,' whispered Mother Nature.

The Minister cleared his throat and swallowed hard. 'You mean murdered?'

'Minister!' gasped Mother Nature. 'That is unthinkable!'

'Oh thank God for that,' he replied.

Delia du Pont, State Pathologist, arrived at the scene of the murder to find Queen Bea and Dr Heron Home struggling to free Princess Min's naked body from the four black silk bondage scarves which held her expertly to the double bed in

the north wing. Out of the corner of her eye, she spotted
Yossarian's corpse abandoned to a pool of blood on the carpet
under the long window.

There was no time for the usual formalities. Delia held up a
small, polished mirror to Princess Min's mouth. Satisfied that
she was still breathing, she methodically unbuttoned her long
yellow raincoat and wrapped it round Yossarian's stiffening
body. She rummaged through her medical box, and ticked
herself off for forgetting to include a replacement raincoat.
They were so much cheaper than bodybags, and, of course,
much more versatile.

'Help us, Delia!' cried Queen Bea. 'We must get these
scarves off before Princess Min comes round and sees them.'

'There's no need to shout,' said Delia, calmly unwinding
the doubleknit turban which she wore for protection against
the wind. 'I can hear you perfectly well.'

'I killed Yossarian,' confessed Queen Bea tearfully.

Delia freed Princess Min from her bonds with a sharp
surgical scissors. Unfussed, she checked the strong, unconscious pulse, clothed the naked princess in a bathrobe donated
by Queen Bea, and looked enquiringly at Heron Home after
she had put her patient into a comfortable recovery position.

'Queen–Bea–left–the–palace–after–the–*Bróg*–to–wave–good
bye–to–Maryann,' strained Heron, recounting each word as if
by rote. 'When Maryann's plane took off, Queen Bea returned
to the east wing where Yossarian had arranged for her to sleep
last night.' Heron looked up, to no one in particular, as if
trying to recall her next line. 'Ah yes, on the way to the east
wing, she passed her own bedroom in the north wing where
she was arrested by strange noises. She entered and saw a
shadowy figure attacking Princess Min on the bed.'

Queen Bea lifted her sister's drowsy head on to her lap and
immediately continued the story for Delia's benefit.

'I said "Stop that!", but it paid no attention to me. I didn't
know how to make it stop and Min was trying to shout but she
had a scarf tied into her mouth. I panicked. I found an old
hatpin on the dresser and I just stabbed with it as hard as I
could.'

Delia sank hopelessly on to the bed. 'And then you realised
you had stabbed Yossarian.'

'Yes,' said Bea stroking Min's velvet black hair. 'I couldn't believe it. It was like a bad dream. I rang Heron, hoping she'd be at home, and she came up here and called you immediately.'

'Queen Bea,' said Delia softly, 'this is a tragedy. You must be in a terrible shock. Of course the charges will be reduced to involuntary manslaughter, I'm sure the legal – '

'That's quite all right, Delia. There won't be any charges. *A Queen cannot be held responsible for her actions because she is the Will of her People.* I'm quite guilty but there's nothing to be done about it.'

Princess Min began to mumble incoherently. 'Thank heavens,' said Heron. 'I think she's going to be all right.'

The cupboard moved. And then it heaved. A familiar groan ensued. Delia was the first to spot the key which had been carelessly thrown to the ground. Picking it up, she rushed towards the cupboard door.

'Montague!' cried Delia. 'It's you!'

Neither Montague du Pont nor Princess Min could recall with any clarity the events of the night before. Between the indignance of the first party and the incoherence of the second, no further light was cast on the scene of the crime.

'Thanks to Queen Bea,' began Montague heatedly, 'I was pushed into the cupboard in the middle of a very important mission – and now I, I don't remember a thing!'

'Yeah, about three in the morning, I followed a ghost in here,' yawned Princess Min. 'And then it's like I just fell asleep, you know?'

Heron Home, Island Manager of Ascourt, took charge. She instructed Delia to make a complete forensic search of the bedroom and conduct interviews with the palace staff.

'Meanwhile, Queen Bea and I will take charge of transporting Yossarian's body to the Institute where we will meet for the cut-up at say, four this afternoon? Let's keep this to ourselves, girls, until we have all the facts. Montague – you handle the publicity if need be.'

Montague rubbed her aching head and nodded.

'We don't suspect foul play,' reminded Heron sternly.

'Until I conduct the post-mortem this afternoon,' agreed Delia, unto whom befell the disagreeable task.

'Poor Nanny Yossarian,' said Queen Bea sadly.

*

Back at the Ascourt Institute, Heron uncovered the yellow raincoat and peeled the corpse of its remaining blood-soaked clothes. Yossarian lay facedown on the slab in Delia's laboratory, naked and innocent as the day she was born. Turning the body over on to its back, Heron recorded two ventral injuries.

'Look, Bea – there's the whole tragic story.'

Under the belly button was a large, red swelling with a hole in it.

'It looks like a bee-sting,' said Bea.

'It is a bee-sting,' said Heron authoritatively. 'Now look here as well.'

Bea looked and retched violently. Yossarian's groin had been torn out.

'Our hatpin story won't get past Delia when she examines the body. What on earth shall we do?'

Queen Bea left the pathologist's laboratory to fetch a mug of black coffee. Entering Dr Home's office she shakily lit a French cigarette and sat huddled in the spacious armchair. She stabbed at the oak desk with the hatpin. It was too much all at once. She wouldn't be able to protect Min once Delia saw the body and realised for herself that Princess Min was guilty of murdering their Nanny. Not even a false confession could protect her sister now. When the telephone rang, she jumped.

'In that case,' she said to the caller, 'you'd better get over here as fast as you can.'

In the royal bedroom of the palace's north wing, Montague remembered the tape recorder wedged in the dishevelled folds of her waistcoat.

'I say, Delia, there might be something on this.'

She put the recorder on the double bed and pressed the playback button. After fifty-two minutes, a funny clicking sound was recorded by the tape.

'It must have turned itself on when I fell,' whispered Montague triumphantly.

'Sshhh!'

They played it three times and made a rough transcription. They both recognised Yossarian's voice saying, 'Heron, it's over. I want to (... ...) with Peter. (... better or ... ...) the (Will?) is (... ... ...) hands now. Come and get me.' There was a click like a phone being hung up and then a long dialling phrase, a twenty-second pause and once more the voice: 'Password (...D?) Mother Nature, Mission Complete.' After a final click, the tape ran itself to the end with no audible sound.

Delia looked at her twin sister disbelievingly. 'What time did you enter the bedroom, Monty? Think hard.'

'It must have been four-thirty – yes it was! I remember the six chimes from the clock – the bedroom window was open.'

Delia shook her head astutely. 'Your recorder would have come on just after four-thirty a.m. Add fifty-two minutes playing time and Heron would have received that phone call from Yossarian at around five-twenty-five a.m. She'd have been in this bedroom no later than six.'

'Good thinking!' remarked Montague keenly.

'And the palace staff mostly agree that Queen Bea arrived back around six-thirty,' said Delia, 'Which means Heron was here *before* Queen Bea, and – '

Montague knew that her sister was leading up to something important. 'Go on!' she urged.

'Well, Heron didn't call me until seven.'

St Gubnet thanked providence that she had packed among her wardrobe an appropriate black wraparound skirt in keeping with an expanding waistline and a funereal occasion. She pinned her soft red tresses into a severe bun which she covered with a thick black shawl. Despite the wind against her, she arrived at the Institute, not a hair out of place and within forty minutes of her phone call to Queen Bea. On examining the corpse, she confirmed Dr Heron Home's conclusion. Princess Min had been raped.

'I am so sorry,' cried Gubnet berating herself. 'I should have spoken sooner to one or other of you. I feel personally responsible for this whole sordid affair. Please believe me when I say I had no part in this – save being ruthlessly manipulated by Mother Nature. Now that I am a citizen of Ascourt my loyalty is to you, Queen Bea. Princess Min doesn't know what's happened to her, I called you because I wanted to help and I didn't know how...'

In this one moment, Bea knew the force of the collective hurt which was charging through her queenly body. In this one moment she knew the agony of being unable to feel for any of it.

'Gubnet, no, it was all my fault,' blubbered Heron untidily. 'Yossarian knew exactly what was happening. The night before she was killed she even said, "Heron, you have no idea, have you?" She was trying to tell me, but you see we'd agreed not to tell each other anything. She saw the Death card in the Tarot reading and she must have known it was her own death, the Goddess, if anyone could have prevented this it was me...'

Queen Bea blew her nose and cleared her throat. St Gubnet ushered them out of the cold, white laboratory and shut the door softly behind her. She pursed her lips and nodded grimly at them.

'Let's get some fresh air. I'll tell you everything I know.'

Montague listened to Delia's analysis of the recent events over a hearty lunch at Swann's Hotel.

'That bit about hearing moans from the bedroom and finding a shadowy figure attacking her on the bed – Princess Min was out cold, she said so herself. It couldn't have happened that way, Monty. Heron got the call at five-twenty-five a.m. and must have waited for Queen Bea to return. They had just enough time to concoct a story between them. Queen Bea confessed, but I'd swear she didn't do it. She wouldn't know how.'

'Quite,' agreed Montague readily. 'My guess is they're protecting someone.'

The morning's endeavours had proved fruitful. But the taped phone calls were not the only discovery. Montague waved the note she found under Queen Bea's pillow.

'It would seem to me that this Maryann character, whoever she is, got herself an introduction to Queen Bea by faking an association with our long-lost Princess Vee. She stole the Will, murdered Yossarian – and then she flew off, ably assisted by our lovelorn Queen, and gets off scot-free.' Montague paused and stabbed a finger at the note. 'Do you realise that Queen Bea actually ordered me to enter her bedroom and obtain footwear? She point blank refused to return my shoes. I couldn't get to the wretched aeroplane to recover the Will. I am in no doubt, Delia, that the Will was on the aeroplane and that Queen Bea is protecting Maryann Leaf.'

'But what for? Stealing a Will is hardly a motive for murder,' said Delia, waving an empty fork.

'Ah,' countered Montague. 'As the Dames rightly supposed to begin with, Maryann Leaf is a spy working for Mother Nature. Let's say Mother Nature wanted a copy of the Will. What better way to get information than to have Her agent bed the monarch? As for Yossarian, I suspect that Maryann Leaf realised that she had been seen destroying the statue – '

'Seen by Yossarian?' questioned Delia.

'Yossarian witnessed a crime – she had to be removed. There's your motive.'

Delia twirled her spaghetti around the fork. 'So why the fancy tie-up job on Princess Min?'

Montague considered this for a moment. 'Well, like she said, she went into the bedroom like me – my guess is that we both got in the way of the murderer.'

'Ok, but how did Heron become involved?'

'I don't know,' said Montague peevishly. 'I can't know everything! Look, I can't think any more. I'm going to call a friend of mine on the mainland, see if she can't get us some information on Maryann Leaf, if that's her real name, of course…' Delia nodded sagely.

At the reception desk of Swann's Hotel, Montague dialled the mainland number to receive a taped telephone message: *'All lines to Ascourt have been temporarily suspended. We apologise for any inconvenience caused.'*

Delia thought about Montague's theory. It was lively, inventive and improbable. The possibilities whirled around like the spaghetti she had no appetite for. Deep down she was hurt and confused because two people she loved and respected had gone to a great deal of trouble to conceal the truth from her. Queen Bea and Heron Home were in some sort of trouble and her deepest instinct was to reach out and help them. Why couldn't they trust her with the truth? How could she support them without the facts?

Delia scribbled a list of instructions on Montague's napkin and left Swann's Hotel alone. Buoyed up by a lively breeze, she arrived at the Institute with a clear mind. As she had correctly surmised, the truth lay naked and exposed in her own laboratory. She immediately saw that it would take no pathologist to put the whole story together. Everything became crystal clear to her.

In the act of fertilisation, a drone's genitals are torn from his body and enter the female intact. This process is often accompanied by a reflexive sting on the part of the female, thus ending the life of the drone. The female was none other than Princess Min. The bonds which tied her to the bed indicated that she had been raped, unleasing the reflexive sting which killed Yossarian which could only mean...

Yossarian had been a drone.

On the misty, cold November afternoon three figures walked beside the crashing surf of the western beaches. St Gubnet shouted gustily. The listeners attended her moving lips at times, distracted by the windcrazed shawl.

'The Superdrones are copyrighted to me personally. I bred them. But Mother Nature and I have been in a relationship since the sixth age of creation – I mean we've never used terms like *yours* or *mine*. I wanted the Superdrones commercially tested on Porschia – no offence, but the results would be more realistic – and Mother Nature kept on about Ascourt and comparative advantage. Well, I was fooled. It's so obvious a child could see it. Mother Nature is having her revenge on Charlotte by forcing you back to the Way of the Bees.'

Heron explained to Queen Bea that comparative advantage meant that the island was so backwards that the test results would look much better on Ascourt than on an efficient and well-run island like Porschia, where the results could be marginal.

'It depends on your priorities,' clarified Heron.

'It was such a minor part of obtaining my Master's degree in genetic engineering, Heron. The Superdrone is just a laboratory cross between a sexy breed of Drone and a Worker. His great advantage is that he behaves like a Worker and eats only half the amount of a normal Drone, so he's a revolutionary and economic proposition.'

'He works hard, he plays hard and he sings for his supper!' said Bea, spinning on a shell.

Gubnet looked intently at the young Queen. Bea had a hidden intelligence which was delightfully and erratically sprung. Mother Nature would die for that jingle.

'But the big problem, you see, is that he can't reproduce other Superdrones like himself – for like all drones his offspring can only be the female Workers,' explained Gubnet.

'And after he's old and tired, you would have to buy another batch of Superdrones from the laboratories of Mother Nature International.'

Heron wrinkled her nose at the whole idea. In other words, a colony of males working and vying for one female Queen. Did Mother Nature seriously think this was a revolution in keeping with the Way of the Bees?

While Heron pondered the unthinkable, Gubnet and Queen Bea walked ahead. With every few steps a flock of red-eyed oystercatchers also moved on nervously.

'Gubnet, do you fancy Min? And wait – ' Queen Bea held up her hand. 'And do you love her more than you love Mother Nature?'

Gubnet smiled indulgently. 'I've been ranting on, haven't I? Well, Princess Min isn't my lover. I feel for her rather the way you do – like an older sister feels protective and caring about a younger one. I don't love Mother Nature any more – but if I did, I'd love them both very differently. Can you understand that?'

Gubnet marvelled at her own smooth delivery, a trick she had picked up from years of convent living. But the outer resonance was in sharp contrast to the inner jangle.

'I think you hate Mother Nature, which means you want to love Her very much but you can't right now. And I think that Min needs to be protected more than any one in the whole wide world and if you don't open your eyes very soon you're going to lose her.'

Bea's unintentional *coup de grace* left Gubnet completely unnerved and struggling for words. 'But you married her off, Bea, just like that…'

Bea put her hands into her jeans pocket and shrugged. Heron caught up and fell into line, but they had reached a standstill at the cliffs. Gubnet took a deep breath of fresh, salty air and continued her tale.

'It was a cold-blooded plan. Mother Nature knew the Superdrones would imprint on Princess Min while she was aboard the yacht. She instructed Min to remain in her naval uniform, knowing full well that we would be fooled into thinking that she was a man. Of course Min had no idea what was going on. Only for the Queen of Porschia's cupidity in blowing up the damn boat in order to get her grubby hands on the loverboys, we would have turned up on Ascourt with Princess Min and her Superdrones and I am certain that Queen Bea would have been deposed shortly afterwards.'

'Well, thankfully, that didn't happen,' said Heron looking protectively towards Queen Bea.

'Exactly. But once the Superdrones were out of the picture, Yossarian filled the breach and impregnated Min, no doubt at Mother Nature's behest. The point is that Min's pregnancy makes her undisputed Queen of Ascourt and that's exactly what Mother Nature wants her to be.'

'And what about me?' asked Queen Bea wistfully.

'I think you should be accompanied by an armed guard from now on.'

Heron and Bea smiled diffidently. There were no firearms on Ascourt and never had been.

'It's OK. Min would never let anyone hurt me, she's a fourth Dan Aikido champion,' said Bea rationally.

'That's right,' said Gubnet, feeling herself flush uncontrollably at the thought of Min's disciplined physique.

The oystercatchers, every one, turned and watched the monstrous wave. It rose, wet, engulfed them and descended to its depths with the bubbles of their logic. All that remained was a sea of emotion.

'How could Yossarian have done that to Min?' cried out Bea. 'How could she? She was our Nanny!'

'Yes indeed! How could she, I mean he – that dirty old drone,' screamed Gubnet. 'That filthy pervert, rapist, defiler. Poor Min. Poor Min. Poor Min. What'll I do? What'll I do? Yes, rape counselling, abortion. Imagine that filthy bastard. Having his children – oh Goddess, no, no…'

Gubnet threw herself on to the rocks.

Bea transformed into stone.

'The Princess Min is not pregnant,' said Heron quietly, checking her watch.

It was almost four o'clock, time to get back to the Institute before the others arrived. The oystercatchers, closeby, lifted their wings to the wind, making ready for the chase.

CHAPTER NINE

An Original Will

The evening of Saturday, November 16th, 1996

Montague followed Delia's instructions, which were short and to the point, and written on the napkin. At four p.m. sharp, the Old Dames Breakfast Club was comfortably seated and waiting in the Ascourt Institute's tiny lecture theatre. At seven minutes past four, Heron, St Gubnet and Queen Bea were met by Montague at the front door of the Institute and escorted on to the public stage of the tiny auditorium where four chairs awaited them. Montague remained in the wings, rehearsing her lines. When Delia arrived and occupied the fourth seat on stage, the whispers in the audience died down, the lights were dimmed and Montague played the eerie recording of Yossarian's last two phone calls.

When the lights came back on, Montague was centre stage, resplendent in a perfumed cravat and the award-winning outfit which she earned in the role of Professor Henry Higgins in last year's production of *My Fair Lady*. She gestured, upstage, to the four seats behind her and turned and faced the jury of Old Dames.

'Dr Heron Home received a phonecall from Yossarian at approximately five-twenty-five a.m. this morning. She is here to explain to us why a one-and-a-half-hour delay was deemed necessary before notifying these events to the proper authorities. Dr Home?'

'Is this drama really necessary, Montague?' said Heron irritably.

Dame Agnetha stood up from the auditorium. 'Yes, I must protest – we want the truth, not an interrogation designed to make trusted friends look ridiculous.'

Montague turned to Delia, occupying the stage seat beside

111

St Gubnet. 'I was only following your instructions!'

Delia raised her eyes to heaven. 'I asked you to organise a Truth Session, not direct the Christmas panto.'

Montague was wounded. She would not be made a show of in front of the Dames. She turned to Queen Bea, who was seated between Gubnet and Heron on the stage, and muttered angrily, 'And if you had given me back my shoe I could have proved once and for all that your lover, Maryann Dingbat, not only stole the Will, but murdered Yossarian as well!'

Queen Bea rose to her full four foot ten and screamed into Montague's noisome cravat, 'Don't you ever talk about my girlfriend like that!'

Dame Clemis rushed on to the stage and addressed herself forcefully to the compere. 'Now let's not make wild and unsubstantiated accusations, shall we, Monty?'

'You duplicitous old hag,' roared Montague, struggling to be free of Clemis's restraining vicegrip. 'You called her a flearidden hippy yourself!'

'I'm going to make us all a cup of tea,' said Dame Murphy, who was joined in her sensibilities by Heron, who knew that the tea was kept in the jar marked *Coffee.*

St Gubnet broke up the fight and escorted Dame Clemis to the powder room to clean up while Dame Agnetha firmly massaged Montague's throbbing temples.

Delia joined the chatter in the auditorium and learned to her bewilderment that the Old Dames had always known that Yossarian was a drone.

'That's why he had beard rash – and all those hairpieces to disguise his pretty heartshaped face,' said Dame Toplis matter-of-factly.

Alone on the stage, accompanied by a burning spotlight, Queen Bea went into a trance. She could see Yossarian holding her six-year-old hand under the statue of Peter, the Last Great Drone.

'Heron, it's over. I want to be buried with Peter. For better of for worse, the Will is out of our hands now,' recited Queen Bea.

In the strange half-light of the ethereal world, Queen Bea could see the figure of Yossarian drawing closer to her. She could see the stubble which had formed a shadow on his pale, drawn face. His kind black eyes were apprehensive; he was sweating and shaking, trying to ask her something.

'Speak your confession, ghost of Yossarian,' uttered Queen Bea gutterally. 'You are beyond harm.'

Dame Murphy, carrying a large tray with eleven teacups, eleven spoons and a jug of milk, froze at the door.

'My real name is Daniel, lover of the Great Drone Peter, who sacrificed his young life for the sake of Ascourt and Charlotte's Dream. After the Great Mating, I waited one month and returned to the palace where the Head Chamberworker remembered her promise to me. In this way, I returned unto the bosom of dear Charlotte, who gave me shelter in the palace and swore no harm would reach me. Queen Charlotte renamed me Yossarian. I was the sister she never had, a trusted confidante and ersatz mother to the three children she eventually bore. When I was appointed to the highest office of Nanny, I dined, thereafter, at her table and no other.

'Fifteen years after the death of Peter, Mother Nature visited Ascourt. She caught me weeping as I was preparing Her suite. It was the anniversary of the day he died. So gentle She was and understanding. I confided in the Mother, our creator, and She gave me hope. She told me that honour comes to those who follow the Way of the Bees.

'I sought solace in Her words; I spoke to the Mother often and at length about Ascourt and Charlotte, about my worries and almost everything I was privy to in the most trusted position of Nanny. Yes, it was I, that same year, who informed Mother Nature of the three eggs which Charlotte laid.

'But the Way of the Bees caught up with me when Mother Nature ordered that only one princess be allowed to remain on Ascourt. They were only six years old. Later that year, Charlotte died. I think she knew my part in it. Soon after, Mother Nature contacted me and asked to see the contents of the Will. I was agitated. I did not think Mother Nature knew of Charlotte's plan for the New Order. I confided in Heron. We made several copies of the Will to make it look as if we had nothing to hide. We sent one to the Mother. The original was kept in the statue of Queen Charlotte, but I removed it, so great by now was my fear of Her all-knowing eye. I kept it under my bed. Not even Heron knew that.

'When Mother Nature read the Will, She learned enough of

Charlotte's Plan to inform me that the three royal daughters of Charlotte must never again be reunited. Now I had every reason to fear for their lives. She threatened to reveal my actions unless I co-operated with Her. From that day on, I was Agent-D – for Daniel and for Drone. I had signed away my life to the Way of the Bees – a Way which would honour me with a traitor's end. I could no longer be trusted. I made Heron promise to reveal nothing to me. We stopped speaking on all but the most superficial of matters. I had nothing to say about Heron, and Mother Nature could get no information from the one who knew the most. I lost Peter, I lost Charlotte and I lost my only surviving friend, Heron Home.

'Towards the end of my life, I became very lonely. I dreamed more and more of lying in the ground with Peter. I was only eighteen when he died. I have had so little warmth in my life. When Mother Nature ordered me to mate with Princess Min, I laughed – how I laughed! And then I realised it was my chance for death, an ending which could not come soon enough for me. It does not make it better, I know, but Princess Min was spared of any pain or knowledge of what happened to her, just as Heron spared my Peter with a fatal injection.

'As soon as Min was unconscious, I recreated the scene of my last lovemaking with Peter. I used the same four black silk scarves that he so proudly wore – the Goddess, but Min looks so like him. Her unconscious reflexes did not fail. Once I came inside, I felt the tearing of my genitals and then her sleeping sting delivered deep into me. I was not in great pain having thoroughly numbed my senses with brandy and valerian. I had no more than five minutes before the fatal sting would rob me of my breath forever. I rang Mother Nature to confirm the deed was done. I hope now She will leave you in peace; Peter and I have honoured Ascourt more than you can know. I rang Heron to say an inadequate goodbye and ask that you uphold my only wish which is to have my statue erected beside his. Charlotte promised me this. Do not forget the drones who gave their lives for Ascourt.

'Honour the memory of Daniel, Last and Bitter Drone of Ascourt, or be cursed with his ghost for all time.'

Gubnet tortured herself with the silent memory of her words to Min only the evening before the murder. It was ironic that she had suggested that Min get rid of Yossarian. When would she learn that her every word was karmic?

After a few minutes, Queen Bea said, 'I think that's it – but it feels like he's still hovering about somewhere.'

'Now that you all know Princess Min killed Yossarian,' sighed Heron, 'I can tell you that Queen Bea and I spent the time between six-thirty and seven this morning making up a story that would protect both of them. Queen Bea confessed to murdering Yossarian with the hatpin so that nobody would be blamed but her. And as we all know, Queen Bea cannot be blamed for anything. I blame myself – I knew Yossarian was being blackmailed for information. And, of course, we both knew Mother Nature had a copy of the Will, because we sent her one when Charlotte died. And when the Superdrones were unexpectedly kidnapped by Porky – '

'Mother Nature forced Yossarian to impregnate Princess Min himself,' finished Gubnet.

'But why Princess Min?' asked Montague.

'Because it says so in Charlotte's Will,' proposed Queen Bea logically. '"My youngest, M, will be the Mother of the future generation of Ascourt", and according to the Way of the Bees there can be only one Queen, so Mother Nature wants the one who'll have babies. And then she has to get rid of me, because I'm the oldest one with the brains.'

'Queen Bea is right of course,' said Heron tactfully. 'And in the directives for Queen Charlotte's New Order, her three daughters, B, V and M must rule together. I expect Mother Nature will try to prevent this from happening.'

'We must watch out for Queen Bea's safety,' warned Gubnet. 'She must never be left on her own.'

There was a strong murmur of agreement. The Head of the Old Dames Breakfast Club paced deliberately around the lecture theatre and addressed herself to Heron.

'Was there any difference between the original Will and the copies that you and Yossarian had made?'

'Apart from the fact that the original was in my hand-writing and the copies were printed, no, Dame Clemis, I can't say that there was,' said Heron ponderously.

'But does Mother Nature know that She is only in possession of a copy?' pressed Dame Clemis.

'No,' replied Heron. 'Not unless Yossarian told Her.'

Dame Clemis stopped striding and unpinned her snow-white bun. 'Please bear with me, everyone. *Let us suppose*, that Mother Nature thought She was in possession of the original. She orders the statue to be destroyed, to make it look as if the Will has just been stolen. She does this to create a diversion – to produce a fog – so that we remain blind to the obvious, and that is that She has planned this all along.'

Montague du Pont threw her eyes up to heaven.

'Proceeding on this theory,' continued Dame Clemis, repinning her bun, 'Mother Nature could not have stolen a Will which She already believed Herself to be in possession of.'

'No!' exploded Montague in frustration. 'I'm telling you, Maryann stole it!' Montague waved the love note under Queen Bea's nose. 'This woman did her homework all right – she knew enough about Ascourt to fool you with a mention of Princess Vee, and you trusted her and she took that Will from right under your nose…'

'She did not!' screamed Bea, frantically snatching at the note.

Montague smugly handed the note to Dame Clemis, who returned it to Queen Bea without even reading it.

'I will thank you not to interrupt me, Montague. Now, what I was going to say was that someone wanted the Will, but it wasn't Mother Nature.'

'The tape that Montague played to us,' said Gubnet, looking at Heron questioningly. 'Didn't Yossarian say to you that the Will was "out of our hands"?'

'He also said he kept the Will under his bed,' reminded Dame Clemis. 'So why would he go to the trouble of smashing the statue?'

'As you just said, Dame Clemis – to have it *look* as if it had been stolen,' snapped Gubnet, losing patience.

Montague stood up and adjusted her cravat with relish. 'Come Delia, let us go home. Our efforts have been wasted. We have cast our pearls before swine.'

Delia hoped the others might understand as she stood up in support of her sister's injured pride. Under her bombastic exterior, Montague cared terribly.

'Wait,' cried Dame Agnetha, coming to the rescue. 'Please don't go, Montague – try and help me, here. If I wanted the original, what do you suppose I'd want it for?'

'Heron's elegant copperplate?' suggested Montague sarcastically.

Once again, Queen Bea slumped into her chair and went into a deep trance. Walking through the mists, she followed Yossarian into her private garden. Yossarian pointed at the trees and hedges and gestured at all the plants. Then the mist enshrouded the garden, dissolving the ghost with it. After a few minutes, she began to recover consciousness. When she opened her eyes, Heron was taking her pulse.

'Yossarian was trying to tell me something. Something about my garden, Heron.'

Heron prayed for the return of her right brain function. She closed her eyes and concentrated on the garden. The tenuous rope to her intuition was fraying fast. She raced out the words in case they might disappear. 'Charlotte's hand drawings of the Princesses' three gardens are in the original, but not in any of the copies.'

Dame Agnetha clapped her hands. 'So you see, the someone who wanted the Will, most especially wanted the garden plans.'

'Definitely not Mother Nature,' said St Gubnet, reminded of her ex-lover's disdain of tended plots.

'I hate to repeat myself,' said Montague, holding the trump card, 'but since Maryann Leaf claims to be a professional horti-culturalist, there is little left to gainsay. She took the Will. And she knew exactly what she was looking for.'

'Perhaps,' countered Heron. 'But as part of her work here, assessing the potential of co-operative organic smallholdings, Maryann had access to the files in the Department of Parks and Lands at Town Hall. Those garden plans are there for any member of the public to peruse, Monty – including you.'

'And Princess Min and I are going straight to Town Hall to get those plans and begin work on her garden,' said Bea, poking a finger into Montague's lavender cravat. 'First thing Monday morning – so there!'

Maryann Leaf landed her light aircraft against high winds and rain at Farranfore Airport, County Kerry. The plane bumped heavily against the tarmacadam and skidded dangerously across the runway. Careering through wet grass, she finally came to a grinding halt against a wall of imposing sandbags. Her restraining belt withstood the force of the crash, but she had a searing pain in her right foot.

The ambulance siren wailed and flashed towards the aircraft. In slow motion, Maryann looked down at her feet to find that a large brown package, displaced by the force of the impact, had landed on her big toe. Not knowing whether to laugh or cry, she picked up the offending package and tried to make out the name which was being smudged by an involuntary cold sweat that clouded her vision. It was addressed to 'The Head of Operation Charlotte'.

Mother Nature returned to 6, St James' Square, London W1, stripped and threw off Her black stilettos. New York, Porschia, Dublin, Oxford and three S/M bars in London and all before twelve midnight GMT. She leaned back, indulging herself in the firm friction of silk underwear against the back of Her leather recliner. The Oxford dons had lapped up the Superdrones, the editor of *Scientific American* had pressed Her with a cash advance and the Director of the Paris Institute of Genetics (affectionately known as the PIG) would be joining Her for luncheon before he flew home the next day. Best of all, not one person had mentioned Ascourt to Her. *Well, dear old Killian, I'll put him on my Christmas list*, vowed Mother Nature solemnly, *and let no one ever accuse the Irish of inefficiency.*

The trip to the S/M Clubs had been purely business. She had offered the owner of each club a five thousand-pound reward for information leading to the whereabouts of Princess Tamarind of Porschia.

Mother Nature closed Her eyes and exhaled slowly. A long burning sensation crept up Her spine like an unfastening zip , loosing Her from Her body.

In step with the drumbeat of Her clitoris, Mother Nature walked briskly back to the Cat Club and ordered a drink at the bar. She knew She wanted relief from the constant burden of responsibility. Perhaps these beautiful women could understand Her pain. She was a Creator. Everyone submitted to Her rule. And if they didn't, She made them. Even Gubnet; but time apart had been time to think. Their ailing sex life was not just because Gubnet wanted a child. It was also because She, Mother Nature, was driven by a powerful and lustful urge to feel safe by submitting to someone else.

Mother Nature's heart was pounding. She was not dressed up and She felt vulnerable. It was a delicious, rare feeling. She sipped Her drink and in the mirror behind the bar, She saw Pearl lean over and nuzzle Her ear. Mother Nature was electrified. Pearl ran the soft leather whip sensuously over her pierced breasts and drawled, 'Trust me, darling, I know just what you need.'

Back at Mother Nature's London apartment, Pearl took off her black leather jacket and silently went to work, dressed in a full body harness. Mother Nature watched in awe as she constructed a spider-sweb pinned to the four corners of the room with a hammer, eight hooks and two pulleys. With skillful, tender knots and kisses, Pearl eventually hoisted the web with Mother Nature tied naked into it.

As Pearl admired her handiwork, Mother Nature melted in front of the ecstatic gaze of Her captor.

'Shut your eyes,' ordered Pearl. 'Don't say a word.'

She could feel Pearl's heavy breath drawing close between Her spreadeagled legs. She trembled like a fly about to be devoured. She stopped breathing when Pearl's wet tongue grazed Her labia, lifting Her into a dizzying ascent. Paralysed and five miles high, Mother Nature did not dare breathe until the web stopped vibrating.

The island manager of Porschia faltered dialling the number which would connect her to Mother Nature's private apartment in London. The phone almost rang itself out before a strangely detached voice answered, 'Pearl, is that you? Chris'sake, what time is it?'

Hayde Lewis choked on her words, 'It's one in the morning. Hayde Lewis here, Eminence, I have urgent information for you.'

'Lewis!' exclaimed Mother Nature, propelling Herself into a more wakeful reality. She must have fallen asleep in Her leather recliner. The spiderweb was gone, as was Pearl.

'The Queens of Porshia and Ascourt have arranged a marriage between the Princesses Tamarind and Min, and I – '

'Are you trying to tell me something I already know, Lewis?'

'Why no, Eminence,' said Hayde caught by surprise.

'Well then, why are you calling me?' asked Mother Nature, cleverly playing for more information.

'The Superdrones are on a hunger strike here on Porschia,' began Hayde tentatively. 'They want Lieutenant Min back, but apparently the Princesses Tamarind and Min are planning to live on Ascourt after the marriage – the Reproductive Programme is in jeopardy, Eminence.'

'The marriage will take place in Porschia, Lewis. See to it,' ordered Mother Nature.

'But how can it, Eminence?' pleaded Hayde's thin voice amid a great fuzz of background interference.

'Is there someone listening in?' asked Mother Nature suspiciously.

The background noise immediately died down.

'Lewis, unlike you I do my job efficiently. I pay you a small fortune and you can't see past your own nose. The Superdrones will co-operate with Princess Min – it'll buy us time. What kind of a gombeen are you? I *bless* this marriage that will take place on December twenty-first in Porschia. I will be there myself. Don't let me down.'

'Eminence, that reminds me – of course I could take it up with accounts, but my paycheck still hasn't arrived – '

'Neither has the insurance money from Lloyds,' said Mother Nature, cutting the line dead.

Hayde Lewis very slowly replaced the receiver. She stood absolutely still, awaiting instructions from the Queen of Porschia, who had maintained a constant presence throughout the phone call by applying an elegant pearl revolver to Hayde's head.

The Queen of Porschia frogmarched Hayde back to her home where the Island Manager had been under house arrest since Her Majesty's return from Ascourt earlier that day. Porky was very pleased with her little ruse. Mother Nature had fallen for it beautifully. The marriage would take place in Porschia, exactly as she planned it.

'I hate Geminis, *Lewis*,' mimicked Porky cruelly. 'And I hate divided loyalties. It's me or *Her*.'

Hayde Lewis considered her appalling situation. Either way she was doomed. She could work without pay for Mother Nature at risk of being bumped off by Porky or she could work without pay for Porky and definitely be bumped off by Mother Nature. As a Gemini, she was inclined to the here and now, and, all things taken into account, Porky had given her a guarantee...

'My loyalty is with you, Majesty,' announced Hayde formally.

'Good thinking,' said Porky pleasantly. 'And in case you change your mind, I shall hold on to the number of your little piggy bank in Switzerland.'

'And you'll honour your promise?' asked Hayde expectantly.

'My dear, I'll have Cook put you back on full rations in the morning!'

In a notorious shebeen in the hills of Kerry, Maryann Leaf was ushered into the parlour. Her boss sat at the poker table flanked by two armed guards. Maryann handed the brown package to the heavies, who checked it for wires under the one naked bulb which dimly lit the room.

'So – how did it go?' enquired the Head of Operation Charlotte without expression.

Maryann grimaced. She was not fooled by the cool demeanour of her boss.

'Bad news,' she reported. 'I located the statue, smashed it and for all that, there was nothing there.'

'Well, fuck it.'

But out of the package came a sheaf of faded parchment. The original black ink had turned sepia with age.

'Jesus Christ, Maryann, what have we here? *The BVM – A New Order by Queen Charlotte*. Well, I'll be damned – this is the fucking original!'

The scrawny hair-lipped red-head danced round the room singing with glee, 'We did it, we did it.' And Maryann broke into a grin and hugged her boss, who ordered *potín* to toast the memory of the virgin Queen Charlotte.

CHAPTER TEN

A Sunday Lunch

Sunday, November 17, 1996

Mother Nature popped the five thousand pound cash advance from the editor of *Scientific American* into an envelope. She turned on Her answering machine and headed out into the deserted streets of London for an early-morning stroll. When She arrived on the doorstep of the Cat Club, the owner nervously ushered Her inside and spoke in a low, hoarse whisper.

'I'm sorry to have got you out of your bed on a Sunday morning and all that – but we had a bit of a night of it last night, as you can see...'

Mother Nature did. It all looked strangely familiar to Her.

'Do I know you?' asked the matronly owner. 'I'd swear I know your face!'

Mother Nature removed the envelope from Her coat and tossed it casually on to a barstool covered in fag ash. Then She sat on it and plainly eyed the proprietor from head to toe. *Nice...*

'I expect you'll be wanting to see the goods?' came the awkward response.

Mother Nature nodded. Her Raybans stopped level between two shirt buttons. A blush of breast under the strain of black lace. For a moment, She had quite forgotten what it was She had come for.

'The thing is she's not due to finish until midday and I'm a bit short-staffed,' explained the owner. 'She's a great little cleaner, you know.'

'The Crown Princess Tamarind has inherited an ancient Irish seat and I must get her back in time for her coronation,' disclosed Mother Nature wryly.

'Well I never!' said the owner of the Cat Club. 'But we do attract all sorts!'

'Precisely,' said Mother Nature, admiring the proprietor's black leather cap. 'So keep it under your hat!'

Mother Nature regretfully slipped Her diminutive figure off the barstool and returned the cash-filled envelope to the breastpocket of Her coat. Unlike the big-willied triple gods, She didn't have time to tarry. Especially not on a Sunday.

'There'll be a dirty big black Merc outside your premises at twelve noon. Open the door, remove this envelope from the back seat and put young Tamarind into it when she's finished her shift. Don't keep her too late – my jet's on standby at Heathrow. Tell her I won't be able to meet her this time – Sunday lunch appointment, terrible bore.... Nice meeting you, sweetie – have a good day!'

Professor Louis Sterne was suspicious by nature. He was a liberal academic in his late thirties, and he railed at the fact that a large corporate enterprise such as Mother Nature International could dictate the direction of science. Not once during the Superdrone seminar at the Oxford Conference did Mother Nature acknowledge that this 'revolutionary break-through' was the work of his most brilliant pupil, St Gubnet of Balleyvourney.

He arrived at London's La Vie en Rose restaurant like a man with a mission. He was going to get answers to the numerous discrepancies that had struck him throughout the seminar. After vichysoisse and the initial pleasantries, Professor Sterne removed his bib and laid it on the table.

'Mother Nature, I must be frank with you. How long more can I keep up this charade? You must know what I am really after, no?'

Mother Nature scrutinised the supervisor of her ex-lover's research work on the Superdrones. He had a sharp nose and a receding mouse-brown hairline. He was lean and intense. His one and only hand-made shirt exuded the hallmark of a premeditated bachelorhood, a fact She confirmed from the unlaundered chronology of sweat rings under his arms. He was a French pen-pusher, suffering the delusions of an academic playboy with ambitions beyond his reach.

'Yes, I think I do,' She replied sardonically. 'But what makes you think I should tell you?'

'I just want to know where she is,' begged Louis pathetically. 'Is she all right?'

'Gubnet is in Ascourt – she has become a recluse,' announced Mother Nature. 'She does not wish to be contacted.'

'An 'ermit? How I will miss her!' exclaimed the Professor with feeling.

'I was involved with her a lot longer than you, Louis – your pain is nothing compared to mine', reflected Mother Nature.

Seizing his moment, Louis Sterne groped in his breastpocket and pulled out a piece of notepaper, it's import betrayed by a half-dozen frenzied crease marks. 'I think you should read this,' he said softly.

It was a letter from the Women's Clinic in Paris confirming that Gubnet was three months pregnant. It was dated July 1996. Louis frowned and looked away.

Mother Nature crushed Her wineglass, reflecting that, in this one moment, Her every suspicion had come to pass.

'It is your child?'

'Yes,' replied Louis, adding to himself, *in a manner of speaking*.

'All right,' conceded Mother Nature cleverly, 'I will do you a deal. We will sign a contract here and now. You will waive any interest in the Superdrones –'

'I assure you,' said Louis, his voice rising an octave, 'I have no interest in the Superdrones – they belong to Gubnet, not me. I merely supervised her research – '

'Don't get fresh with me, Louis,' scolded Mother Nature. 'You have admitted to being the father of her child. If you married her in France, you would automatically own half her property – which includes the official copyright to produce the Superdrones. We both know it's in her name. Do you take me for a fool, Louis?'

'I cannot dispute the truth,' admitted Louis baldly.

'I will waive any interest in your child and you will waive any interest, present or future, in the Superdrones,' stated Mother Nature.

The contract was signed and witnessed by the dessert waiter. After coffee, the meeting was at an end.

'Madam, you are ruthless,' said Professor Sterne, pulling out Mother Nature's chair as She stood up to leave.

Professor Sterne arrived at Heathrow Airport in time for the Sunday-afternoon flight to Paris. He was in celebratory humour. He kicked his heels in the air. Mother Nature had passed his little test with flying colours. Thanks to Her, he now knew that Gubnet was in Ascourt, and the future of the Ovum-to-Ovum Project was safe. Mother Nature did not even know it existed.

Once on board, he ordered champagne, sat back, fiddled with the combination lock on his black attaché case and removed three documents.

The first was a paper entitled 'Home, H. 1979. *Ovum-to-Ovum Fertilisation – Why Not?* J. Women's Studies, **2**: 1– 37'. He picked up the paper and ceremoniously toasted Dr Home with a glass of champagne.

The second document was the uncompleted PhD thesis of his gifted ex-pupil, Gubnet. It was entitled *Woman-to-Woman Reproduction – Techniques and Procedures.* But Gubnet had always referred to it as Ovum-to-Ovum.

Professor Sterne poured himself another glass and reread the third document on his little pull-out table. It was the letter from the clinic confirming her pregnancy. He knew it off by heart. Kissing the note he said aloud, *'Voilà*, Gubnet! Ovum-to-Ovum is no longer a theory!'

That same Sunday afternoon, the phone lines were dead and the flow of electricity had ceased on the island of Ascourt. The citizens were of one mind that they had been cruelly cut off from the rest of the world. They were not, however, agreed on the vexing question of Yossarian/Daniel's last request. In fact, a deep division had emerged.

Heron Home, among others including Queen Bea, Montague du Pont and most of the palace staff, not only wished to acknowledge Yossarian's life-long service but also argued that Ascourt could not claim itself to be drone-free until the ghost was put to rest. They advocated fulfilling his wishes for a funeral and a statue in his honour.

On the other hand, while Gubnet, the Old Dames Breakfast Club, Queen Bea and most of the Ascourt Institute agreed that a statue and funeral might seem less suspicious to Mother Nature, they disagreed on the basis that rape was violence to women and could not be justified in any way whatever. They advocated a cremation and pointed out that since Ascourt was *incommunicado*, it didn't matter what Mother Nature thought as She had no way of finding out.

Despite this grave division, everyone was civil and on speaking terms. The Old Dames were quick to realise that this was because the islanders were displaying an atavistic return to a hive instinct in the face of a certain calamity – *united we stand and divided we fall*. The essence of this first day of Ascourt's solitary confinement was clear. As Old Dames, every one, they knew that the strength of their people lay in the group consciousness – the hive instinct – where life carries on regardless of collective fears or individual wishes. The motion was unanimously agreed. Henceforth, the general populace would be invited to join the Old Dames each morning for a traditional breakfast meeting in the Northern Territories.

The rest of their meeting, held in the privacy of Sorrel's woodcabin, was confidentially given over to the bizarre and complicated event of Princess Min's rape. The Old Dames concluded that she would have to be told the truth. Her body would never forget it had been physically violated. Dame Agnetha suggested rape-crisis counselling and Dame Meleka offered her services as a medical herbalist.

That evening, despite the skulking grey presence of the warship now in full view of Ascourt, an utter calm descended upon the island. The Old Dames retired to Swann's and played duplicate bridge by candlelight. Small groups wandered into the Northern Territories to watch the sunset. In Town Square, the strumming of guitars could be heard all the way up the two hundred and sixteen steps to the palace.

CHAPTER ELEVEN

Princess Min's Garden

Monday, November 18, 1996

On the second morning of Ascourt's solitary confinement, the Old Dames were joined by nearly all the islanders on their trek to the Northern Territories. To their knowingness and delight, the communal breakfast in the open autumn air turned into a feast of food and ideas, and even the unaware were aware that the siege of Ascourt was returning them to themselves.

The citizens agreed on a daily work routine and voted unanimously to observe the Rule of Three, for as Dame Agnetha reminded them: 'When two people talk, they behave mutually, they conspire. When three people get together it becomes difficult to play such a game. Two will agree but three must co-operate in a far more conscious way.'

Everyone was in favour of communal meals and a group conscience before bedtime. This very positive attitude, on the doorstep of disaster, had a harmonising effect that brought out the best in one and all.

Delia du Pont suggested that Yossarian's body be embalmed until a more permanent solution was agreed upon. This found an immediate consensus and was followed by a complicated group ritual for the continuation of cold weather.

Dame Clemis reflected that the Old Dames had taken a wise decision to step back. Nobody had told anybody else what to do. For the first time in as long as she could remember, Ascourt was showing signs of its true potential. Empathy weaved with synchronicity. Each person just sensed their place in the order of things and was determined to play their part. Except for the potato-picking...

Dame Clemis drew lots for groups of three. Queen Bea asked for a dispensation. This left a breach in the potato-picking group. Dames Meleka and Murphy tossed a coin.

After some argument, Dame Meleka joined the potato-pickers and Dame Murphy left for the Town Hall in the company of Princess Min and Queen Bea. The nutgatherers were the first to start work. St Gubnet's cleaning detail joined forces with Heron Home's kitchen gang, as nobody had so much as washed a dish since Cook's departure to Porschia.

Following a thorough search of the relevant Town Hall archives, Queen Bea's gang of three emerged victorious. With the Garden Plans tucked safely under the arm of her fake fur, Queen Bea remarked that it was just as well that Montague had surrendered the Garden Plans as her presence in Town Hall was in breach of the Rule of Three.

Climbing the two hundred and sixteen steps of the palace, Dame Murphy revealed that her colleague, Dame Meleka, had not abided by the decision of the toss. The older Dame had refused point blank to join Queen Bea's group, asserting her age and rank in order to avoid the gruelling first stages of digging Princess Min's garden.

'She said I'd have to swap with her because she hates digging you see.'

'But there's even more digging involved in potato-picking!' puffed Princess Min, whose fresh blue overalls were one size too small for an adequate intake of breath.

'And there's no palace kitchen nearby for a quick cup of tea when you're tired,' pointed out Queen Bea.

'I think Dame Meleka is anxious to discuss the price of psilocybin mushrooms with the Guide of the Northern Territories.' disclosed Dame Murphy readily. 'And since the potato field is adjacent to Sorrel's cabin, it follows, does it not, that discussion rather than digging may be the order of the morning, and I daresay over quite a few cups of tea at that.'

They made their way to the palace nursery where three garden staff assembled the items biologically and otherwise apposite to the Plans. A heavily laden procession made its way to the site of work, situated in the front lawn adjacent to the cannon. Before they could down tools, the head gardener organised them into a straight line facing out to sea where a grey warship lurked on bright topaz waves. It brought back memories. Princess Min knew just what it felt like to be on a big boat like that.

'Poor guys – I bet they've nothing better to do than watch

us with their binoculars!'

'Take aim,' ordered the head gardener, 'and on the count of three – we'll salute our friends a fine good morning!'

Each one lifted their garden tool and waved it madly at the warship. This put them all in great high spirits and by midday, the entire ten-by-ten metre plot was dug and turned.

During the busy communal lunch at the palace, Dame Meleka donned her white herbalist's overcoat and announced she would be holding a women's clinic for the rest of the afternoon. Princess Min was first on the list. Dr Heron Home volunteered to help out with light secretarial duties, and joined them in the Smoking Room, observing the Rule of Three. Princess Min steeled herself for the internal examination. She had been through this indignity in Japan. She remembered the cold, metal speculum and the wrenching of her unsuspecting vaginal wall. Warily, she took off the muddy overalls and removed her underwear.

Dame Meleka laid the Princess on an old soft couch, and gently stroked the inside of her thigh. She had never found any use for a speculum in her practice and in consequence did not possess one. She entered Min by stages, feeling around with her sensitive, clawlike fingers.

'It takes much longer with the rubber gloves,' she complained, 'but that's potato-picking for you.'

Princess Min smiled behind her eyes. She allowed her mind to wander about the price of hallucinogenic mushrooms. Finally, Dame Meleka withdrew her fingers and held out a black insect-like object, about an inch long.

'His parts,' she said, wrinkling her beak.

It was then that Princess Min reacted, heaving most of her lunch on to the Persian rug. She insisted on cleaning it up. She dressed herself and turned to the others before she left the room, 'Please, don't worry for me. I have accepted this – ' She frowned at Heron, who was about to interrupt her. 'I am the youngest daughter and it is my duty to my ancestors to bear the future generation of Ascourt.'

'Princess Min,' interrupted Heron, 'you're not made that way!'

'I accept my burden with honour. That is my pride as a warrior, Heron.'

'You have not been fertilised,' explained Dame Meleka firmly. 'Believe me, I can spot a pregnant woman a mile off – and that is something I pride myself on!'

Gubnet collided into Min as she ran out of the makeshift clinic, and held her fast in a deep, warm hug.

'It's me next, love, will you come in and hold my hand?' asked Gubnet in a way that Min could not refuse.

Dame Meleka did not examine St Gubnet of Balleyvourney. She conducted her conversation seated on the sofa between her two clients.

'You are almost eight months pregnant,' she observed, 'and the spirit of the girlchild lives inside you.'

'It's strange, you know, but of course the minute I named her, the sickness stopped,' laughed Gubnet. 'I thought it would never end!'

'It will be an easy birth, you won't need me anyway!' continued the Dame in a lighthearted vein.

'Who's the lucky father?' popped Heron, winking at Min, who glared back at her.

'*Father*, Heron? You, of all people, ought to know better than that!' admonished Gubnet.

'Goddess, I'm sorry – curiosity killed the cat, what?'

Princess Min fired an imaginary revolver at Heron's head.

'Oh dear,' apologised Heron again, 'I'm an awful gombeen, I know.'

Dame Meleka was perched on the very edge of her seat. The tension was unbearable. The question had been on the tip of her tongue. If there was no father, then it could only be the one thing, and since Gubnet was a saint…

'It's a virgin birth!' she burst out.

'Not quite,' said Gubnet, flattered, none the less. 'Heron, do you remember a paper you wrote called *Ovum-to-Ovum Fertilisation – Why Not?*'

A nascent smile appeared on Heron's disbelieving face. Gubnet positively beamed. She had been waiting for this moment for months – the moment when one scientist tells the other how her theory became a fact.

'First, I obtained a frozen, unfertilised egg from the egg donor bank at the Paris Institute of Genetics. Then, with the help of Professor Louis Sterne, my supervisor there, I was put under anaesthetic and a single unfertilised egg was recovered from my ovary.'

Gubnet looked up and enjoyed the pregnant pause.

'We put the two miraculous unfertilised eggs under a microscope and with tiny scalpels, removed their outer membrane coverings and mixed their genetic material together. Then we transferred the lot into a nutritious, cosy, new casing which we'd artificially constructed.'

Dame Meleka put a restraining hand on Princess Min's knee, which was tapping violently.

'Once we were sure that the entity was happily dividing away, we implanted the embryo back into my womb – and I'm very pregnant, as you can see!'

There were streams of proud tears pouring down Heron's beaming pink face. 'I think this calls for a celebration,' she said, heading for the drinks cabinet. 'You do realise that you are the first woman to be fertilised by another woman?'

'Ovum-to-Ovum,' pronounced Dame Meleka, carefully memorising the gynaecological innovation.

'*Mná-mná*,' said Gubnet in plain Irish.

'Does this other woman know that she fertilised you?' asked Min tightly.

'Absolutely not!' cried Gubnet over Dame Meleka's birdlike figure. 'Many, many women donate their eggs to the Institute for research, or posterity, or both – but they all sign a declaration waiving any interest, you see?'

'Yes, OK – you don't know who she is and she doesn't know who you are,' said Min, hands raised in a gesture of finality. *Let's leave it at that.*

'Look, I'll confess to knowing who She is – She's a donor at the Egg Bank and She has a name. But believe me, She has no idea I am carrying our child,' stated Gubnet defensively.

St Gubnet reached over Dame Meleka and took the hand of the young Princess who, to her surprise, did not snatch it away. She knew she was provoking her own confession and the walls to her defences were crumbling fast. Dear old Louis Sterne was the only other living person who knew the secret which was bursting her heart with sadness.

'It's Mother Nature's, isn't it?' said Heron, quietly putting it all together.

'Yes, it is.'

131

Princess Min pulled her hand away from Gubnet's and refused to look up. Dame Meleka manoeuvred awkwardly between them. Finally, she took Gubnet's outstretched hand into her lap and squeezed it sympathetically.

'It was when I – when I came back from Paris,' began Gubnet haltingly. 'I was going to tell Her – I mean, it was an experiment, a possible project for a PhD thesis. Louis Sterne and I never thought it would actually work. But it did, so I told Mother Nature how much I wanted to have a child with Her and She wouldn't have it. No discussion – just no, no, no. She wouldn't hear of it. What could I do? I couldn't tell Her I was already pregnant – She didn't seem to know – and then I was so hurt that She didn't want it...'

'So you left Her,' chirped Dame Meleka with some satisfaction, 'and came to Ascourt – where you hoped we might have you on board.'

'Oh no, I didn't think you would at all,' protested Gubnet in full flood. 'I was sure I'd be asked to leave – '

'Hush, hush, Gubnet!' smoothed the Old Dame. 'You are among friends of course.'

Princess Min threw herself into the gardening for the rest of the afternoon. She was upset, humiliated and cheated by the rape. How dare Yossarian die of the bee-sting she delivered while she was still unconscious! She carted the biggest rocks and sweated more than the head gardener. The thoughts passed only to be replaced by more. Why was she jealous of Mother Nature, jealous of Gubnet's child and so utterly disappointed at not being pregnant herself? Princess Min looked round for a suitable rock to crown the top of the spiral rockery. She tortured herself about wanting to get rid of Yossarian before she died. She shovelled sand and earth into the crevices of the ornate spiral, but the usual satisfaction of a job well done was replaced by tumultuous waves of panic and confusion. How could she think when her every waking thought was with St Gubnet of Balleyvourney?

The head gardener marvelled at the show of silent strength. She saw in Min a kindred spirit, a royal princess with horticultural potential. She had the one characteristic which any true gardener would instantly recognise – she rarely spoke while gardening.

As Queen Bea and Dame Murphy chatted over the Garden Plans during their frequent rest breaks, the head gardener struck up an easy rhythm of work with Princess Min. When the paving slabs were levelled and laid, a nudge might follow a wink and the pair would move on to another section, pinning trellis and planting vines. During the official afternoon break, they sat across from one another unravelling knots from a large garden net, gulping hot tea in place of words. They were like a pair of ancient mermaids, conspiring in the comfort of their labours.

Princess Min had a waking dream. She challenged Mother Nature to a duel. She fought for Gubnet's honour. After Mother Nature's funeral, she married Gubnet and acknowledged the baby Athena as her own. Athena grew up strong and laid thousands of eggs. Gubnet and Min lived happily to a ripe old age, grandmothers of the future generation of Ascourt.

'Min! Wake up!' shouted Queen Bea. 'I can't lift up that thing by myself.'

'Surely they haven't fallen asleep on the job?' enquired Dame Murphy, poking the head gardener, who remained motionless.

In fact, neither so much as stirred a muscle until the sun disappeared below the western horizon two hours later. They woke astonished to find that the garden had been completed in their absence. Princess Min admired the little temple in the centre.

'Look at this,' she urged the head gardener. 'It's beautiful!'

The head gardener, in her haste, tripped and landed on something soft and heavy. To her surprise, it was Dame Murphy.

'Oh, my dears,' said the Dame rising unsteadily, 'I couldn't leave you, what with the Rule of Three. The others left when we finished.'

Princess Min ran her hands over the ornate wrought-iron grate on the floor of the miniature temple. 'How on earth did you get this in here?' she asked Dame Murphy. 'This barbeque must weigh half a ton!'

Dame Murphy laughed self-effacingly and said, 'My dear! That is not a barbeque – *that* is the Sacred Flame of Vesta!'

The head gardener dug deep into her overalls pocket and recovered a muddy box of safety matches. She twiddled a knob on the grate and invited Princess Min to strike the first match. In the darkening mist, a pristine flame shot up a full two metres high. Three long shadows stood witness. The periwinkles twinkled and the tiny leaves of parthenocissus lit up like rippling fires melting the snowbush beside it.

It was a garden of the night.

It was Montague du Pont's idea that captured everyone's imagination for the group conscience in Town Square. Sitting in blankets with torches and candles, the citizens of Ascourt listened as their local journalist read aloud from a book she had found in the Town Hall library. It was a first edition of *The BVM – A New Order* by Queen Charlotte.

'"There is a place for science in my dream. But only in that, science can offer an explanation after the fact. It is a dream helper, but in itself, poor science – it is incapable of diversity. Poor, neurotic science who has lost the key to it's own imagination.

'"For it is our dreams that hold the key to all Creation. It is a fact that we can manifest whatever we are capable of imagining – for better or for worse. Even a child will dream of walking before it can actually do so. A rich and diverse world will feed itself on the fertile subsoil of myth, dream and legend. From the labile depths of our subconscious, all things are possible. A woman can dream she is a river, and in this way she can explore the world.

'"My dream for the New Order is based on an old Judaic story – neither new nor original. But I believe that Ascourt's future is securely based on a legend which half the twentieth century inhabitants of our world accept as possible.

'"The story is about a woman called Mary who conceived a child without fertilisation. I have named my three royal daughters after her, the Blessed Virgin Mary. On each of their arms is tattooed the initials B, V and M. The future of my dream for a New Order is based on the legend of the mother who was not impregnated. The BVM. *There is no other way*.

'"My eldest, B, is blessed with wisdom, she is older than her years. She will rule with vision as Queen. Listen and obey all she says. My middle daughter, V, now she is the Shaman. Under her rule, Ascourt will never come to harm. Question not her actions, for all she does is for the protection of this island. My youngest, M, will be the Mother of the future generation of Ascourt. She will conceive and abundantly bear forth my dream. Under her rule, Ascourt will overflow with bounty and joy.

'"These three will rule together as one. But the Essence of the Rule of Three can only be revealed when each one, B, V and M, finds out her true name. They will gain the Seven Rules of Creation and Mother Nature will bless them Herself. Only then will the New Order be born."'

Montague placed a marker at the end of Chapter Two and closed the book shut.

'I think I know what it means!' said Meleka the medical herbalist excitedly, 'Princess Min is not "M". That's it!'

'Princess Min is not the Mother of the future generation!' parroted Dame Toplis beside her.

When the news reached Min, who was sitting close to the front, she said to Gubnet, 'You know, I'm kind of relieved. I was so upset about not being pregnant and I felt guilty because I hadn't done my duty as youngest daughter.'

'How do you feel now?' asked Dame Agnetha keeping a close watch on Min's emotional reactions.

Princess Min gritted her teeth. 'If I ever got my hands on Yossarian, I'd kill him.'

'Dame Meleka said you had tiny ovaries,' offered Bea informatively. 'She said she'd never seen anything like it in a grown woman!'

'Well, I'm glad,' said Min defensively. 'I never wanted to be a Mother anyway.'

'Me neither!' said Queen Bea, wistfully hugging her. 'But a Shaman sounds nice, doesn't it?'

Montague du Pont could not agree more.

'You have to die to become a Shaman,' she offered scurrilously.

'I do believe you're right, Montague,' confirmed Dame Agnetha, 'although the process is not entirely gratuitous.'

'A Shaman sacrifices her life in order to learn the secrets of the Underworld,' said Gubnet in a solemn address to the two sisters. 'The death is symbolic.'

'I know that,' said Bea, squirming in the voluminous folds

of her fake fur, 'which is why I'm perfectly happy to be the Queen.'

Gubnet left the royal sisters and joined an intense conversation between Dr Heron Home PhD and Dame Clemis on the improbable merits of Charlotte's Dream. But they failed to acknowledge her point.

'Don't you see that I could use Ovum-to-Ovum to recover unfertilised eggs from the ovaries of Queen Bea or Princess Min, and fertilise them each with a donor egg of their choice?'

Heron and Clemis did not.

'How can you be serious about this ridiculous dream of Charlotte's when I could have both those girls pregnant in the morning?, said Gubnet authoritatively. 'What are we waiting around for?'

'Not so fast, St Gubnet of Balleyvourney,' said Dame Clemis, putting her finger on Gubnet's lips. She swept her other arm in a great arc around the crowd in Town Square. ' Don't *you* see that this is about a way of life? Your science can't solve a problem by getting any one of us pregnant!'

'Ovum-to-Ovum is for humans, Gubnet,' added Heron quickly, 'like you and me. I agree though – we could have everyone pregnant in the morning. Each one of these women, pregnant with one egg, each producing one baby. And then what?'

'And then,' continued Dame Clemis, 'we will have succeeded in creating a horse by removing the stripes of a zebra.'

'These are Bee People, Gubnet,' said Heron sternly, 'and their Queen lays eggs – hundreds at a time. Charlotte's Dream isn't changing *who* they are, it is changing *how* and *why* they are.'

'Don't patronise me with some idle excuse to sit around and dream the impossible dream,' rebuked the patron saint of bees.

'This Dream will be a great comfort to our people in these troubled times,' said Dame Clemis, ominously gesturing towards the sea.

'The Mother helps those who help themselves!' quarrelled Gubnet. 'Those girls will not get pregnant on their own!'

'*There is no other way*,' murmured Heron reverentially.

'It is *not* the only option you have left,' retorted Gubnet, irate with the hocus-pocus and fatalism of the island mentality.

'Mother Nature made Yossarian rape Princess Min, and if we go back to the Way of the Bees, then She's going to get rid of me too. Do you want that?' said Queen Bea, challenging Montague du Pont.

'No,' stumbled Montague under the stern gaze of Princess Min, 'I wouldn't put it in quite those terms.'

'It's a great dream and I am the will of the people,' said Queen Bea. 'So if I believe in it, then it must be because all of you believe in it too!'

But Montague wagged a smug finger under Bea's nose. 'According to your mother's Will, you're not who you think you are,' and, turning to Princess Min, she added for good measure, 'and neither are you.'

As the narrow crescent moon culminated in the night sky, the State Pathologist and the herbalist combined their respective talents of forensics and physiology to formulate an original solution to the vexing question of royal identity.

'If Queen Bea's ovaries are undeveloped and juvenile as are Princess Min's,' began Dame Meleka, 'then we can conclude, by default, that Princess V must be the Mother of the future generation of Ascourt.'

'But if Queen Bea's ovaries are developed,' said Delia, 'then she is Mother, which can only mean that B, as we know her now, is actually M.'

'Yes, but the only basis we have for fact is my examination of Princess Min this morning, which proves conclusively that, whatever else, Min cannot be M.'

'I agree,' said Delia earnestly. 'Queen Bea should undergo a thorough internal examination as soon as possible.'

Gubnet pinned Heron down as soon as Clemis had left to join a beckoning Dame at the far side of the Square.

'You *must* know which one of them is which,' she said accusingly. 'How else could you have known Min wasn't pregnant before she was examined?'

Heron sighed. 'I really don't know, Gubnet – Charlotte just

named them arbitrarily and said that when the time was right they'd find out who they really were. She did it to protect them.'

'Oh come now, Heron, didn't you say Min "wasn't made that way"?'

Heron knew she would get no peace until she surrendered the truth to her former colleague at MIT. St Gubnet would not let up until she did. Shrugging her shoulders, she said, 'Do you remember the bit in the book where Charlotte said that science was a dream-helper?'

Gubnet nodded.

'Well,' continued Heron uncertainly, 'Charlotte told me to use my science to cross her last three unfertilised eggs with three different wild strains of bee. Each strain was specially selected for temperament and characteristic, producing B, V and M, do you see?'

'I do,' said Gubnet. 'But I was labouring under the impression that you had used Ovum-to-Ovum to cross Charlotte's eggs with your own!'

'Oh dear no!' laughed Heron nervously. 'So that's where all the rumours came from!'

'But if you bred them, Heron, how can you not know which one of them is which?' said Gubnet, returning to the point.

'The other thing Charlotte asked of her scientific dream-helper was that I ensure all three eggs were completely sterile.'

Gubnet gasped. 'Sterile? How sterile?'

'All three would present as juvenile ovarian development – and that is to say no egg production. I really don't know which one of them is meant to be which, Gubnet, but obviously none of them could have become pregnant from the rape – or drones – or even Ovum-to-Ovum, for that matter.'

'For the Goddess's sake – all three of them sterile? What on earth was Charlotte trying to achieve by that?'

'It means that there is *no other way* for Ascourt. A Princess with no eggs cannot be made pregnant by any earthly means. We must believe that Charlotte's Dream is possible – like it was for the Blessed Virgin Mary. Should one of the royal sisters conceive and bear eggs, it will be because the whole of Ascourt will have wished it to be so.'

Gubnet sucked in her breath softly. An essential truth

descended, answering all of her questions at once. It wasn't that there were flaws in her technological grasp of the situation; and neither had Heron gone mad. The point was that there were never any obstacles in a dream. It was so simple she had very nearly missed it.

Queen Bea ascended the steps and held up her hand for silence. Looking pointedly at Montague she said, 'I have decided that I am still the Queen since I don't feel any different. Now I'm very tired and I want to go to bed, so the meeting's over and it's time to go home.'

Within minutes, the occupants of Town Square began to disperse. Approximately half of them headed westwards, down the long, windy road to Seaview Suburbs. The rest began to climb the two hundred and sixteen steps of the palace.

Unlike Queen Bea, Princess Min felt very different. Changed, in fact. There was a lightness in her step and a sense of release which comes when a skin has been shed. When she caught up with the caped figure in front of her, she simply said, 'I'm glad I don't have to be who I was before.'

They didn't say much. Min slipped an arm around Gubnet's waist, closing the ancient distance between them.

CHAPTER TWELVE

The Great Sleep:
The Body Snatchers

Tuesday, November 19 – Sunday, December 8, 1996

It was long past midnight when Queen Bea lay down on the very comfortable long red sofa of the palace's smoking room. She decided that her old bedroom in the north wing would have to be converted into a games room for children if and when they were laid. Tired as she was, the problem of the tiny three-bedroomed palace bothered her greatly. No one, after all, would ever want to sleep in the room of the murder, nor of the murdered rapist. That left the east wing, which was Min's anyway. The grim prospect of rebuilding two new bedrooms condensed itself into a frightening fog of rape and murder.

On the brink of sleep, Queen Bea tossed and turned. She became aware of a more physical source of displeasure. She opened her eyes and glared at the invisible draught tormenting her from the open window. She reached for her cigarettes; the pack was empty. More vexing still, her bladder was full.

'Damnation,' she muttered arising.

Hobbling in her coat down the long cold corridor to the toilet, Queen Bea noticed a figure in the shadows creeping stealthily behind her.

The lights of the east wing remained burning in a timeless delerium of slow-dripping honey. Gubnet leaned over and unbuttoned Min's shirt. She pressed a cool hand under the open top and slid it smoothly across the muscular sternum until a nipple lodged tightly between the groove in her fingers.

It threw them both into the breach of two beds impulsively joined as one.

Princess Min lay back and shut her wanting eyes. The fiery

140

tresses grazed her cheek and burned like hot lava spilling molten kisses down her neck.

They lingered over this caress, for there was a passion building.

They uncoiled their length for there was uncertainty, minor adjustment and lightning checks.

They held their breath for there was that awesome calm before the stormbreak of desire.

Queen Bea was very relieved to see a light under the door of the bedroom of the east wing. She didn't remember to knock, and in her excitement and haste, tripped over her bootlaces and landed noiselessly on a deep shag pile carpet in the middle of the bedroom. She recovered her spectacles, stood up and saw the oblivious lovers deep in a kiss. Queen Bea cleared her throat and coughed.

'Help,' she tried, loudly, a couple of times.

Sensing a disturbance, Princess Min leapt out of bed in a state of semi-undress. Her trousers fly was open, revealing soft crimson knickers and silken black pubic hairs.

'You're supposed to be looking after *me*,' wailed Bea in distress.

Gubnet popped a tousled head over the covers and dangled the missing top at Min, who gratefully put it back on, restoring a modicum of sibling decency.

Queen Bea invited herself on to the edge of the bed and told them of her worries.

'I can't sleep, it's effing freezing cold, I've run out of fags and bloody Yossarian's ghost is following me everywhere.'

Princess Min looked around fearlessly. 'I can't see him, Bea, are you sure it's him?'

'He won't come in here,' assured Bea. 'You see he hasn't the nerve to face you after what he did.'

'Perhaps he wants something,' said Gubnet, pulling Min back into the bed.

'Oh yes,' said Bea wearily, 'he's threatening to haunt me until his statue is erected beside Peter's.'

'You should never give in to a blackmailer,' admonished Gubnet while squeezing Min's leg under the blankets.

'Well actually, I said I'd have a word with everyone about it tomorrow. He promised to go away if we did what he asked.'

'He's a blackmailer, a rapist and a drone,' pronounced Gubnet witheringly. 'He deserves nothing but our utter contempt.'

Queen Bea weighed it all up and decided that it was an opportune moment to make the request she had originally intended.

'Would you mind terribly if I stayed in the east wing?' she said to Min. 'Yossarian won't bother me if I'm in here and I desperately need to get some sleep. I'm so, so tired after all that gardening today.'

Min looked despondently at Gubnet who nodded hopelessly back at her.

'And it'll be all right by me if Gubnet wants to stay too,' yawned Bea graciously.

'I'd better fix up the camp bed,' said Princess Min awkwardly.

'No!' cried Bea. 'You see I have to sleep with you because you're supposed to protect me from Mother Nature.'

Gubnet resigned herself to the situation and snuggled up to Min on one side of the bed, making room for Bea on the other. They all said goodnight and turned out the lights. As sleep overtook the troubled lovers, a plaintive voice emerged from the dark.

'I want to sleep in the middle,' whined Bea.

'Only if you release me from my marriage to Tamarind,' growled Min back at her.

'But I can't do that,' protested Bea miserably.

'Then there's no deal,' said Min, adhering herself firmly to Gubnet's waist. 'And if I hear one more word out of you before sunrise I will separate these two beds, *mei-mei*.'

'What did you just call me?'

'*Mei-mei* – that's chinese for little sister, get it?'

'Then what are you?' enquired Bea, sitting bolt upright in the bed.

'Bigger than you – for the Goddess's sake, Bea, go to sleep!'

Gubnet patted Min's bottom approvingly. Assertion in a woman always turned her on.

By two in the morning, everyone on Ascourt was asleep.

To the untrained eye, the night was no more or less than a restless series of uncoordinated rolls and shifts. An unorchestrated slumber of incoherent sighs and snores, perhaps. But it was much more than that; for life flickers on and off, blinking so fast that one doesn't usually notice the intervals in between. The trained eye can spot this gap. An hour which seems longer than the one preceding it, for instance...

Ascourt was not really asleep. The seemingly dormant citizens were vitally alive in an undisturbable time gap of enormous complexity and infinite creativity.

What precisely caused this prolonged sleep was the willing desire of the community to empathise with an existential crisis so profound that its understanding was beyond any one mind alone. This event is not a likely occurrence in a given neighbourhood.

Of those who visited Ascourt's distant shores during the long hibernation, few understood. Those who did were not human.

The core energy which attracted Ascourt into a stationary transit emanated from the palace's east wing and the precise physical being of St Gubnet of Balleyvourney. This inconsistency was later put down to the fact that Gubnet, although human, had worked with bees all her life. Still others maintained that it was due to the powerful insistence of Athena, unborn but no less a personage than the daughter of Mother Nature Herself.

As St Gubnet's body was the living sanctuary of a marriage between two different systems of reality, it was also the magnetic physical co-ordinate upon which a collision course had been fixed. Every strain and nuance resided in the subtexture of her being, and all of Ascourt rested inside her.

Maryann Leaf pored over the original manuscript, paying especial attention to Charlotte's hand-drawn plans of the three royal gardens. On her desk lay the instruments of her unsuccessful investigations. A protractor, T-square, compass and ruler could not eke out the esoteric geometry, nor reveal to her a pattern within the horticultural designs.

Each of the three Princesses' gardens contained a folly. Queen Bea's garden sported a statue of Pallas-Athene, Princess Min's garden had a barbeque and Vee's, a sundial. She had not realised the significance of the garden plans which had caught her eye a week ago in the Town Hall archives. Even the smallest difference between the archive copies and the original now in her possession would be something to go on. She just couldn't remember. She played with possible alignments of sunlight, but no trick of the sun nor moon made anything more apparent. She left her cottage in the hills of Kerry and began the forty-kilometre drive to the shebeen which doubled up as a clandestine headquarters for Operation Charlotte.

The badly tuned car radio crackled in concert with the throaty exhaust of Maryann's battered pink Volkswagen. Up the long and tortuous Connor Pass, she twiddled the dials absentmindedly. She thought she heard a female voice and the word 'Ascourt'. Startled, she pulled the car over into an adjacent lay-by and turned the engine off. In the utter quiet of the hills, she listened attentively to the almost inaudible radio interview. The first voice was neutral, investigative and business-like:

'Mother Nature, can you confirm that there has been an outbreak of the BADS virus?'

'Yes – there has been a death on one of my many island colonies. The colony in question is under quarantine and we are awaiting developments.'

'What hope is there for the islanders of Ascourt to survive?' rose the first voice over what sounded like an electrical storm.

'Containment of the infection depends on keeping the identity of the island a secret,' came the smarting reply. 'The last thing we need is the well-meaning but curious visitor who will spread the infection unbeknownst to themselves. There is a strict quarantine in operation.'

'Yes,' swooped the first voice, 'the public is warned to stay away from the infected area of Ascourt. Naval gunboats surrounding the island have orders to open fire upon unauthorised personnel.'

'This is a very serious disease,' warned Mother Nature. 'The last infectious outbreak of the 1950s decimated the Irish economy. We have reason to believe that most of Ascourt is infected.'

'For the benefit of our listeners, could you describe the symptoms of the BADS virus?'

'It is a highly contagious disease of bees,' boomed the deep, lush voice of Mother Nature. 'The only symptom is lethargy quickly followed by death.'

'Mother Nature, what are the World Health Organisation recommendations?'

'The WHO priority, and my own, is to contain the spread of infection. They have recommended no viral testing for a six-month period. Obviously the more personnel on and off the island will substantially increase the chances of spread. Anyway, viral testing would only serve to confirm what we already know.'

'And finally, is it possible for you to agree with the WHO recommendation to lethally fumigate the island should the BADS virus be confirmed in the near future?'

'Regrettably, it is. The island in question has an ageing population with a sterile Queen. They are of little consequence to the national economy and I intend to do whatever is in my power to allay the fears of the international community.'

'Thank you Mother Nature. This is the BBC World Service, it is two pee-em and here are the news headlines. Irish naval boats will join the UN peacekeeping forces in the Gulf next week. At home, the Queen is once again in the news... '

Maryann switched off the radio. She could not believe what she had just heard.

All through the Great Sleep, Banba maintained a vigil over Ascourt. At first, the ghost of Yossarian joined her. Banba loved her job as the Spirit of Death and this assignment was out of the ordinary. She wanted to tune into the communal dream and just listen. But Yossarian droned on and on. She tried to make him take an interest in the mine-laying activities of the warboat, but he kept returning to her side. He barely raised an eyebrow when a naval launch of three handsome officers arrived on the island. She became annoyed with his endless prattle about Great Drones and ancient promises out of the mouths of those long dead. Banba left him at South Harbour and flew up to the palace. On her way she passed the uniformed men kidnapping the body of a sleeping citizen. She wondered if Yossarian would even notice she was gone.

On hearing about the radio broadcast, the hare-lipped chieftain in charge of Operation Charlotte grew tense and edgy.

'But this Gulf thing could be very timely for us,' she said, tapping the headlines of the daily newspaper.

Maryann thought hard before expressing an opinion. The Irish Navy had only five boats. If they were going to join the peacekeeping forces, then it was very likely that the fifth gunboat presently anchored off Ascourt would be called away in the next couple of days.

'Won't it be dangerous for you?' asked Maryann nervously.

'We'll have to take that chance,' replied her boss, rolling up her sleeves.

The chieftain sweated over the nautical almanac and plotted a course to Ascourt. Maryann knew that her boss would never admit to fear. She certainly had a temper and was very highly strung. Maryann tenderly rubbed the tattoo on her boss's wiry forearm.

'What if you catch the BADS virus?' she demanded tenderly. 'Where'll Operation Charlotte be then?'

'In the hands of the woman I trust more than I trust myself,' said the boss, making eye contact.

Maryann sighed. Flattery and tenderness were a rare commodity these days. They hadn't slept together since her return from Ascourt.

Princess Min and Queen Bea had managed to curl up in a ball in the crack at the bottom of the beds. They were not cold, so Banba spread her white cloak evenly over Gubnet's sleeping body. Poor mite! Banba held both sides of her temples and breathed into Gubnet's body, which was stiff with physical tension. There was an imbalance as a result of crossing over into two realities. Gubnet was a human now living as a bee Person in a land of great change, with a young foetus alive and growing in her slender frame.

She has lost a great deal of weight, thought Banba, *even since the céilí.*

The protestations of the dream world became audible. St Gubnet had contributed reproductive technology to both the bee and the human world. Her first concern was with the product of her Master's thesis – the Superdrones. It was genetic simplicity – crossing the genes of a Worker with those of a Drone. Anyone could have done it. Why did she?

You are human, whispered Banba in the strange dream tongue, *you weren't to know.*

The Superdrones – what an idea. It was tantamount to wiping out the female Worker bees. It was just a game, a game to get my Masters. Why did Mother Nature latch on to it – what for? The Way of the Bees is perfect. Did She see the Superdrones as some sort of expression of Her love for me? Is it possible that Mother Nature did this for me? I know I am to blame.

Banba said, *All Ascourt awaits you, St Gubnet of Balleyvourney. Your troubles are too big to squeeze through the gates of the Underworld. Let them go; sleep and rest.*

Mother Nature was whisked to Bantry in a black stretch limousine. Looking through the one-way glass, She admired the beautiful scenery of West Cork as it all too quickly flew past. It reminded Her of Herself: rugged coastlines, heather-bound mountains; naked, windswept and utterly inseparable from the stark reality of nature. High above the speeding car, turbulent storm clouds were in pursuit. Mother Nature sensed their tension and urgency. The air sparkled visibly with current. It was a perfect creative moment. The elements were gathering round the alchemist's wand.

She reeled off the elements thus:

1. The extraordinary marriage between Princess Min of Ascourt and Tamarind of Porschia.

2. Growing international interest in the Superdrones.

3. The end of Ascourt.

4. The end of the Way of the Bees, the end of predictability and productivity!

The current bullish speculation in Mother Nature International shares was a direct result of international confidence in the revolutionary Superdrones. Research and marketing would be aided by the stable marriage between Princess Tamarind and Princess Min upon whom the only living batch of Superdrones had imprinted themselves. Ascourt's ultimate fate was now in the hands of the World Health Organisation. They had endorsed Her view that an immediate quarantine was cheaper and more effective than a tedious and costly investigation of the BADS virus on a remote island with a sterile queen and an ageing population. In the short term, Ascourt was out of the way. In the longer term, it was ideally suited as an Atlantic Bird Sanctuary. And a quick, profitable sale to the State.

Productivity and *Profitability* – the *Modern* Way of the Bees.

Mother Nature performed the operations of a ledger in her mind's eye. It wasn't the money. As an immortal creator, She pondered that the price of survival was change. And yet, the Way of the Bees was as perfect and stable as a hexagon. And yet... Mother Nature acknowledged the incessant whisper of the cosmos through the partially rolled down window:

You seek perfection so that you might cease to create.

Yes, agonised Mother Nature, *I have been so tired and weary. And yet... this new imperfection, this new birth... it makes me feel young and sexy and ... tenderly ruthless.*

Racing past the wintery skeletons of roadside scrub, Mother Nature saw that what is perfect is just so because no more can be created from it. Perfection was death. And the Way of the Bees was perfectly dead. From now on, She would be the spearhead of change itself in the Seventh Age of Creation. From now on, it was Productivity and *Profitability* – the *Modern* Way of the Bees.

The winds howled over Ascourt. Trees of shallow root were torn from the soil and callously thrown to the ground. Lightning whipped up the firmament and all was ablaze in a nightmare of genocidal proportion. Banba took shelter in the palace. She settled in the Smoking Room and cocked her head up to the east wing. Ascourt was reaching the bottom of the abyss. It was sinking fast, thought Banba.

The uncloseable window in the Smoking Room was letting in a gusty draft. Banba didn't, by nature, feel the cold, but strong air currents tended to disrupt her ethereal composition. When the door slammed, she jumped, realising she had split into two. Her other half was in the corridor, following Gubnet's sleepwalking body into the kitchen.

The lightning storm had turned the milk sour, but Gubnet didn't notice. She drank and talked. Her spirits were low. This was the straw she had grasped: the Bee World was inexorably changing, a fact which Gubnet was entirely coincidental to. Ascourt wanted change. Mother Nature wanted change. The only tragedy was that Mother Nature had latched on to the wretched Superdrones.

Banba saw that Gubnet had chewed on a bitter grain of truth. She led her by the hand back to the Smoking Room and made her open the door. When she had merged with her other half, she felt whole again. She led Gubnet back up to bed and tucked her in. Queen Bea slept with a beatific smile. Princess Min looked disturbed.

The Navy gunboat docked in Bantry and unloaded its live cargo onto the pier beside Mother Nature's black Mercedes. The Admiral confirmed Her worst suspicions.

'Best we could do was leave the island surrounded by skull and crossbones, yellow quarantine flags and a few underwater mines,' he reassured Her. 'A bit of bad timing – but then the Gulf usually is.'

'Is she unconscious?' enquired Mother Nature of the casket.

'Funny thing you should say that,' remarked the Admiral. 'Apparently the whole damned island was fast asleep, right in the middle of the day.'

Mother Nature ordered the wicker casket be opened.

'I hope my lads got the right one,' he said stuffily. 'They didn't have much time, you know.'

Mother Nature looked at the rosy face with satisfaction. When it was safely locked in the boot of Her car, She invited the Admiral for a few gin slings at the harbour's Anchor Bar.

Banba opened the pilot's door of the red helicopter on the front lawn of the palace and sat noiselessly beside the Cook. She removed her brass fob watch and dangled it in front of the supersensitive epicurean genius. Banba waved a sprig of rosemary under Cook's nose. She didn't even flinch.

'Welcome back to Ascourt, Cook,' said Banba courteously. 'What is the purpose of your visit?'

'Porky has come to fetch Princess Min for the wedding.'

'And you, dear Cook?'

Cook kneaded the air with both fists. 'I am making a wedding cake for Min and Tamarind.'

Banba put a small blue crystal into her clenched fist. 'This is a present from the Underworld. Put it into the cake mix. When I count to ten, you will have forgotten you ever saw me.'

The Queen of Porschia struggled with the deadweight on her back. She tripped down the last few stairs which were wet from the incessant storms which beset the island. Porky landed hard on her well-covered bottom. Unbelievably, Princess Min remained firmly lodged on her well-rounded shoulders.

'I suppose it would be too much to ask that a superior officer of the Underworld might give me an earthly hand?' she exhorted.

But Gubnet cried out in her sleep, and Banba flew up the stairs to be at her side.

When you put one female egg with another, that is Ovum-to-Ovum, my contribution to the world of humans – a world I rightly belong to but hardly know. Ovum-to-Ovum is useless to Ascourt. I see the fruit of Ovum-to-Ovum in my womb and I know that Mother Nature will destroy us to preserve Her own way of change. A way I created in a human laboratory. A monstrous Superdrone.

From a distance, Banba heard the helicopter rising into the air. After the experience with the door, it made her shudder to think of the effects of a pair of rotary blades. When it left at last, all became quiet. Banba relaxed and allowed Ascourt's dream thoughts to filter through her. She felt their shallow inhalation of despair. But Banba was from the Underworld. This was a sensation she was entirely comfortable with. She leaned back on the bed, spreading her cloak between Gubnet and Queen Bea. There was room enough now that Princess Min had been taken.

Banba knew they were nearly there, for her cloak was turning from white to blue – the official colour of the Underworld. She hoped they would not be disappointed with the myriad wonders of her land. Ascourt had made a courageous decision, and although their collective descent into the Underworld had been entirely unforeseen, she remained optimistic that she could teach them the Seven Rules of Creation in accordance with Queen Charlotte's Will. Banba yawned, pleasurably anticipating the rich depths of the wise abyss. It was the furthest thought from her mind that if they did not succeed, they would remain in the Underworld forever.

One night, an unmarked motor boat glided silently into Ascourt. Two civilians crept up the hill from South Harbour and returned with a dead body. Banba watched to see what

Yossarian would do. She nudged him quietly. To her delight, he sailed with them, hovering neurotically about the robbers of his own corpse.

In the interest of self-preservation, Yossarian ensured that the yacht was steered precisely and accurately past the under-water mines. It was a sorry fact of being a ghost around people who shamefacedly displayed such spiritual ineptitude. He would rather not have had to listen to the angry words now being exchanged by thieves. In fortuitous retrospect, Banba's lack of interest had forced Yossarian to expand his worldview and take in other activities on a day that the Navy was engaged in burying underwater mines around the island. Yossarian concentrated on the steering, and did his best not to listen.

'Where did you disappear to?' asked the fierce-looking one. 'You went off without telling me – I dragged the body all by myself.'

Yossarian winced. The skin of both his corpse's heels was torn loose and flapping in blood.

'If you must know, I went to see if Queen Bea was all right.'

'Something going on between you and her?' said the helmswoman, letting go of the rudder. Yossarian grabbed it and neatly dodged another mine.

'She was fast asleep, all right?'

Yossarian waited with interest for the other one to reply.

'You haven't come near me since your happy holiday in Ascourt – don't think I haven't noticed.'

'You haven't let me near you,' protested Maryann. 'You've been totally preoccupied with your mother's bloody Will which I'm beginning to think is the greatest piece of fiction I've ever read!'

'You don't think well of me, admit it!' roared the chieftain above the crash of a wave.

The body rolled sideways. The right arm dangled danger-ously over the edge of the shallow boat. The wave disap-peared and the boat crashed on top of a mine. Yossarian held her eyes shut tight.

'I used to admire you, Vee. You had such dreams and ideals, but look where it's got you. You're all bitter and twisted. You're a brute with more enthusiasm for a dead body than for a sister you haven't seen in twelve whole years!'

Yossarian nodded in agreement. As a child, Princess Vee had been cold and calculating. Some things never changed. When Vee and Min had been forced to leave Ascourt, Vee had never waved goodbye. She had neither looked back nor shed a tear.

Princess Vee sullenly took hold of the rudder and steered purposefully for the shore. The pit in her stomach burned a hole in her heart. She knew she was a difficult person to love. Maryann had been the only one to ever get close. It wasn't jealousy. It was jealousy. And it was the horrible thought that not one person in the world might think well of her. Suddenly, she wanted Maryann Leaf like she had never wanted her before. But there was one question. One burning question. Did she dare to ask it?

'Maryann,' she spluttered, 'are you in love with Queen Bea?'

Yossarian slipped himself into the narrow seat beside Princess Vee, and felt all the emotions going through Vee. This was an iron heart which if broken would never heal.

Maryann covered her face with her hands and cried, 'For the sake of the Goddess, I'm in love with you both!'

Chapter Thirteen

The Great Sleep: The Underworld

Tuesday, November 19 – Sunday, December 8, 1996

Islands are, in part, physical outcrops of certain indefinable temperamental aspects of the Underworld. The storms that cut them off completely, from time to time, are vital in maintaining the emotional vibrations that connect the Underworld with its work on earth. During her training, Banba had perfected the art of summonsing storms. Her visitors had exactly twenty-four hours in the Underworld, which amounted to twenty earth days. It was imperative that no outsiders arrive on Ascourt during this time. The sea complied immediately. Great waves started to roll and foam outside the ring of flags surrounding the island. The storm would protect the island for twenty days and twenty nights. Looking out to the twelve-foot waves, Banba did not think of herself as an adept, but instead, highly privileged to be among those who had chosen a terrifyingly difficult path of no certain reward.

Following the rays from the tip of the sun, Banba quickly left the water in a straight line and returned to shore. The moment of entry to the Underworld was *now*, before the sun rose any higher. She swept her magic cloak over Ascourt, firmly locking the sun on to the eastern horizon. When the citizens stirred from their beds, they found themselves in a strangely transformed land where the sun never rose and the light was dim. It was dark but clear, and surprisingly easy to see. Somewhere from afar, a storm raged about them, yet the weather was clement and the island untouched.

Out of habit, the sleep-sodden bodies gathered in Town Square, looking about them at the startling changes in the trees and the different feel of the land at their feet. Just as Ascourt was not really asleep during the sinking into the Underworld, it is true to say, that on arrival, they were not really awake either. One or two felt a sensation which defied gravity and, in consequence, began to float upwards. It very soon transpired that Banba was their guide. She hovered ahead, leading them up the steps of the palace. Moving was easy; it was a matter of cardinality and inner motive force. That is to say, once a direction had been decided, one simply wished to be on one's way. There was a lightness among them, a decided euphoria, a determination to make the best of things. Looking back over her shoulder, she was pleased with their smooth acclimatisation. They were learning fast.

It was a new experience for Banba too. She had never led a group of voluntary tourists into the Underworld. It was a much maligned place, and rarely visited except, of course, by the dead.

The entrance to the Underworld is reached after an extremely long and narrow descent, by whatever route. The most popular trail is probably The Valley of Tears. Dark and uncomfortable, its adherents are commonly frustrated by a hugely expansive fear which prevents further access. One has to be as slight and limber, or dead, to enter. There is a saying which claims that should the sun ever rise in the Underworld it would be because an ego must have passed through its gates!

Ascourt had entered the Underworld in a unique way, through a very precise time gap. Their communal willingness to sink so far had led them here, and it would be a precisely timed affair to get them out. There was much to experience and learn before they left. Banba took out her fob watch. If they were not to become permanent residents, she must teach them the Seven Rules of Creation in twenty-four hours!

As they climbed the steps of the palace, the citizens of Ascourt coalesced into one communal mind. They each retained their separate bodies, yet no individuality was expressed. They had become their own amoebic barometer to every nuance, or even half-thought. They were also preoccupied with a very new approach to movement. As Banba whisked them upwards and onwards, they realised they were flying with their feet dangling beneath them. They were ready for their next lesson. She picked a low-hanging cloud with a bird's-eye view of the island. She knew they would be startled by the effect their emotions would have on what lay beneath them.

The group experienced a rapid succession of feelings as Ascourt melted and moulded into a thousand probable realities. After the initial bewildering magic, they slowed down to one of sadness and surrender, the feeling that led them into the Underworld in the first place. They looked down to see birds growing fat on the flesh of their dead and decomposing bodies. Ascourt transformed itself into a giant aviary blessed with only those flowers which can grow in the pungent nutriment of birdshit. The smell was vile.

On experiencing fear, the scene below them transformed audibly. Ships sailed in and out of South Harbour. The island was abuzz with a distinctive droning sound that made them feel nauseous to the pits of their hovering stomachs. Was this Mother Nature's reality? An island of Superdrones swarming, ever swarming around a captive queen controlled by dollars and power and productivity?

Reminiscing, they looked down once more and saw themselves as they had been before. In the calm passing of time, they aged, wrinkled and died. The population dwindled steadily. It became harder and harder for those left to get around or feed themselves. The island grew wild until almost all of it looked like the Northern Territories. An enormous flock of seagulls moved into the palace, and the group were facing, full circle, the sadness of their first vision.

This heaviness felt like a lead weight. The collective anchor sank them gently back into Town Square.

Banba sat quietly beside them. The group were not demonstrating a readiness to progress to the next lesson. What they had seen was that sadness gave way to fear which gave way to reminiscing of times gone by which led them back to sadness. She watched as the group wandered round and round Town Square. They were a circle of despair, with no apparent means of detaching themselves and assimilating the simple meaning of the lesson: *Negative emotions attract negative events.*

Banba turned away from them, trained as she was to wait for all time if necessary. But she felt an urge to check on her fob watch – they didn't have all of time!

A sudden light drizzle of rain turned into a downpour. The

River Naiad swelled her banks and overflowed into Town Square. The group were very clearly experiencing their emotions, thought Banba wryly. As the water crept up the steps of the palace, they began to swim. They showed no signs of fear, for the River Naiad was a friendly water spirit they had lived with all their lives.

When the river spoke to them, she said, 'Good people of Ascourt, your land is now a Valley of Tears, as you have so wished it.'

Banba climbed out of the water on to a dry step. Creation was childstuff in the Underworld, yet this was a game they must learn to play before they left. The rules were simple – and once learned, never forgotten.

Collectively, they wished the river peace and the return to her valley in the centre of the island. But the harder they wished, the higher and mightier the river grew, until she was forced to address them again.

'My friends,' she burbled, 'you do me great honour. I am the strength of your emotions. I flow with them. Will you see what I am saying?'

The group tried again. When they were satisfied that their feelings were of peace and calm, they collectively rewished the river a safe return to her usual pastures. Banba knew this wouldn't work, but she was heartened to think that they had absorbed the third lesson sitting up on the cloud. They were using their emotions now to colour events. However, there was more to it than that.

After a while, the river transformed into a smooth and glassy millpond. But she did not retreat one inch. And she refused to speak to them again. She grew cold and rigid, forcing the bathers on to dry land. They remained calm and followed Banba's lead towards the higher and drier steps of the palace. The river did not follow them.

Once again, they were miraculously floating up into the atmosphere. Then, looking down on to the river-soaked island, they all felt something at once. Within minutes, the river collected her sprawling volume and receded back into the valley which cut the island into two. Banba winked and crooked her little finger at them. *Well done!* They responded with a strange sound, like linen torn free from the fabric of worry.

But Banba did not hesitate to test them again. Time was running its race. High up in the dark sky of the Underworld, Banba spun thrice round and faced them, disguised as Mother Nature. They had learned that their emotions influence and coloured the nature of events – but had they really understood what the river was showing them? Banba circled them menacingly. She struck fear into their racing hearts. She said the sun would never rise and she cursed them for all time.

The group from Ascourt skilfully concentrated their emotions and turned them into respect and love for their Creator. The cursing stopped, but still it seemed as if Mother Nature would not leave them in peace.

'You are my creations,' mimicked Banba, hissing and spitting, 'you cannot have a dream unless I dreamed it. You are powerless to act unless I say so, and I say *you all fall down!*'

At this command the group, by now inured to the ups and downs of the Underworld, freefell gently on to Town Square which was still somewhat waterlogged. They had truly succeeded in not being afraid of Mother Nature and felt understandably despondent when they found her impatiently awaiting them at their landing point.

Banba took pity on them and removed her disguise. They looked at her like a class of bewildered and upset four-year-olds, but Banba could not, was not, allowed to explain. The Rules of Creation could be learned only by playing the game. Banba's brass watch told her that they had used up two-thirds of their time and not yet consolidated the lesson of the river. Banba felt sorry for Naiad, whose explanation was elegant and did not warrant any misunderstanding. Yet somewhere, somehow they must have managed to stop believing that their land was a valley of tears – for this was the only premise upon which Naiad would have withdrawn to her banks. Similarly, if they had believed that their dream for Ascourt's future was secure, 'Mother Nature's threats would have been meaningless too, and they would not have been afraid in the first place!

It wasn't enough to change their feelings – as the river had tried to show them. They were *not* their emotions, and it was this missing link in their comprehension that prevented them from coming fully to terms with their third lesson.

They were inadequately equipped to foresee that it was, in fact, their beliefs that dictated their emotions. And nor was it the other way around. Transforming their feelings of great sorrow into calm had soothed them – just as the river herself, mirroring their emotions, had been pacified when they wished her to go back the second time. But as long as they believed in a Valley of Tears, the river would comply – just as emotions will always follow on from beliefs. The flood Event they found themselves in was an exact replica of their very own belief. *Events* were influenced by *emotions* which sprang from *beliefs*. It was maddeningly simple. And all too crucial a fourth lesson for the creation of the future they dreamed of.

Banba thought hard about the Seven Rules of Creation. The group had succeeded in learning the first three. One: creators are communal. Two: direction and will can take you places. Three: emotions colour the events you attract into your life. But they had stuck on the fourth: to change the emotions which attract and influence certain events, you must first discover the belief or beliefs that are at the root of those emotions.

The lessons had to be learned in sequence. Banba rubbed her forehead and swore she would never volunteer for special duty again. When Banba next looked up, she noticed that the group were busy wiggling their little fingers. It gave her an idea. Excitedly, she pointed towards South Harbour and soon the group were in flight behind her, gliding smoothly down the hill. They followed her across the sands, flying over the water, until she landed within the ring of markers dividing the calm sea from the raging storm beyond.

One looked bemusedly at the other. They were walking on water. Banba pointed at the yellow flags and quarantine notices bobbing furiously in the waves. Cautiously, they linked arms and made a precarious passage into the rougher waters. The notices read: 'Quarantine Island. Do not enter. BADS virus Area. Highly Contagious, Notifiable Disease.'

Back on the beach, the group was depressed, now believing that on top of everything else, they were mortally infected with the BADS virus. Banba collected stones, twigs and driftwood. She built a blazing fire and invited the group to sit with her in a circle. In intense meditation, speeded up by the addition of rosemary and yarrow to the flames, the group learned the wisdom of virus medicine. Each saw that their genes were made up of coded building blocks called DNA. Each cell was a chemical factory of limitless possibility. Simply by wishing what you wanted, the DNA would order itself into a plan from which any number of identical copies could be made and transported to other cells for high-volume, high-tech production. They realised that their feelings of illness were being translated by their cells as a direct order to make a chemical blueprint of the BADS virus!

Banba was struck by their hesitance. In a playful way, she held up her little finger, threw back her head and laughed. The virus in her finger transmuted rapidly, the DNA was immediately reordered and resequenced to produce a soothing brain chemical. The group copied her and for the first time in a week, experienced a sensation of well-being and calm.

Banba was baffled – surely it wasn't possible to learn the fifth lesson of Creation without a thorough grounding in the fourth? Yet here they were, *creating their own physical reality*! In order to deprogramme the virus, they needed to believe they could create physical reality at will, and clearly they had strong beliefs in their ability to do just that. It was important progress, and Banba was pleased. Charlotte's Dream would require them to believe absolutely in their Queen's ability to produce daughters without prior fertilisation.

But the fourth Rule stated that *'your beliefs create your emotions'*, and what worried Banba was that, without an understanding of the fourth Rule, which they seemed incapable of grasping, anyone could take their dream away from them. Not least Mother Nature. The fourth Rule would consolidate their belief in a vision, producing appropriate feelings and a smooth passage of creative events. They were still hooked on believing in their feelings, unable to detach enough to see that their feelings were caused by their beliefs. It was a horrible jumble. *Mission impossible*, she reflected.

Even more significant, however, was that they would not be able to leave the Underworld until they believed they could. Banba checked her watch. There were only two hours left. If they missed the precise time of departure, they would never wake again.

Banba pulled her sky-blue cloak around her shoulders and left the group to themselves. The Rules of the Underworld were carefully considered. Yet she knew she would have to break them in order to pass on the lessons they needed to learn. The Sixth Rule of Creation could be summarised in eight words, yet it required a precise mathematical explanation based on an understanding that all time happened at once. It would take far longer than two hours to explain in accordance with the strict prescriptions of the Underworld.

Wielding a screwdriver in the smoking room of the palace, she knew that the consequences of her actions would be answerable to the Underworld. She could lose her job over a decision to explain a Rule in this way. She was not allowed to communicate directly, she was not allowed to use physical symbols – in fact, she was not allowed to do anything other than witness their own understanding, as they *naturally* came to it, according to their need. In the kitchen, she found a pair of scissors and neatly cut a large square of blue material from her cloak.

The Seventh Rule of Creation said: if a Belief is in anyway limiting, then it is not a true belief about reality.

But it is binding for the duration that the Belief is held, said Banba under her breath, *for every fibre of our being-ness will joyfully cooperate in the manifestation of whatever we believe, whether or not it is true.*

She wrote three hieroglyphs and wrapped up the package that contained the sixth Rule. As for the seventh... well, time had run out. Without the fourth, what use was the seventh – except in her own defence in the Underworld; their rules were, after all, limiting!

She left the parcel in Town Square, and flew back to the beach to join the group. She stood among them in her sky-blue cloak and prayed.

You put your faith in St Gubnet. When she was finally able to give up control, you collectively sunk into the Underworld. Now you must leave. You have not gained the Seven Rules of Creation as I wished. I have failed, and in consequence one of you must die in order to gain the Seven Rules of Creation in accordance with Charlotte's Dream. There is no other way. I cannot tell you how sorry I am.

Banba gently herded the group to the edge of the water. Her brass fob watch told her that it was now or never; for the sun, at this very moment, would be rising on Ascourt. It was all she could do to believe in their faith that the sun would rise, returning them to their island home. She beamed a great love and waved them to the edge of the dark water. *You must go home! Go home now!*

160

CHAPTER FOURTEEN

Three Breakfasts

Monday, December 9, 1996

Heron woke sweating and palpably terrified. Her cot was surrounded by a bank of barking amplifiers in a little glass room looking out onto a gleaming new laboratory. A burly guard paced up and down between rows of test-tubes and incubators. Mother Nature sat at the end of the bed with a breakfast tray looking for all the world like Little Red Riding Hood. When the sound died, Mother Nature removed her earplugs and threw a violently orange splotched CD at her.

The label read: *Oklahoma – original acid house remix*.

'That's what it took to wake you up,' She cackled. 'Oh what a beautiful morning!'

During Mother Nature's subsequent monologue, Heron gathered that it was a Monday morning, she had overslept and it was time to go to work. Mother Nature loomed closer with a bowl of horrible porridge. She was so close that Heron could see Her pearly white teeth.

'Ascourt that has been hit by the BADS virus,' She went on. 'It is out of my hands. The Irish government itself could not rescue them. As you were the only human, and not susceptible to BADS, I made a case to have you taken off the island. You were fast asleep and there wasn't time for niceties. You are a valued employee of Mother Nature International and you are honoured to be the only survivor of Ascourt,' She said with emotion. 'The whole island is asleep, Heron, they are dying even now as we speak and there is not a thing I can do for any of them. I have done all I can.'

'You mean you left Gubnet on Ascourt too?' said Heron opening her mouth for a spoonful of the horrible goo.

Mother Nature smiled clinically as She fed Her victim. 'Unfortunately, Gubnet was not officially resident on Ascourt. It follows, does it not, that she could not be officially removed.'

'I see,' chewed Heron. 'So that explains why we were cut off from communication.'

Mother Nature nodded grimly. 'Yes. There is already one dead. Ascourt is finished, we must accept that. It is time to move on. If your questions are answered, I'll leave you to eat your breakfast. We cannot afford to look back, Heron, there is much work to be done.'

'Doing what exactly?' enquired Heron carefully looking about. It was certainly secure. The chances of getting past the guard were remote. She spat a mouthful of horrible porridge into a tissue.

'You will be breeding Superdrones, here in the Convent,' announced Mother Nature, proudly looking out on to her fully equipped and up-to-date laboratory.

A short discussion about pay and prospects ensued. Dr Heron Home PhD reasoned correctly. She had been kidnapped from Ascourt to work as a prisoner for the rest of her days, breeding Superdrones in the convent's laboratory in Ballyvourney.

'Consider it a job transfer and be heartened to think that your pay will be offset against Ascourt's back taxes,' She pouted good-humouredly.

'But we were going to pay you the full five hundred thousand pounds with the dowry from Princess Min's marriage,' said Heron, wary that the pursuit of logic was a dangerous pasttime, particularly in the presence of a Creator.

'I admire your sentiment, Heron, for I too believe that one should settle one's debts,' said Mother Nature approvingly. 'And I have done everything in my power to facilitate this marriage between Ascourt and Porschia – I personally located Princess Tamarind, you know.'

Mother Nature stood at the door, glimmering in a crimson radiance. Heron saw a sparkling blur, a sensation she felt when her right brain function was about to take over. The inward tremble ceased and Heron became the wolf, unafraid to confront or attack. She salivated at the prospects of eating Mother Nature for breakfast.

'Our future lies with the Modern Way of the Bees – the Superdrones – and you are to be my scientific dream helper. It is a dream of change, and all change must come through me, however, unfortunately...' Mother Nature looked Heron sadly in the eyes. 'Productivity and profitability prevented the rescue of Princess Min, which is a shame, since her very own Superdrones are wasting away on Porschia as we speak. These are challenging times, especially for the Bee People who are, as you know, my chosen ones. But I have taken a leaf out of Charlotte's book and, as I'm sure she would have wished, I have chosen you to co-operate with my dream, Heron, which is why you are here. Any questions?'

'Just one,' said Heron feeling her whiskers quiver. 'How will you explain that Yossarian died of BADS when his autopsy shows otherwise? *You* were responsible for Yossarian's death – he died because you ordered him to mate with Princess Min. And how do you propose to explain that Ascourt succumbed to BADS when they were all vaccinated against it at birth?'

Little Red Riding Hood blinked her long lashes.

'And if Gubnet dies, everyone knows you will inherit the Superdrones,' said Heron, baring her fangs.

'On the contrary,' said Mother Nature aware of some change in Heron's demeanour, 'those of us who are prepared to change have everything to gain. For that is the price of creation.'

'Ovum-to-Ovum!' growled the wolf as she pounced out of bed. But Red Riding Hood was quicker. Mother Nature threw herself at Heron and grabbed her by the throat.

'What are you saying?' said Mother Nature, throttling her viciously.

'Gubnet is carrying your child,' grimaced Heron, but the words came out devoid of sound.

Princess Min stretched out an arm to envelope the object of her affections in an early-morning embrace. But the bed in which she had fallen asleep was not the empty bed she awoke in. She remembered fragments of a dream about a strange place where the sun would never rise – but where?

With one eye open, she watched the sun's rising orb through a set of three french windows. The room filled with a bright natural light which brought a sense of renewal and vigour to her sleepy frame. Sitting up in the vacant bed, she rubbed her hands vigorously and applied them to her left eye which was still glued with sleep. When the heat melted the nocturnal adhesive, she bounded out of bed and peered through the window. From what she could make out, she was on the ground floor of a ranch-style house which was low and long. Beyond her were lush green fields dotted with sheep and windswept trees. The fields were divided by handmade stone walls, typical of the west of Ireland. She could smell the sea, but she could not see or hear it.

Princess Min determined that she was neither dreaming nor on the Island of Ascourt. Beyond this, she did not give a thought to her newfound circumstances. Her body felt as if it had been asleep for weeks. She lustily threw open the centre window and saluted the life-giving sun. The urge for action surged through her veins. It was not a time to think.

She lined up the prayer mat and performed one hundred and eight salutations to the sun. Even as she lay on the floor an hour later, panting for breath, she sensed the miraculous nature of her being – everlasting Qi and the total transcendence of life. She wondered if this state of infinite wellbeing and calm was heaven and earth within her. Deep in pyschic meditation, she sensed the yin of yang and the yang of yin. She performed a complete bodycheck in her mind's eye and began a return to consciousness, moving her fingers and toes, absorbing the sounds in the room. She also sensed a heavily made-up pair of eyes staring down on her.

Thinking first it was Mother Nature, Princess Min jumped to her feet and faced the foe. It stuck out a snake-bangled arm and said:

'Hi, I'm Tamarind. You've been asleep for ages!'

Princess Min was overcome with shyness. Her once pristine-white vest and knickers were a dull grey and totally inappropriate for the purposes of meeting one's future wife. She grabbed a towel and covered herself.

'It's OK,' said Princess Tamarind, patting her shoulder, 'nothing I haven't seen before!'

Princess Min pulled away. So, she was on the island of Porschia. She knew nothing of their customs but this familiarity was far from dignified.

'Take a shower and come on down for breakfast,' said Tamarind, putting a friendly arm around Min's waist. 'You're not much fun when you're asleep, you know!'

Princess Min shut her eyes against the stinging needles of water and watched a parade of the past float through her mind. After her training in Kyoto, she had joined the Japanese Navy. Two years later, Mother Nature had requested her return to Ascourt. So much had happened in such a short time. She saw Sien Sun, her last Aikido master in Kyoto – a passion delicately built, ricepaper on ricepaper. Her first unrequited love. Then came the flat-breasted Major who chased her with alacrity all over the boat. It was flattering, nerve-wracking fun. But Min never allowed herself to be caught, until… Gubnet. From the moment they met, it had been just Gubnet, only Gubnet, all Gubnet…

Then this? This Princess Tamarind? Min tried to imagine them in bed; she even tried to conjure up the feelings of wet and warmth and openness, like with Gubnet, but instead she saw herself fumbling and unsure, unable to negotiate the hundred bangles and steely zips adorning a spirit completely unfamiliar to her. They had nothing in common.

Princess Min stepped out of the shower and peppered her body with talcum powder. She dressed formally and focused herself on the challenge ahead. It was a job, after all. She must marry this Porschian princess and expedite their return to Ascourt.

Princess Tamarind lolled in the kitchen while Cook prepared breakfast.

'She is lovely,' remarked Tamarind. 'You should see her body!'

'I have,' said Cook, whose hands never ceased in culinary movement: stir, chop, spread, knead.

'I think she's a bit young for her age,' continued Tamarind. 'I much prefer older women, they know exactly what they want.'

'I know,' said Cook, flipping a pancake in a perfect arc.

'Still, I suppose it'll be fun to be Queen. Mum's retiring you know.'

'I do,' said Cook, shoving a tower of pancakes into the oven.

'Where do you think she'll go?' asked Tamarind.

Cook felt the large blue crystal in her pocket, which reminded her to weigh the fruit for the wedding cake.

'We're thinking of Florida, dear,' said Cook, munching a raisin.

'We?' said Tamarind, raising her eyebrows.

'That's right,' confirmed Cook. 'There's no ghosts in Florida, far as we know.'

Breakfast was eaten in silence, to the relief of Princess Min. The Queen of Porschia removed a napkin from her ample cleavage and addressed the two young people.

'Now, why don't you go out and play?' she boomed. 'It's a lovely, dry winter morning.'

'What do you think, Min?' said Tamarind, suggestively wetting her crimson lipstick. 'Quick game of kisscatch?'

The Queen of Porschia frowned at her daughter, whom London had changed insufficiently, and turned her attentions to her future daughter-in-law.

'I trust you are well rested, Min,' she said. 'Cook and I went to pick you up and found the whole of Ascourt fast asleep. I ran into that dreadful woman, Banba, who has made a habit of terrorising Cook, and realised at once what was going on.'

Princess Min looked at the Queen of Porschia as if she were speaking in a foreign tongue.

'Of course, you've never seen it before,' she said with an air of reassuring authority. 'Ascourt was in the Underworld. You lot must have been up to something very wicked to get a punishment like that.'

Princess Min was not in a position to contradict her. In Japan she had learned that the word of an elder was law. And all the more so if that elder was one's prospective mother-in-law.

'Still, you've made amends, and you're all back now,' said the Queen, pausing for breath. 'I remember a story my mother told me about an island near here which entered the Underworld and never came back. Now the Queen of the island at the time – '

'Right,' said Tamarind, firmly pushing out her chair, 'we're off to play outside. All right, Mum?'

Princess Min blushed. This was too much, to insult one's ancestors in this way.

'I'm very sorry, Your Majesty,' Princess Min apologised for the blunder of her future wife.

Her Majesty nodded, opened the *Irish Herald*, located the Gardening Section and withdrew from all further communication.

Queen Bea was crouched on the beach, watching the sun's fiery tip on the edge of the horizon. It made her think a strange thought. What would happen if the sun didn't rise? What if it all depended on *her*? It was a terrible thing to contemplate. She stood up, straightening her back, and pointed to the east.

'Rise!' she ordered majestically, just in case.

The rays of the early sun crept across the water and kissed her feet on the early morning shoreline. Queen Bea giggled. Thinking of breakfast after a good morning's work, she turned to find herself facing a crowd of islanders.

She jumped in surprise. 'What are you all doing here?'

But not a one of them could remember actually leaving her bed.

Still of one mind, the citizens of Ascourt left the beach and chatted politely among one another. They herded together following the only road which led them around Seaview Suburbs and up the hill towards Town Square on the other side of the island. As the collective fog dispersed, each individual began to feel the strain of the climb, the pressure of long-unused muscles and a flow of pure oxygen to the brain. Egos were stretching and flexing. Individual tensions became manifest and halfway up the hill, a difference of opinion regarding the dreams of 'the night before' was evident.

'I don't know. It was biblical, I really felt that,' said Montague, stressing the word *felt* for the purposes of authenticity.

'Not quite,' breathed Dame Agnetha excitedly. 'But it's coming back to me, yes, it was a workshop like the ones I do here, only *more so*…'

A light wind gusted at the exact point from which the River Naiad sparkled beneath them. Delia du Pont instinctively reached for her turban to discover, instead, a prickly row of damp bedtime curlers which shocked her into remembering something.

'I dreamed that the river flooded its banks!' she cried out.

'We were swimming in our emotions,' corrected Dame Murphy, whose long johns were rolled up to her knees. 'I remember it quite clearly. I lay on my back and pretended I was on an island paradise having a lovely dream.'

The group felt singularly tired, and had difficulty mustering the strength to climb the long stretch of hill still ahead of them.

'The less we talk, the faster we'll get to breakfast. I feel like

I haven't eaten in a week,' snapped St Gubnet irritably.

'I felt like Moses receiving the Ten Commandments,' persisted Montague. 'I am convinced I was being told *something* by *someone* very important!'

'You are on to it, Montague,' resounded Dame Agnetha, 'Except that they were *Rules*...'

'Neither one of you was in my dream,' rankled St Gubnet. 'I dreamed my own dream; I was some sort of very big flying thing.'

'So was I! It goes something like this...' said Dame Murphy, wobbling on her bare tiptoes. 'You sort of aim and wish yourself there...'

But nothing happened.

'Pity you can't remember, Dame Murphy, because I really don't think I have the energy for another step, and if I don't eat soon I might lose my temper at someone,' puffed Gubnet, who felt significantly more pregnant than she had the night before.

Dame Clemis, who had simply listened, said, 'We were surely in this together. I don't recall anything myself, yet I feel at one with everyone's version of the events.'

'And we all woke up on the beach together,' said Dame Thwaites, shaking the sand out of her pink satin nightie.

Queen Bea stopped in her tracks. *Together*... Inexplicably, it was all very clear to her.

'It will only work if we all fly together, at the same time!' she explained.

Dame Murphy stood in front of the group and tried again. When they were all up wobbling on one foot, she said, 'Now, think of your direction and will yourself there.'

At first it didn't work. But there was a sort of lightheadedness, and they tried it again.

'Together to the very top step of the palace,' said Dame Murphy, encouraging a united vision. 'One, two...six!'

Montague snickered.

Queen Bea glared at her. 'Just this once, Montague, it would be really *too good of you* to join in with the spirit of things.'

And the defiance of gravity was as simple as that. Lift-off was straightforward; they glided perilously close to the beech tree in Town Square, and in the blink of an eyelid, they were up the two hundred and sixteen steps of the palace.

'I don't believe this!' muttered St Gubnet of Balleyvourney, reading the note on the kitchen table.

'*Princess Min and Cook with me. Both well. Change of plans: wedding in Porschia, December twenty-first – Winter Solstice. You're all invited. Love, Porky. P.S. Money for Tamarind's dowry all yours when knot is tied. See you there. Must run.*'

Gubnet sank into her chair. There were times in life when reality was more than a match for the simple miracles of a dream. This was one of them. The Old Dames Breakfast Club clucked around her in a concerted effort to produce a hearty meal. Shelves were swept of their contents, cupboard doors were opened and disappointedly banged shut again. Forays into the pantry returned empty-handed. They had not been restocked since Cook left their shores.

'The Queen of Porschia took Min from right under our noses and neither one of us woke up,' said Gubnet questioningly to Bea. 'Which is highly unlikely because I'm a very light sleeper.'

Bea considered this for a moment and said, 'Today is November nineteenth, which gives us one month and three days to practice flying to the wedding in Porschia.'

'And that's another thing,' said Gubnet. 'It's all very well for you lot to be flying around, but I'm human and we don't fly – we just don't. It's quite upsetting.'

'I told you already,' said Queen Bea matronisingly, 'Min wouldn't have left if you'd have just let yourself believe that you loved her.'

'I can't think what that has to do with flying,' said Gubnet who was almost too tired to be annoyed with Bea's highly random cerebral malfunctions.

'It's not what you are,' said Queen Bea, explaining herself slowly. 'It's what you *believe* you are.'

Montague, who had been earwigging at the door, just couldn't resist. 'What about your girlfriend, Bea? We haven't seen her round in a while – or didn't you believe you loved her enough?'

'I do believe I truly love her,' said Bea, going red in the face. 'She didn't steal anything and I know she'll be back as soon as she can.'

'How on earth can you tell if what you believe in is true?' said Gubnet. 'You'd only believe it if you thought it was true in the first place.'

'But that's just it,' said Dame Agnetha, rejecting a pot for its congealed contents. 'I'm sure that was one of the Rules – the only way you can tell if what you believe in is true is if it *doesn't limit* the possibilities you have in mind for the making of your life.'

Montague du Pont remembered. It hit her like a flash of lightning. 'It was in Charlotte's Will all along,' she cried excitedly.

'What was?' asked Queen Bea, all of a flutter.

'"You will gain the Seven Rules of Creation!"' she quoted from memory.

'And did you?'

Everyone turned and faced Montague expectantly.

'Well, I can't be expected to remember everything they told me,' she stammered awkwardly.

'Look what I found under Cook's bed,' said Dame Thwaites, producing a commercial pack of cornflakes and a box of Belgian chocolates. They were in business. Breakfast was served.

The sun lost no time in its steady ascent to the zenith. By midday, Banba's gift was discovered, wrapped in a cloth of memorable blue, lying where she had placed it, under the beech tree in Town Square. Word spread, and a sizeable crowd gathered, at first just staring. Then followed disbelief, incredulity and doubt. A motion was put forward.

'I propose to open it,' announced Queen Bea, 'if for no other reason than it is addressed to me.'

The letters B, V and M were smudgily etched in thin black marker on a corner of the blue material.

The wrapping was removed and passed round, evoking in each participant the desire to merge and be as one. Comprehension was instant and simultaneous. It was nothing less than a sign.

It was a particular blue, a blue with an age-long association. Without a single word spoken, they sat in a circle listening to the thoughts of their organic whole. It was that they had been given a dream by the Blessed Virgin Mary, the BVM. She had left them a sign of her presence – a symbol of her love and protection wrapped in a fragment of her heavenly blue cloak.

Queen Bea stretched out a finger to touch the parcel.

'Don't do that!' shouted Montague, 'it's not yours!'

But it was too late, and Queen Bea was sent reeling from a bolt of electricity. The parcel was alive.

The Old Dames Breakfast Club retired to Swann's Hotel to discuss the essence of the parcel. Efforts were then made to locate Dr Heron Home, PhD, which resulted in the discovery that she was not on the island. Undaunted, the Old Dames sought the opinion of the State Pathologist.

'I suspect,' concluded Delia scientifically, 'that the package contains some source of electricity, and it would best be opened by a person or persons clad in rubber-soled footwear.'

'Agreed!' concurred the Dames all at once, looking down at their shoes.

'I could have a look around the Institute,' suggested Delia helpfully. 'We used to have a stock of white laboratory wellington boots.'

When Delia left, the Dames opened up a full and frank discussion.

'I do hope,' said Dame Toplis, 'that Delia does not find the wellies.'

'Quite,' said Dame Thwaites. 'It would not do to have Montague crowing about her sister as the one chosen to open the parcel.'

'It is unfortunate that not one of us is in possession of the specified footwear,' said Dame Murphy regretfully.

'Nor Queen Bea,' said Dame Agnetha, recalling the electric shock.

'The identity of the Chosen One will be a mystery,' sighed Dame Murphy, romantically adding, 'I wonder who is wearing rubber shoes?'

The essence of the parcel was abundantly clear to Dame Clemis, who did not believe in allowing chance a hand in the selection of the Chosen One. The Dames swept up to Town Square and conducted a comprehensive survey of footwear among the citizenry.

As chance indeed had it, or fate as Dame Clemis later described it, the Chosen One was none other than Montague du Pont, wearing a pair of red size-three Adidas, with leather uppers and thick rubber soles. Delia du Pont arrived in Town

Square, sans footwear, but with an agitated announcement which did not help matters.

'The Institute has been ransacked,' she groaned. 'Heron's files are scattered about in her office, the wellies are missing and someone has made off with Yossarian's body.'

'That makes a total of three people missing,' counted St Gubnet. 'Min, Heron and Yossarian.'

'That's a shame about Yossarian,' said Queen Bea. 'Because I made up my mind last night that we really ought to give her a decent burial and a statue of her own beside Peter's.'

'*He*,' said Gubnet astringently, 'is a rapist and *we* are not for one minute in agreement about his interment.'

'I only thought we should do it so that I could get some sleep,' said Queen Bea plaintively. 'After all, it's not *you* he wants to talk to all night along.'

Montague approached the parcel intrepidly. She placed the blue cloth to one side and nervously touched the package. Unharmed, she opened the top and stood back as the others crowded around it. In it was a white plastic square with three holes punched in a triangle. Dame Clemis nudged Montague towards the parcel. It was a test for the Chosen One. Montague steeled herself to put her hand into the box and withdraw the object. She suffered a moment of fear and a moment of resentment for all the times she had proved herself, only to be stultified in her moment of glory.

She dived into the box and held the gift aloft. There were oohs and ahs, murmurings and whispers. Suddenly, Montague let out a yelp and dropped the sacred omen. The crowd jumped backwards, all at once.

'What did you do that for?' howled Montague at Queen Bea, who had stepped on her foot.

'Those are my shoes. I lent them to you at the céilí and you never returned them.'

Opinions varied on the nature of the object. Dame Agnetha was quick to grasp that the three small holes were symbolic of the BVM. Delia du Pont offered her learned scientific opinion. 'Actually, it is one of those things, more usually seen screwed into a wall, for holding a plug.'

'A powerpoint?' offered the technically minded Dame Murphy.

'I don't see how it can be,' said Queen Bea logically. 'After all it's not connected to anything.'

'But it delivered an electric shock,' pointed out Delia.

'It is a gift to us,' reasoned Dame Agnetha, 'a gift with strange powers.'

Queen Bea was disconcerted. Perhaps it was a trap. 'What if Mother Nature was trying to sting me again?'

Gubnet put an arm around her, 'No Bea, you got an electric shock because you weren't wearing rubber-soled shoes. Trust me, Mother Nature would never resort to cheap plastic gimmicks.'

'Still, *I* should have opened the parcel,' said Bea resentfully, pointing at Montague, 'because those are *my* shoes.'

Montague circled the parcel slowly. Words were forming in her mind. A present from the BVM., a Powerpoint, a cloth of blue. She opened herself to the cosmos and felt a power that is known only to those who are chosen. The sentences surged through her. If anyone had asked, she could have sung the harmony of its colour. The colour blue, sky-blue...

'There is a Powerpoint in the Present,' she said in deep, low tones. She did not attempt to sing it. If anyone had so much as touched her, they would have fried in her radiance. And again, 'There is a Powerpoint in the Present.'

Dame Clemis thought fast. She had correctly assessed the essence of the present, but despite their best efforts, a certain unsatisfactory detail remained. Dame Agnetha agreed. There was no point in bemoaning the fact. There was nothing else to be done. The Old Dames Breakfast Club must admit to its ranks the Chosen One.

'We have been given a very great sign from the BVM,' began Dame Agnetha, prompted by Dame Clemis, 'a gift of power. A power which we can wield for the creation of our future *in her name.*'

'Montague du Pont,' announced Dame Clemis solemnly, 'kneel for your Dame-making.'

A rolling sweat broke out on the overheated body of the Chosen One. Montague registered disbelief. Followed by a fleeting moment of humility. Dame Clemis traced an imaginary circle with her official stick of hazel. It was almost too much for Montague to bear. Then the Head of the Old Dames Breakfast Club addressed her again.

'Montague the Leo,' chanted the tall thin figure of Dame Clemis dramatically, 'Montague of the Shoe, Montague the Chosen One!'

Dame Clemis sprinkled the kneeling figure with a handful of rue.

'Rise now as *Dame* Montague, Keeper of the Powerpoint.'

The ceremonies went on until dusk. There were complicated rituals and ancient procedures which the Breakfast Club insisted upon for their first ever Dame-making since Queen Charlotte's death.

It was an unpopular decision with Queen Bea, who insisted it could not possibly be the 'Will of the People' unless Montague returned her Adidas footwear. Eyebrows were similarly raised when Dame Clemis offered herself as Montague's bridge partner in one of the rituals concerning this practice.

Later that evening, Dame Montague hobnobbed with the other Old Dames at a private function in the luxurious tearooms of Swann's Hotel.

'You are one of us now,' said Dame Clemis proudly. Dame Agnetha gave her a small token of their esteem. It was *The Compleat Book of Player's Bridge*.

'Read and digest,' said Agnetha, with a hint of a friendly warning, 'for it is bridge that wins respect from the inner sanctum.'

Montague blushed. She knew it was so; she had watched them for years, convinced that one day she would be among their number. It had come to pass and she was not unprepared. All inner sancta played games. It was unavoidable. The Old Dames played bridge and so did Montague du Pont. She had absorbed every book on the subject available in the local library.

Confidently she said, 'I will not let you down.'

Dames Montague and Clemis achieved the highest ever score in the evening's rubber. Montague effused about the obvious and karmic nature of the partnership, and Dame Clemis, though genuinely pleased with the 'more-than-chance' element of beginner's luck, did not forget the important issue.

'Dame Montague,' she said earnestly, 'I think it best that your Adidas shoes be kept in the hotel safe.'

Montague undid her laces and handed over the shoes. Queen Bea would probably stop at nothing to get them back, she thought grievously to herself.

'No, that's not it, Dame Montague,' said Dame Clemis, intercepting her less than charitable thought. 'And you can put the Powerpoint into the safe as well, if you wouldn't mind.'

Divested of her sovereign accoutrements, Montague felt naked and vulnerable. In fact, she felt *ordinary*. Dame Clemis closed the safe and locked it.

'Queen Bea won't get near them. Don't worry, my dear.'

'I'm very relieved to hear you say that,' admitted the novice Dame Montague. 'I have noticed that Queen Bea tends to allow her personal motives to get in the way.'

'We all do, Dame Montague, Keeper of the Powerpoint,' instructed the Oldest Dame benevolently, 'and that is why it pays to take precautionary measures.'

'Of course,' flushed the initiate reverently.

'Then you'll agree that these items are now the official property of the Old Dames Breakfast Club?'

'Well, quite,' concurred the younger Dame generously.

'And you don't so much as breathe on them unless we give you the say-so,' dismissed Clemis severely. 'Got it?'

Mother Nature picked up the receiver on Her private phone line.

'Are you Mother Nature of Mother Nature International?' came the rasping voice.

'Who's that?' She replied.

'We want to make you an offer you can't refuse,' said the caller in a thick country accent.

'I don't make a habit of talking to strangers,' warned Mother Nature. 'And speak up, I can hardly hear you.'

'My organisation wants to buy that island that's in the news – Ascourt, right? Just name your price.'

'It's not for sale,' said Mother Nature. 'Who are you – Provos or what?'

'Your island is distant and remote, and we need a training ground. Money's no object. Think about it, we'll be in touch.'

The phone clicked dead on the other side. Mother Nature looked out on the soft mists of Balleyvourney and grinned from ear to ear. The universe had conspired with Her and She had not missed the point of their little joke. An island fit for guerillas, eh? She had not been far wrong. The end of Ascourt was in sight at last.

PART THREE

PART THREE

CHAPTER FIFTEEN

The Porschian Cartel

December 10 – 15, 1996

Cook was not out of place in Zurich's Ambassador Hotel which was hosting the EU finals for Rustic Chef of '96. She carried her bag firmly through the foyer and steadily navigated her way to suite 107. She checked the room thoroughly and followed a simple list of instructions from Dion Fortune's down-to-earth manual on the management of unwanted spirits. Reassured by the invasive smell of garlic, she ran a long hot bath and recited a list of numbers to herself.

Cook dressed simply for the evening's formal presentation. Back in the hotel foyer, the electronic billboard flashed messages every thirty seconds. Lounge One was hosting Nobel prize nominations at eight o'clock. Cook anxiously tapped her foot. Ascourt began with an A, she would be first to speak and she could not be late. The billboard blinked again. It began to run through a list of the Nobel entries. Cook approached reception, and spoke in a clear west of Ireland accent:

'How many lounges are there in this hotel?'

'There are two, madam,' came the reply in perfect English.

'*Merci,*' she offered in faultless French.

Lounge Two was packed to capacity. Cook was introduced, the audience clapped politely and reached for their headphones as she began her speech of introduction.

'Irish cuisine is a romantic fancy of the stomachs of those who have long left our shores. In reality, there is no such thing as an authentic Irish cuisine. Irish cooking is a testament to the ingenuity of poverty, oppression and colonisation. I make no apology for this. We are famous for our stews, because as every chef in the audience very well knows, no one should

179

reveal what is in a stew, especially if it has been begged, borrowed or stolen.'

This raised an eyebrow or two among the international jurists, but Cook pressed on to the finish.

'Without giving too much away, my menu in tomorrow's competition will be a culinary statement about Irish rustic simplicity. Thank you.'

The jurists gratefully unhooked their headphones. The audience in Lounge Two clapped apprehensively. Cook left the podium and headed for Lounge One, where the Nobel prize nominations had just begun.

It was midnight when Cook turned the key to the door of suite 107. Her olfactory organ twitched. Someone had disturbed the neat line of white pepper powder that she had carefully laid under the door. Cook sneezed. The acrid vapour was all-pervasive. On the bed, her portfolio lay open and rifled. But nothing was missing – not the menu for tomorrow's competition, not her passport, travellers' cheques or airline ticket. Getting into bed, Cook straightened up the photograph of the Queen of Porschia and turned the pages of her manual until she came upon the section dispensing advanced instruction for the removal of disquieting spirits. 'Above all,' she recited, 'one must be firm!'

Early next morning, Cook breakfasted lightly on toast and coffee. She read a few pages from *The Islandwoman* by Peig Sayers. Inspired, she set to work in the airless, basement kitchens of the Hotel Ambassador. She could hear the rolling waves hurtling along the shore, she could smell the fresh clumps of seaweed and most of all, the searing winds which cut right through her frame. It was Cook's philosophy that hunger was the inspirational premise of culinary perception.

Cook left the Hotel with a sturdy hat box and an hour to spare. Walking briskly, she recited to herself a long list of numbers. A uniformed porter ushered her into the vaults of the Zurich Grossebank. She reeled off the numbers to a cashier, produced an identification in the name of Hayde Lewis and withdrew the entire account in Swiss francs. She left the bank and made her way to the Central Post Office where she availed of a discount rate for the posting of 'paper matter'. Cook did not believe in taking chances. She had little faith in banks, couriers or the Customs and Excise. She favoured the postal system which was old-fashioned, reliable and discreet. The package, containing the equivalent of just under one million Irish punts, would reach Porschia in less than a week.

In Lounge Two, chefs in tall white hats inspected the competition. Cook stood at the back of the crowd which surrounded the Irish table, unable to get an inch closer to her winning display: an appetiser of stone-ground Irish brown bread with beechnut puree butter, a starter of *Allium sativum* or wild garlic soup, and a main course of Sea Pie – a delicately enclosed pudding of potatoes and seaweed steamed in brine, strong herbs and black pepper. Dessert was a plain oatmeal cookie and a glass of milk from a matron of the rare but indigenous breed of Kerry cows. Cook agreed with all the superlatives arising from her fare. Minimalist! *Vegetarische!* Macrobiotic even! *Gut und preiswert! Nouvelle cuisine*! Aah and Ooh! The simple presentation was cleverly juxtaposed by a pair of goldrimmed spectacles and a copy of *The Islandwoman* on an empty wicker seat.

'Are you the chef from Ascourt?' came a nervous whisper from the back of the crowd.

'I am,' said Cook in her competition hat.

'Can you get a message to St Gubnet?' he asked anxiously.

Cook proffered a pencil and paper, 'You can write it down on that, love. I'll no doubt see her soon.'

Professor Louis Sterne scribbled madly. 'Tell her to ring me at this number.'

'Would you mind if I had a look at the soles of your shoes?' requested Cook suddenly.

Louis Sterne removed a shoe for inspection. Cook sniffed suspiciously.

'There's pepper on your shoes – you were in my room last night, weren't you?'

Suddenly there was a loud cheer from Lounge One. *Vive la France!* was roared heavenward amid a rumba of *Olé, Olé, Olé, Olé!*

'I took the liberty of ensuring that you were who I thought you might be,' said Professor Sterne, mopping his receding hairline. 'Please forgive a desperate man – I think our French–Irish project has just been nominated for the Nobel prize next door…'

'French–Irish?' said Cook, gripping his expensively tailored suit.

'Me, St Gubnet and Dr Heron Home,' reeled off the Professor. 'Ovum-to-Ovum Fertilisation – '

'In that case,' said Cook, gripping his other shoulder and kissing him on both his shaven cheeks, 'I'll be in touch!'

Cook was in Zurich to cash in Hayde Lewis' sizeable bank account. She most adamantly did not come to Zurich to win an excuse of a cookery contest; and it was not the upset of missing out on the first prize but the disgrace of being disqualified over a technicality to do with the dessert that annoyed her. The judges claimed, and rightly, that the oatmeal biscuit had been purchased and not baked. Cook counterclaimed, and with some justification, that the Irish were congenitally incapable of making so much as an apple pie and that 'pudding' was assembled from an assortment of packages which one bought in a supermarket.

'Anyway, dessert is a British notion!' said Cook scathingly.

'But Madam, could you not have chosen a piece of Irish cheese?' wondered a helpful jurist.

'Swiss supermarkets do not stock Irish cheese,' fulminated Cook among a gathering rash of journalists.

'Is it true that you are violently anti-British?' accused the lightbulbs popping into her eyes.

'No publicity,' said Cook, pulling her chef's hat over her eyes, 'no publicity.'

Cook spent the rest of the day locked into her hotel bedroom, performing research on Ovum-to-Ovum Fertilisation by telephone. The next day she flew home. The kind air hostess on the Aer Lingus flight to Shannon poured her a nutritious glass of Guinness stout.

'Would Madam like a newspaper? We have European, British and Irish publications.'

'One of each,' said Cook, who was an avid reader.

The headline in the Irish paper read: 'TOP IRISH CHEF SAYS BRITISH APPLE PIE IS BEST.'

That's not quite what I meant, said Cook to herself.

The Continental paper said: 'IRISH EXPERTS SAY SWISS SUPERMARKETS LACK IMAGINATION.'

'Experts? But there was only one of me,' said Cook quietly.

The British paper sniped: 'NO SURRENDER SAY CHEATING IRISH.'

'That's an outright typical British racist lie!' accused Cook, noting with satisfaction that all three papers were owned by Rupert Murdoch. 'That's libel, slander and incitement to racial unrest,' she continued excitedly.

The passenger beside her croaked sympathetically, 'That's the gutter press for you.'

'Indeed'n it is,' agreed Cook. 'You wouldn't believe what that should have read…'

'Tell me, dear,' said the aged one. 'I was a suffragette once myself.'

'No *Publicity* say Cheating Irish,' enunciated Cook with propriety.

'Oh, it's hard to find honesty these days, dear.'

The Queen of Porschia had mixed reactions about Cook's return. On the one hand, she missed her. On the other, she was greatly vexed. The blend of these two feelings emerged as a coolness which Cook subconsciously tried to melt by lighting the kitchen fires and incinerating the events which she had left behind her in Zurich.

'Mother Nature Herself couldn't have bought the amount of publicity that you managed to attract,' said the Queen of Porschia with more than a hint of disapproval in her voice.

'I did everything I could not to win that blasted competition,' said Cook. 'I made a dog's dinner, I insulted the jury and I showed a rude disinterest in the entire proceedings.'

'But you didn't win – you were disqualified!' exploded Porky. 'It's in every newspaper in the land!'

'I got us the money,' returned Cook evenly.

'And a lot of publicity – what if someone in the Swiss bank identifies you?'

'Never mind all that,' said Cook. 'I found out something far more important – something much more interesting…'

Cook put her hand in the pocket of her pristine white overalls. She felt the smooth lump of blue crystal and was suddenly reminded of the wedding.

'The cake,' she blurted. 'The wedding's in ten day's time…'

She fetched Delia Smith's cookery book from the kitchen shelf and looked up 'A Rich Fruit Cake'.

She pounded a heavy scales on the counter and got to work.

'I suppose you'll be too busy to talk to me now,' said a chastened Porky amid a flurry of fat, flour and raisins.

The apparition which burst through the kitchen door and straight into Cook's arms for a hug failed to kindle in Porky the basic maternal instinct required to nurture an offspring parading as a streetwise cockatoo in designer-shredded leathers.

'So glad you're back,' enthused Tamarind. 'Oh Cook – do you think you could make us a packed lunch, please? Min and I are off for the afternoon to inspect the Superdrones.'

Cook ignored the Queen of Porschia and handed Tamarind a spoon of the wedding-cake mixture. 'Try that, poppet – it's delicious. Now you just sit down there and have a cup of tea till I prepare a basket for your lunch.'

In an attempt to be included, the Queen of Porschia addressed her daughter: 'Well, dear, how are you and Princess Min getting along?'

Cook sliced bread, whipped a chickpea and garlic spread, packed a carton of olives and two slices of melon, drizzled a plain sponge with lemon juice and iced it. She packed cutlery, wine glasses, a pot of honey and serviettes.

'She's not exactly my dream girl,' said Tamarind, 'if that's what you mean.'

'I didn't mean anything at all,' replied Porky defensively. 'I don't know anything about that sort of thing.'

'Oh come on, Mum, what do you call what's going on between you and Cook then?'

'Business,' retorted the Queen of Porschia.

'*Relationship,*' insisted Tamarind.

'Business relationship,' said Cook, finding space in the basket for a bottle of St Emilion 1985.

'I presume you're not having sex together,' said Tamarind matter-of-factly.

'We most certainly are not,' smouldered Porky.

'Well neither are we – does that answer your question then?'

When Tamarind left, Porky tried to make it up to Cook.

'Perhaps I could give you a hand, what?'

'You never so much as asked me...' trailed off Cook despondently.

Porky got out of her chair and put her arms around Cook's shoulder.

'I meant to, but we were interrupted – tell me now, dear, tell me what you discovered in Zurich,' said Porky conspiratorially.

Cook shook her head and reached for the blue crystal in her pocket. She dropped it into the wedding-cake mix, along with a tear, and stirred it one last time.

'Whatever's the matter?' asked Porky.

'I was very frightened, I thought there were ghosts everywhere,' sobbed Cook, 'And I faced them all for you, and...*us*.'

At first, Tamarind's irreverent attitude to life had been a source of annoyance, not to mention embarrassment, to Min. Yet it had been Tamarind's persistence over the last few days which had led to an ease of friendship between them. They talked about everything, but mostly about love.

Princess Min didn't find it difficult to admit that she wanted to settle down with Gubnet and have a palaceful of pets and children because that thought filled her up with love.

Tamarind admitted that she had never been 'in love'. 'In love' was...

'You and a very special woman, Tam,' was all Min could say to explain it.

The two princesses agreed that they would be firm friends. Their marriage was royal. And that meant they would both be in love with other people. It meant they would help each other out if other people let them down.

They trudged through a muddy field of ewes overwintering on turnips. Princess Min offered to carry the picnic hamper and Tamarind told the story of her childhood.

'Everyone thinks I'm tougher than a punk. And I dress like one to make sure they leave me alone. But the real me is more like these sheep,' said Tamarind poignantly. 'They shut their eyes and dream of grass in the endless winter of their lives. Tell me Min, am I strong enough to survive on dreams alone?'

'What is strength?' questioned Princess Min reflectively. 'When you train in a dojo, Tammy, you enter a state of mind; you take your spirit with you, you respect your worthy opponent – and you never lose. Then Mother Nature organises for you to be raped in your sleep...'

'You should get angry or get even,' urged Tamarind with conviction.

But it wasn't just *anybody* they were talking about. The vagaries of living deities were a hazard of life, like getting run over by a bus.

'Lots of religions have living gods, Tam. The Japs, the Greeks – us – and they all have one thing in common: their gods elect to live on earth. They get up to no good, they make mistakes – just like we do.'

'So how come they never get to pay for them?'

'Maybe they do – in ways we don't understand.'

'Min I'm telling you now, girl, I'm going to confront that cow at the wedding – I'm going to give Her a piece of my mind.'

Min grappled with this idea and laughed. Once upon a time, she vowed to fight Mother Nature herself for Gubnet's honour. And not so long ago it would have been unthinkable to allow another woman to fight for hers...

They picnicked in an ancient circle of holly trees, on top of a sacred mound, surrounded by sheep.

'What are we going to do with your Superdrones once we get married, Min?'

'I'll teach them there's more to life than love,' said Princess Min, whose humour was restored by Cook's excellent hamper.

That afternoon, Cook told Porky that she ought to rethink her plans for the Superdrones in view of what she had learned from Professor Sterne about Ovum-to-Ovum in Zurich.

'I see,' said Porky reasonably, 'but where is the profit to be made in bringing together the eggs of two women in order to produce a *single* female offspring?'

'Humans are not quite like us,' explained Cook patiently. 'They only expect one offspring at a time...'

'The old quality versus quantity argument,' discerned

Porky. 'Still, I can't see our people wanting it. With the Superdrones, all of a Queen's eggs can be fertilised at once, an island's food supply will no longer be depleted and what's more the buggers will work.'

'We've got to expand our horizons, start looking at new vistas, exploit the human population.'

'I take your point. But...'

'What Bee People do you know that have any money?' pressed Cook, 'apart from Porschians? If there's any profit to be made in the Bee World, you can be sure that Mother Nature is going to make it. She's going to force you to retire in favour of Tamarind and you won't see a penny out of the Superdrones.'

Porky knew this was true – but the beauty of her own little ruse was that it was the most expedient route to the inevitable. Hayde Lewis had told her as much the day she arrived back from Ascourt, which was why she had rescued Princess Min who would kick those Superdrones into shape. It was also why she had tricked Mother Nature into agreeing that the wedding should be in Porschia, where She would discover for Herself the wonders of a model island, up and running with Superdrones. Mother Nature would be impressed enough to accept her resignation in exchange for a passport to the comfortable pastures of Florida where she and Cook would graze happily ever after on the ill-gotten gains of Hayde Lewis's Swiss francs...

The Queen of Porschia saw in her own plan the prospect of an easy retirement but a premature coronary. She tugged breathlessly on her choker of pearls. Every one of her tailored frocks was straining against the truth of being fat and forty-something. No indeed! Cook was right. She was far too young to roll over and play dead into Mother Nature's hands.

'We must be ahead of the posse, Porky. You and I. Business relationship. We will be the ones to market Ovum-to-Ovum fertilisation to the human population.'

Cook's idea was an exciting new ball game. Porky shed ten mental pounds and felt fitter than she had for years. It was nothing short of a new lease of life. But deep inside, perhaps in her uterus, she experienced a consumer's resistance to the whole idea of Ovum-to-Ovum.

'Would these humans really want this?' asked the Queen of Porschia incredulously.

'They'd kill for it,' swore Cook.

Porky and Cook spent the afternoon hatching a modified plan while the wedding cake baked itself to perfection.

'We need help, Porky, we can't do this on our own.'

'I'll form a cartel – trusted family and friends only.'

'Now, St Gubnet owns the technology,' went on Cook, 'and when the Princesses Tamarind and Min marry next week, you will rightfully own fifty per cent of any genetic technology in Ascourt, providing you pay the dowry money as agreed.'

Porky's face dropped, 'All five hundred thousand pounds of it? That's my entire life's savings!'

'All of it,' insisted Cook. 'That makes us legal.'

'And if Mother Nature tries to stop us,' enthused the Queen, 'we'll tell Her that Captain McCarthy is on his way to London to inform Lloyds that one of Her own people planted the yacht with explosives!'

'We mustn't forget about Gubnet and Home,' said Cook. 'They may have their own plans for Ovum-to-Ovum, particularly if they win the Nobel prize.'

'Right,' sighed Porky. 'And once Mother Nature gets wind of it…'

'She won't,' said Cook proudly. 'Thanks to my culinary debacle in Zurich, the Ovum-to-Ovum nomination received little or no publicity. But we must act fast. Once we own Ascourt, we'll have the major say-so as to how the technology is used.'

'You mean just like that – we buy Ascourt?' said Porky. 'With what? I have nothing left!'

'With Hayde's money,' whispered Cook. 'The parcel will be here by the end of the week.'

'No,' groaned Porky, 'I'll be a bankrupt after this wedding.'

'We'll be millionaires three times over in a couple of years,' said Cook. 'Ascourt's going cheap, Mother Nature wants shot of it. This is a once-in-a-lifetime opportunity, Porky. It won't come again.'

The Superdrones were over the top at the sight of Princess Min, whom they still addressed as 'Lieutenant'. Min could not help suppressing a wry grin as she ordered, 'No droning, boys,' lest they start up in a chorus of appreciation. They resembled a grateful horde of refugees, too thin and neglected to expand into the empty prison compound allotted them. They were not fit for work; a series of hunger strikes had left them with nothing more than an endearing belief in their hero's return.

The prison's concrete recreation yard led directly into a long low building with cells either side of a cental passage. The doors were not locked. Princess Tamarind inspected each room in turn and was surprised by a constant symmetry and in-built sense of order.

'Didn't you know?' remarked Min, casually expert, 'Superdrones are obsessive tidiers, fastidiously clean – total neurotics.'

'I'd almost think you were fond of them,' teased Tamarind, turning the handle of the last door.

But it was locked. Tamarind looked askance at Min before she slid back the peephole. Inside there was a man sitting on his bed, wrapped in a blanket. Tamarind shrugged her shoulders and stood back for Min to take a look.

'Mum said they didn't have prisoners any more!'

Min stared hard in disbelief.

Princess Min found the central-heating switch and turned it up to high. When the part-time prison warden came on duty later that evening, Min ordered a diet of fresh bananas, honeycomb and yogurt for the Superdrones. She found extra blankets and put them to bed early while Tamarind persuaded the guard to hand over a set of keys. Together they entered the last eight-foot-square cell on the corridor.

'Lieutenant Min,' he smiled weakly.

'Captain McCarthy,' she returned with a firm handshake, 'I thought you were drowned.'

The Captain looked distrustfully at Tamarind, who bore a slight resemblance to her mother.

'It's all right,' reassured Min, 'Tamarind and her mum don't have much in common apart from good looks. I give you my word you can trust us both. '

'Well, the Queen of Porschia comes every day and every day, the same question – What happened to the yacht? And every day I reply, You tell me, it was one of your lot blew it up. Then she says, Who blew it up?, and I say I don't know, and she says That's right, and laughs and off she goes. You tell me.'

Min handed him a blanket and said, 'I'll find out what I can, Captain.'

The Princesses tramped home in the dark of the mid-winter evening. Min told Tamarind about the voyage which had ended in an explosion, the sinking of the yacht and the brave rescue of the passengers and cargo by Porky and her crack helicopter crew. But even the redoubtable Queen of Porschia must have been aware that the Captain's thinly veiled accusations were well founded. Min told Tamarind that only downright pre-science could have had such a well-organised rescue crew onstream within ten minutes of a mayday SOS call.

'She never actually said he drowned, but we all presumed that he did.'

'Mum's up to something,' said Tamarind, 'isn't she?'

Min bit her tongue. *Your mother blew up that boat, Tammy, and I think she knows I'm the only one who can prove it.* Instead, she replied with an abrupt change of subject. 'Some mothers are always up to something. Did I ever tell you that my mother knew our Nanny was a *drone?*'

The Porschian Cartel was officially formed on Sunday, December 15th at a luncheon party at Porky's ranch. The presiding centrepiece was a parcel from Zurich. Dishes and conversation revolved around it like satellites. No pair of eyes could resist its undisturbable allure. It was never once moved.

Porky toasted the Swiss postal service, the forthcoming wedding and the Porschian Cartel. She instructed Hayde Lewis to purchase the island of Ascourt from Mother Nature, using Captain McCarthy as a lever for a fair price. She acknowledged Hayde Lewis's personal contribution to raising the necessary venture capital. Hayde made a gracious speech of acceptance and became a member of the Cartel.

'Nothing ventured, nothing gained, Your Majesty,' she said, enviously eyeing her parcel of Swiss francs.

'You two children just get married – no quarrelling or bickering before the big day. And tidy up those Superdrones, I want them looking predictable and productive at the wedding. From now on, we five are going to be one big happy family. Every penny of profit this Cartel makes is going to be split five ways – right, Cook?'

Cook nodded as she came through the swing doors with a trolley of very hot Bombe Alaska. She had just come off the phone to Professor Louis Sterne in Paris. She winked at Porky. His attendance at the wedding would ensure a comprehensive press coverage of *all* the highlights planned that day. Porky tapped her nose, acknowledging one more detail which would not be shared with the others.

'I can't join the Cartel unless you level with me,' demanded Princess Min. 'For one thing, why are we buying Ascourt?'

'To save our sisters!' cried Porky earnestly.

'To make all our dreams come true,' said Hayde, determined to prove herself an asset in any scheme involving a million punts of her personal cash.

'To get rich,' said Cook, cutting through the fast-melting confection.

'This Cartel is going to break Mother Nature once and for all,' vowed Porky, cracking her knuckles.

'I'm in!' said Tamarind, persuaded on the last count.

'All for one and one for all?' said Porky, raising an eye at her future daughter-in-law.

'All right then, me too,' agreed Princess Min with a hesitant nod. She wondered what she would say to poor old Captain McCarthy. *Family was family, after all?*

CHAPTER SIXTEEN

The Purchase of Ascourt
Monday, December 16, 1996

The row had begun in bed over the terms of their relationship. Had an assumed monogamy evolved over the years or was it simply assumption? The ghost of Yossarian agreed with Princess Vee. Such misunderstandings arose due to lack of communication, and the offending party should have made time to direct an inquiry to base. One might have, came the reply, if a one-sided interaction over the course of five years could be said to amount to a relationship.

Princess Vee was sorry. The haggard looks over the breakfast table were the beginnings of a contrition, not so much for the unkind words of the night before, but rather in a partial empathy for the fact that both were facing into a big day ahead.

She followed Maryann out to the car and wished her good luck at the hearing in Tralee.

'Look it, meet me in The Olde Tea House when you're through yourself,' said Maryann, cajoling the VW into life.

'You're very confident,' said Vee, landing a spit on the rear tyre.

'Well, if I don't make it, bad cess to them and you can visit me behind bars. Good luck yourself.'

'Don't worry about me.'

'Always the big woman for sure,' said Maryann through the purr-Phut-VROOM of the engine.

The injured party shuffled back to the kitchen in a pair of bedroom slippers, rolled up a narrow smoke and bluntly spoke her mind.

'*You* were a great help last night. She thought I was talking to myself, said I was rambling – sure wasn't I having a three-way conversation, thanks to you!'

'If it was a facilitator you wanted,' observed the acrid ghost of Yossarian, 'then you should have told her who you were talking to.'

Princess Vee snorted rudely. 'And just how would I put it to her? The house is haunted, don't you worry, darlin'?'

'If you don't need me then I'll be about the housework and do a little tidying in the parlour,' said Yossarian, ignoring her.

'No, wait – I really would like to know what you think.'

'I think she'll get off scott-free,' said Yossarian, with the benefit of ghostly foresight.

'No, I mean what would you say my chances with Maryann are against Bea?'

Yossarian grimaced. It was not going to be a fun morning. He hovered between the kitchen table and the parlour where his body was laid out.

'Come on now and tell me the truth. Did she really sleep with my sister? I'd nearly tell her I was seeing another woman myself only you're a drone, more's the pity.'

Yossarian draped himself over Vee's shoulder and whispered, 'Maryann thinks you're exciting in bed, OK?'

'I knew it!' swiped Vee angrily. 'They *did* sleep together!'

Yossarian slipped off the chair and left the room with a cleaning rag. Princess Vee was short on respect for other people's misery. His body might rot, or more likely fall apart, before the parlour got a decent dusting.

'I suppose you were watching them, were you?' insinuated Princess Vee loudly.

The unwholesome implication gathered Yossarian into the force of a domestic typhoon which blew him angrily back into the kitchen. He tied himself as tight as a net around his former charge, stuffed the cleaning rag into her mouth and squeezed a little bit harder everytime Princess Vee tried to speak.

An hour later, Princess Vee strode down the hill to catch the bus into Tralee. Yossarian hated walking and bickered all the way. The bus ride was scenic, and the only other passenger on board convinced himself that the red-haired woman talking to herself in the back was the result of a hangover from the night before.

'It was tough being the middle daughter,' confided Vee. 'I was nowhere. Bea got to stay in Ascourt and be Queen. Min

193

was spoiled rotten. Imagine, going to Japan? And I was dumped in a cheap boarding school on the mainland. I ran away, and joined the lads. I've killed a man; that makes you dead inside. I'm a reject, Yossarian – that's what I've lived with every day since I was born.'

Yossarian listened, but he had a lot else on his mind. In a way he wished he hadn't opened this brooding can of worms.

'I act like I'm rejected, I cut myself off. Maryann's been saying it for ages – only I couldn't admit it because I was doing the rejection for her when she wasn't doing it at all. Reject, reject, reject.'

'Oh, quit your snivelling will you?' snapped Yossarian. 'You're lucky to be alive which is more than I can say for myself.'

'Well, why don't we talk about you then?' responded Vee tartly. 'Nothing like a twenty-year relationship with a dead man to put you in touch with reality!'

The passenger in the bus moved back three rows on the pretext of dropping a coin.

'You're afraid to admit that things were better with Peter when he was dead. That's why you can't let go – you'd rather avoid him, wouldn't you? You're too scared to admit that you don't want a relationship with him after all these years.'

Yossarian wept the deeply cleansing tears of a neatly opened wound. It was the first refreshing breath of life after death.

Princess Vee's tears followed an internal route down a damp back alley inside her head.

The eavesdropping passenger blew hard into his crumpled hanky.

The bus fogged up.

'You and I have never liked one another have we?' said Yossarian fumbling with his handbag. 'And maybe that's best, because I'm going to leave now and confront the ghosts of my past. And you are going to Ascourt where your future is. You're needed there, Vee – they can't do this without you. I was the one who sent you the Will, because I knew...'

'You?' said Vee, smacking herself on the forehead. 'Of course!'

'I found a note from Maryann under Bea's pillow. She said she knew you, so I put the Will on her aeroplane and hoped it would reach you.'

'But why me?' implored Vee.

'Because it was meant to be. It's your part in the story of Charlotte's Plan – she said the Will would be safe with you, only no one knew where you were. Now don't ask me any more!'

The bus pulled into Tralee, depositing two passengers and a ghost into a heavy local shower.

'Don't go, Yossarian, I need you for this meeting,' begged Vee alone in the downpour.

'You'll do just fine without me,' said the ex-nanny. 'And don't worry about Maryann, the judge won five numbers in the lottery last night and he'll let everyone go this morning. Now really, Vee, you'll have to get used to the idea of letting me go too!'

Princess Vee felt a tap on her shoulder. 'Excuse me,' said the man, lifting up his umbrella, 'I was on the bus with you and I couldn't help overhearing your chat. Would you mind if I asked your spirit a question?'

Before Vee could fob him off, the empty space beside her answered, 'Rags to Riches, Newmarket, two o'clock.'

'Thanks, missus,' he said, 'I'll remember you in me prayers.'

When Princess Vee looked round, he was gone. And so was the ghost of Yossarian.

Sitting an arm's length away from Her in the solicitor's office, the young woman read over the documents concerning the sale of Ascourt, sat back in the chair beside her own solicitor and sighed an enormous sigh of relief. Mother Nature, in turn, read the independent pathologist's report stating that Yossarian's death was due to a bee-sting delivered in the process of mating. An elisa test for the presence of the BADS virus was negative, although alcohol levels were significant.

Mother Nature read the damning evidence without a single change of expression. It was a matter of *habeus corpus*. Mother Nature had no choice but to agree without quibble to hand over Ascourt lock, stock and barrel, in exchange for Yossarian's body and the report which could ruin Her.

'Blackmail is an unpalatable business at the best of times,' remarked Mother Nature sourly, 'but it is distasteful in the extreme not to know who one is being blackmailed *by*.'

'Q-quite,' said the young woman, appealing to her solicitor for help.

'Let's get on, shall we,' said the solicitor manfully, 'and complete the deal.'

The papers were duly signed and both parties shook hands. Mother Nature leaned forward and brushed Her lips against the face which looked older than its years.

'Tell me something,' whispered Mother Nature, slipping a practised finger up the young woman's trembling forearm, 'how old were you in 1984?'

'I was s-s-six.'

Mother Nature smiled narrowly at Her youthful adversary. Flushing out the last of the little foxes had taken care and patience and, of course, those particular attributes least affected by the erosion of time. A good memory, for one thing. A harelip and a tattoo for another.

'Princess Vee of Ascourt,' purred Mother Nature. 'We meet again.'

Princess Vee stood at the top of the mall, trying to figure out whether The Olde Tea House was to the right or left of the junction, when a black limo pulled up beside her. Mother Nature popped Her head out of the window and said, 'Sorry, sweetie, I forgot to ask you what I should do with your house keys once I'd collected the body.'

Princess Vee felt an invisible coil caressing her neck into a lingering paralysis. Mother Nature possessed the sort of presence that a nest of cobras could only hope to aspire to. It was immediate and disarming. And unwholesomely seductive.

'Under the mat, th-thanks,' stuttered Princess Vee, wishing the ground would swallow her up.

'No, indeed – please accept my thanks,' said Mother Nature, breasting a cleavage. 'A fair exchange is no robbery – you made that very easy for me. A word of advice, perhaps–'

Princess Vee looked down at her shoes and blushed for the first time in her entire life. She would never again do business in odd socks.

'In the matter of solicitors,' advised Mother Nature. 'I'd make it a policy never to hire a man myself.'

Princess Vee ran all the way to The Olde Tea House, where she found Maryann in a state of partial shock.

'I don't quite understand it,' said Maryann breathlessly. 'It was all over in less than fifteen minutes. The judge asked me if the cannabis was for my personal use, and I said yes it was, and then he asked me if I'd ever been attacked, and then he gave a speech and dismissed the case!'

'What did he say exactly?' asked Princess Vee cautiously.

'Tell me your news first,' pressed Maryann excitedly. 'Well?'

'How about a cup of tea for the new owner of Ascourt,' said Princess Vee, biting her lip modestly.

'I don't believe it!' shrieked Maryann, hugging her. 'We've done it!'

Service was an unhurried commodity in The Olde Tea House. Both staff and custom had evolved the art of waiting through a learned compromise. Intimacy was a protracted pleasure, to be unravelled in the secret confines of a warm and timeless booth. Princess Vee watched Maryann speak, the lips fast and impersonal, oblivious to nuance. With scarcely a delay, a fuss of teacakes and crockery arrived, and an arresting pinafore stopped and worked a knowing cloth, briskly removing the embarrassing remains of an unused privilege. The admission was subtle. Princess Vee stowed it away, lifted her elbows from the table and mentally tuned into the conversation.

'The Judge said that an honest government would put a tax on cannabis so the Gardaí could concentrate on serious crimes instead,' said Maryann, 'like rape. He told them that it wasn't good enough to be prosecuting female tax-payers when the streets of Kerry weren't safe enough to walk home in at night.'

'They must have been gobsmacked,' laughed Princess Vee. 'Like that man on the bus today – oh Jeez, that reminds me of something. Have you any money on you?'

With fifty pounds in her pocket, Princess Vee strolled into the bookmakers with a few minutes to spare before the two o'clock at Newmarket. She recognised the bus passenger at the top of the queue placing his bet. He tipped his cap at her and put a bundle of notes on the counter. She winked back at him. Fifty pounds on Rags to Riches at 100/1 was a tidy winnings of five thousand pounds – enough to cover the solicitor and the pathologist's report, and maybe even the purchase of a small boat.

'Don't do it,' came a familiar voice, startling her out of her reveries.

'What's wrong now?' snapped Vee rudely. 'Anyway I thought you'd gone for good.'

The bus passenger put his betting slip into his breast pocket, smiled again at the redhead talking to herself in the queue and sat in the back of the shop with his eyes glued to the telly.

'I'm only thinking of you, dear,' said Yossarian. 'I think you ought to leave before it happens.'

'What happens? What?' fumed Vee impatiently.

'Noble Lad is going to win the two o'clock and it's hardly worth your while at 5/6 on,' hissed Yossarian.

'Why didn't you tell him? He's just put all his money on Rags to Riches,' scolded Vee, 'on your advice!'

'Fortune comes in many a guise, one man's wealth is another's demise. Now get out while the going's good,' urged Yossarian.

Still clutching the borrowed fifty pounds, Princess Vee left the shop and stared disbelievingly at the blank space beside her.

'This had better be good,' she said to the ghost.

'It is. You see the cashier takes pity on him because he loses all his money. Now that's how they meet. Later, she marries him and he gives up gambling for good. Now I really have got to be getting along. I can't keep on rescuing you, Vee. For the last time, your future is in Ascourt. Do try to remember that.'

Princess Vee shook her head, 'You're right. I'll leave first thing tomorrow. Listen, I forgot to ask you – it's just that after our conversation I thought you might have changed your mind. Do you still want a statue next to yer man in Ascourt?'

'Oh yes, near Peter,' whistled the wind, 'where I can keep an eye on him, darling.'

Princess Vee followed the signs for the city carpark where she had agreed to rendezvous with Maryann. The problem was not the future. She relaxed her pace and imagined herself on Ascourt. Her memories of the island were dimmed, but when she shut her eyes she could still hear the rhythmic sound of the waves.

Passing the hotel, she stepped up her pace. Along the main boulevard, the present enclosed her like the defoliated poplars either side of the short stretch of road that was in it. There was no meaning in the here and now. Nothing and no one in her immediate life made sense. The deeper she dug, the more ridiculously complicated the questions became.

She reached the carpark and several decisions simultaneously. Cut and run.

There were few words exchanged between them on the long drive home through the mountains. Princess Vee craned her neck out of the window of the VW, trying to catch a glimpse of the sea below. Maryann studiously concentrated on the road ahead, operating the windscreen wipers with her right hand and a box of Kleenex with the left. It wasn't raining any more, but it should have been. The fine clear weather brought an added level of unreality to the situation. Only the insane or the cruel could have chosen such a moment to pronounce a relationship over. In Maryann's mind, her ex-lover was both.

The front-door keys were under the mat as promised. There were no traces of Mother Nature's visit save that Yossarian's body was gone. An empty feeling sucked the house and its inhabitants of life. There was nothing more to say nor do in the presence of the other. Snatches of conversations started and then drifted into the evening air. For a time they watched the clouds gathering over the sunset, but the ensuing night would make no concessions to the accelerating phenomenon of estrangement.

When Maryann eventually slept, the other prowled the house, collecting a few last precious memories to squeeze into a carry bag which contained, among other items, the garden plans of Charlotte's Will. She slipped the car keys out of Maryann's coat and shut the front door quietly behind her. The VW rolled silently down the hill and contracted into a reassuring bumpstart some minutes later. Alone in the night, her black balaclava pulled down close above her eyes, Princess Vee felt the instinctive call of the wild, the urge to freedom and an unwillingness to deal with reality till it made its inevitable appearance with the dawn. She drove through the night, taking in deep, restorative lungfuls of negative ions. She arrived in Bantry in time for breakfast and a stroll on the pier.

Princess Vee did not notice the black limo with registration plates MNI 1 muscling through Bantry's double-parked main street. But it was a familiar sight to the locals, who scurried about in the hopes that it might stop on its way through. Mother Nature was a popular figure in the area. Her vast industries gave considerable local employment, and supplications to Her generosity were often favourably met.

A village guard of honour formed a simple line into the parlour of the Anchor Bar. With a single wave, Mother Nature indicated that business was the order of the day. The locals were dismissed to a free pint of stout in the public bar.

Her secret rendezvous with the Porschian Island Manager was the talk of the town. In return for one Captain McCarthy and an estimated one million pounds, Ascourt was sold to a cartel headed by the Queen of Porschia. The parlour where this exchange took place had been recently made sound-proof at Mother Nature's personal expense, but the following extract from their conversation made the rounds thanks to a loiterer in the gent's toilet.

'Hayde, let me tell you the difference between a worm and a wyrm. A worm wiggles round until it is caught, put on a hook and fed to the fish. But you are not that kind of ordinary worm. No, you are a special kind of wyrm. So clever that we are left wondering why you wiggle, why you get caught, why you put yourself on a hook and why you are fed to the fish. You are a wyrm with a y who will fool most of the people most of the time, but you will never fool a fish because fish can't spell, Hayde, and I am a very big fish in a very big pond. Do I make myself clear?'

It was midday when Mother Nature's entourage left the sleepy town of Bantry. The owner of the local garage was at pains to explain that he 'never once disturbed the dead body in the Merc', even though the spare tyre was low on air. The publican reckoned Captain McCarthy was 'on something,' but given all the drink he'd consumed down the years, 'sher it was hard to refuse the poor divil a pint.' And as the veracity of a man of the cloth was beyond question, everyone agreed with the parish priest that the whole charabanc was headed for Lloyds of London, 'dead body and all.'

Unaware of the morning's events, Princess Vee negotiated a passage to Ascourt on an unlicensed fishing vessel sometime after lunch.

With her eyes fixed on the indescribable beauty of the peninsulas and islets around them, Princess Vee attempted to settle the past and secure the future. She would tell Bea about her five-year relationship with Maryann. They would console one another as sisters do. Ascourt's future depended on the strength of the three sibling bonds. There was no mention of girlfriends in their mother's Will. They should stick up for one another. Blood runs thicker than water.

These comforts held until land disappeared and the small boat plunged itself into deeper waters. Princess Vee was not a sailor born, and many unwanted thoughts were dredged up from the pit of her stomach. One of these was that she had not said goodbye, another was the fact of stealing Maryann's car. The worst of it was Maryann's insistence from the beginning that she find her roots and deal with the past. Operation Charlotte was conceived and Maryann applied for the horti-culturalist's post on Ascourt in order to retrieve the Will. In fact if it hadn't been for Maryann's support and courage, she probably wouldn't be on this boat, finally going home after twelve lost years. The nocturnal flight of the night before lost its sparkle. A miscreant wave slapped her face with a fresh salty sting, rebuking a cowardly act of ingratitude.

She was well and truly trapped on a sea between two unknowns. The mysterious future which lay in Ascourt had been secured through months of meticulous planning. Yet that past which led to this future was clouded by the memory of Mother Nature inexplicably mocking all her efforts. In a calm swell, Princess Vee pondered on Yossarian's words: ...*it was always meant to be*. For a moment she thought she could just make out the shape of an island ahead. For a moment she allowed herself to let go of both past and future, and in that moment she felt strangely whole and right. But it was too much like fate – that concept designed to keep mindless puppets on their strings. She could not accept it.

The boat cut its motor and drifted towards the harbour.

Princess Vee choked back the tears. It was a frightening moment: the long-dreamed-of homecoming, the stuff of nightmare and fantasy alike. Her eyes re-absorbed the blanked-out spaces and restored the faded outline of a six-year-old's memory. She felt the magic of the island all over her skin. She breathed it in, she bit her lip, she remembered, she forgot, she shook her head and finally let out a whoop of delight.

The couple coming down the long hill towards the harbour waved frantically at her. Princess Vee waved back at them. The shock didn't register fully until some few minutes later when she was standing beside them, openly weeping on the pier.

'We've been expecting you,' said Maryann, cheerfully tossing her long dark curls. 'Vee, meet your older sister, Bea.'

The introduction was awkwardly formal. Princess Vee was stunned by the ease and familiarity between Maryann and Queen Bea. She sensed she was dealing with an immoveable and united force. She was visiting their relationship. The real reunion had already happened.

'Sorry, Vee, but I didn't see much point in staying either,' explained Maryann gently. 'I've told Bea all about us, and, well…life goes on.'

'But I took the car…' spluttered Vee. 'How on earth did you get here before me?'

'I'm the one who flies,' chided Maryann humorously, 'remember?'

CHAPTER SEVENTEEN

The Laboratory in the Convent for the Keepers of Bees

Wednesday, December 18, 1996

The radical restructuring of the Convent in Balleyvourney had spawned a tripartite caste system over which Mother Nature ruled without compromise. But Heron Home was neither prisoner, prison guard nor domestic staff.

In words described to her through the offices of power, Heron was classified as a special voluntary worker in the ultramodern laboratories of MNI (Balleyvourney). She ate, slept and woke in the basement complex where laboratory machines hummed and flickered, and the only sign of human life was the steely eye of the guard – an eye inflexible as the regime imposed upon them both. She suffered sensory deprivation in the airless, windowless ambience of a technological amphitheatre. It predisposed an even larger gap between her normal right–left brain discrepancy. The lights were never dimmed; the post-modern clock was unable to reveal its position either post or ante the meridian.

In terms plainly outlined through the offices of an ICI laboratory calendar, Heron Home classed herself as an un-remarkable convent prisoner of approximately one week's inexperience.

Throughout the seven indistinguishable nights and days, Heron had dreamed of her death, only to be answered each time by a familiar voice in her head: *Your work is with Mother Nature. Cooperate with Her*. And Heron had. At the far end of the laboratory, an incubator bleeped a mechanically pitched reminder. Twenty-two batches of Superdrones were about to be hatched. Against her will and better judgement. This was no mere game of survival. Charlotte's Dream surged through her veins like a nightmare, and she was being kept alive to fulfil it.

All at once, Heron's head felt light and dreamy. She reset the thermostat and turned towards a spinning centrifuge in the certain knowledge that something important depended on it. While the hatching Superdrones cooled down, Heron switched off the centrifuge and discreetly removed from it four test tubes containing spun-down genetic material from a broken fingernail which had come into her possession by way of an intended strangulation, and whose owner was unaware of the secrets which Heron intended to eke from it.

The tiny strands of genetic material, flushed from their keratinous casing, would provide the answer to a hitherto undreamed of speculation: was or was not Mother Nature a member of the species *Homo sapiens*?

Heron took a magician's delight in the speed of the genetic gadgetry, but considered the question carefully before looking down the microscope to where the answer now lay. She reassured herself that this extramural line of enquiry, conducted at Mother Nature's expense, was not some elegant means of survival by which she was surreptitiously defying her captor. She raised an eyebrow at the guard, challenging him to acknowledge that a game was at hand. He was a monolith of indifference.

Heron shrugged and looked down the microscope. She counted the wriggling chromosomes and photographed them. They were decidedly and anticlimactically human. It occurred to her that she must have known this all along. After all, if Mother Nature didn't have chromosomes, and human chromosomes at that, then how on earth could Gubnet have performed a genetic merging between them? Hadn't Mother Nature Herself always said, *You are creations in my own image?*

Heron shook her head and grunted disagreeably. In truth, she was no more capable of asking a stupid question than she was of answering the paradoxical finding of a genetic experiment which she had just performed for no good reason known to herself.

Was it more disturbing that Mother Nature, a living deity, was proved inconsequentially human by experiment, or that

Heron Home, a human being, was proved insane by virtue of the need for inconsequential experiment?

It was true she had been hearing voices. Charlotte's, Yossarian's, Banba's, a host of others. Somewhere between her right and left brain lay a wide-open space which was destined to be filled by an indiscriminate assortment of external psychic suggestion. Was it possible that she was picking up on someone else's train of thought? Was her mind being used by a person or persons unknown? But who? And why?

Heron put the negatives of Mother Nature's chromosomes into her coat pocket. She cleared away the evidence of her experiment like a robot. *I am just a pawn in someone else's karma,* she muttered confusedly. The guard unlocked the door and brought in lunch. Shrimps and chips.

Mother Nature arrived back to the Convent in Balleyvourney after a long and exhausting trip involving perjury, double-dealing and international business. She locked the door to Her office, kicked off Her shoes and replaced the dreaded PC on Her desk with an antique abacus.

Mother Nature counted out the sack of Swiss francs which She had received from Hayde Lewis on Tuesday, December 16th at the Anchor Bar, Bantry. She performed a complicated conversion, flicking rows of beads and revealing that in exchange for Captain McCarthy, the Porschian Cartel had bought the island of Ascourt for the equivalent of just under IR£1m.

For his freedom and a new identity, Captain McCarthy had lied to the investigators at Lloyds of London, assuring them that the yacht was sunk due to bad weather. Mother Nature reset the rows of counting beads, fished out the insurance cheque from Her brassière, performed a conversion and added a figure of ten million pounds to the profits thus far calculated.

Mother Nature grimaced at the losses of Her two-day whirlwind operation. Yossarian's cremation had come to IR£650. The cost of obtaining a falsified government report certifying that the cause of death was due to the BADS virus was a staggering IR£25,000. The beads of the abacus were uncompromisingly accurate. Mother Nature moved on.

The neat brown envelope tucked into Her bodysnug corset contained twenty-two cheques in twenty-two denominations representing the first twenty-two international orders for Superdrones. The beads whirled, quivered and came to rest, confirming initial payments to MNI of IR£5m.

There was one last debt. IR£9.99, as stated on the chemist's receipt for the purchase of one pregnancy-testing kit. Mother Nature wrote down the net profit on a scrap of paper, put away Her abacus and unscrewed a sample jar of urine. She followed the test instructions to the letter. The result confirmed Her worst suspicions.

Mother Nature left Her office with Charlotte's Will, the pregnancy-testing kit and the sample of urine. She swept past the guard, pushed the buttons for the security code and entered the basement laboratory complex to find Dr Heron Home removing tiny Superdrone larvae from the hexagonal incubators.

'Real work is so fulfilling, Heron, don't you think?' said Mother Nature, genuinely pleased at the progress. 'Now, dear, would you do a pregnancy test on this sample of Princess Min's urine and confirm it for me *in situ*.'

'But how did you get this?' stumbled Heron anxiously.

'Hayde Lewis,' said Mother Nature, appraising the reaction, 'my contact in Porschia. She's playing a rather dangerous game of being a double agent, wouldn't you say?'

'Princess Min is in Porschia?'

Mother Nature unscrewed the sample jar and impatiently handed Heron a coloured cardboard stick.

'Dip!' She ordered in a testy falsetto.

As the negative result came as no surprise to either of them, Mother Nature looked narrowly at Her recalcitrant employee, who timidly looked away from Her. But She had seen the evidence for Herself. Yossarian's genitals were severed from his body and his abdomen carried the mark of a royal female sting. He had carried out his part of the bargain. *But perhaps...*

'He mated with Queen Bea instead of Princess Min, by mistake,' suggested Mother Nature even-temperedly. 'You will have to learn to co-operate with me, Heron. I am sick of this weary fandango of childish half-truths and tiresome lies. The truth, Heron!'

Heron remained absolutely still. The blood supply to her

brain pounded out the awful mantra. *Your work is with Mother Nature. Cooperate with Her.* The pressure behind her eyeballs mounted. Tell the truth and betray Ascourt. Tell a lie and Mother Nature would read it straight from her eyes. Nothing could be hidden from Her.

'The truth,' said Heron, holding onto the desk, 'is Yossarian raped Princess Min, on your orders.'

'Then why isn't she pregnant?' screamed Mother Nature in blind rage.

'Because Princess Min is sterile,' confessed Heron, sinking into the seat beneath her.

'My eldest, B,' read out Heron from the book handed to her by Mother Nature, 'is blessed with wisdom, she is older than her years. She will rule with vision as Queen. Listen and obey all she says. My middle daughter, V, now she is the Shaman. Under her rule, Ascourt will never come to harm. Question not her actions, for all she does is for the protection of this island. My youngest, M, will be the Mother of the future generation of Ascourt. She will conceive and abundantly bear forth my dream. Under her rule, Ascourt will overflow with bounty and joy. These three – '

'Stop there,' instructed Mother Nature, drawing her nose up to Heron's until the two women eyeballed one another. The Will specifically stated that the youngest daughter, Min, would reproduce and become Mother of the future generation of Ascourt. And up to this point, She had facilitated them. She had located Min; She had even arranged for the young Princess to become pregnant. Many eons ago She learned that force was best directed through its most natural channel.

'Heron,' She whispered, 'I have been wondering about the significance of these lines. There is more intelligence in my little finger than in all of you put together. The game is up. I have been labouring under the impression that Min was M. Well, clearly she is not.'

'We don't know which of them is which, either,' trembled Heron, 'honestly we don't. No one does, not even the Princesses themselves…'

Mother Nature rapped Her knuckles like a pistol-shot on the desk. 'You are trying my patience! The one who can have babies is M. Haven't you heard of fertility testing?'

'No use,' said Heron logically. 'They're *all* sterile…'

'These three will rule together as one,' continued Heron, reading aloud as Mother Nature paced the laboratory, 'but the Essence of the Rule of Three can only be revealed when each one, B, V and M, finds out her true name. They will gain the Seven Rules of Creation and Mother Nature will bless them Herself. Only then will the New Order be born.'

Mother Nature came to a halt beside the desk and acerbically summed up Her thoughts. 'So there are three princesses, one of whom will be mother of Ascourt, none of whom knows her actual identity, and all of whom are infertile. Do you really expect me to buy that one little island can cause so much trouble over an idea as ridiculous as this?'

'It does sound implausible,' agreed Heron, putting down the book, 'but what's to say it's not possible?'

'It's not possible because I will not agree to it,' said Mother Nature, firmly gripping Her employee by the collar of her regulation white laboratory coat. It wasn't the obvious that was bothering Her. Charlotte's Dream was among the top three thorns in Her side. But now it was imperative that Charlotte's Dream go no further. Ascourt remained stubbornly impervious to the fact that their Dream could not happen unless She, Creator and Goddess Herself, endorsed it.

'I will not bless them, Heron, don't you see?' She said, applying an even pressure to the collar bone under Her fingers.

'But it says that you will, when the three Princesses get together,' squirmed Heron.

'I knew you'd see it my way,' said Mother Nature, casually brushing a speck of dust off Heron's lapel, 'which is why we must ensure that they don't get together – ever.'

'We won't have a batch of Superdrones ready for the wedding. No matter. Princess Tamarind may not be ready to mate until she has completed a proper period of mourning,' resumed Mother Nature ruthlessly. 'And since we cannot identify which Princess is which, then one of them will have to go. The only one with any reasonable chance of turning up to her own wedding is Min, so Min is the obvious choice. Now consider this, Heron – the afternoon of the wedding, I will see to it that

Princess Min gets a special glass of her favourite imported chrysanthemum tea, spiked with digitalis. There will be no traceable cause of death. Ascourt's dream will go to the grave with her. The young widow Tamarind will soon realise the importance of her own Superdrones, as quickly as we can get them to her. She will be Queen of a model island and richly rewarded, like her foolish mother once was before her. Maybe they will all learn the lesson at last. What I say goes. There is only one Way.'

Mother Nature showed no hint of regret, guilt or remorse. She was a cosmic force applying itself in a straight line, like a river. Some people get drowned.

'Straighten up, Heron, and repeat the company motto after me,' said Mother Nature sternly. 'Productivity and Profitability – The Modern Way of the Bees. This little chat has been very reassuring, dear. Never forget you are a trusted employee. I know you will be very happy here, doing an honest day's work, helping to create a valuable and viable future for us all.'

The work in the laboratory was routine and boring. The thought of an entire life spent in the service of a Superdrone culture was more than she could bear. In the moments which flicker between the pulse of life, Heron found herself staring into the past. The sight of Charlotte and Yossarian were so clear to her – but where were they now? She remembered Peter, and oh, how important and epoch-making it all was then. The past was alive to her. The future was the moribund eye of the guard.

Heron watched herself move mechanically around the spacious laboratory. She was disappearing on a magic carpet, relinquishing the controls over the body below her. But a slow, persistent spiral of thought ascended into her mind: *Your work is with Mother Nature. Cooperate with Her.*

Thinking about it, she suddenly found herself back in reality, contemplating a plug in her hand. If the future of Ascourt depended on Mother Nature, then what if she, Heron Home PhD, was here to make Mother Nature agree with Ascourt, so that Charlotte's Dream would succeed? Heron felt instinctively guilty. Tampering with the plans of a Creator was hubris. And such acts of mortal arrogance did not go unpunished by the gods. But the truth, as ever, was even less palatable. She no longer cared, and much less still believed, that she was anything other than superfluous to the New Order.

She existed, lived and breathed – the eternal wait of a fly sacrificed on a web. Had Yossarian felt this too? And there was something else she couldn't quite put a finger on. It was as if some other future harkened like the oceanic urgings of a landlost seashell. She listened intently for its faint call. Nothing else mattered. She was wooing death and a life beyond.

But the courtship between Heron Home and death was short-lived. Without warning, the plug in her hand exploded 220 lethal volts, flinging her body clear across the room.

'My dears, we've killed her,' said Clemis regretfully.

The Old Dames crowded round Heron's body while Dame Meleka, the herbalist, tried to find a pulse and initiate emergency resuscitation procedures.

'She's hanging on by a thread,' cried Dame Meleka, 'we may have a chance.'

After several rib-cracking attempts, the heart of Heron Home resumed with a thump.

'She'll be fine,' reported Dame Meleka, 'but she's had a terrible shock.'

'I'll say,' said Dame Toplis, looking accusingly at Dame Montague.

'That's hardly fair,' retorted Montague, who was in possession of the Powerpoint. 'There's bound to be operational problems with new technology.'

Dame Murphy, an engineer at heart, agreed. 'You see, our Powerpoint happened to make an exact fit with the plug in Heron's hand. An unfortunate coincidence, really…'

'Dame Meleka, you must expedite her recovery. We've rather a lot to do,' urged Dame Clemis.

'Try this,' said Dame Agnetha with her ever-ready vial of Bach's Rescue Remedy.

In her capacity as owner of Swann's Hotel, Dame Thwaites took it upon herself to organise refreshment while the others brought Heron back to life.

'Porter!' she cried, tapping on the plate glass to catch his attention, 'open this door immediately!'

The guard undid the safety catch of his revolver and towered over the head of Dame Thwaites.

'What's goin' on in there?' he said, straining his eyes at the sight of a bunch of elderly women.

'Doctor Home has had an electric shock and is receiving medical aid,' reported Dame Thwaites matter-of-factly.

'Who are you, then?' he growled down at her.

'We are a group of very hungry Old Dames,' she replied, 'and we have a long day ahead of us.'

The guard tensed his biceps and tightened the grip on his revolver.

'My good man, kindly see to it that we are brought tea for eight people and a round of tomato sandwiches,' she said, undeterred by his feral attitude.

The guard blinked.

'You'll be wanting a pepper mill then,' he said, checking with her before he locked the door. 'Security, ma'am. I won't be two ticks.'

Montague showed Heron the Powerpoint and explained to her how it worked.

'First we visualised you, and then we wished ourselves into your presence. I'm the only one it'll work for, though,' said Dame Montague proudly.

'That's not quite true, Monty,' interrupted Dame Toplis. 'As you are well aware, it doesn't seem to work unless there is a unilateral agreement about the purpose to which we apply it.'

'Which is why we are here,' hinted Dame Agnetha.

'In a roundabout sort of way,' muttered Dame Murphy, who preferred straight lines herself.

'Well, actually we fancy our chances at the Irish Bridge Teams-of-Four,' put in Dame Thwaites, 'which begins at seven-thirty this evening in Dublin.'

Heron moved her head like a tennis spectator with a hangover.

'The point is,' began Clemis, as elder spokesperson, 'well, the point is that they agreed to our going to the bridge championships on the condition that we do St Gubnet a favour – '

'See here, Heron,' said Montague, holding up the

211

Powerpoint. 'We think we may have been stranded in the Underworld. We're three weeks behind.'

'Which we'd never have realised if Queen Bea's girlfriend hadn't turned up when she did,' put in Dame Toplis. 'Right, Monty?'

'Thing is,' continued Dame Montague, ignoring the jibe, 'we promised to get back to Ascourt in time to get the others to the wedding, and if we get through to the bridge finals, we could be cutting things very fine.'

Dame Meleka pragmatically assisted Heron to her feet and propped her up against the incubator. She waved two sample jars in front of Heron, who remained safely wedged between Dames Agnetha and Murphy.

'Gubnet asked that you make a chromosome map from this sample, which is from her body, and this smaller one here, which is the baby's. She said you'd need a chromosome map for Mother Nature as well, but she wasn't sure how you'd get it. We promised to deliver the lot to Professor Louis Sterne in Paris before we played the tournament tonight. That's it!'

'I've got the negatives of Mother Nature's chromosomes in the pocket of my lab coat!' said Heron in amazement. It was a relief to think that at least some part of her recent cerebral chaos could be attributed to the Old Dames Breakfast Club.

'But what's it all about?' asked Dame Toplis. Biology was not her thing in life. Assisting Dame Meleka and Delia du Pont with their first-ever joint amniocentesis was a recent experience she cared not to repeat.

'If Professor Sterne has the chromosome maps of Mother Nature and St Gubnet, then he can prove beyond a doubt that they are both the parent's of St Gubnet's child,' explained Heron.

'But why would Gubnet want him to do that, I wonder?' asked Dame Murphy.

'The less we talk, the faster we work,' said Clemis school-marmishly.

'Let us prepare for our tea, shall we? The Porter will be arriving any minute now,' said Dame Thwaites, clearing a laboratory bench.

'Porter?' exclaimed Heron. 'That man is a hired assassin without a trace of human emotion. Dame Thwaites, he is a dangerous animal.'

'Correct,' asserted Dame Thwaites. 'Extraordinarily responsive to a tone of authority.'

Heron had prepared and photographed three sets of chromosome maps by the time the Old Dames finished their feast. Dame Agnetha gave her an extra long hug.

'No time for tearful goodbyes,' prompted Dame Clemis. 'We really must go.'

Heron waved and the Old Dames concentrated on the Powerpoint.

'Cardinality and motive force,' hummed Dame Murphy the navigator. 'Think of your direction and will yourself there.'

'Wait a minute,' cried Heron, 'how can you play bridge with seven people?'

'Gosh,' said Dame Meleka, breaking her concentration. 'You're right Heron. At home, we play three-handed bridge, but you can't do that in an official competition!'

'Do you play the light or the strong no trump?' asked Heron, hinting at a certain prowess in card play.

Dame Agnetha stroked her cheek. 'Oh, love, don't think we hadn't considered asking you to play. It's just that – '

'The Powerpoint cannot accommodate travel arrangements for any persons who were not involved in our period in the Underworld,' explained Dame Montague, Official Keeper of the Device.

Clemis shook her head and ruefully agreed: 'It wouldn't work for Princess Vee either.'

'That's right,' said Dame Murphy. 'Princess Vee will have to fly to the wedding – '

'In Maryann's plane,' snickered Montague. 'Bea's very upset about it!'

'Oh do stop it, Montague,' snapped Dame Clemis, 'I'm sure Heron isn't interested in the latest palace gossip.'

'I might have been in the Underworld,' speculated Heron earnestly. 'The most peculiar things have been happening to me lately.'

'I don't think so,' said Dame Agnetha kindly. 'You see, while we were in the Underworld, Princess Vee and Maryann came to Ascourt and took Yossarian's body, and then the Queen of Porschia left us a note that she had come for Princess Min, and by the looks of things, Mother Nature must have kidnapped you.'

'Never mind then,' said Heron, filling with tears. 'Safe trip, eh? See you soon!'

'Very soon,' promised Dame Agnetha, blowing her a kiss.

The Old Dames positioned themselves once again for take-off. Dame Murphy issued the flight instructions.

'Now let's see, yes. Paris. Forty-eight degrees and fifty-two minutes north, and two degrees and twenty minutes east.'

Montague raised the Powerpoint but the Dames remained firmly in the laboratory.

'Why don't you visualise the Eiffel Tower?' said Heron, pointing it out on the ICI laboratory calendar. 'It's actually quite close to the Institute for Genetics.'

'The Eiffel Tower,' reiterated Dame Toplis. 'One, two...six!'

When the guard next looked through the plate glass doors, he saw the empty prospect of his future with Mother Nature International. Every last one of the women had disappeared.

'Pinch me,' said Heron to Agnetha.

'Takes a bit of getting used to,' shouted back Dame Agnetha.

'How fast are we travelling?' cried Heron.

'At the speed of light,' bellowed Dame Murphy.

'I think I know where Professor Sterne's office is,' said Heron as they slowed over Paris a few minutes later. 'We could be out of here in half an hour.'

'Excellent,' said Dame Clemis. 'We'll wait for you here at the Tower.'

'I think it would be best if Dame Montague accompanied me,' requested Heron sensibly. 'The Powerpoint might be handy in view of unforeseen hazards.'

Dressed in a blue robe and Adidas footwear, Dame Montague du Pont felt at home in the streets of Paris. Chic black numbers hooted mobilettes in deference to her style and *savoir-faire*. Dr Heron Home, PhD, strolled easily, taking in the sunset and a newfound sense of freedom.

'I must have been in the Underworld after all, Monty,' she said. 'I couldn't have got here otherwise.'

Montague waved her Powerpoint at three women sitting on a bench.

'*Electricité!*' they giggled.

214

'Monty,' interrupted Heron awkwardly, 'I rather asked you along so that you might fill me in on the palace gossip actually...'

'The Nobel Prize for Ovum-to-Ovum?' stammered Dr Heron Home. 'But how did you get in touch with St Gubnet?'

'Simple,' beamed Professor Sterne. 'I met the Cook in Zurich. There I asked her to relay the good news to Gubnet when she got back to Ascourt. *Voilà*, and now you have come with the proof at last!'

'But Cook left Ascourt after the céilí,' said Dame Montague, 'and, to my certain knowledge, hasn't been in touch with any one of us since.'

Professor Sterne threw up his hands and shook his head in amazement. 'It is a mystery. But these negatives are exactly what we need to convince the Nobel Committee to announce the names of Gubnet, Home and Sterne on December twenty-first,' he said excitedly, 'in alphabetical order, of course.'

'But that's the day of the wedding,' remembered Dame Montague.

'Something's up,' mumbled Heron inaudibly.

'You both know – but of course!' seized Professor Sterne eagerly. 'I thought that Cook phoned me in the strictest confidence. Pah! I have done everything she asked! We three, Gubnet, Home and Sterne, will be in Porschia attending the wedding. And what if we win? Of course – the Swedes must be prepared! The Nobel Committee have thus agreed to a live satellite linkup in case...!'

It was seven twenty-seven p.m. when the Old Dames and Dr Heron Home arrived at the doors of the Shelbourne Hotel in Dublin. The President of the Bridge Club arrived three minutes later.

'You see, we're not late!' hissed Dame Thwaites defensively.

'We're three minutes early,' said Dame Toplis, agreeing with her partner.

After an excellent night of bridge, Dames Thwaites and Toplis were not among their colleagues enjoying gin and tonics at the bar.

'They've gone to their rooms,' reported Heron. 'They were

too tired to join us.'

'Well, they wouldn't dare after what they did to us in Paris,' swaggered Montague with two grand slams to her credit.

'Quite a to-do,' agreed Dame Murphy, 'although their choice of café was excellent, I must admit.'

'It was on the other side of Paris,' snapped Clemis. 'The metro took nearly an hour if I remember correctly.'

'Oh, but it was heavenly,' said Dame Meleka, remembering the croissants which had all but melted in her mouth.

'They held us up to ransom with their demands to loiter in Paris,' agitated Dame Montague, testing her recent rise in the pecking order. 'They jeopardised the entire competition. They knew we couldn't go anywhere without them. We damn nearly didn't get here at all.'

'That's true,' agreed Dame Agnetha gently, 'but we are a democratic club and – '

'A democratic continuum,' put in Dame Clemis.

'It is not democratic if a minority can dictate to the majority,' countered Dame Montague, recalling the rudiments of a political philosophy, 'it is socialist.'

'Well done, Dame Montague, you have grasped our Essence: – *and so to each according to her needs*,' said Dame Agnetha, damping the fires of the young pretender.

CHAPTER EIGHTEEN

Princess Vee's Garden

Thursday, December 19, 1996

Despite Maryann's repeated requests for more private accommodation, Queen Bea would not return to the north wing for fear of Yossarian's ghost. She felt safer in the makeshift lovenest of the smoking room, whose door could be clearly seen from the kitchen. Bea's sole source of unrest stemmed from the unsettling revelation that Maryann's former lover was none other than her long-lost sister, Princess Vee.

Maryann could not relax while Princess Vee was within earshot of them. There would be no respite as long as Vee was thundering around in her hobnail boots, banging their door with a clapped-out brush and pan. Maryann was convinced they would get no rest until Bea was able to accept her own part in the *mènage à trois* and stop blaming other people's pasts for her own difficulties with the present.

The winter weather had taken its toll in terms of progress not yet made on the landscaping, planting and building of Princess Vee's garden. The ground was soft and the rain was mixed with sleet, and this second morning in a row, St Gubnet and Princess Vee breakfasted alone in the palace kitchen.

'I take it they're sleeping in again,' remarked Gubnet, who was not a one to ignore the obvious.

It was possible that Vee did not hear her. The rain clanged on to the makeshift tin roof of the kitchen, hurled itself into rusting gutters and gurgled its way forcibly into every congested pore of soil.

What St Gubnet saw across the breakfast table was a solitary young woman with a nervous constitution, dry skin and tangled hair. Princess Vee was underweight, unwashed and unaware that, after two days on Ascourt, her threadbare

217

pullover had assumed a nondescript shade of green.

Gubnet reflected that Princess Vee lacked the essential skills of survival in a cold and draught-ridden palace. On such a morning, it was essential to brush one's hair before breakfast and apply buckets under leaks in the roof after it. Winter maintenance and repair was not glorious work, but it got one through the dismal fog of your average personal tragedy.

'Do you want me to tell you what your problem is, Vee?' needled Gubnet.

'I'm bored and I'm angry,' shot Vee at the one person she had come to admire since her arrival in Ascourt.

'I can cure the boredom,' said Gubnet, handing her a bucket, 'and I can give you some advice about your anger, if you care to listen.'

'What can you possibly say to me that I don't already know?' said Vee with a miserable acid rising in her throat. 'I'm angry because I'm rejected? I'm not stupid. But what am I supposed to do about it? They do nothing but bonk and I can't get away from it 'cos it's done nothing but rain since I got here.'

'Maybe that's why it's raining outside,' nudged Gubnet kindly.

'So now it's my fault it's raining,' said Vee darkly.

'Oh Vee love, of course not,' said Gubnet, squeezing her shoulder. 'I've been here too long and I forget how the rest of the world lives. You see, on Ascourt we would each of us take it for granted that the rain meant something special. The Old Dames call it the Essence.'

'As I see it, the rain came essentially so's that Maryann and Bea could stay in bed for forty-eight hours.'

'And,' held Gubnet, 'so that you were brought closer to your real feelings.'

'I *am* angry, can't you see?'

'No, love, I can't. I think you need to get angrier,' said Gubnet with concern. 'Because if it wasn't raining outside, you'd probably be digging the garden and be just as controlled as you are now. Frankly, if you are angry, then be angry.'

Princess Vee held herself in check. She took her time, formulating the right words to explain her predicament. She needed desperately to confess something and be understood.

'Gubnet, there is anger and anger,' she said slowly. 'I once killed a man in blind fury.'

'No one just kills in blind fury,' said Gubnet. 'Something must have been going on between you and this man, something that was building – '

'All right,' admitted Vee, 'you've got a point.'

'Of course I have. Anger is only safe as long as it's fresh. It's the stale stuff that's poisonous.'

'Maybe you're right,' conceded Princess Vee uncertainly.

'A fire cannot rage in the rain. Not today, anyway. Trust me, sister, I'm a red-head too.'

'Right then, you'd best get out of the way,' said Vee steering her pregnant adviser out through the kitchen door.

'I'll be in Cook's old bedroom if you need me,' replied Gubnet stoutly.

Tangled in the asphyxiating warmth of a deeply knotted cocoon, the two bodies paused in sympathy with another heartbeat whose more metallic quality reverberated audibly outside the room. It was an intrusive rhythm, not of their making yet in complete accord with a third-party agenda throwing pots around the kitchen on their behalf.

'Was I that bad last night?' asked Bea intrepidly of her inamorata.

'Oh darling,' said Maryann tactfully groping for the right words, 'these things take time, don't you think?'

'I wouldn't know,' admitted Queen Bea honestly. 'I was hoping you might give me a few pointers...'

'It's not about technique,' sighed Maryann, closing her eyes. 'I wish it would stop raining.'

Queen Bea sat up among the cushions and blankets and vowed to herself that she would do everything to make Maryann happy. She was in love with the tall, handsome horticulturalist. She stroked the perfect curls on her lover's forehead and wished they would never be straight. She was deeply in love with the woman who flew to Ascourt in a glider. She nuzzled the strong brown hand against her cheek. She was a Queen in love with Maryann Leaf, mother of two and former lover of...

'Was Vee good in bed?' probed Bea, delicately kissing a temple.

'It was good for us both while the passion lasted,' murmured Maryann testily.

'And then your passion ran out?' tendered Bea grazing an ear.

'Actually *her* passion ran out,' snapped Maryann. ' And it was a long time before I could admit to the fact.'

'And when was that?'

'When I first laid my eyes on you, Bea.'

An ominous, magnetic silence emanated from the kitchen across the hall. The two lovers faced each other in the deadly calm that bespeaks the eye of the storm.

'You still want her, don't you?' accused Bea suddenly.

'What's that supposed to mean?'

'You're in love with us both,' challenged Bea. 'It's my personality and her body, isn't it?'

'Bea, give us a chance! Maybe my body does still want her, but the rest of me certainly doesn't.'

'Well, I'm not going to share you with her!' cried Bea adamantly.

'Your insecurity is most unattractive,' hissed Maryann across the cushion between them.

'Nothing about me is attractive to you,' cried Bea wildly, 'and it's just too bad that I'm useless in bed, isn't it?'

'You know the last person I slept with who was as concerned about their performance as you are was a man,' replied Maryann sarcastically.

'What are you doing in here then?' screamed Bea hysterically. 'Get out!'

'Right if that's your attitude – '

'Not you – them!'

But it was too late. The lovers were caught by an icy-cold tubful of water, flung into their nest courtesy of Princess Vee, who was aided and abetted by St Gubnet, standing against the door with her arms smugly crossed.

'Now fucking get out of that fucking bed,' ordered Vee furiously. 'I'm fucking sick of it. You're both so fucking selfish.'

Just as the two lovers flapped about in the frozen wet of inaction, shock and mutual helplessness, so Princess Vee's rage transformed into grief when confronted by the scene of their actual intimacy. She turned to St Gubnet, who wiped her tears with a clean hanky and led her reassuringly to the window.

'See? What did I tell you?' she said by way of encouragement. 'It's stopped raining – look!'

'I think they're trying to tell us something,' confided Bea to Maryann who was furiously shaking the wet out of her hair.

'It's time to begin work on Princess Vee's Garden,' said Gubnet giving no quarter.

'Are there any dry knickers in the laundry, Gubnet?' asked Bea off-handedly.

'Tell her there's no toothpaste either,' whispered Maryann, nudging Bea.

'If it's a nursery yez want,' said St Gubnet with an edge of flint in her voice, 'then from now on, you will all make your beds, do your chores and be fully dressed for breakfast which will be served at eight-thirty a.m. There is to be no smoking at the table. Have I made myself quite clear?'

Having set her three charges to preparing breakfast, Gubnet strolled out into the fresh air where she encountered a giant rainbow lounging in the garden. She felt Athena's reaction before she felt her own. The child stretched. She was two people now. It was three times the joy. There was even room in her heart for Mother Nature and Princess Min, who had both abandoned her for destinies of their own making. The sea all round her was calm with the fullness of rain. Nature asserted its unimpeachable right to bestow one perfect moment. St Gubnet was transported.

'Coo-eee,' puffed the bright yellow turban ascending the two hundred and sixteen steps of the palace. But the lone figure in the garden did not stir.

'Yoo-hoo,' it called again, mindful of the numerous statues in the palace grounds.

'Well Gubnet, thank goodness it's you!' panted Delia du Pont after a squint and a poke. 'One can never be certain of anything these days. I heard some very good news on the radio this morning – Montague and Clemis have made it through to the bridge finals! Ascourt is on the map, what?' Delia foraged around in her voluminous carpet bag from which she produced two freshly baked brown loaves and a winsome pot of honey. 'I have been missing our little get-togethers,' she confided. 'I couldn't wait to see you when the rain stopped.'

221

Gubnet held Delia's hand in the crook of her arm and strolled the long way round to the kitchen door.

'You're glowing,' remarked Delia. 'I do hope you're not running round after those girls!'

The chorus which greeted them in the kitchen brought an unbelieving smile to Gubnet's face. Queen Bea ran round the table with cutlery, Maryann tended the kettle and Princess Vee had brushed her hair.

'Won't you join us for breakfast, Delia?' invited Gubnet serenely.

After breakfast, they set to work on the garden plans that Princess Vee had found in the original copy of Charlotte's Will. The design was simplicity itself. Princess Vee's garden was significantly smaller than the other two, consisting of a small apiary, statue number 222 and a triangular plot of barley, specified as *Hordeum vulgare*. There were no other plants save a miniature hedge enclosing the whole in the shape of a horse's shoe.

Maryann concentrated with a frown. St Gubnet roused the head gardener in the hopes of locating the numbered statue and Delia du Pont traced her fingers around the very obvious shapes in the garden plan that Queen Charlotte had drawn before she died.

'You're right,' said Maryann, 'the cereal plot is triangular, the apiary is round, even the hedge has a recognisable shape. But what could it possibly mean?'

Delia wetted her lips. There was nothing her pathologist's soul liked better than a good puzzle.

'It could be a star alignment,' she said. 'If you look carefully at this drawing you will see that these faded lines here are actually a continuation of the hedge – '

'It's not a horseshoe!' grasped Maryann, 'it's a womb-shape with a long cervix.'

'Precisely. And when the asteroid Ceres makes an alignment into the cervix, that could be the exact time when the fertilisation of 'M' occurs. Which, of course,' added Delia, 'is a simple matter of calculation with the help of modern ephemerides.'

Maryann let out a long low whistle.

'Ceres is the Goddess of Agriculture, right?'

222

'And fertility,' added Delia. 'That's why Queen Charlotte included the apiary and the plot of *Hordeum*.'

'Beehives and Barley, of course!'

Delia laid the three garden plans out on the ground, one beside the other. She could barely contain her excitement at the revelations contained within them.

'Ceres, Vesta, Pallas-Athene and Juno are a group of asteroids which lie between the planets Mars and Jupiter. Are you with me so far?' said Delia, taking in Maryann's nod. She then put her finger on the plan for Queen Bea's garden. 'The statue in Bea's garden is Pallas-Athene, see?'

'Right,' agreed Maryann. 'It's written in Queen Charlotte's own hand.'

'But look here at Princess Min's garden – now what do you suppose that is?' said Delia, pointing it out.

'Why, that's the barbecue!'

'Or, as Dame Murphy believes, it is the Fire of Vesta,' said Delia with relish. 'And so, in Princess Vee's garden – '

'Statue number two-two-two is Ceres!' cried Maryann with goosebumps running up her back.

'All in a day's work,' said the unassuming pathologist. 'Now wherever has Gubnet got to?'

Gubnet went through the palace inventory with the head gardener. All the building materials and nursery stock required for the construction of Princess Vee's garden were present and correct. They were agreed that while the planting should be left until spring, there was no reason why the apiary could not be put into place – nor, for that matter, the statue.

The head gardener hunted the palace stores for pegs and strings to assist in the marking out of the various geometric dimensions and, in so doing, located statue number 222 under a pile of rusted scaffolding. It was shrouded in a sheet of thick canvas and appeared to be all of a piece. St Gubnet put her shoulder to the pile and strained against the weight of tangled metal.

'It'll take four grown women and me to shift that,' intervened the head gardener catching, Gubnet by the wrist. 'You're not to lift a thing, not in your condition.'

Bea took her responsibilities as Queen and sister to heart and invited Vee on a tour of her own established garden. The winter shrubbery glistened in the aftermath of rain; the tall *Mahonia japonica* cast down its perfume from a cascade of yellow flower spikes and the sculptured streams pulsed a watery life into the well of Pallas-Athene.

'St Gubnet named her child after my statue,' said Queen Bea proudly.

'It's a very beautiful garden, Bea. It really suits you,' replied Vee, trying to make up for her earlier rudeness.

'Yes, it's much more *mature* than the other gardens,' said Bea. 'Of course, it was planted up when I was six.'

Princess Vee suspended disbelief and wondered how her short, plump, bespectacled sister had formulated a life guaranteeing popularity among her friends, while at the same time circumventing almost certain assassination by her enemies. Queen Bea was instinctively and unerringly drawn to explode into other people's cracks, while remaining peculiarly invulnerable to her own. She was psychic dynamite. Princess Vee surmised that a defensive stance would be to risk certain exposure to Bea's next provocative dart, whereas a direct confrontation would serve only to raise the embarrassing question of what exactly there was to confront. There was no dealing with her. Or was there…?

'Would you like me to show you Min's garden? There's not much to see, though,' warned Bea.

'Yes, I'd like that,' said Vee, trying hard to be sisterly. 'It would mean a lot to me.'

Princess Min's garden needed the atmospheric cast of an evening's fire to light up the creepers and oddly shaped shrubs. It was at a natural disadvantage under water. Princess Vee stooped down to encourage the trailing stems of periwinkle swimming in the mud. Hers was an admiration for survivors.

'She's awfully strong and brave. She wears Japanese robes, she has a crew-cut and a black belt, she's in love with Gubnet and she eats seaweed,' said Bea informatively.

'But what's she like?' pressed Vee. 'I mean do you think we'd get along?'

'Min protects me from Mother Nature, who's going to come here and kill me one day. Everyone knows that.'

Princess Vee intuited something important. Could it be that

her sister understood the world only in relation to how it func-
tioned in terms of her survival? But of course – she had been
Queen Bea since she was knee high to a grasshopper! 'You
don't have to worry about Mother Nature even if Min isn't
here,' assured Vee quietly.

'I don't?' said Bea in a fog behind her spectacles.

'Mother Nature doesn't own Ascourt any more, Bea. I do.
That's why I'm here, do you understand?'

'Not quite,' said Bea diffidently.

'If Min wasn't here to protect you, then She'd have to deal
with me,' said Princess Vee finally getting it right. 'And if
Mother Nature put one foot on Ascourt I'd have no choice but
to take Her to court for illegal trespass on private property.'

'Oh, Vee – how did we ever get along without you?' wept
Bea in full and grateful floods.

Princess Vee hugged her sister close to her heart. Queen
Bea took liberties because she was a property of the public and
because the public was her property. It all made absolute Bee
Person sense. Bea wasn't vindictive – she just *was* the entire
community that lived and breathed through her Queenly
Essence.

'I've been away too long,' sobbed Vee. 'I'd forgotten everything. Bea – will you forgive me…?'

'My precious Vee,' said Bea, almost choking. 'And none of
us will be right till we get Min back!'

An atmosphere of sisterly tranquility prevailed throughout
lunch. Fortified by thick wedges of bread and root soup, the
women trudged across the mud with a drying west wind in
their faces. In the palace stores they set to work removing the
heap of metal by whatever means were at hand. The statue
was eventually persuaded from its rest by cajoling, hacksaws,
pleas and expletives. St Gubnet supervised the entire
manoeuvre, and, one step at a time, they dragged, heaved,
stumbled and pulled it towards its place of glory in Princess
Vee's garden.

Statue number 222 was laid flat in the mud. The head
gardener cut the ropes and Princess Vee proudly removed the
front of the canvas cover. The face of the statue was missing
one glass eye, but this imperfection did not detract from its
imposing majesty. It was over three metres high.

With a log and a pulley, they raised the statue on to its plinth, the remaining canvas falling off its shoulders like a loose cape. They formed a circle around the base and chanted an old bee song about blessing a statue's new career, adding an impromptu verse to do with the trials of looking out to sea with one blue eye.

Maryann asked the statue for a blessing: 'Oh, Ceres, Goddess of Fertility and Agriculture, please bless the little garden plots that I plan to grow and feed us in your name. And please protect them from the winds.'

Queen Bea said: 'Ceres, big and strong and tall, protect this garden which is *especially* small.'

'The nicest things arrive in the smallest packages,' said Vee, tolerantly amused.

'That's what I said,' insisted Bea. 'You're who "M" is – because the youngest sister would have the smallest garden, so you're going to lay the eggs!'

The lines, which she had off by heart, flashed a bright purple through Princess Vee's brain:

My youngest, M, will be the Mother of the future generation of Ascourt. She will conceive and abundantly bear forth my dream. Under her rule, Ascourt will overflow with bounty and joy.

Princess Vee's breath left her body like a punch in the abdomen. She had never, not for one instant, considered the possibility that she might one day be a mother. But hadn't Yossarian said it himself that day in Tralee: *You're needed there, Vee – they can't do this without you.*

Princess Vee wobbled and fell into the sturdy arms of the head gardener. She was unconscious for only a couple of minutes, but in this time, she felt Yossarian's presence. He stroked her brow and whispered in his unmistakeable voice: *Thank you, thank you, I can't tell you how much this means to me.*

When Princess Vee came round, she found herself mumbling Yossarian's name.

'I see it now!' said Gubnet with a contorted look of fury on her face.

'Yossarian's back, isn't he?' said Bea regretfully.

Gubnet stood up and pointed grimly at the statue. 'Yes, and there he is!'

'It's not Ceres after all,' sagged Maryann, looking helplessly at Delia.

226

'We have aided and abetted a rapist,' ranted St Gubnet, grabbing the head gardener by the arm. 'This is a horrible mistake, Maryann. Come, Delia, we must cleanse ourselves of his presence and think again.'

Queen Bea waited behind while Princess Vee stared hard at the statue. Having ascertained that she was feeling better, Bea clambered on to her sister's shoulders and looked over the hedge.

'Now can you see what his missing eye is looking at?' said Vee, balancing in the soft ground at her feet.

'Why, yes!' cried Bea. 'The blue eye is looking out to sea and the missing one is staring straight over the top of the hedge at the statue of the Great Drone, Peter!'

'I thought as much,' said Vee, bending to let Queen Bea dismount. 'The last thing he said to me was to put him somewhere near Peter, so that he could keep an eye on him!'

'Yossarian always dressed like a goddess,' remarked Bea, 'even when he wasn't well.'

'He was very good to me, Bea. He made me see how much I counted, and it was down to his nagging that I actually got here.'

'Well if you don't mind about him being in your garden,' said Bea supportively, 'then neither do I.'

'Thanks, Bea.'

'He promised to stop bothering me if he got a statue,' said Bea. 'Actually.'

Over high tea, St Gubnet raised the indelicate matter of Queen Charlotte's mental health in the drawing of the garden plans. Unsatisfied with the general reception, she proceeded to ridicule the Goddess–Asteroid theory, treating Delia's protests with sceptical contempt, the whole effect of which accumulated in Maryann's alimentary canal as a case of severe and acid indigestion. Princess Vee wisely kept her counsel and a straight face throughout Queen Bea's undignified performance of snickering loudly into a handkerchief on the pretence of blowing her nose. The instant at which Gubnet did *not* throw her plate across the kitchen, Queen Bea accidentally shattered a mug of milk, causing Maryann to jump out of her seat and leave the kitchen in fright. It was only a matter of time before

Delia excused herself, and, in need of fresh air, Princess Vee accompanied her on the long walk home.

Neither questioned, nor offered solace. They both knew, but did not articulate, that further discussion was meaningless until St Gubnet acknowledged that Yossarian was a red rag to her feelings which ran deep and true for Princess Min. They arrived at the cottage in Seaview Suburbs, silent in the watch of a golden sunset.

Princess Vee plugged in the wireless in the hopes of picking up a weather forecast. High winds would mean delaying the flight to Porschia which she and Maryann had planned for early the following morning. With no response from the radio, she pulled out the plug, and glanced around for an alternative source of power. Delia assured her that there were no batteries in the house, the last two having been used up by Montague's tape recorder, on the night of the murder.

'As we are without electricity,' advised Delia, 'the only hope of an accurate weather forecast would be from Sorrel, the Guide of the Northern Territories.'

Princess Vee bid Delia farewell and set a brisk pace in order to reach her destination before the light failed completely. Criss-crossing in between cottages, she forded the river Naiad at its most shallow point on the western beaches. She climbed up to the long northern ridge, hacked her way through heather and gorse, and halfway along, beyond a dense green thicket, she could just make out a tiny wisp of smoke from the chimney in Sorrel's wood cabin.

Delia had warned her about the Guide of the Northern Territories. She was nature's shaman; a recluse and animal speaker. She knew plant medicine and weathertelling but was otherwise not forthcoming. The journey back to the palace, via the eastern chalkhills, was treacherous by night, so Princess Vee kept her enquiry short and to the point.

'Any idea what the weather will be like for flying tomorrow?'

The figure crouched over the woodpile did not answer her. A steady stream of red liquid poured on to the ground from a crown of tight brown bloodmatted curls. The chunky face was pale and drawn tight with shock. The guilty culprit was an axe, covered in the blood of its owner.

Princess Vee went into overdrive. She carried Sorrel

indoors and wrapped her in blankets beside the open fire. She cleaned her face and pressed sprigs of rosemary and pine into the wound. She led the cats into the kitchen and fed them. By the time the emergency had passed its peak, the stars were glittering in a pitch black night and Sorrel had passed out cold.

There was nothing for it but to stay the night. Princess Vee eased Sorrel's head on to her lap and made space for the inevitable feline invasion. She sipped a dram of poitín, and was strangely contented by the crackling of the fire, the gently breathing body and the raucous sound of unorchestrated purrs.

It was still dark outside when Princess Vee found herself cossetted in the blankets that were meant for her patient. She woke with a start to a furry paw tickling the scar on her lip. She could hear a body moving round in the kitchen. A few minutes later, Sorrel padded in with a teapot and a plate of biscuits. She slipped on to the floor beside her, removed the cat on Vee's chest and sat up on one elbow, an endearing grin on her face.

'You have beautiful lips,' she whispered, just brushing them. 'Felice and I have been watching you sleep.'

Princess Vee closed her eyes and breathed deep into her ribcage. The healing scent of a pine perfume rushed into her lower body from the skin next to her own. A series of mini-explosions went off inside her. She reached out and slowly drew the unbuttoned check shirt towards her.

The kiss was a long and telling introduction. They lingered, branding the shape of a mutual desire. The heat from their bodies rose, the cats prowled invisible auras, and a wind circled the cabin, rattling a pane which was loose in its groove.

Sorrel unzipped Vee's trousers, sending a racing thrill down her legs. She could feel Sorrel's palm cradling the top of her thighs, the other hand slipping into wetness, when finally she was rocked like a baby on the edge of a torrent. Vee held time until she came inside, in tears, on the molten shores of a blissful cascade.

'Thank you,' she murmured in a litter of rosemary. But the rocking didn't stop.

CHAPTER NINETEEN

Solstice Eve

Friday, December 20, 1996

Maryann and Queen Bea tapped the window loudly until the sleeping mass of blankets stirred on the floor of the old wood cabin.

'It's the Queen of Ascourt,' urged Sorrel, shaking her companion awake.

'My sister!'

'Your sister?' gasped Sorrel, 'Then you're a Princess…?'

'Vee,' affirmed Vee, swiftly grabbing her pullover.

'Oh shit!' said Sorrel, hitching up her trousers as the visitors entered unasked.

'What are you doing here?' demanded Queen Bea of her wayward sister.

'Half the island's chasing round looking for you,' added Maryann in a certain tone of voice for good measure.

A small family of cats also invited themselves in after a long and hungry morning. Because of strong winds, a breakfast of the feathered variety had not come their way. They marched straight into the kitchen, where exquisite drips of milk awaited their combined talents of agility and smell. After a chase around the pantry, the pride made a dignified return to the parlour, where four inviting laps were there to be jumped on, clawed and jumped off again. The cat on Sorrel's lap purred a belated apology. Sorrel scratched its ears by way of a gracious acceptance.

'I was up on the roof securing the cabin when little Felice here tripped me up and I fell head first on to something sharp…'

'An axe,' said Vee, squaring her shoulder as Sorrel leaned up beside her.

'But I'm quite all right now.'

'Just a minute,' said Maryann seriously. 'If you were securing your cabin, then are we expecting a storm?'

'Storm?' laughed Sorrel. 'More like a hurricane!'

'I came up last night to get a weather report and…'

'How long before it hits?' interrupted Maryann checking her watch.

'No more than a couple of hours,' replied Sorrel, sniffing the wind. 'It's blowing in from the north and getting stronger by the minute.'

Maryann looked worriedly across to Princess Vee. If they were to get to the wedding ahead of the storm, they would have to leave Ascourt immediately. Sorrel offered to push out the glider and wind up the propeller. Maryann made Queen Bea promise never, never to stray out of sight of the people who loved her and were looking out for her safety. Princess Vee traced a pensive finger along the handsome wrinkles of wise old age and pressed her lips against Sorrel's cheek.

'I can't bear to be parted from you,' she whispered longingly. 'You won't come to the wedding and I'm concerned about you.'

Queen Bea wasn't worried at all. 'Safe trip!' she cried. And it would be now that Princess Vee's mind was no longer on her Maryann Leaf.

With the others out searching for Princess Vee, St Gubnet waddled despairingly around the breakfast table. She thought of Princess Min and winced. Even her trusty wraparound skirt could no longer accomodate her gargantuan girth. Delia had meant well, but a curtain was a curtain and Gubnet's eyes receded like two black holes in the durable canvas which her friend euphemistically called a kaftan.

St Gubnet removed the kitchen mirror from the wall, sat down and sighed. But the minute she took the weight off her feet, she dozed off, oblivious to the quickly gathering storm. She dreamed of Banba thrice circling the island in an attempt to ward off a tornado. The black wind whipped like a top destroying every living thing in its path. Banba fled to Gubnet's side, whispering, 'Wake up, wake up, too late, it's here!'

Gubnet sat up with a start to a ricochet of doors slamming in the wind. The roof of the kitchen tore at its seams and was lifted off in one almighty wrench. Slapping gusts whooped

231

through the kitchen, sending pots and pans flying, and as Gubnet ran for cover, the kitchen window was sucked clean out of its sill.

Gubnet fled into the ballroom and crawled under a low banquet table. She barely caught the tail end of a black serpent flashing past her before it flew upstairs towards the overhanging balcony. It hovered outside the door to Queen Bea's old bedroom in the north wing. All at once, the vast, gusting ballroom assumed an ominous silence. In a panic, Gubnet followed it up the stairs and into the bedroom. She was immediately lifted an inch off the ground by the force of an angrily whirring black spectre.

'Where's Queen Bea?' it crackled.

'What do you want with her?' replied Gubnet courageously.

'Answer my question!' it exploded, throwing Gubnet clear across the room. Before she could rise to her feet, another explosion buckled Queen Bea's brass bed into a twisted heap of metal. This second outburst brought about a momentary deacceleration of speed. Gubnet grimaced on her knees at the familiar face revolving within the swirl of a bilious ether.

'We'd better have a cup of tea,' she scolded, heaving herself to her feet. 'There's no talking to you in this state.'

The shadow followed Gubnet, unleasing a last coil of tension in an elegant spin and arriving down the steps just ahead of her.

'You don't even recognise me, do you?' said Gubnet, jabbing it with a finger.

'Gubnet?'

'*Saint* Gubnet to you, Your Eminence!'

Mother Nature, now unspun, could not believe Her eyes. 'You look awful!'

'I'm about to have a baby,' pronounced Gubnet irately, 'I can't sleep a wink at night and I haven't had a bath since you had our electricity cut off. What did you expect – Ingrid Bergman?'

St Gubnet carefully observed Mother Nature's behaviour as she boiled the kettle. The wind had subsided both indoors and out. Her ex-lover contentedly picked through the kitchen rubble like a crow on a bombsite. She proudly retrieved and handed over two chipped china mugs and the last teabag in the palace. Mother Nature seemed relaxed, almost child-like, but there was no disguising the eyes, which glistened with an unbecoming dementia.

'I can smell Queen Bea,' She twitched, adding an unnatural amount of sugar to Her tea.

'And what would you be wanting with a wee thing like her?' asked Gubnet softly.

'Where is Queen Bea?' wondered Mother Nature out loud. 'Where could she be?'

Gubnet watched with alarm as Mother Nature burrowed Her spoon into the sugar bowl, unearthing every grain until She reached the bottom.

'I haven't seen you in ages,' said Gubnet, in an effort to distract Her. 'How have you been?'

Mother Nature spoke candidly, crushing neat rows of sugar granules under Her spoon. From time to time She paused to draw breath, as if the excitement was too much for Her.

'So you see,' She ended, 'the escaped Dr Heron Home, PhD, is no doubt in Porschia warning Princess Min as we speak. But no matter. Queen Bea is here. Problem solved.'

'Do go on,' nodded Gubnet, rubbing her hands together. The temperature in the newly modified open-plan kitchen was as chilling as Mother Nature's disturbing revelations. Gubnet monitored a flicker of lucidness as the eyes across from her own began to blink; and the voice, though earnest, had moderated in pitch.

'Gubnet, I alone must ensure that Charlotte's Plan never comes to pass. Those girls must never reunite. They don't understand the consequences of their mother's foolish vendetta. *I am* the Modern Way of the Bees. All change must come through me.'

'I agree,' placated Gubnet. 'Ascourt must change with your consent. But if you destroy Charlotte's daughters, then you are giving the world a sign of your weakness. You are, in effect, admitting to the threat of their very existence.'

'Don't exaggerate, dear,' said Mother Nature loftily, 'Every Creator has a destructive side. Hecate, Kali, Erishkegal – the list is endless. Anyway, I only need to get rid of one of them. Hardly what you'd call a carnage, now is it?'

St Gubnet almost choked with the expedient irony of her ex-lover's miscalculated logic. It was clear to her that Mother

Nature had no idea that the Royal Princesses of Ascourt were the least of Her problems. But could she risk her life and her daughter's in order to spare Queen Bea? Should she play her trump card? She knew that she must.

'Why wouldn't you have a child with me?' challenged Gubnet, bracing herself for the mother of all battles.

'Why must we rehash this tired old subject?' mimicked Mother Nature, throwing Her eyes up to heaven.

'Because,' said Gubnet laying out the incontrovertible fact, 'a child would spell the end of your career as a Creator. Because *your* child is the only living thing that would force you to give up control.'

Mother Nature shrugged Her shoulders. 'I suppose so.' Pearl was a voluntary pleasure, and Gubnet didn't know about her, after all.

'You suppose so? You know so!' shot Gubnet. 'Every Creator since time immemorial has been forced into retirement by their kids. Uranus by His son Saturn, God the Father by His son Jesus, and next is Mother Nature by Her daughter, Athena.'

'Don't waste your breath – I happen to know the child isn't mine.'

'Aeons of unconditional love and support wasn't priority enough for you to take the biggest step of your life to retire and have our child!'

'That's right,' sleazed Mother Nature, 'so you run off with some jumped up French professor and try to pass his brat off as mine? Loyalty? Don't make me laugh!'

Gubnet lifted herself slowly off the chair and broke into lung-stabbing sobs. It was all over. She had played out her ace in a game with no rules. *Oh, why did I have the child behind Her back and think it would all work out in the end? By the time She sees the inevitable, Ascourt will be destroyed and all who live on her…*

Sorrel entered the kitchen intrepidly. Overcome with shyness, she nodded to the slim good-looker with the wild black hair, figuring St Gubnet as the matron she had come to give her message to.

'Um, I just came down to tell you not to worry about Maryann and Princess Vee, they left for Porschia this morning. And Queen Bea's up in my place. I hope you weren't too worried, I got here just as soon as the storm died down enough to walk the cliffs.'

'The storm has not died, but all is quiet in the eye of the storm,' glittered Mother Nature maniacally. 'Queen Bea up in your place, what good news! And who are you?'

Sorrel gave her name and pointed out her cabin across the valley. St Gubnet looked in horror at the unwitting messenger and threw herself at Mother Nature's feet.

'Kill me and Athena. We are your only threat! For pity's sake, leave the others be!'

'Oh cheer up, Gubnet!' said Mother Nature, patting her head, 'Go back to the mainland and stop playing at being a Bee Person. You're a human being – this stuff is none of your business any more. I'll make a nice settlement for you and Louis Sterne and the brat. Take my advice and you'll never have to work again. And thank you, Sorrel. What a pretty name. Now I shall be on my way.'

A split second later, Mother Nature had transformed once more into a raging tornado, taking the kitchen door with Her as She twisted violently towards Queen Bea and the Northern Territories. The low sound of a rumbling thunder was intermittently pierced by earsplitting cracks. Every tree in the forest was uprooted in Her path. The wood cabin collapsed on impact and was blown piecemeal over the cliff. Sorrel winced, closing her arms around Gubnet, who had already closed her eyes.

When the storm departed, Sorrel and Gubnet crossed the eastern chalkhills, protecting their eyes against the gritty fallout from its wake. The sea below them foamed a white saliva, spitting as it swallowed whole trees, bits of fence and lumpen concrete. There were voices everywhere; whispering, taunting, crying, pleading – around them, below them, above them. Seven ungainly birds squawked overhead, like grouse to the scatter of shot. St Gubnet froze as the creatures plummeted from their flightless arc, headfirst into the river Naiad.

'Poor herons!' she murmured, clutching her heart.

They met the vacant site of Sorrel's abode with trepidation. There was no earthly way to put anything right. Sorrel wandered round, whistling and calling – some of her friends appeared, others were too frightened. St Gubnet prayed and kept a watch on the sea.

On the other side of the island, the residents of Seaview

Suburbs, headed by Delia du Pont, reacted quickly to the crisis. Armed with coats and towels they made a beeline for the river Naiad. The rescue operation was a complete success – just one minor head wound and a few ruffled feathers. They wrapped the seven traumatised Old Dames in blankets and walked them back to Seaview Suburbs for hot toddies and a change of dry clothes.

'It was Mother Nature,' affirmed a shaken Dame Clemis to the Seaview rescue team.

'We could see Her in the middle of the storm,' quivered Dame Thwaites. 'She was too quick for us.'

'She grabbed the Powerpoint out of my hand – '

'Then She crushed it,' said Dame Toplis, manually demonstrating.

'She threw us to the four winds and shouted, *Make your own way home!*' continued Dame Meleka, flapping her arms.

'Actually I thought She said, *Where's Heron Home?*' put in Dame Agnetha mildly.

Dame Murphy rubbed the bruise on her head, admitting, 'You're probably right, Aggie, but I could have sworn She said, *I'll teach you bloody Herons a lesson unless you go Home.*'

'You see we couldn't fly without the Powerpoint, so we crashlanded over the eastern chalkhills and thankfully into the river,' said Dame Montague to her sister, Delia.

'Good job She doesn't know that Heron Home is in Dublin,' said Dame Thwaites in breach of the secret oath.

'Meeting Professor Sterne and the all-woman camera crew from Sweden...'

'The Goddess be with them!'

'Which one?'

'The Blessed Virgin Mary,' said Dame Clemis.

Night fell quickly on the eve of the December Solstice. The residents of Seaview Suburbs shared their last scraps of food at the communal bonfire on the western beach. Banba sat listlessly by the fire as they cooked. It was the last supper; it was very dark with hardly a star yet risen. The dying quiet was pierced by the monotonous explosions of naval mines making contact with the floating debris of the storm. Everyone known to be alive on the island was present. It completed a full and despairing picture. Queen Bea was beyond rescue, there was no getting to the wedding without the Powerpoint, and nobody, except Dame Montague, wanted to talk about any of it. It was the end of the world and lifelessly cold.

'The electricity might come back on tonight,' she announced brightly.

'And pigs might fly,' snapped St Gubnet.

'No, really,' protested Dame Montague. 'That's what took us so long – you tell her, Clemis.'

Dame Clemis straightened up her stiff back while Dame Meleka rubbed it with lavender oil, warmed from the fire. 'Not that it matters,' she said, imparting a withering look at Montague, 'but we approached the Electricity Supply Board in Dublin and settled our so-called arrears with the cash we won at the Bridge championship.'

'Which means we've nothing to buy food with,' surmised Gubnet pessimistically.

'Look here, Gubnet – we found Heron and we got the chromosome pictures to Professor Sterne in Paris. He said they were conclusive proof that you and Mother Nature are the biological parents of Athena. We did everything you asked, and more besides. But the best news of all is – '

'This is hardly the time, Montague,' ordered Dame Clemis sharply.

'Why ever not?' smarted the Keeper of the Powerpoint.

'We're in mourning, Montague,' said Dame Agnetha, casting a gentle reminder. 'Queen Bea is, was…'

The silence grew impregnable, the censure and the agony complete. Without their Queen, the Bee People were unable to function as a coherent whole. It was their way. Ascourt had never been separated from its Queen. They were paralysed without her.

Dame Montague left the circle on the beach and walked pluckily up the hill. She didn't know where she was going, save to remove herself from a hopeless spirit of collective pessimism. The dark engulfed her, but she knew every crook and turn in the narrow, windy road. There was not a one of them who understood what it was like to be singled out – a stultified object of suspicion and derision, a conscientious objector in the midst of overpowering communal-mindedness. She had paid a high price to join the Dames when the truth was she didn't give a fig for Queen Bea, or royalty, or loyal herds of sheep…

A soft, encouraging glow shone the way before her, and

237

Dame Montague du Pont determined that with or without them, there was always hope. Climbing up the two hundred and sixteen steps of the palace, Montague realised the value of her uniqueness with a crystal clarity.

You are susceptible to their jibes, but you are not susceptible to their paralysis. You have always stood alone. Because of this, you are their only hope.

Banba glowed brighter still at these words of self-realisation, and lit Dame Montague's path into the smoking room of the palace. She beamed herself on to the spot from which she had unscrewed the original Powerpoint, and Montague was quick to realise the implication. There were four similar Powerpoints in this one room alone…

At the front gates of the palace, Dame Montague held Powerpoint Two up to the stars. She repeated the formula of direction and motive force, willing herself back to the circle on the beach. She felt the familiar uplift, the pull of clothes on her body. When she opened her eyes, the tiny dwellings beneath her flight were alight with the lamps of a hundred bulbs.

Banba's only thought as she flew alongside Dame Montague was that if the electricity had come on five minutes earlier, her mortal companion might now be on a one-way flight to the Underworld instead. Dame Montague, engrossed in more earthly thoughts, imagined herself flicking on the immersion heater and enjoying a long, hot bath with her sister at Ambling Cottage.

The group on the beach witnessed a double comet sweeping its magnificent blue arc across the nightsky. It was a sign from the Blessed Virgin Mary and, however recently adopted, the BVM could not appear if Queen Bea was dead, for such was the Essence of a triple goddess. Once again, She had blessed them in their hour of need. Queen Bea was alive! They would attend the wedding with Powerpoint Two. B, V and M would be reunited and they would be whole again, ready to greet the dawn of the New Order.

Princess Tamarind's hen party was well under way when Maryann landed the glider. The storm had pursued them most of the way, mysteriously blowing itself out as they approached the island of Porschia. Princess Vee leapt out of the plane, barely exchanged a handshake with the Queen of Porschia and ran down the red carpet muttering and swearing.

'We meet again,' said the Queen of Porschia to Maryann. 'Your new friend is – unwell?'

'That is Princess Vee and I think she needs to throw up,' said Maryann, matter-of-factly.

'Of course – I meant, Queen Bea is not in your company?'

'The rest of the party's flying here tomorrow,' said Maryann ignoring the innuendo.

'By magic carpet?' said the Queen condescendingly of her future poor relations.

'Speaking of mysteries,' said Maryann, raising her eyebrows, 'how about a tour of those underwater camellias, Porky?'

Princess Vee did not wait for the others to catch up. She proceeded from the toilet through customs, where no one, it appeared, was working, and found her way to the front door where a row of shiny jeeps were parked, ready to transport members of the wedding party to their pre-arranged destinations. The dapper little Superdrone who claimed her person and baggage seemed the envy of the other chauffeurs, and honked his horn with aplomb as they swept across the roundabout on to Porschia's main motorway. Princess Vee was a little taken aback by his over-the-shoulder chatter and flagrant lack of concern for the highway code.

'You're a real princess, aren't you?' he said, devouring her with his eyes.

'Aren't they feeding you enough?' she said haughtily. 'Here, have a bar of chocolate – '

'No thank you, Highness Vee, I must always watch my figure,' he said, patting his flat belly.

'Where are you taking me?'

The driver pressed his hand on her knee and puckered his lips. 'How far do you want to go?'

Princess Vee slapped his face and caught him in a stranglehold from the backseat. 'I want to see my sister, Princess Min,' she growled.

'Yes, I want her too,' said the Superdrone, eagerly pressing the accelerator pedal to the floor.

Queen Bea stood up and bumped her head on the low ceiling of the glider's fuselage. She was not certain how long she had been asleep and it took her a moment to remember where she was. She crawled to the front of the glider, opened the door and jumped twice her own height to the ground below her. It was an aircraft hangar, and it was awfully dark.

She walked across the runway towards a large building with a flickering neon sign which read *Porschia International Airport*. They were just locking up.

'Airport's closed, dear,' said a helpful cleaning worker.

Tempted by a free canteen dinner and a lift into town on the worker's bus, Queen Bea grabbed a mop and got to work in the main foyer.

At the end of the dayshift, the Superdrones had changed uniforms and cheerfully transformed into extra barstaff for the Hotel's hen party. Princess Min lined them up in the kitchen and swung her sword meaningfully in front of them.

'Castration,' she threatened, 'for anyone who interrupts me or my sister tonight, understood?'

The Superdrones squirmed with pride.

By nine o'clock that evening, Maryann Leaf had left the Queen of Porschia's horticultural tour and joined the princesses who were comfortably seated in the bar of the Paradise Hotel.

'But you must have thought about it,' pressed Princess Vee, leaning over their reserved table.

'Okay, okay – I think I could be "M",' admitted Princess Min with difficulty.

'You do? So do I!'

'Really?'

'Of course – but why do you think you're "M"?'

'No, you tell me first.'

'Well, it doesn't make much sense,' said Princess Vee biting her lip, 'but if I'm "M", then I'd be Mother of all Ascourt. Me, a mother? I used to think that was impossible – do you know what I'm saying?'

'Sister, I know I do.'

The jazz band tuned up, the bar was serving doubles and the party started to swing. Maryann and Tamarind hardly got a word in edgeways. Vee and Min talked non-stop, discovering they had much in common.

'You mean Mother Nature sold Ascourt to you too?' expostulated Min on behalf of the Porschian Cartel.

'But Vee told me it was the best deal she'd ever done!' said

Maryann, attempting to join in.

'Do you mind?' said Princess Vee rudely to her ex.

'It's a hen party,' protested Tamarind. 'We should be having fun!'

'Not now!' glared the Sisters.

'Well, suit yourselves,' retorted Princess Tamarind, taking Maryann Leaf firmly by the hand. 'Let's you and me find us a party.'

'We can't be too cautious,' apologised Porky to a guest, 'we are expecting Mother Nature to arrive at any minute.'

Each invitation was checked off the Island Manager's list at the hotel's front door before receiving a secure welcome from the Queen of Porschia.

'Hayde!' shrieked the Queen suddenly. 'Get rid of that riff-raff immediately!'

A worker's bus had just pulled up in the main driveway.

'And before Vee and Min got stuck in,' said Maryann walking down the road, 'I spent most of the evening with your mother. She really is an accomplished breeder.'

'They're all breeders round here,' snorted Princess Tamarind. 'Don't suppose you'd be into a little incest would you?'

'Been there, done that…' admitted Maryann ruefully.

'Let's hitch,' said Tamarind suddenly. 'Someone's bound to recognise me.'

'Yeah, look – that bus is pulling over already!'

The overcrowded vehicle stopped and picked up the two hitchers. By the time they reached the beach, Queen Bea had explained the whole lengthy tale.

'…so my new friends invited me to their Solstice Party instead.'

'Mum will be a bit distressed when she finds out who she threw out of my party,' giggled Tamarind gleefully.

'I adore your life, darling,' sighed Maryann, squeezing Bea's hand, 'but when I said stay close to the ones who loved you, I didn't mean become a stowaway on my plane!'

The beach was alive with drums and dancing. It would go on until the very last worker collapsed with exhaustion, just as the Sun had itself on this longest night of the year. Queen

Bea's new friends were determined to introduce her to everyone. No sooner than they had received the hospitalities of one bonfire than they were shuffled along to the next for another bite to eat, a quick joint and just one more toast... Queen Bea thought she would pop.

'Apparently there's room for us all in the last beach house on the row,' said Maryann to Tamarind.

'I should think so too – it's mine,' replied Tamarind with a wide grin. 'Look I'm off for a walk, see you later, right?'

Princess Tamarind walked away from the party and into the dark, moonless night. She waded drunkenly through the surf, feeling it gush like a giant hole in her heart. It wasn't the fact that Queen Bea had become an overnight celebrity and the Porschian workers had hardly recognised their own future Queen. It really wasn't. Only the sea had ever understood, for only the sea would willingly pour itself into her vast and empty soul.

If you were my lover then I should be full, she said aloud.

She took off her shoes and felt the numbing chill of icy water on her feet. She clambered over a rocky ridge and sat listening to the intense and wooing music of the ocean. She never felt alone with the sea. But something else was moving. And it was making a low keening noise not three feet away from her.

'Who are you?' asked the Princess fearlessly. The face of the woman was otherworldly, the hair sea-sprayed on to her head. She was moving ever so slightly, on all fours. She was indescribably beautiful, a little confused and completely naked. 'You must be freezing!' said Tamarind, covering the gentle creature with her cloak.

It didn't take much persuasion, for the woman was weak and the wind cut against them. They walked slowly across the beach, saluted the last few revellers and knocked on the door of the last house on the row. The woman leaned against her and melted into her side. She was light as a feather. Princess Tamarind picked her up and put her weight against the door until it gave way. She laid her on the sofa, and slipped under the blanket enfolding the cold body in the warmth of her own bare flesh. There wasn't a stir in the house. She felt the quiet breath of the woman against her neck. It deepened and warmed. It filled her heart. It whispered, 'I ran out of wind, Pearl,' but Princess Tamarind was fast asleep.

242

CHAPTER TWENTY

The Solstice Wedding
Saturday, December 21th, 1996

By 8:30 a.m., Maryann Leaf had done all she could to rouse Queen Bea, who remained soundly and solidly snoring in the upstairs bedroom of the seaside bungalow.

'But we can't leave without her!' she panicked.

'Come on, we haven't got time for this – I'll send a jeep over to pick them up later,' whispered Tamarind, creeping past the sleeping body on the couch downstairs. The wedding ceremony was due to begin at 8:45 and they were very, very late.

On the morning of the 21st of December each year, the sun rose between 8:55 and 9:00, creeping through the cervical tunnel and eventually lighting up the entire uterine crypt, which otherwise spent the year in darkness. The Porshian passage tomb accommodated eleven people standing up, but was not in any other way suited to a wedding party. It was pitch black both outside and in, but there wasn't a cloud in sight. The five people present anticipated a dramatic ceremony, the couple being forged in holy union by the Sun – a non-sectarian entity of life-giving proportion and warmly recognised by all. The idea was theirs alone, the Queen of Porschia had given it her blessing and all that remained was for Princess Min's other half to turn up. Which she did, at 8:54 exactly.

Hayde Lewis, acting as usher, shone a torch down the passage and announced the arrival of Princess Tamarind and Maryann Leaf. Princess Vee grimaced at her sister, Min, and the Queen of Porschia arrested the latecomers at the narrow entrance with a look that positively glowered in the dark.

'And where did you two end up last night?'

'I can't say,' replied Tamarind pushing past her mother.

243

Princess Min giggled. Princess Vee did not. Everyone knew something but no one knew for sure.

'Three down and one to go?' hissed Vee sarcastically at Maryann, who decided then and there to stand beside Princess Min instead.

'Well – who was she?' winked Princess Min at her irreverent bride-to-be.

'I really don't know, beloved,' replied Princess Tamarind with a beatific smile.

'She can't say!' mimicked Porky sarcastically. 'The morning of her wedding she deigns to turn up looking like she's been dragged through a bush by the roots of her hair and she doesn't know who she slept with last night?'

'And who did you sleep with last night?' bristled Tamarind under the spikes of her bridal coiffure.

Cook quickly spotted the first thin golden ray creeping up the passage. 'It's time to give the children your blessings, dear.'

The Queen of Porschia joined Cook at the passage entrance to inspect the approaching beam.

'I think you two should move out of the way of the light, Porky,' suggested Princess Vee tactfully.

'Unless, of course you and Cook want to make your little thing official before we do,' added Tamarind to even the score.

The Queen of Porschia stepped back with dignity. 'Don't let it upset you, Cook. We mustn't forget we are marrying into a family that sleeps round with commoners.'

Maryann gasped. Princess Min let out a low whistle and Princess Vee snorted indignantly.

'Shhh!' said Hayde Lewis at 9:02. The chamber filled with a soft, golden light. The Princesses Min and Tamarind exchanged silver rings, and the royal couple were officially wed.

After the ceremony, Princess Vee and Maryann Leaf returned to pick up Queen Bea on their way to the wedding party at the Paradise Hotel. But the last beach house on the row was deserted.

'I swear to you Vee, she was here this morning when we left!'

They searched for her among the faces of the crowd that were gathered along the shoreline not fifty metres from the bungalow where Maryann recognised a few haggard faces from the night before. They all seemed too busy to talk to her. Some were donning wetsuits, and those not in possession of binoculars were praying. Further out to sea, a flotilla of fishing boats pitched vigilantly under the cliffs.

'They're looking for a body,' said Vee, gritting her teeth. 'Someone fell off the cliffs about a half-hour ago.'

Mother Nature sat into the back seat of the chauffeur-driven jeep awaiting Her arrival at the Porschian International Airport. She forgave Herself for thinking Ascourt could ever be a model island for Superdrones. But then She'd had Her reasons at the time and this was not a day for regrets.

'It is an eighteen-minute journey from the airport to the Hotel, Excellency,' he informed Her.

Mother Nature smiled graciously. Porschia was everything She dreamed of – a beautiful island modelled on Productivity and Profitability – the Modern Way of the Bees. Its future was as smooth and streamlined as the Superdrone driving the jeep. There could be no doubt; prospective clients would come here and buy the dream they were looking for. But no amount of money could underwrite the risks She had taken to revolutionise an already perfect system. She had risen to the ultimate challenge; meddling with the apotheosis of Her own Creation, for what is perfect can no longer create anew. The Old Way of the Bees was dead. And hexagons weren't the most space-efficient shapes after all…

Mother Nature stretched out Her legs on the back seat and exhaled the last of Her tension and stress. It was all over. But who would have thought it possible? A miracle at the last hour – the morning of the wedding itself. No one could have been more surprised and delighted than She to have been awakened by Queen Bea appearing out of nowhere with a breakfast tray… They had even talked a little before Queen Bea ran up to the top of the cliffs and threw herself screaming onto the rocks below.

'Nothing more frightening than the pursuit of a vicious hornet,' said Mother Nature aloud, savouring the chase.

The Superdrone driver, overhearing Her, turned round and shook his head with conviction. 'Lieutenant Min worse,' he grumbled.

Mother Nature acknowledged Her chauffeur 's remark with a frown, guaranteeing no further disruption to Her morning rumination.

Still disguised as a hornet, She had darted among the horrified onlookers on the beach below, leaving them in no doubt as to the cause of Queen Bea's tragic accident. But there had been no time to gloat.

She had flown quickly to the Airport, where Her arrival had been expected, and into a cubicle in the ladies' loo. The hand that cranked the wheel of fortune had been turning it steadily in Her favour. For in that cubicle had been Hayde Lewis, clutching a briefcase and a one-way ticket out of Porschia. The intimidating hornet had transformed itself back into Mother Nature causing Hayde to drop the briefcase in fright. The spilled contents had comprised the dowry to be paid by the Queen of Porschia to Ascourt in one lump sum, on the day of the marriage, as was the custom. Five hundred thousand pounds, to be exact.

'I see you have more than enough cash in hand to get me some clothes,' had been Her naked pronouncement in the cramped cubicle, and when Hayde had returned with a startling black cocktail dress unpegged from the duty-free boutique, it had pleased Her so much that She had reconsidered Her employee's plight over drinks in the airport lounge.

'You're a villain, Lewis. So you see, I trust you completely.'

'But why?' Hayde had protested, sensing she was not about to be let off lightly.

'Because you're utterly predictable.'

'But I don't know the first thing about breeding Superdrones!'

'At a quarter of a million pounds a batch, you'll learn quickly enough.'

Mother Nature had waved as the aeroplane took off. Hayde Lewis had made the right decision. As newly appointed vice-president of Mother Nature International, Hayde would travel the world, live in luxury and have guaranteed immunity against the forces of law and order. She was the right type and, thanks to this morning's strange twist of events, her loyalty was absolutely guaranteed.

'Coming up on your right, Excellency – the passage tomb where the royal couple were married this morning,' informed the Superdrone chauffeur.

Mother Nature inwardly wished the couple an abiding love and a model union. Then, as quickly as they sped past the small green mound in the big empty field, Mother Nature flushed with the unexpected thought of Pearl. In that lost and lonely night, she had never seemed so real. So soft, so warm...

Love inspired Her with a generosity of spirit. It was a time for giving and forgiving. In this one moment, She saw beyond their petty motives and misunderstandings. If Heron hadn't run away, if Gubnet hadn't left Her, if Princess Min had been disposed of, if Queen Bea hadn't, if the Queen of Porschia was principled, if Hayde Lewis hadn't milked the honeypot – the cupidity, the stupidity, the naivety! Whatever their motives, each of their paths had twined inexorably around Her own. Only this morning, Queen Bea admitted, *I always knew this would be my fate!* Mother Nature squeezed a tear. How very touching!

'Excellency, we have arrived,' said the dapper little Superdrone, jumping out to open Her door.

The Queen of Porschia had taken the precaution of issuing the chauffeurs with a strict code of conduct in the presence of Mother Nature. No requests for autographs, no idle chatter and, above all, no car radios. It was paramount to their plan that not one word about the Nobel Prize reach Mother Nature's all-hearing ears. Porky flapped across the red carpet towards the jeep which had just pulled up on the Paradise Hotel's front drive.

'Eminence!' she puffed. 'The children were so upset you missed their little ceremony this morning, but then they're such early risers. I don't know where they are! None of our guests has quite got here yet. Do come indoors, I'm sure you'll take a cup of tea. We've planned a little publicity in your honour, I hope you won't mind having a few words with the press, if they arrive. Such a mess, the wedding brunch will be later than scheduled, I'm sure. You haven't seen Queen Bea, have you?'

The Queen of Porschia led the way to a sealed-off room in the bowels of the Hotel for a specially rigged private audience with Mother Nature with whom she intended to clear up a few loose ends.

'What I mean to say, that is,' hesitated Porky, 'there seems to be some confusion over who owns Ascourt. Princess Vee tells me – '

'The Creator sometimes moves in mysterious ways,' said Mother Nature, exposing a shapely knee while reaching for Her tea. 'I am very impressed with the work you have achieved here, Porky. The Superdrones are a credit to you.'

'Why, Eminence!' blushed Porky.

'You have my word that you are the sole and rightful owner of Ascourt,' pronounced Mother Nature. 'It is yours to do with as you please.'

The Queen of Porschia discreetly pressed the hidden button under her frilly collar, and in so doing, switched off the miniature recording device which had settled the matter of ownership, obviated the need for further threat or tactic and enabled a speedy progression to the main purpose of the discussion.

'The deal is Min and Tamarind stay on in Porschia with the Superdrones, and I manage Ascourt in my own right.'

'It's up to you, of course, although I'm a little surprised at your about-face,' replied Mother Nature candidly. 'I was under the impression that you had an almost *proprietary* interest in the Superdrones from the start... Now all you talk about is that unmentionable island. Tell me, what on earth would one *do* there?'

'I'm tired, Eminence. I just want a quiet retirement on Ascourt. I see now that the Superdrones are a young woman's game and the children don't need me interfering and getting in the way.'

A specially concealed green light flashed three times. On cue, Porky rose stiffly from her chair and suggested they prepare to meet the press.

'Whatever you think best,' said Mother Nature, graciously helping the aged dowager to her feet. In a very slow but regal procession out to the front lawn of the hotel, Mother Nature thought about the speech She had written for the wedding brunch and decided it would not require alteration for the purposes of a local media event.

Professor Sterne and Doctor Heron Home had taken a great liking to the Swedish camera crew who had not been in the least put out when the party from Ascourt had landed in an untidy heap on the front lawn of the Hotel on top of all their equipment. They worked quickly and efficiently. In a matter of twenty minutes, they had established the necessary electronic links to Stockholm and were waiting tensely for the news. The crowd swayed nervously around the three Nobel hopefuls. The Swedish presenter listened to her earphone and clearly repeated each word of the live transmission:

'We, the Nobel Committee are proud to announce that this year's Peace Prize has been awarded to Home, Gubnet and Sterne for Ovum-to-Ovum Fertilisation, a joint venture between the Paris Institute of Genetics and Mother Nature International, Ireland. We are hoping to make a special satellite link to Porschia where we are hopefully meeting the winners and having an exclusive interview with Mother Nature and the prize-winners. Over to you Matilde, in Ireland.'

'Why are they interviewing Mother Nature?' shouted Gubnet irately. 'She's got nothing to do with it!'

'Shh!' hushed Heron, trying to get a better view.

Professor Louis Sterne just grinned all over his freshly shaved and perfumed face.

'Yes, this is me, Matilde, live from the island of Porschia,' smiled the presenter at the rolling cameras, 'and we are waiting patiently to speak to Mother Nature about the Nobel Prize. Yes! Look out, now there She is on the left, and the other on Her right is the Queen of Porschia. Oh my God, cut – cut!!'

But nothing could be heard above the sudden roar of laughter on the lawn. In front of millions of viewers all over the world, Mother Nature had just punched Porky on the nose.

Princess Tamarind and Princess Min left the empty wedding marquee erected on the sweeping back lawn of the hotel. Not a single guest had arrived. They were both very worried. On a number of accounts. Princess Tamarind twirled self-consciously in her off-white tutu and black fishnet tights. Princess Min took off her shoes and pressed her bare feet into the cool, moist lawn.

'I know this is the worst time for it, but I think I'm getting a migraine,' said Min rubbing her forehead.

'Bea could have bumped into the woman I was with last night,' said Tamarind, pirouetting unsteadily. 'They probably just went for a stroll together.'

'I hope so,' hesitated Min. 'Actually, Tammy, now that we're married I have to tell you something in confidence – '

'Well, you know there's something I want to share with you too – '

'I know your mother blew up the yacht, Tam, and that's the truth,' said Min, finally glad to get it off her chest.

'What?' spluttered Tamarind. 'Your sister's missing and you're worried about some boat?'

Princess Min crouched on the lawn and rubbed her throbbing temples. 'Listen to me. Vee and I did a lot of serious talking last night. I think we have enough evidence to send Her to prison for life.'

'Bad and all as she is, she's my mum,' frowned Tamarind. 'Come to think of it, she's your mum too, now.'

'No, no – I didn't mean Porky, I meant Mother Nature,' said Min intently.

'Now that's one wicked old bitch,' agreed Tamarind, stroking the velvet black temple of her bride, 'and I'll support you all the way, my friend.'

'So you were with someone last night?' asked Min curiously.

'Yeah, but I didn't get her name,' confided Tamarind shyly. 'I felt like I'd known her all my life…'

'That's wonderful!' cried Min. 'We'll toast your happiness with champagne!'

'Not with that migraine,' ordered Tamarind sternly. 'It'll be chrysanthemum tea for you, my dear.'

The newly-weds stood up, shook off the damp grass and strolled hand in hand towards the main building where their guests had adjourned to the hotel bar.

Gubnet watched them walking towards the hotel from the long window of the public bar. In her eyes, the happy couple assumed the awkward mould of young love; at once looking away or down, overcoming each blushful glance with terrible giggles and grimaces. She felt wretched watching them. She fled into the loo and shut her eyes to the harsh reflection of the washroom mirror. *Princess Min will have no time for you now*, she told the despondent, bloated Viking in the mirror. It was a small mercy, arriving too late to attend the dreaded wedding ceremony. Under the cold pure jets of water, she absolved herself of a simple emotional reaction. She was jealous, despite the attempts she had made to destroy the memory of Min. She towelled her pale face vigorously. It brought the blood courageously close to her skin.

The bar clucked like a hungry hen coop with the whole of Ascourt exchanging news and gossip over drinks, peanuts and crisps. The noise died down a fraction when Princess Min held up her hand for silence and proposed a toast. 'To love,' she said looking deep into Tamarind's eyes. 'And to old friends – better late than never!' As she brought the glass to her lips, Dr Heron Home, PhD, lunged through the crowd, bringing Min to her knees in the first and finest rugby tackle ever witnessed on the island of Porschia.

'Don't drink the tea,' shouted Heron. 'It's poisoned!'

'Oh no! My beautiful white linen jacket,' moaned Princess Min, who was soaked through.

'Mother Nature – '

'Of course,' said Min, calmly headed for the changing room. 'Who else?'

The film stopped rolling for the live broadcast while Mother Nature locked horns with the Queen of Porschia on the deserted front lawn of the Paradise Hotel. Porky deserved to spend the rest of her days on Ascourt, and her new in-laws were welcome to her. But Porky's stake in Ovum-to-Ovum had been negotiated in exchange for a royal marriage and a dowry worth half a million pounds. A little bird at the airport had wagged its tongue before it flew the coop.

'You tricked me into thinking it was a little press thing for the wedding,' accused Mother Nature vitriolically.

'Did I?' replied Porky innocently, 'It must have slipped my mind – it's my age you know, imagine that – and you didn't even know we'd won the Nobel Prize!'

'What I don't know is irrelevant,' smarted Mother Nature. 'What I do know is that this shoddy stunt is about using my good name as invaluable publicity to endorse your latest and leanest money-making endeavour. '

'Fair's fair,' retorted the Queen, holding on to her nose. 'I paid good money to buy Ascourt.'

'To retire peacefully? Or to become a rich woman with a

fifty per cent stake in Ovum-to-Ovum?' glared Mother Nature dangerously.

'You must be slipping, it took you long enough to find out,' taunted Porky nasally.

'That may be so,' conceded Mother Nature, 'but so must you. The dowry that will pay for your fifty per cent stake disappeared on a flight out of Porschia this morning with Hayde Lewis.'

Mother Nature curled Her lips in a narrow smile at Her vanquished opponent. The knife had been inserted. And it would be twisted. She turned Her back on the Queen of Porschia and faced the cameras.

'Roll it there, Matilde,' ordered Mother Nature disdainfully. 'I am ready to make my statement to the world.'

Princess Min swayed headily beside St Gubnet in front of the mirror in the the ladies' loo. Their shoulders touched lightly, but Min's eyes filled with tears when she realised what Gubnet was saying to her.

'Really,' pleaded Min, 'we're just best friends!'

'You're married to her – besides, I'm too old for you.'

'Tammy's in love with someone else, and I'm in love with you, Gubnet.'

'But you said you never thought about me while you were in Porschia.'

'I tried,' begged Min, 'not to think about you.'

'I tried too.'

'It was too scary.'

'I haven't been myself since you left.'

'Then we're meant for one another!'

'It's too late now!'

Heron Home tapped politely and stuck her head round the loo door. 'Hurry on, you two – Mother Nature's back on screen.'

Mother Nature faced the cameras with equanimity. She admitted Her surprise at a 'brave little backroom project' winning international recognition and spoke at length of the importance of inter-species and inter-European co-operation. She thanked the Nobel Committee and went on to explain their possible reasons for the award, making maximum use of free airtime to propagate Her own views on the matter.

'We must not forget that Ovum-to-Ovum Fertilisation is not a complex leap forward in scientific thought. It is a simple matter of engineering to mechanically rupture the walls of two eggs, mix their genetic contents and reimplant the whole, new, living embryo in a superficial casing. However, it is not a straightforward matter for the female participants involved. There is a maximum of surgical intervention, a minimum guarantee of success and a prohibitive cost outlay.

'But this is not to take from the project in any way whatever. The award we proudly received today was the Nobel Peace Prize. It is not a scientific accolade, but a humanitarian one, in recognition of the fact that women can now choose to be fertilised by women, the result of which is female progeny. It is clearer now than ever before that men must choose peace, or we will reproduce our own kind and we will do it without them.'

By one o'clock everyone, except Queen Bea, had arrived at the hotel and was seated in the marquee on the back lawn for the wedding brunch. The married couple sat at the top of the main table, flanked by Princess Vee and Maryann to one side, and the three Nobel Prize-winners on the other. The Superdrones ran around the marquee with bottles of champagne and cold plates.

The Old Dames occupied their own table but got most of the attention from the photographers, due to a lively assortment of hats. After a brief meeting with the Queen of Porschia in the hotel lobby not ten minutes earlier, Dame Clemis had reported the embarrassing position to the others, taking care to point out that while Porky 's explanation of the stolen dowry was inadequate, it did mean that Princess Tamarind's membership of the Old Dames Breakfast Club might be indefinitely compromised.

Cook proudly wheeled in the magnificent wedding cake, removed her apron and joined the Queen of Porschia at the far end of the table.

'The hotel safe is empty,' cried Porky miserably. 'Hayde Lewis took the lot!'

'That is serious,' observed Cook thoughtfully. But the money was not her main priority. Did Porky love her or was it a one-sided affair?

*

When Princess Min stood up to cut the cake, Tamarind glanced discreetly at the beautiful woman who was being seated between Cook and her mother at the far end of the table. It had come as a terrible blow to discover who She was. She hadn't said a word to the others. She didn't know how to tell them. Gubnet mistook her behaviour for shyness and tried to get a conversation started. But Tamarind was in shock.

'Min tells me you're in love,' coaxed Gubnet gently.

'Actually, Tammy doesn't know who she is yet,' whispered Princess Min, leaning over them with the cake slice.

'Queen Bea is missing,' interrupted Maryann harshly, 'and we're sitting round like nothing's happened. For the Goddess's sake, why aren't we down on the beach helping the others to look for her?'

'No, wait, Maryann,' said Tamarind finally, 'I believe there is someone in this very room who can tell us exactly what happened...'

The woman who woke up on my sofa to discover She was alone in the house with Queen Bea.

Mother Nature was ravenously hungry and took Her time eating three whole slices of the delicious wedding cake. She sat back, wiped Her lips on an expensive white linen napkin and digested the fact that Pearl, who was sitting at the other end of the table, was none other than Princess Tamarind. What a way to have created reality! Once again, the entire sense of the unity of all Her creaturedom overwhelmed Mother Nature with its innate meaningfulness. Only for Heron's timely escape, She might have turned up with a batch of Superdrones ready to imprint on Tamarind! How embarrassing! And since Porky's non-payment of the dowry would render the marriage null and void, Princess Min would just have to marry someone else! Mother Nature was filling fast with Her love for Pearl – or would it be Tamarind? – but first there was business to attend to. She must ask Cook for the recipe for the wedding cake. And then She would deliver Her *coup de grace* into Porky's twisting ribs. What joy, and all in a day's work!

'I suppose you will return to Ascourt to be at Porky's side?' enquired Mother Nature of Cook.

'Not unless I get a public commitment from the new owner,' said Cook, putting her nascent relationship to the test.

Porky had no appetite for cake. She felt that something important was slipping through the fingers of her hand. Something called Control.

'Yes,' agreed Mother Nature ominously, 'a new owner does have certain responsibilities. Like clearing up bad debts.'

'What bad debts?' asked Porky defensively.

'Well, as new owner, I presumed you knew about the *back taxes*,' said Mother Nature, savouring the words on Her palate. 'Ascourt agreed to pay me in full as soon as they received the dowry from you, my dear.'

'How much?' squealed Porky.

'Half a million pounds,' said Mother Nature slowly, 'with interest as of today.'

Porky almost howled with the sheer misery of it all. Mother Nature had knotted the noose. There was no way out except to save her own skin...

'Mother Nature please have mercy,' squirmed Porky tearfully. 'I wanted nothing more than to stay on in Porschia with the Superdrones – it was Cook who made me buy Ascourt, she planned it all. She said if things went wrong we could always go to Lloyds of London and tell them I blew up the boat, and you'd have to return the insurance money and maybe even go to jail because you made Captain McCarthy perjure himself...'

'Ingenious!' praised Mother Nature. 'And are you going to London, Cook?'

'No,' said Cook, sadly making up her mind. 'I have decided to go to Florida, and I am going to go alone.'

'Don't forget to leave me the recipe before you go, Cook,' requested Mother Nature.

'It would be my pleasure, Eminence. And as for you,' said Cook, grabbing Porky's sore nose and squeezing it tenaciously, 'you can have your cake and eat it any way you like on Ascourt.'

'Do you mean to say you are handing in your notice?' bellowed Porky nasally.

'That is correct,' replied Cook indignantly. 'End of business relationship.'

Cook took her leave and she did not look back.

'And so, Porky – young, free, single and heading across the water to Lloyds of London?' enquired Mother Nature sarcastically.

'I assure you, Excellency, no! I'm too old for the duck pond...'

Just as Princess Tamarind made up her mind to confront Mother Nature, the Swedish presenter rounded up the Nobel Prize-winners for an interview in the wedding marquee. The stars waited patiently under the lights while Mother Nature powdered Her nose. The camerawoman wanted Dr Heron Home PhD and Professor Louis Sterne to stand either side of 'the two mothers,' at which Mother Nature demanded an explanation and was given one.

'More lies!' decried Mother Nature to the Presenter. 'The truth is that Professor Sterne is the father of this child whom these Nobel cheats are claiming as a result of Ovum-to-Ovum Fertilisation. He was having an affair with Gubnet behind my back.'

'I was only involved with Gubnet and the project in a fatherly way,' explained Louis calmly.

'I am not the mother of that child,' stated Mother Nature, 'unless someone knows better than I.'

'I sent them your gene samples,' owned up Heron gleefully, 'which I extracted from a broken fingernail the day you tried to strangle me.'

'The Nobel Committee are satisfied the child is the result of a cross between St Gubnet and Mother Nature,' said the Presenter objectively. 'We have all the facts.'

'Now will you believe me?' asked Gubnet confidently of her immortal ex-girlfriend.

'But I never wanted a child,' protested Mother Nature.

'Quite,' agreed Gubnet. 'So I used one of the eggs you donated to the Institute a few years back – remember, in your idealistic days? You thought it might help human nature in the quest for the superior being?'

The Swedish crew spared neither film nor flash. Every word was captured and recorded, for nothing short of a nuclear war would keep this story from making headlines the world over.

As the camera crew were otherwise engaged, Dame Thwaites rooted around in her handbag, found her disposable Le Clic camera and lost no time in capturing the romantic event on celluloid. A tastefully framed colour photo of Princess Min sharing her slice of the wedding cake with Princess Tamarind would look just perfect back home in the honeymoon suite of Swann's Hotel.

Princess Min ruined the shot. There was something stuck in her windpipe, close to her heart. She turned glassy-eyed. To her great surprise, she didn't fight for breath but found herself outside her paralysed body in a calmly suspended vacuum where she could both see and hear quite clearly.

Princess Min watched them grabbing and pulling at her body. When all attempts at rescusitation failed, they gathered behind Dame Montague's Powerpoint and faced Mother Nature with a condemnatory silence. Nobody moved when Mother Nature grabbed Powerpoint Two and crushed it under Her shoe. Dame Montague's knees shook under her blue cloak when she bravely informed Mother Nature of her discovery that the world was full of Powerpoints. All one needed was a screwdriver.

Even from her ethereal vantage, Princess Min was overwhelmed by the power of so much emotion. She saw their auras merge into a mighty rainbow. They were neither desperate nor afraid. They no longer believed in what Mother Nature stood for.

Princess Min saw that St Gubnet already knew this through the child she carried in her womb. The child whose birth ordained the inevitable end of Mother Nature's increasingly capricious rule. But it was doubly heartbreaking for Gubnet, now cradling the dead body in her arms, for in the beginning all she wanted was for Mother Nature to want it too.

'Queen Bea would say it's never too late,' she whispered on to Min's dead lips. 'I love you more than you can ever know.'

Mother Nature faded visibly in front of everybody's eyes. She was losing power fast. Dame Montague, no longer in any fear of the Creator, accused Her, outright, of the kidnap of Heron Home.

'And enslavery,' added Heron, finding her voice.

'What about causing an international health scare with a phoney virus?' decried Delia du Pont.

'Selling an island twice is an imprisonable offence,' stated Princess Vee.

'So is extortion,' returned Porky self-righteously.

'You killed Queen Bea, didn't you?' demanded Princess Tamarind, eyes blazing.

And to all the charges, Mother Nature nodded weakly and looked faint.

'You blackmailed Yossarian,' said Heron.

'He raped Min,' hissed Gubnet.

'And you knew he would die carrying out your orders,' said Dame Clemis to the Creator of All Things.

Princess Vee, Dr Heron Home and Professor Louis Sterne walked round Mother Nature slowly and deliberately.

'I think we have enough evidence to go to the cops,' said Princess Vee.

'I agree,' said Louis Sterne.

'I'll phone them,' said Heron, staring into the eyes of her former captor. 'They should be here in a couple of hours.'

Mother Nature was tied up into a chair and encircled by a guard of Old Dames. She asked to speak to Tamarind, and this request was granted. Princess Min stood in her ethereal body beside Princess Tamarind and looked at the petite divinity that had once struck fear into the hearts of so many. Mother Nature made a moving case for love.

'These chains do not bind me, Pearl,' said Mother Nature indicating the ropes that tied Her, 'but yours do.'

Tamarind was silent in her anguish. They had been in each other's dreams. Captor and captive. Oyster and pearl.

'Come with me, Pearl, far away from here – '

But Princess Tamarind knew where the fantasy ended and reality began. She said: 'Why did you kill Min? Wasn't it enough to destroy Queen Charlotte's Dream, to kill Queen Bea and Yossarian – to so totally fuck everyone up and think you could just walk out of here with me in your arms?'

'I didn't kill Princess Min,' said Mother Nature categorically.

'Aren't you in the least bit sorry for what you've done?' asked Tamarind, appalled at Mother Nature's attitude.

'Yeah – a bit,' shrugged Mother Nature. 'But I can't change the past. C'mon, Pearl – we're one of a kind. Let's get outta here.'

'Can you bring back the dead?' asked Tamarind sarcastically.

'It isn't easy, of course, but for you…'

'I know – anything,' said Tamarind, throwing her eyes up to heaven. 'You know I hate myself for finding you even the least bit attractive.'

'But it's a start,' said Mother Nature, sensing a tiny shift in what She would only describe as a gruesomely misplaced and moral sentimentalism. And it was true, a Creator needed only one person to believe in them in order to start over…

Princess Min left them when she saw the woman in the white coat beckon to her from the corner of the marquee. It was Banba.

'You're teasing me again,' said Min, recalling their last encounter.

'You've a *grá* for the older woman and it works a treat,' replied Banba flatteringly. 'Didn't I say I'd come and get you when you were a little bit older?'

They left the marquee and flew across the shining seas to Ascourt. Princess Min asked many questions, all of which Banba explained in depth. This was allowed, as Min was dead and officially part of the Underworld. Banba told her that the others would soon follow with her corpse, and that everything was going exactly to plan.

'But why did Mother Nature kill me when She'd already killed Bea?' grieved Min.

'She didn't kill you,' replied Banba shortly, 'I did. I gave Cook the Blue Stone and she put it in the cake which you ate.'

'And then what?' said Min, spotting the white chalkcliffs of Ascourt in the distance.

'The Blue Stone will let you speak the secrets of the Underworld.'

'Not much good if I'm dead, is it?' said Min.

'Do you feel dead, dear?' asked Banba.

'I've never felt better, actually.'

'Good,' said Banba. 'Then we'll start by studying the Seven Rules of Creation.'

Princess Min shut her eyes as they gathered speed and hurtled through the cliffs of Ascourt. When she opened them, she was deep in the Underworld. It was familiar and warm and dark. The memories came flooding back. She'd been here before.

The Great Swarm began that afternoon from the Porschian International Airport. The glider, carrying the chief mourners, was the first to take off. They were followed by a group gathered on the runway under the aegis of Powerpoint Three, donated to them by the staff and management of the Paradise Hotel. Dame Montague laid her blue cloak on the tarmac and the fliers took up their positions around it. On the call of one, two…six! the circle hovered above the ground, gathering the cloak into a transportable hammock within which was St Gubnet, who would not be parted from the body of Princess Min.

The Queen of Porschia put her entire helicopter fleet at the disposal of everyone else, including the grateful Swedish cameracrew, who wanted to get home, those who had not visited the Underworld and learned how to fly and, of course, criminals. Mother Nature was on board, securely handcuffed and a fugitive from the forces of law and order.

Dr Heron Home and Professor Louis Sterne waved everyone a tearful goodbye on the tarmac. They had stayed behind to press criminal charges on Mother Nature when the Guards arrived.

'Tell me, Doctor Home,' asked Professor Sterne, 'is it realistic to give Mother Nature Her freedom in exchange for this crazy promise? Can She really bring your Princess Min or Queen Bea back to life?'

Heron Home looked out on to the empty runway. It was a relief they'd all gone, taking the mad whirlwinds of the New Order with them. Then came the words which could only have been Charlotte's: *Your work is with Mother Nature, co-operate with Her.* And it was this she had needed to understand: that Ascourt and Mother Nature were one. The impossibility of it! Yet Charlotte in her infinite wisdom must have known this all along. And now Heron knew that it had been her special role to bring them together – Mother Nature had no choice but to follow Tamarind to Ascourt and be granted refuge from the forces of law and order. And this was what Charlotte had asked of her trusted lover – to knot Ascourt's destiny to Mother Nature's. And who else but she would have agreed with such blind faith and devotion?

'You know, Louis, the police couldn't hold Mother Nature

against Her Will any more than we could,' she replied.

'I don't understand,' said Louis shaking his head. 'We are waiting here to report Her to the police and then we are to tell them we don't know where She is?'

Heron laughed affably and buttoned up her tweed jacket. She was looking forward to her own freedom. Deep down she had known, although not in words, that she would not be returning to Ascourt. Like Yossarian, she saw no place for herself in the brave New Order. The thought of death had been a comfort to her in the long and lonely period she had spent without Charlotte. And now her work was done. She had only one regret, and that was not having said a proper goodbye to old friends.

'I'm going home, Louis,' said Heron joyously.

'And home is not Ascourt?' discerned Louis sensitively.

'No, ducks,' said Heron. 'It's where the heart is.'

CHAPTER TWENTY-ONE

The New Order

Maryann landed the glider with little trouble. Mother Nature's storm had swathed an almost perfect runway through the forest which had once grown proudly in the Northern Territories. Princess Vee pointed across the valley to where the palace lay in ruins. Looking down into the valley, the river was choked with rubble, boulders and entire tree trunks. Naiad was reduced to a pathetic, trickling stream. They had been gone only a couple of days, yet the dust hung in a murky haze over the devastated island of Ascourt.

They walked a short distance uphill and found Sorrel putting the finishing touches on a well-crafted hexagonal lean-to. Seeing them, she put her finger firmly on her lips and quietly led them into a makeshift bender where they whispered their grief over a boiling pot of tea.

Sorrel looked puzzled as Maryann sobbed her way incoherently through the story of Queen Bea's death on the cliffs of Porschia. When Maryann could no longer speak, Sorrel held her in her arms and fed her tea by the spoonful.

'You should drink it too,' counselled Sorrel to Vee, 'you are also in shock.'

But throughout the visit to Porschia, Princess Vee had fought with an iron heart, unable to give in to the agonising grief of two dead sisters and so many shattered dreams. She wanted to take refuge in Sorrel's strength. But when she thought of Gubnet who had realised her love too late, or Maryann, whose troubled affair with Bea had ended without even a body to mourn, she was angry that she herself had survived. She was fucked up that Sorrel loved her and she wanted to hit out at those tender, kind eyes so full of questions and patience.

'You couldn't possibly understand,' said Vee icily. 'Min is dead too.'

Sorrel did not reply. She left the bender and walked across to the hexagonal brood chamber with Maryann. When they entered the dimly lit interior, their nostrils were filled with the aromatic pine scent of freshly felled wood. Sorrel looked at the bloated body and then anxiously at Maryann. Queen Bea was asleep, but her condition was worsening.

'Will you stay with her while Vee and I get help?'

Mother Nature pragmatically assessed the nature of the miracle expected of Her. First, She would have to remove the object blocking Princess Min's windpipe. She decided on the Heimlich manoeuvre. She placed both hands on the Princess's diaphragm and squeezed hard. Out popped a large blue stone. Then the Queen of Porschia remembered something important.

'I saw Cook drop that into the wedding cake,' said Porky, telling tales out of school.

While Tamarind and her mother examined the Blue Stone, Mother Nature administered the kiss of life. A flush of colour crept into Min's face and soon she was breathing rhythmically. Tamarind burst into tears and threw herself into Mother Nature's arms.

'You did it!' she cried. 'You kept your promise!'

Sorrel and Princess Vee walked quickly back over the cliffs with the Old Dames. In the lean-to, Maryann held Bea's hand while Dame Meleka examined her by candlelight. The Old Dames listened intently while Sorrel explained how Queen Bea had disappeared during the storm and then reappeared two days later in a dreadful condition, demanding that Sorrel build her a brood chamber to *exact* specifications.

'We all thought you were dead,' sobbed Maryann on the edge of the bed.

'I think you're pregnant,' announced Dame Meleka after careful consideration.

'I can't think of anything except toast and honey,' squirmed Queen Bea uneasily.

Every dwelling from Seaview Suburbs to the palace itself was uninhabitable as a result of the storm. One by one, the islanders trekked into the Northern Territories with provisions and blankets. Everyone helped, even the Queen of Porschia. Sorrel demonstrated the finer points of bender construction, and by sundown, the isolated Northern Territories had transformed into a bustling shantytown preparing for its evening meal. The Queen of Porschia landed her helicopter perilously close to the central bonfire and nearly put it out. Disapproving looks were replaced by grins and smiles when a cargo of groceries and two very special passengers emerged. Each being adamant that the other needed more help than herself, St Gubnet and Princess Min got stuck in the narrow door of the helicopter.

'You're both so butch,' remarked Porky under her breath as she prised them loose.

Queen Bea was allowed to receive only one wellwisher at a time. In between visits, Maryann toasted bread on the fire while passing on important bits of news. They heard that Bea claimed to have mastered the art of flying.

'That's impossible,' said Dame Montague, Keeper of the Powerpoint(s).

'You don't need that mumbo-jumbo,' said Mother Nature good-naturedly. 'Flying is in your genes.'

'It's not in mine,' said St Gubnet unequivocally.

'Ah, but you always had great willpower,' plamaused Mother Nature.

Princess Min dipped a knife into a large pot of honey and spread it generously on four evenly browned pieces of toast. She began to think out loud. 'You see, Rule Two of Creation says that Direction and Will can take you places – '

'Yes,' cried Dame Murphy, 'Cardinality and motive force, one, two...six!'

'But the Powerpoint you found in the present in Town Square was meant as a clue to Rule Six,' said Min, looking kindly at Dame Montague, 'and that is that *Your Point of Power is in the Present.*'

'How do you know all this stuff?' asked Mother Nature worriedly. For it was true; the Seven Rules of Creation were privy only to Creators. Dame Montague was also worried. Only the first Powerpoint had been in the present.

Princess Min did not reply to either of them. She saw Gubnet, her true love, dozing on Dame Agnetha's lap. She saw

Banba, her spirit guide, in the bright corona of the fire. She saw Vee become whole in the arms of Sorrel. She saw herself as a shaman who had faced death to return with the Seven Rules of Creation. She saw Ascourt rise to bless Charlotte's Dream on the night of the Moon's eclipse. Princess Min gathered up the slices of honeyed toast and took her place in the queue outside Queen Bea's chamber.

Gubnet woke to the stirring of the child in her womb, but Agnetha had joined the Old Dames to watch the Moon over the cliffs, and Mother Nature now sat in her place, offering her a bowl of soup. Gubnet was speechless, for in all their years together she couldn't recall Mother Nature ever once tending a sickbed.

'It's my child too,' explained Mother Nature hastily.

Gubnet nodded but she wanted so much to know if Mother Nature were happy – was She content? Would She be proud of Athena? What would She do next? Had She and Tamarind made love? Was She still angry? Does She miss me?

They sat in mutual silence, drinking soup and intuiting each other's thoughts. For a long while they watched the far-off silhouette of Princess Min talking intently among the Old Dames.

'She will be Athena's teacher,' acknowledged Mother Nature with supreme difficulty.

'And mother,' insisted Gubnet.

Queen Bea could hear her body's machinations as clearly as her own heartbeat. If Dame Meleka was right, then thousands of eggs were in the making and she was about to become Mother of all Ascourt. Meantime, she tried hard not to think about the thirty-eight slices of toast and honey and the fact that she could not see her toes. Bea's body had swollen so much that she was no longer surprised at the shocked stares and mumbled words of each incoming visitor. But Tamarind hardly seemed to notice. She rushed in, pulled up a chair and asked for advice on a 'matter of the heart'. What would she do about her feelings for Mother Nature? Bea listened with both horror and fascination. Tamarind was very upset. Yes, she had always known that she was one half of another, but Mother Nature? Surely that was a kismet too cruel to contemplate.

'You could always take out a life-insurance policy,' counselled Bea wisely, 'or even talk to the Old Dames – they're experts on relationships.'

But Tamarind wanted Bea's opinion because Bea suffered a profound antipathy towards Mother Nature, and Tamarind was relying on the fact that Bea would not compromise with her.

'Min thinks it's great I've found someone,' explained Tamarind, 'and Porky can't wait, 'cos that might get her off the financial hook, never mind the kudos, and I'm going demented because it's like I'll have to choose between my new friends and a lunatic who's made all your lives hell!'

Bea huffed and puffed. Her lower half was about to explode. There was no time to think anything through, so she waited for the contraction to subside, drew breath and said: 'Tell Mother Nature that we must have a sign from the BVM – and you will wait here with us until we get one.'

As the Moon began its eclipse, Princess Min recited the Seven Rules of Creation.

'Number One: Creation is Communal.

'Number Two: Direction and Will can take you places.

'Number Three: Emotions colour and influence the Events which you attract into your Life.

'Number Four: Your Beliefs create your Emotions – it is not the other way round.

'Number Five: You Create Your Own Reality.

'Number Six: Your Point of Power is in the Present.

'Number Seven: If a Belief is in anyway limiting, then it is not a true belief about Reality.'

Dame Montague expressed the opinion that none of this was new to her. And the others, perhaps more wisely, agreed.

When the Moon disappeared inside its fiery red halo, Princess Vee declared that the Ways of Mother Nature were dead.

'And when the Moon reappears, the New Order will be born,' said Sorrel wondrously.

'But what's my place in it all?' puzzled Vee. 'There's Bea becoming a mother, and Min spouting every kind of wisdom. Who am I?'

'You're special to me,' said Sorrel, and she was right.

*

Two hours later, St Gubnet went into labour and, with the help of Princess Min and Delia du Pont, gave birth to a healthy twelve-pound red-headed Athena.

Maryann poked her head out of the hexagonal brood chamber to announce that Queen Bea had just laid a perfectly shaped egg, and Dame Meleka was satisfied that mother and egg were normal and healthy.

'Just one egg?' asked Porky incredulously. It was unheard of. A queen would lay hundreds, if not thousands, at any one time.

'Twelve ounces,' cried Maryann proudly. 'And we're naming her Pallas, after the statue in Bea's garden.'

Princess Min wrapped baby Athena into her chest. 'You and Pallas are going to be the best of friends.'

Mother Nature looked at the little creature nervously. It was time to make plans, to hit the road, to get the hell out before Her offspring initiated the kind of parental catastrophe that only the children of Divinities were capable of. But She had one last thing to do before She left…

Tamarind wanted a sign from the BVM and Mother Nature knew just where to look for it. She had listened and watched. She was the most intelligent woman on all earth, and Seven Rules of Creation or no, they had consistently missed the signs they were looking for. Mother Nature closed Her eyes. She would show them what they could not see, beginning with the statue of Pallas-Athene. She would invest them with the power of creation. Really, it was child's play.

As soon as it was light, Mother Nature banded together a select group of volunteers and climbed to the very top of the eastern chalkcliffs.

'We are going to fly to the palace, using Rules Two and Six – Direction and Will, remembering that your Point of Power is in the Present.'

Dame Montague slipped her hand into her coat and clutched the hidden Powerpoint. She was the first to lift off. Queen Bea felt herself hovering, but then she felt light all over, having lost a great deal of weight after laying her egg. Maryann and Princess Vee remained firmly perched on a rocky ledge. Mother Nature was losing patience. She ordered Princess Min to jump. Min refused.

'And take that thing out of your pocket,' shouted Mother Nature at Dame Montague.

Suddenly a tremendous gust of wind appeared out of nowhere and blew them all off the cliff. Mother Nature cackled. She had applied the Rule of Natural Selection. There would be no free ride for failures.

During the flight, which was brief, Queen Bea told Montague that she had known about flying without the Powerpoint for quite some time.

'Oh yes,' she admitted. 'When Mother Nature chased me off the cliff, all I could think of was wanting to be home and safe in Ascourt. And as soon as I thought that, I stopped falling and found myself flying home across the ocean.'

'That's how she got on board the glider, the day we flew to the wedding,' added Maryann, who was simultaneously experiencing an unwanted angular velocity. 'I made her promise to stay with the people she loved, so she imagined herself on board with Princess Vee and I, and next thing – she was!'

When they landed, Dame Montague was silent. It didn't matter what she did, someone else, especially Bea, could always do it better. Dame Montague felt small and useless. She felt like a cheat, because she hadn't dared let go of Powerpoint Three, and even Maryann, who was a human, had flown without one. She strayed off, a little behind the group. Then Mother Nature called her to one side.

'I rarely do this sort of thing, because I don't believe it helps, but in your case,' said Mother Nature, furrowing Her brow, 'it just might. I'm going to grant you a wish, Dame Montague. And I hope you understand that I am compelled to make it for you.'

Mother Nature spun on Her heels three times with Her arms akimbo. When She came to a halt, Dame Montague became aware that the people around her looked different. Their eyes, in particular, shone through to their souls.

'I know what they're thinking!' exclaimed Montague, who was taken aback to discover that they were not, after all, thinking about her.

'Be careful,' warned Mother Nature, 'for soon you may find you don't want to know…'

'That's what happened to you, isn't it?' said Dame Montague with a newfound compassion.

Mother Nature began the search with the statue of Pallas-Athene in Queen Bea's garden. She hummed and hawed, poked at plants, walked up and down and shook Her head from time to time. When She came to a halt, the others stopped too.

'One day, Zeus suffered a terrible headache,' began Mother Nature, 'so he ordered that his head be split open, and lo and behold, out popped the infant goddess, Minerva – also known as Pallas-Athene, after the cities she presided over.'

Mother Nature pointed at the hedge and asked Maryann to identify it.

'It's a myrtle hedge,' said Maryann, nonplussed.

'And what, pray, is that thing climbing all over it?' said Mother Nature, who had an aversion for tended gardens.

'A *clematis montana*.'

'And that bushy thing – '

'A *choisya ternata*,' replied Maryann, 'Otherwise known as a Mexican Orange.'

Mother Nature rubbed her hands together and then spread them for silence.

'I conclude, then, that Bea here is "M" and no other.'

'I knew I was "M" from the beginning,' said Bea, who had not spent all night laying an egg for nothing. Dame Montague saw straight away that Bea was lying and she felt immediately relieved of the need to rise to the bait.

Mother Nature guided the group to the next garden, which was Princess Min's. She performed an identical ritual to the one before and then said, 'Now you have the general idea – so can anyone of you tell me who Min is?'

Dame Montague knew but she didn't like to say, as she was privy to the letter imprinted on Mother Nature's conscious mind. She also knew that the others had it wrong.

Maryann repeated the exercise of naming the plants from Princess Min's garden. There was a Snowbush, the periwinkle was almost washed out of the ground with rain, and there were the naked brown stems of *pathenocissus* all along the wall. It didn't make sense. Princess Min was quicker.

'Bea has Minerva in her garden, so she's "M",' stated Min logically, 'and I have a barbeque in mine, so I'm "B" – right?'

It was not until they reached Princess Vee's tiny garden that Maryann stumbled on the answer.

'I don't believe it!' she swore. 'It was in that bloody Will all along!'

'It most certainly was not,' said Mother Nature. 'I read it from cover to cover – '

'The Garden Plans were in the original,' disclosed Princess Vee with some satisfaction. 'You only had a copy, thanks to Yossarian.'

Mother Nature propped Herself against the statue of Yossarian and laughed uproariously. She could leave them now to figure out who was who, but in all the world they would never understand what it meant without Her help. *Rule One – Creators are Communal.*

'Humour me,' She said. 'I want you all to close your eyes and count to a hundred. When you open them, I will reveal everything, I promise.' And Dame Montague could see that it was almost true.

At the count of a hundred, Mother Nature was standing in the exact spot She had left them. She began by asking Maryann to share her revelations.

'This may seem too simple,' said Maryann, recalling Delia's astronomical theories, 'but all three shapes in Vee's garden begin with the letter "B". The round apiary is nothing more than a *B*eehive, the little horseshoe hedge is *B*uxus or *B*ox and even the triangular plot of cereal is common or garden *B*arley. The statue of Yossarian, I guess he's a *B*oy...'

'Princess Vee is "B",' confirmed Dame Montague.

'I'm the Q-Queen of Ascourt?' stammered Vee incredulously.

'It's a very important position,' conceded Queen Bea.

'It's certainly the most important garden of the three,' revealed Mother Nature after a good look round.

She asked Princess Min for the Blue Stone which she had choked on and showed her how it fit exactly into the missing eye of the statue of Yossarian. Then Mother Nature looked at Bea and said, 'The hedge is a womb shape with a long cervix, and you will be fertilised once a year when the Sun's rays creep up the chamber on the midwinter solstice. It's quite scientific, really.'

Maryann gasped. Delia had not been mistaken after all. She had simply given the right answer to the wrong question.

'The Queen's garden must contain aspects of all her

peoples,' explained Mother Nature, shaking Her head. And then it struck Her why Charlotte had gone to so much trouble to hide her plans, for She would have seen through them instantly. But it was too late for regrets. Even if She could have prevented Ascourt's rebellion, She could not have foreseen that Gubnet would have conceived Her child. And that was the real cruncher...

'What about the Ceres theme of agriculture?' pursued Maryann intently. 'The beehive, the barley, the womb-shaped hedge?'

'The barley is your part in all this, Maryann – to establish a self-sufficient island agriculture,' informed Mother Nature. 'But each of the symbols is quite unique. The hedge represents Bea's fertility and the statue contains Min's Blue Stone, reinforcing the island's link with the Underworld. The Queen's allegiance is ultimately to the Beehive, represented by the Triple Goddess. '

'That's us!' cried Bea enthusiastically, 'the BVM!'

Mother Nature asked the others to leave the real Queen of Ascourt in her garden for a few minutes of meditation and contemplation. Vee was radiant, regal and over the Moon.

Princess Min raced into her garden excitedly. She knew she had to be 'V' – but where were all these clues?

Maryann pointed out that *parthenocissus* was commonly known as Virginia Creeper, the Snowbush was a souped-up Viburnum, and periwinkles came from a botanical family called Vinca. Then Min remembered something Dame Murphy had laughed about when the garden was under construction.

'She told me that my barbeque was the sacred hearth of Vesta, and I thought she was just trying to be nice!'

Mother Nature then asked that Princess Min be allowed some time to explore her garden on her own and realise a deeper meaning. Queen Bea didn't have to be asked. She marched into her garden and looked up at the tall, spiky Mahonia. 'Mary,' she said. She traced the curves of the delicate *Clematis montana*; 'Madame,' she decided. And through the lightly coloured leaves of the Mexican Orange, she chose Misty as a name to remember it by. Lastly, she waded up the trickling stream to the little wooden statue of Pallas-Athene. Minerva, she reminded herself, and in its tiny folded wooden hands, she saw – a sign from the BVM.

271

That evening, Dame Clemis called an open meeting of the Old Dames Breakfast Club. There were two items on the agenda: the Essence of the day, and Princess Tamarind's appointment as an Old Dame, as agreed under the terms of the marriage contract. The proceedings began with an opening speech from the Queen of Ascourt, whose job it was to summarise the feelings of the community. Vee was extremely nervous.

'Just tell them the first thing that comes into your head,' urged Bea. 'The Queen is never wrong!'

From her vantage in the eastern chalkcliffs, Vee surveyed the ruined dwellings across the length of the island. In the ocean around her, she saw the seamines and quarantine notices still bobbing up and down, threatening their peace and wellbeing. Looking down into the denuded valley, the river Naiad almost sobbed with the effort of making its way past the rubble from the storm. The first thing that came into Vee's mind was disaster, destruction and chaos.

'We will make our home in the Northern Territories,' began Vee. 'We wish to be left in peace to build our lives as befitting our vision of the New Order. The naval mines and quarantine notices will be left in their place, for it will discourage the merely curious. We agree that the Queen of Porschia be the legal owner and Guardian of Ascourt. Dealing with the world from her base in Porschia, she is in a good position to ensure that Ascourt is not interfered with in any way. We know her secrets, and she knows ours. She will be our Guardian, in whom we place our trust.'

Porky, who was seated between her daughter and Mother Nature, snuffled into her sleeve. This was such an honour. If it meant what she hoped it did. 'Do you think it's a sign that I should return to Porschia and take up the reins?' she bluffed.

'Probably,' replied Tamarind, winking at Mother Nature.

'But do you think it means I should manage the Superdrones for your empire?' enquired Porky rather more directly of Mother Nature Herself.

'Hayde Lewis is the boss now,' said Mother Nature. 'Talk to her.'

'I will,' said Porky gratefully. After all, she owed money to Mother Nature and there was the outstanding dowry for Tamarind, not that it counted since the marriage seemed to have broken up. Porky felt an old thrill returning. She was back in business with an irrepressible grin. She decided not to raise the matter of money unless someone else did. These were strange times, but it was no excuse for impoliteness.

'Guardian, eh?' said Porky, who really liked the sound of her new title.

Dame Clemis requested order and proceeded to deal with the first item on the agenda. Much to the relief of the Old Dames, Princess Tamarind announced that she did not wish to become one of their number. She had received a sign from the BVM and her first priority was a long holiday with Mother Nature in a remote and sunny tropical paradise.

'I'm sorry I couldn't keep the sign myself,' said Bea looking impishly at Mother Nature, 'since the BVM left it in *my* garden.'

The matter of the money was quickly settled. Mother Nature generously waived all outstanding debts, on condition that Porky set up an index-linked trust fund worth half a million a year to Ascourt.

'But that's not going to help any of you become self-sufficient,' appealed Porky to the circle.

'Oh but it will,' said Princess Min encouragingly. 'And if you need any help in remembering how to be a good guardian, then don't forget who saw you plant those explosives on Mother Nature's yacht.'

At this embarrassing juncture, Dame Clemis suggested they move on to Item two and it was clear from their response that everyone wanted to speak. The Essence of the day was the birth of the New Order, it was the end of the Old Ways, it was a celebration of nature, it was a new Queen, it was –

'Reproduction,' said Gubnet. 'Let us not forget that we have received the Nobel Prize for revolutionising reproduction. Let us not forget that woman can choose to reproduce with woman in order to give birth to woman. Let us not forget that last night I gave birth to Athena. Let us not forget this new word in our vocabulary – *Ovum-to-Ovum*.'

Bea listened, her shiny white egg in her lap. She had laid this egg, but she hadn't won a Nobel prize. She had swelled up with this one egg till she might have burst, but it hadn't given her wisdom like Min. She looked at Vee and asked: 'Am I still Queen Bea?'

And Vee replied, 'The one who lays the eggs is always the

queen bee.'

And Min said, 'The Essence is really about the Rule of Three – '

'But we should first thank Queen Bea for who she is and who she will be,' said Vee sensitively.

And Montague said, 'Thankfully she is no longer who she was.'

And Bea burst into inconsolable tears. Montague realised that the gift had changed what she saw, but it hadn't changed how she felt.

Princess Min expounded on the Rule of Three, engaging the attention of all the Old Dames whose invention it had been. She reminded them of Ascourt's long association with the number three. She explained that the BVM was not meant as a representation of the Blessed Virgin Mary.

'The BVM is not a goddess-figure,' said Min. 'The BVM is us – the power of we three alive in us all to make Charlotte's Dream come true. I am the living principle of the Underworld.'

'And I, as Queen, am the principle of interconnection in the living organism of our community,' said Vee.

'I just have the babies,' said Bea, smoothing her tear-stained egg. 'As many as everyone thinks we need.'

Gubnet felt the heat rising in her chest. She was aflame. She tucked Athena into her shoulder and left her place in the circle to sit beside Queen Bea. In a conspiratorial wink between mothers, Bea took Athena while Gubnet lifted the egg gently out of Bea's lap.

'This is the miracle of the BVM,' said Gubnet, holding the egg for all to see, 'and it's been under our noses for centuries. The first woman in written records to have conceived without fertilisation was the Blessed Virgin Mary – the BVM. And now Bea has done it too. And I believe that only Bea could, because she's the living Essence of the Seventh Rule of Creation – She doesn't believe in limitations – and anyone who does should reconsider their reasons for wanting to be here.'

And so began the New Order of Ascourt. It was the Seventh Age of Creation and nothing was impossible any more. All those who stayed on Ascourt lived happily ever after.

THE END

Those who did not stay

Dame Montague did swear allegiance to the New Order but later took up residence on the mainland of Ireland. She became an international Bridge professional and wrote a book called *Know What's On Your Opponent's Mind*.

Her sister, *Delia du Pont* (MD), also travelled abroad, furthering her knowledge of the surgical procedures used in Ovum-to-Ovum.

Mná-mná (Woman-to-Woman) Ltd was a Florida-registered company set up by Cook which specialised in Ovum-to-Ovum. Cook employed a network of international saleswomen and regularly used the services of Delia du Pont (MD).

The Queen of Porschia won the franchise from Mná-mná Ltd (Florida) to run Birthing Holidays in Ascourt for couples who had conceived by Ovum-to-Ovum. She wrote to her daughter every Christmas.

Hayde Lewis ran Mother Nature International with panache. The key to her success was diversification and research. The Queen of Porschia was one of two new Vice Presidents appointed with special responsibility for Superdrones. Hayde also bought a small company in Florida called Mná-mná Ltd.

Professor Louis Sterne left the Paris Institute of Genetics and went on the lucrative Nobel Winners lecture circuit. He accepted a sinecure from Mother Nature International and became Vice President in charge of Research in his spare time. He is widely believed to be the last person to have seen Heron Home alive.

Dr Heron Home, PhD, has disappeared.

Epilogue

Mother Nature and Tamarind flew slowly away from Ascourt, frequently looking back to the island which was fading like a tiny dot in the ocean. They were both calm, floating in the undemanding space between earth and sky, the past and future. Mother Nature took one last look at Ascourt and shook Her head with a rueful smile.

'Why didn't you tell them?' asked Tamarind who had wanted to herself.

'They'll find out soon enough,' said Mother Nature solemnly, 'and probably before Athena cuts her first tooth.'

'You're embarrassed about it!' teased Tamarind benignly.

'I promised you I'd help them understand the power of their own creation,' corrected Mother Nature.

'And you did, they know the BVM is their story and it's inside them,' conceded Tamarind. 'But you shouldn't be ashamed of your story either. You're still their goddess.'

'A triple goddess!' snorted Mother Nature in disgust. 'When I was goddess in my own right, I was very productive and things were always perfect. I was happy in those days.'

'You were not!' retorted Tamarind. 'You told me you were very lonely until Gubnet came along!'

'And it's all her fault,' lamented the Creator of All Things. 'She wanted a family and now she has one. They'll be talking about us like the holy trinity. Hecate, Demeter and Persephone...'

'Mother Nature, Gubnet and Athena,' chanted the young Princess solemnly.

Tamarind had never flown so high. She saved her breath by trying not to talk, but she had a thousand questions on her mind. She looked at Mother Nature shimmering in the black cocktail dress beside her. She wanted to know everything about Her. She was a sight to behold. She was the most beautiful woman on all earth, and yet most people only ever referred to Her intelligence. Everyone was afraid of Her. Perhaps it was because Mother Nature was like Hecate – She was the whole of Nature, both destructive and creative and beyond all the rules. She was a fugitive from the forces of law and order!

'Why did you blush when Gubnet mentioned the Seventh Rule of Creation?' asked Tamarind inquisitively.

'I'd rather not say,' replied Mother Nature, tensing Her shoulders.

'We shouldn't have secrets from one another,' said Tamarind, running an enormous pearl between her fingers, 'like the sign from the BVM – '

'When Queen Bea found that pearl in her statue of Pallas-Athene, she knew it was a sign from the BVM of my *special name for you…*'

'Look, I know how the pearl got to be there, and it had nothing to do with the BVM!'

'How do you know?' asked Mother Nature suspiciously.

'Bea told me,' revealed Tamarind. 'She opened her eyes while the others were still counting and she followed you!'

Mother Nature groaned. In the old days it was quite the thing for a girl to have Her secrets, but nowadays! Pick, pick, pick! 'The Seventh Rule of Creation, oh well,' she sighed. 'A long story, not exactly to my credit…'

The telling of the tale took up most of the journey to the tropical island paradise on which Mother Nature and Tamarind proposed to unwind and get to know each other better. It began with the story of Queen Charlotte and her distress about the Mating which her mother had planned for her.

'Unknown to anyone,' whispered Mother Nature, 'Charlotte came to me. She told me it was degrading to be assaulted by an army of drones all with the one thing on their minds. She said it was a form of medieval rape which had no place in the modern world. She begged me to allow her to conceive by an artificial means. And I refused. I told her that the Way of the Bees was perfect and productive. Charlotte insisted that there must be a better way and I was adamant that it was wrong thinking to believe you could better something that was already perfect. I told her it was an impossible thing to ask of me.'

'You were very proud of the Way of the Bees, and the

hexagons and all of that,' empathised Tamarind as best she could.

'Precisely,' agreed Mother Nature. 'But then Charlotte accused me of defying the Seventh Rule of Creation...!'

'If a Belief about Reality is an anyway limiting, then it is not a true Belief about Reality, right?'

'So she said,' pondered Mother Nature. 'And then she swore to me she'd prove it.'

'Well, she certainly did that,' remarked Tamarind.

'Yeah, and fuck her anyway.'

Together they swooped down to their tropical island paradise. It was sun, sand and surf. It was a much-needed holiday. It was the playground of the goddesses, and Mother Nature looked at Tamarind with a steamy glint in Her eye. But Tamarind had something else in mind.

'Don't you see that the wonderful things that came out of Charlotte's Dream would never have happened without you?'

And whenever Mother Nature really thought about it, She didn't feel so bad.